T0277967

BREAK TO YOU

NEAL SHUSTERMAN

BREAK TO YOU
BREAK TO YOU
BREAK TO YOU

DEBRA YOUNG
MICHELLE KNOWLDEN

Quill Tree Books
An Imprint of HarperCollinsPublishers

Quill Tree Books is an imprint of HarperCollins Publishers.

Break to You
Copyright © 2024 by Temple Hill Publishing LLC
All rights reserved. Printed in the United States of America.
No part of this book may be used or reproduced in any manner whatsoever without
written permission except in the case of brief quotations embodied in critical
articles and reviews. For information address HarperCollins Children's Books,
a division of HarperCollins Publishers, 195 Broadway, New York, NY 10007.
www.epicreads.com

Library of Congress Control Number: 2023943333
ISBN 978-0-06-287576-1

Typography by Joel Tippie
24 25 26 27 28 LBC 5 4 3 2 1
First Edition

For Julie Miller, Marianne Crandall Wilson, Deb Svec, Helen Zientek, and all librarians and media specialists past and present, who continue to fight against those who believe banning books solves anything for anyone

—N.S.

For my family, with gratitude

—D.Y.

For my incredible family,
with love

—M.K.

PART ONE

ADRIANA

INTAKE

The clerk turns the manila envelope upside down, and it spews forth the remainders of Adriana's life onto the counter. Then the woman carelessly flicks through it all, as if panning for gold through a sieve. Gold that she's apparently never found.

A stranger's touching my stuff, Adriana thinks. She wants to slap the woman's hands away but controls the impulse. Not an easy thing for Adriana to do.

"Did you look at the list of things you are and are not allowed to bring into the detention facility?"

The clerk's name plate says *Paula Laplante.* She somehow seems both under thirty and over fifty at the same time. Like being a juvenile detention intake clerk has sent her soul through a time-space wormhole. When she speaks, she addresses Lana, Adriana's stepmother, still not making eye contact with Adriana.

Lana leans down so she can talk through the slot in the bulletproof glass. It's the kind of partition they have in banks. Adriana wonders if there's a little button under the counter to call in a SWAT team if anyone on her side of the glass gets out of hand.

"Yes," Lana says, "we read it." Lana's mouth is so close to the little voice grille in the glass, it looks like she's kissing it.

Paula Laplante gives Lana a dubious glance, then pushes aside some photos and a pill bottle to reveal a small soft-covered leather journal. She picks it up, and even though she doesn't open it, Adriana feels violated. She wants to shove Lana aside and reach through the slot in the window to break Paula Laplante's fingers.

Pretend it doesn't matter. They can't hurt you if they think you don't care.

But the woman must sense Adriana bristling, because she finally looks at Adriana, studying her. Then she pushes the journal and pill bottle back through the little window slot.

"Nope," she says dismissively. "The photos are okay, but any meds in your profile will be prescribed on-site. And personal notebooks aren't allowed."

Adriana reaches for the journal, but Lana puts her hand on Adriana's—as if taking the journal back through the slot is an admission of defeat. Lana grabs the pills, but the journal stays put. Now it sits there in the slot halfway between two incompatible worlds.

Adriana's dad should be there to help, but he had to stay

home with her half brother, who's only three. Of course, they could have found someone else to watch him, but after the trial, it was pretty clear that her father was done with court orders, done with signing forms, done with her.

"Is there a problem?" Paula the intake troll asks. "The instructions on personal belongings are very clear."

"The journal is from her doctor," Lana blurts out. "Her *therapist*. She's supposed to write down everything she thinks." That might be possible for Lana. Her thoughts are limited to her toddler, social media, and her job—which she's about to be late for, as evidenced by how many times she's looked at her watch in the past five minutes. Adriana's thoughts, however, could fill phone books. That is, if she could get them out of her head. Most of the time she just looks at the blank page, lucky to get a paragraph out. But damn, do those paragraphs feel good.

Lana turns from the exchange between Adriana and Paula, glancing at the door as if she's hoping Adriana's father will show up and take charge of her intake. Weird, but in the moment, Adriana can't exactly remember what her father looks like. In the diffused light, Lana's face has gone a bit blurry, too, like a television dream scene. Why is her family dissolving, while the detention center and its soulless little troll look so clear she can see cracks in the walls, and the spinach in Paula Laplante's teeth?

"I'm sorry, it's not allowable," says Paula. "Can you imagine what it would be like if we made exceptions for some, but not for others?"

3

Adriana bites the inside of her cheek till she tastes blood. She has to have that journal, but she won't beg. She'll say nothing more. Not. One. Syllable.

The journal remains in the slot, between this world and the other. It becomes the touchstone in a game of chicken. Who will blink first? Who will commit the journal into their world?

It turns out that Paula Laplante doesn't care enough to press the issue. She takes the journal to clear the slot for an onslaught of paperwork—but she doesn't put the journal with the rest of Adriana's belongings. She puts it to the side, like a petulant child in time-out.

Lana pats Adriana's hand gently as if to say it will be okay. Adriana doesn't pull her hand away each time Lana tries to comfort her, but she doesn't respond to it either. Lana's various attempts at affection are always like cockroaches skittering across the floor. Small, irritating, and betraying a frantic need to escape.

Behind the blue door leading into the detention center, a buzzer sounds. It's machine-gun loud, followed by a racket of doors slamming and a stampede of steps. Sounds like normal school. Except nothing feels normal about it.

There are a dozen pages for Lana to fill out. Signatures, disclaimers, releases of liability. The kind of stuff you sign at the doctor's so that you can't sue them if they kill you or leave their car keys in your intestines or whatever.

"It took less time to marry your father," Lana jokes, but neither Adriana nor the intake troll laughs. In fact, Adriana finds it insulting.

"Is she allowed to sign stuff for me?" Adriana asks Paula. "I mean, she's not my *real* mother."

Lana takes a deep breath and releases it. She says nothing.

"A legal guardian is all you need," Paula says. Adriana wants to tell her that she needs a whole lot more than that, but what would be the point?

Lana finishes signing without reading any of the small print—and it's all small print—then shoves the pages back through the slot. Paula looks through them, as if to make sure Lana correctly signed her own name.

"The order says you'll be with us for seven months," Paula says to Adriana. She picks at her teeth but misses the spinach. "You're aware of that, right?"

Now Adriana knows the real reason for the glass partition. It's not about bullets—it's because Paula Laplante would be slapped senseless by everyone who encountered her if it weren't for the glass. Seven months. The rest of her junior year, and the beginning of her senior year. Suddenly *homecoming* has an actual meaning.

"Yeah, I know."

Could it be that the reason Adriana is having trouble remembering her father and seeing her stepmother is that, in a way, she's seeing them through a glass too? The one separating her from her old life. By court order she'll live in a world of locked doors where little pen pushers decide whether you can have a stupid journal or not. Where seven months isn't a measure of time, it's just a list of things that don't belong to you anymore.

From this moment on, she will only see her family like one

might from inside a science experiment: scrutinized in rooms low on oxygen, high on perspiration, and in precisely measured fractions of time. That is, if they bother to come at all.

Paula Laplante regards the journal once more, wrinkling her nose like a jackal sniffing dead meat.

"I'll pass the diary to the staff psychiatrist," she says. "He'll decide what to do about it."

Journal, not diary, Adriana wants to scream. A diary is a pink thing that princesses and spoiled suburban girls fill with Christmas lists. This little book is no-nonsense brown leather.

"Yeah, sure, whatever," Adriana mumbles.

"Thank you," Lana says, as if translating for Adriana—but when Paula the intake goblin turns to the phone, Lana flips her the middle finger. Adriana refuses to say anything, but her lip quirks for a nanosecond before gravity pulls it down again.

"Adriana Zarahn is ready to be processed," Paula announces into the phone.

Processed. Like American cheese or Spam. This is it. You're no longer a real person.

In a few moments an angular Black woman appears at the narrow window of the detention center door. No, not door—air lock. A pair of doors on either end of a short corridor, keeping one world from infecting the other. The clerk buzzes the woman into the reception area. She spots Adriana right away and offers a practiced smile—the first one Adriana's seen today—although it's about as fake as Lana's nails.

The woman wears a blue polo shirt and tan pants—a uniform

trying to not look like a uniform. She's at least six inches taller than Adriana. Paula passes her a single sheet and Adriana's manila envelope. The woman takes only a moment to glance at the sheet.

"Adriana, I'm Jameara Abeku, your unit counselor." Without waiting for a response, she turns to Lana. "Are you family? You're welcome to join us while I show Adriana around. If you have the time, that is."

"She doesn't." Adriana says before Lana can make the excuse herself. "She's late for work."

Jameara goes still except for one raised eyebrow.

Lana gives a humorless laugh. "She's right." Then Lana hugs Adriana, who is careful not to hug her back. "We'll see you very soon, yes?" she says, speaking for her absent father as well. Lana peels herself away then trots quickly out to the parking lot, leaving only the florid scent of her perfume on Adriana's top.

"Shall we?" says Jameara, as if Adriana has a choice. Then they step into the air lock that marks the interface between what was and what is.

MORE DOORS THAN WALLS

"Take everything off, put your clothes in the bag, then put on the gown and have a seat," Jameara says. "Nurse Thomas will be in to examine you. I'll be back when you're done."

Jameara steps out, closing the door. Adriana strips, puts on the gown, and sits in the hard chair. This is her new life. She might as well get used to being ordered around and treated like a thing. Nurse Thomas—does that mean that the nurse about to examine her is some guy? No way a guy nurse is touching her. But she doesn't have a choice about it, does she?

She tenses at the sound of footsteps outside the door.

Stay calm. Be cool. Don't scream. When he comes in, she'll ask for a woman. They'll have to give her one, won't they?

She takes a deep breath of the cold antiseptic air and laces her fingers together. The door opens after a perfunctory knock, and a woman enters. Adriana tries to hide how relieved she is. Thomas must be her last name. She wears green scrubs, her hair is pulled into a tight bun at the nape of her neck, and she throws a no-nonsense look at Adriana.

"Hello, Adriana. I'm going to check you out and then you'll be good to go."

"You mean good to stay," Adriana points out.

"You got me there." As she speaks, she pulls on thin, vanilla-colored rubber gloves. "First I'm going to check your head for lice."

Lice? thinks Adriana. *Lice!*

She must read Adriana's indignation because she says, "Health code compliance. Doesn't matter how squeaky-clean you are, we've got to check."

Adriana sits as if made of stone, feeling Nurse Thomas's gloved fingers methodically parting her hair all the way down to the roots, and moving through it with a literal fine-tooth comb. Adriana wonders if that's where the expression comes from. A fine-tooth comb searching for lice. When she's satisfied that Adriana is louse-free, Nurse Thomas puts down the comb and takes a step back. "Okay, stand up, please, and hold your arms straight out, palms up."

Nurse Thomas checks the inside of her arms and her wrists. Adriana knows what she's looking for. Track marks.

"I don't use," says Adriana.

"We have to check," responds Nurse Thomas. "Health code."

Next, she examines between Adriana's toes, inspecting her

9

toenails for fungus, or toe jam, or whatever the hell else that might be a health code violation. Finally the nurse snaps off the gloves and drops them into a trash can, along with whatever is left of Adriana's dignity.

"To the right is the shower room. There's soap, towels, and a plastic bag holding your uniform. I'll tell Jameara you're almost ready."

After a shower where the water only hinted at getting warm, Adriana puts on her uniform: a Day-Glo yellow sweatshirt so bright it could be visible from space, puke-olive pants with an elastic waist, and generic sneakers.

As promised, Jameara's waiting for her. "That wasn't so hard, was it?" Jameara leads her out of the infirmary, tapping her badge to the reader near each door. They turn down another hallway, going past a single giant daisy painted on the wall—but it's not a full-fledged bloom; it's just a yellow outline of the blossom on the ice-white wall, drawn in a wiggly style like Jack Frost painted it, and the stem isn't exactly green; it's brown daubed with green like it's got some sad daisy disease. *Well, they tried,* she thinks. But to be honest, they didn't try hard enough.

Jameara stops at another door; her card whisks through the reader. The place is like a maze of cages connected by locked doors, with cameras everywhere. A cold draft breathes over Adriana, and she shivers.

Does this place ever warm up?

They step into a tunnel brightened by a series of round lights set into the ceiling. The lights gleam over a full mural painted in vibrant colors the entire length of the tunnel. Better, at least, than the desolate daisy.

"I know it might not feel like it, but you're lucky you were assigned to Compass," Jameara says. "Our facility's a little different from the others. A new way of thinking about juvenile detention."

She goes on to explain that there's more self-reliance and less rigidity than other facilities—although it all seems pretty rigid to Adriana. She doesn't want to imagine things being worse.

"Usually pre-adjudicated kids are housed separately from those who've already been sentenced—but we have special dispensation to blend the populations."

"And that's good . . . how?" asks Adriana.

"It gives the sentenced kids hope, and makes the kids awaiting trial less scared, because they know if they're found guilty, they'll be coming back to familiar faces."

Adriana wasn't quite "sentenced" but she did stand before a judge. It was all about lawyers making deals. At least she got to present herself this morning, rather than arriving in chains. Did they do that? She had no idea. At any rate, she likes the idea of a "mixed population," and that not every girl around her has already gotten the thumbs-down.

Another door, another card swish, and down a short hall ending at the most solid-looking door yet.

"We're in the girls' building now," says Jameara.

The sound of girls' voices and a blaring television spill through as they enter a large three-storied common area with steel stairs leading to the other levels, and doors on each wall, on every level. Adriana hangs behind Jameara. The last thing in the world she wants to do is meet a bunch of strangers all at once.

"This is the Rec Hub. You can spend free time in here—watch TV, and there are art supplies. Your pod also has a little living room—but that's just for the other girls you share the pod with."

Pods. What are we, whales?

Jameara sends another practiced smile her way, as if TV and colored pencils would solve everything.

I just need my journal, thank you very much. I'm already done with this tour. Can I go to my room now?

The Rec Hub has beige chairs and sofas, like if you looked up "furniture" on Google, these are the pictures you'd get. On one wall, a vertical band of glass maybe four inches wide lets in some daylight to compete with the fluorescent lighting.

"Girls," calls out Jameara, her voice commanding attention. Eyes fix on Adriana and silence falls, except for a Disney character on the TV. Adriana gets the feeling that television here is highly curated.

"Say hello to Adriana," says Jameara. "She's just joining us."

A couple of noncommittal hellos and heys float from the group. They all wear the same olive pants and yellow sweatshirts. Her gaze skates over the group, a blur of faces in various shades, and she wishes she were anywhere but here. She hates meeting people. They are always a disappointment. Her stomach tightens and tension grips her, but she flips up her hand in a *s'up* gesture, carefully keeping her smile to herself. She's not the needy type, and she wants them to know it.

Her eyes snag on a slight girl, underweight to the point of looking malnourished, and maybe a little bit hunched. Her feet dangle several inches from the floor, and her face seems as misplaced and innocent as that sad wall daisy back in the infirmary hallway. Compared to the other girls, she's almost ghostlike. Her ethnicity is a mystery. She could be any race, or any combination. But then, so could Adriana. So could half the girls here. The ghost girl gives Adriana a kind smile, and Adriana wonders what on earth this girl could have done to get her locked up.

Adriana realizes she's staring and looks away, inadvertently meeting dark eyes in a brown face that won every genetic lottery. The eyes preside over high cheekbones and a perfectly proportioned mouth holding a hint of a grin. This girl sits in an ugly armchair as if it were a throne, her legs resting in a feminine slant the way ladies sit in old movies; an elegant beauty attended by the girls around her.

Prom Princess with her court, thinks Adriana, taking in the other girls sitting around her. There's neither curiosity nor welcome in their faces, but the prom princess looks at her with a touch of interest, one slim-fingered hand idly stroking a long braid of glossy black hair.

Jameara gestures to the door. "I'll show you your room now."

Adriana is happy to have an excuse to get away from the stares, but she feels their eyes on her as she follows Jameara. Adriana brushes a hand through her hair, regaining her composure.

13

"Each floor has four pods, and each pod has five bedrooms." Jameara brings them through a door on the main floor of the Rec Hub, labeled with a bright yellow *C*, which leads to another air lock. "Each pod has a letter so you'll know which one you're in—you're in Pod C." She opens the door to reveal a pathetic mini living room with doors to several bedrooms.

More doors than walls in this place.

"Not all the rooms are occupied," Jameara tells her. "There are three other girls in Pod C, so you'll be the fourth. The fifth bedroom is used for storage."

She takes Adriana to a door embossed with a yellow number four. Jameara's card hisses through the reader. "Here we are. C4," she says. "This is home."

Adriana steps in, dragging her feet on the concrete floor.

A built-in platform bed grows out of the windowless wall. It's unmade, with a bedroll and a single pillow. A low cinder-block divider only partially hides a stainless-steel toilet and, a few feet away, a sink attached to the wall. No desk, no chair.

She casts Jameara a you've-got-to-be-kidding gaze. "It looks like a kennel."

Without stepping into the cell, Jameara leans against the doorframe in a way that's both casual and not casual at all. "It's just a place to sleep. You won't be spending all that much time here—and the bedrolls are comfortable; that's what matters."

"So I'm a dog, but a comfortable dog."

Jameara ignores her. It must be part of her training. No negative attention given.

"Right there is your detainee handbook," says Jameara, pointing to a pamphlet lying on the pillow. "Read it," she continues. "I'm happy to answer any questions, but I think the handbook's pretty clear."

When Jameara straightens, Adriana stiffens. The woman looks like she's going to give a pep talk, and that raises Adriana's walls high.

"I know things seem bleak to you right now—believe me—I know how painful life can be for young people, especially a young girl like yourself." Jameara looks so serious, her tone so quiet, Adriana can't help but be drawn in. She waits silently for the rest of what Jameara might say, barbed wire now atop her walls.

"I want you to know and to believe that your future lies in you. Right now, you're looking for it, but don't worry; in time you'll find it." Jameara smiles. "Okay?"

Adriana crosses her arms over her chest, hunching her shoulders. "Sure," she says, but she doesn't believe it. Her stepmother would say something like that. She's full of touchy-feely crap too.

As uninviting as her room is, Adriana wishes she could just stay here for the rest of the day, but Jameara is already on to the next item on her agenda.

"It's nearly lunchtime." Jameara steps back from the doorframe. "Normally you'd be escorted with the rest of the girls, but just this once I'll take you to the cafeteria myself."

Leaving Adriana's room, Jameara pulls the door closed

behind them and Adriana hears the lock click into place. It must be her least favorite sound in the world.

The cafeteria is a large room of rectangular tables with no-nonsense bolts securing them to the floor. Flimsy plastic chairs are upside-down on top of each table, their legs sticking up in the air. *Why are the tables solid and bolted, but the chairs so cheap?* she wonders. There must be some detention center logic she's missing. Or maybe it's just bureaucratic stupidity. It makes her think of her school library. The school made a big deal about its renovation, only to discover that the designers had failed to put in electrical outlets. When questioned, they had said, "Why would you need outlets in a library?" The thought of her old school gives her a sudden pang. She wonders if this place even has a library. She wants to pretend she doesn't care, but she does.

It suddenly occurs to Adriana that the reason for cheap plastic chairs is to prevent kids from weaponizing them. Or at least from causing too much damage if they try. Now she wishes she hadn't figured it out.

Two girls at the far end of the cafeteria have begun taking down the lightweight chairs and arranging them at each table. A food station runs the length of one wall; its metal front shines dully in the faint daylight falling through the thin band of window glass set just below the ceiling.

"We have chores here, including cafeteria work. You'll find out how we do things at orientation tomorrow. Breakfast is at

16

seven, lunch at eleven, and dinner at five."

"Why so early?" Adriana asks.

"The cafeteria is one of several areas we share with the boys. Girls get seven, eleven, and five; boys get eight, noon, and six."

"Sucks that they get better hours."

Jameara grins. "Yeah, but they do all the after-meal cleanup. To remind them that you girls are not their maids."

Although they're a few minutes early for lunch, the food's ready, so Jameara takes her to the service counter. Adriana glances at the girls setting up for lunch. One of them puts a chair down and stares at Adriana, her face a mask. She turns her head, catches the other girl's eye, and jerks a nod toward Adriana as if to say, *Check out the fresh meat.*

"Go ahead," says Jameara. "The others will be here in a minute."

Adriana takes a tray from the stack, breathing in the aroma of institutional food, which is an oasis in the midst of other less appealing odors that permeate the center.

"So new girls get to go first?" asks Adriana.

"Well, I figure you must be hungry. I've dragged you all over the place."

Behind the counter, a hefty woman in a white apron with a net covering her hair presides over the warming trays. Lunch ladies are the same throughout the universe.

"Dorella, this is Adriana. She just joined us."

"Hey there, Adriana," says Dorella.

Behind her, two more staff workers at a long steel table place lettuce and tomato chunks in the corner section of rectangular partitioned plates, finishing them off with a dollop of Thousand Island dressing. Dorella grabs one of the plates.

"Spaghetti and meatballs, or fish sticks?" Dorella asks—and Jameara points out that kids at other facilities don't get to choose what they eat. It's part of the Compass experience.

Adriana chooses the pasta, and Dorella piles on spaghetti, slops on sauce and meatballs, then adds a slice of garlic toast, and hands the plate to Adriana. She hates Thousand Island dressing, but that's not one of the things she gets to choose.

Adriana takes a napkin-wrapped plastic fork and a plastic cup from the last counter. After filling the cup with water, she sits at a table, unwraps the fork, and takes a tentative taste. The food smells good, but the meatball tastes like cardboard, and the spaghetti's texture is beyond sad.

How do they manage to get the spaghetti mushy and crunchy at the same time?

"Good job, girls," Jameara says to the chair flippers. All the chairs are down and neatly placed. The girls now stand with their hands behind their backs. Adriana can tell they're trying not to stare at her, but she feels their eyes on her anyway.

What're they waiting for . . . orders? Adriana wonders.

The cafeteria door opens, and a female guard in a khaki uniform with a shield-shaped badge on a shirt sleeve leads in a line of girls, all walking with their hands behind their backs and all absolutely quiet. The two chair flippers join them at the end of the line.

"At ease, ladies," says the guard.

The girls file past Adriana to the food counter, casting curious looks her way. She recognizes Prom Princess and her court from the communal area.

Jameara flashes a quick smile at Adriana. "Everyone at a table remains standing until either it's filled or they're given permission to sit. But you get a pass for the first meal."

Adriana grimaces. A "pass" just singles her out.

"I'm going to leave you now." Jameara nods toward the guard. "Officer Bonivich will be here," she says, departing. Adriana wonders why Jameara thinks she might need a security guard.

Having to share the room with a pack that has yet to accept her makes the meal seem even less appetizing than it already is. She looks down at her plate and focuses on winding spaghetti on the tines of her fork, taking her time to eat as slowly as she can, because sitting there with nothing to focus on is the stuff of nightmares.

Behind her she hears the rattle of trays and the shuffling of feet as the girls move along the line. Then she looks up to see two girls approaching her table. One is a girl with limp blond hair, carrying a tray. The other is the small ghostly girl, who doesn't carry anything.

"Hi," says the sickly girl. "I'm Pip. This is Jolene."

Jolene, who's managing to hold Pip's tray as well as her own, gives her a timid smile. "Adriana, right?"

"Right," says Adriana.

Jolene puts Pip's tray on the table in front of Pip.

"Such personal service," Adriana comments, standing up, so as not to be rude, since they have to stand until the table is full.

Pip shrugs. "Jolene just likes to help. Sometimes carrying a tray is hard for me."

Adriana wants to ask why but suspects it would be out of line, so instead she says, "Pip's a cute name. Is it real, or a nickname?"

This earns Adriana a cheerful grin, reminding her of her three-year-old half brother whose face lights up the same way. *How old is she?* Adriana wonders.

"A little bit of both, I guess," says Pip. "It's short for Penelope."

Then the Prom Princess approaches with a few members of her court, and they join Pip, Jolene, and Adriana at their table. The girl gives Adriana a warm smile. She's Latina, but there's a hint of something else there too. Indian? Filipina? Adriana wonders why she's programmed to care.

When a tall, thin girl with wide attitude arrives at the last spot at the table, everyone sits. Then the tall girl gives Adriana a look as cold and flat as the room's walls. "Who said you could sit with us?"

This girl looks like a mix of every ethnicity under the sun. No way to know how she identifies, except for being the prime shadow to the Princess's glimmer. "I asked you a question!"

Adriana gets it right away—this is the girl who keeps the court in line, so the Princess doesn't have to do it herself. Her challenging tone ruffles Adriana's nerves in spite of herself.

"Didn't think I needed permission," replies Adriana—not as

a challenge, but in a mild tone of voice. "Besides, I didn't 'sit with you'—I was already here. You guys came and sat with me."

The girl just glares at her, contempt plain in her eyes. Does she not know she's a cliché? Or maybe she does, and she's just owning it.

Finally Prom Princess speaks up. "I'm Bianca," she says. "This my girl, Monessa." She waves a hand toward Tall Girl. "And you're right, we sat by you—because they tell me you're in Monessa's and my pod," she tells Adriana. Adriana's not sure that's good news. "Which means you can sit with us anytime."

Monessa's eyes don't lose their coldness, but she backs down.

"Okay, thanks," Adriana says.

Then, out of nowhere, Monessa takes her fork, reaches over to Adriana's tray, stabs one of Adriana's anemic meatballs, and eats it in one bite.

But before Adriana can even react, Pip speaks up. "Monessa, don't be that way!" Then Pip takes one of her own meatballs and plops it onto Adriana's tray to replace the stolen one. "Here, I didn't want it anyway," Pip says with a smile.

And then everyone waits to see what Adriana will do.

She turns to Monessa. "You gonna take this one too?"

Monessa shrugs. "Not hungry no more."

Adriana knows that this is some kind of test, with Bianca the silent judge and jury. The question is, what's the right move? Should she eat it? Should she give it back to Pip? Should she smash her tray over Monessa's head to show these girls that she can't be messed with? In the end, she goes with her

21

gut, and just gives the meatball back to Pip.

"No thanks, Pip," Adriana says. "I'm not the kind of dirtbag who takes another person's food."

Monessa's face turns all sorts of purple. "What did you call me?"

"Nothing—I'm talking about meatballs," Adriana says.

Monessa postures for a fight—but just then the guard walks over.

"Got a problem here?"

She's a stocky woman, round face, short brown curly hair; her khaki uniform is sharply pressed and fits her snugly. Her name tag indicates that this is the Officer Bonivich that Jameara spoke of.

Adriana thinks that Bianca might be the one to deflect Bonivich's attention, but instead it's Pip who speaks up.

"Hello, Officer Bonivich. We're good here," Pip says with a big old smile. "We were just working out portions. Some of us got more than others, so we're trying to even it out."

Bonivich considers it, nods without another word, and walks off.

And then, wonder of wonders, Bianca smiles.

"Well, that was fun." And at that decree, Monessa drops her hackles, but not without a warning stare in Adriana's direction.

3

"TELL ME WHY YOU'RE HERE"

Meet me in the park, you said,
So I sped.
I'm your friend, you said,
And friends help friends
To the dank dirty end,
So I rode my way down
To the pitiful patch
Of crabgrass
And grabass
Misnamed a park,
Where boys wanting action,
Their own satisfaction,
Infest the sickly sycamores at night,
While in the day,

Little kids,
Oblivious to the lascivious,
Teeter in the playground,
Spinning round and round,
They laugh and swing,
And the thing—the STING
Is as far from their minds
As from mine.
But you know what's coming.
You sense it,
No matter how dense it's left me,
I am your plan, your ploy,
Your escape,
Some low-res shape
In your pitiful patch.
Now you're there by the curb
Where dogs crap and drunks bleed,
Your scraps of weed and powder and pills,
All changed for bills,
Jackson and Grant,
Hey, girl, can't you help
And be my eyes?
You ask,
As you pimp your packets of pain.
Because friends do right by friends
By night and by day and never say
No.

Until shit goes down,
Nose-down, closed down,
As trust goes bust,
And we're busted.

The sting
Has venom,
All black and white
And spinning lights,
We're read our rights,
And the world melts down
To the lies on your lips
That called me your friend.
And now they say
It will all be okay,
But for you, only you,
Because I still don't know
Your hidden finger—the second stinger,
points to me.
Your accusation abomination
Replaces me in your damnation.
I'm your friend, you said,
But what you meant
Was bent
Into a hinge on that black door,
A trap door,
For your magical disappearance,

While I ran interference,
Never knowing I was the one being played,
Being made,
With no crime
But the dime bags YOU put in my pocket.
What a shock it was to see your betrayal
Of your perfect besties portrayal.
It's only in cuffs
That I finally know,
When you said friend,
You meant dead end.

The jangling of bells jerks Adriana out of sleep. She presses her hands against her ears for all the good it doesn't do. *What the hell?* The morning bell echoes within the concrete walls of her room and abruptly stops, leaving a shaken silence. The door clicks. For a moment she thinks someone's there—but no. It's the door automatically unlocking for her.

She reflexively looks for her journal, to catalog her feelings about all of this, but quickly realizes that it's gone. Confiscated by Paula the intake troll. Did she read it? Adriana wonders. Her private thoughts violated by people who couldn't care less. Best not to think about that.

She scrambles off the platform bed, pushes her feet into thin rubber slippers, and, dressed in her pajamas, goes to stand outside the door, facing it with her hands behind her back in the required hand-to-wrist hold. Something she learned quickly, without having to be told. *Damn, it feels like the crack of dawn.* She rests her head against the door and closes her eyes.

"Head up, Zareen!"

Officer Bonivich's voice snaps her to attention.

"Zarahn," Adriana corrects, then regrets it. Does she really want to get on Bonivich's bad side so quickly?

"My mistake," Bonivich says. "Zarahn."

Adriana can't tell whether she's being genuine or sarcastic. She has the kind of voice that makes everything she says sound mocking.

"Let's go, ladies!"

They march to the showers. Ten minutes later Adriana is back in her room. She dresses in a fresh set of clothes, then deftly plaits her wet hair into a single braid but decides that looks a little too much like Bianca, so she undoes it. Then she goes to stand once more outside her door, waiting to be escorted to breakfast. Yesterday after dinner, Jameara dropped by and told her she'd have her first session with Dr. Alvarado, the staff psychiatrist, after her first class. She hopes she gets her journal back.

Day two, she thinks. Probably not a good idea to count the days. Her time will only seem longer.

Behind her she hears a cough and faint wheeze. She glances back. Pip catches her gaze and winks at her. *Strange girl,* Adriana thinks. *But at least she's friendly.*

◆ ◆ ◆

27

In the cafeteria at breakfast, Adriana takes a moment to gather the big picture that she didn't get at lunch or dinner the day before, probably because most of her cafeteria time was spent looking into her food or trying to deal with the group of girls she was sitting with. Adriana knows an awful lot can be learned about a place from cafeteria dynamics, and Bianca's court is only a subset of the larger population.

The faces around her range from vampiric pale to pure cacao, with every shade in between. More brown faces than white—clearly this place isn't a cross section of America, but more a cross section of who America kicks to the curb.

While prisons tend to break sharply along racial lines, that kind of thing is strongly discouraged here. "We are a community at Compass," Jameara explained. "Not factions." Even so, there are tables of Black girls, white girls, and Latina girls, each insisting upon their own—but most everyone else seems to put race aside in the cafeteria, saving it, perhaps, for when it matters.

For a lot of the girls, it's hard to tell how they identify. But then, Adriana isn't much different. Her father's family is Moroccan, her mother's Greek and Spanish. Her "Mediterranean" look can legitimately be seen as many things. She has found, however, that ambiguity is a double-edged sword. Yes, she can fit in with crowds that want her to—but can also be seen as "other" by crowds that don't.

"Empty spot here, pod-mate!" Bianca indicates the space to her right at the table where she and her regulars stand, waiting for the last spot to fill. Adriana realizes that Bianca intentionally saved the space for her.

"Thanks," she says, avoiding Monessa's disapproving stare.

Adriana's arrival allows them all to sit. She looks at her tray. Cheesy scrambled eggs bracketed by two triangles of toast and a couple of strips of bacon. The aroma of cheese mingled with bacon makes her stomach growl.

The girls make small talk in between bites. Adriana keeps waiting for someone to ask her what landed her here at Compass. But maybe it's an unspoken rule that you don't ask. Still, she wonders how she'd answer if they did. There are various reasons Adriana is here, all of which are true. Skipping school, hanging out with "bad influences," bailing from the foster homes she'd been forced to live in until her father cleaned up his act, leaving her with a stepmother she doesn't like. And then the final reason.

When the conversation around the table lags, the other girls also begin to brood on their own thoughts as they eat. A dark interior is something they must all have in common.

An hour later, they're sitting at desks in history class. Apparently Monessa isn't allowed to be near Bianca in class because their desks are across the room from each other. Adriana's assigned spot is next to Bianca—which is good, because being close to the Queen Bee is wise. And because it's bound to piss off Monessa.

The teacher is not actually in the room. She's on a big TV

screen, a meticulously coiffed woman with a background almost as fake as her eyebrows. She drones on about historical child exploitation, such as forced marriages, and occasionally she poses questions to individuals in the group, perhaps to remind them that this is an interactive feed, and that she can see them. Even so, sometimes she seems like a recording of a talking head. There's a room monitor in case a physical presence is required. Mostly she keeps track of pens and does crosswords.

As the teacher goes on and on about child brides, Bianca gives an exaggerated roll of her eyes. "I hate listening to this."

Adriana glances at her sympathetically. "Me too. As if we need to be reminded how shitty things have been for women."

Then Bianca leans a bit closer. "I almost got trafficked myself."

"Really?"

"Yep. One of my mom's losers talked her into pimping me out. They pretended like I was going to a girls'-night-out party. Dressed me up in this glittery minidress, Mom did my makeup. I was kind of excited 'cause she hardly paid that kind of attention to me." Bianca looks up to make sure the teacher is too involved in the lecture to notice what's going on in the room.

"Anyway, we get there, and as soon as I walk in, I knew what was going on. There were lots of girls dressed like me, you know, streetwalker style, and one of the guys, looked like some college boy, wanted me to come over to him."

"What did you do?" asks Adriana.

"I tried to run out of there. Got to the front door but it was locked."

"Seriously?"

Bianca nods. "Stone locked, girl. I had to climb out a bathroom window." Her eyes glaze with the memory. "My own mother."

"That sucks, Bianca." For a moment Adriana feels a crack in the wall Bianca lives behind. The walls they *both* live behind. But the moment passes; Bianca brushes at her eyes and glances sideways away from Adriana's gaze the way a person does when they want to act as if it means nothing.

"Ladies," pipes up the teacher, "are you with us today?"

"Where the hell else would we be?" Bianca says, clearly displacing her thoughts about her mother on the teacher.

"Language, Bianca."

"Yeah, yeah."

The teacher considers Bianca, then decides that Bianca's not a boat you rock. Instead, she gestures to Adriana.

"Miss Zarahn, please take a different seat."

The room monitor takes that as a cue to stand and point to a new spot for Adriana. After Adriana moves, she glances at Bianca, who gives her a grin. Because having your seat changed by the teacher—even remotely—is a badge of honor.

After history class ends, Officer Bonivich escorts Adriana to the staff psychiatrist's office. Adriana walks next to her, hands behind her back, matching her steps to the officer's. The odor of cigarette smoke slaps her in the face as soon as they step into Alvarado's office—like oxygen-masks-should-drop-from-the-ceiling kind of stench. It's only on his clothes—no smoking at

Compass—but damn did those threads suck in the funk.

Alvarado dismisses Bonivich and gestures to one of two armchairs arranged around a table. "Please take a seat, Miss Zarahn." On his cluttered desk is an open folder with Adriana's name on it.

So is Adriana's journal.

It pokes out from a haphazard pile of paperwork. She wants to grab it and leave but knows that would probably ensure he'd take it away from her for good.

Alvarado grabs her case file with his nicotine-stained fingers, but instead of going over it, closes it and folds his arms, leaning back in his chair.

"Tell me why you're here."

Adriana thinks this must be a trick question. Or the guy's just too lazy to read it for himself. She points to the folder. "Isn't it all in there?"

"I've already read it," Alvarado says, then flips his hand like swatting away a fly. "Affidavits, reports, forms. Words, words, words. But not the words I'm interested in." He pauses, fixing eye contact. "Why are you here?"

Adriana fixes her gaze on the droopy mustache framing his mouth like the jowls of a walrus. She doesn't know what answer will free her from this little puzzle box of a room.

"I can wait," says Alvarado. "We don't have all day, but our appointment lasts for twenty minutes. We could sit here staring at each other, bored to death during that time, or you can answer the question, Adriana."

The idea of staring at Alvarado—and the overly white teeth that keep peeking out from beneath his mustache—for twenty minutes motivates her to give an answer.

"I didn't do what they said I did, and I got screwed."

"Nope," says Alvarado, far too pleasantly.

"So, you just want me to say I *was* selling drugs in that park? Is that it?"

Alvarado shrugs. "Irrelevant. The other girl says it was you, you say it was her. Either way, that's not the real reason you're here."

That "other girl" Alvarado mentioned was, in theory, Adriana's friend. She didn't have all that many, but this girl she seemed to connect with. And even after Adriana knew she was making some change with dime bags, Adriana didn't end the friendship, because in Adriana's life, friends have been few and far between. Sometimes you deny what you know until it's too late. And when this so-called friend asked her to keep a lookout for cops, or anything suspicious that day, Adriana did—because isn't that what friends do? Favors? Even when they might get you in trouble? In the end, the girl said she wasn't dealing at all—that *she* was the one helping Adriana. And had a better lawyer. She got probation. Adriana got sent here.

"I picked the wrong friends," Adriana offers Alvarado.

He shows a little more of his over-white teeth. "Now we're getting somewhere. Keep going."

Now that Adriana knows the type of bullshit answers Alvarado wants, she can flip them out to him like cards.

"I pissed off my stepmother."

"I lied to my father."

"I disrespected my teachers."

"I punched some dude for no reason."

Adriana has no idea if any of that is in her file, but what does it matter? It's all true. Which means they're not bullshit answers at all.

"So, can you wrap that all up into a single 'I' statement?" Alvarado asks.

"Uh . . . I'm a complete loser?"

The man gives off a condescending chuckle that makes her want to rip off his mustache like they do in cartoons. "No, Adriana. Nothing so severe."

And when she doesn't continue the game, he finally answers for her.

"You're here," he says, "because of your own bad choices. Even if you're innocent of the crime that landed you at Compass, you're still here because of a habitual tendency to make poor decisions."

He pauses as if Adriana's head is so thick, his words need time to sink in. She really dislikes this man in a profound and fundamental way.

"Other than that, you strike me as a nice girl with a fine future, unless you continue to sabotage yourself."

So there it is. Alvarado's final judgment. Now everything about her will have to revolve around that simplistic assessment. It's good, in a way. It means that following the rules and keeping her file clean will allow Alvarado to check all the necessary boxes for her. Maybe even get her out early on his recommendation. That is, unless he's right, and she sabotages herself.

"So," says Alvarado, "considering what we now know about you, why are you here?"

Again that question.

"I mean that in a grander, universal way," Alvarado clarifies, gesturing broadly with his hands.

And although Adriana wants to tell him to shove his grand universe up his ass, she says, "I'm here to learn how to make better choices."

Alvarado smiles. "Simple as that." He leans back, incredibly self-satisfied. Glancing down at a paper on his desk, he says, "Your antianxiety RX from home was low-dosage and as-needed. I'll take you off it for now. We can prescribe it later if you need it."

Great. So now some juvie joker gets to decide what meds she needs—a doc-in-a-box who probably couldn't get a real job outside of this place. If Compass is supposed to be all "new concept," couldn't they spring for someone better than this guy? Everything about him, from his messy office to his fake smile, screams bargain basement.

"I'll see you next week," Alvarado says, then he calls for Bonivich to escort her out—because although it hasn't been twenty minutes, he got what he wanted from her. Adriana feels dirty somehow. As if she was just an accomplice in her own humiliation.

But before Bonivich comes in, Adriana asks the one thing that matters to her.

"My journal," she says, and points to it, within the debris on his desk. "Can I have it back now?"

Alvarado pulls out the small brown leather book from the pile it's under.

"Ah yes, your journal." He holds it a moment, looking at it, no doubt deciding whether or not to give it back to her.

Adriana waits, watching him. She won't ask again. Asking again would show weakness. Even more than she's already shown.

"If thoughts are worth having, they're certainly worth writing down," he says, then holds it out to her. Stepping up, Adriana takes it, feeling relief wash over her. Until he says, "Of course, I can't give you a pen. They're all monitored."

Always a catch. Adriana wonders if he's enjoying this. "So how—?"

"You can check out a pen in class or in the library. But it has to stay there when you leave." Then he waits for her reaction, but she gives him none. He takes a moment, pretending to ponder, then puts up a finger as if just coming up with an idea. "I think I can solve your problem." He scrounges around on his train wreck of a desk and comes up with a cheap ballpoint pen. Then he pulls on the tip until the floppy ink insert slides out of the hard plastic sheath. He holds the ink insert out to Adriana. "Writing instruments can be used as weapons—but I don't think you can do any damage with this."

It flops in his hand, a spineless thing. A pen with erectile dysfunction. She has to purse her lips to keep from smirking, because now that's how she'll always think of him. She takes it, and although she doesn't want to offer the man any gratitude, she gives him an obligatory "Thank you."

"Anyone asks, tell them you got it from me."

Then, as she looks at the journal in her other hand, something occurs to her. Something she wished had never entered her mind.

"You read it!" Adriana exclaims before she can stop herself, her tone full of accusation. She hugs her journal to her chest, outrage burning in her.

"That would be an invasion of privacy, Miss Zarahn," Alvarado says. "Under the circumstances, it might be warranted, but it would also be unprofessional."

And although he makes it sound like he hasn't read it, Adriana notices that he never said that. In fact, he never actually denied it.

This man is dangerous, thinks Adriana. *Not because of what he does, but because of what he can do. Not because of the things he says, but because of the things he doesn't.*

PLATITUDES AND ATTITUDES

I am Compass,
Brick and mortar,
Blood and bone.
Aware but alone,
Just the scrapings of souls
Who left bits of themselves behind,
Like the faint whisper of flesh on pavement
When a child skins a knee.
Enslavement,
This is me.
I do not question my awareness.
Or the unfairness.
I only know that I see but don't feel.
When they stumble and fall,
I don't crumble at all

Under the weight of what I witness.
I pretend to be witless.
I was built to be the brutal frame
For a futile game of hide-and-seek,
Though no one comes seeking.
It's more about hiding.
And chiding.
And dividing.
Those abiding within my walls
Question the direction
Of my so-called correction.
   "Who am I now?"
   "Do I still exist?"
They are unmissed, unfixed
By my detention dimension.
I am here to erase the world's memory
Of the kids it refuses to think about.
Some are rejected.
Some are ejected.
The rest are digested.

Sitting cross-legged on the bed with the journal propped open on her knee, Adriana writes with the floppy pen cartridge that cramps her fingers to use. She has to write the date at the top of the page each day, because the days have already begun to blend together, passing in a numbing rain of emotional sleet. She swore she wouldn't count the days, but now she has to, just to know that time is actually moving.

Sometimes she writes about her impressions of the other girls. Sometimes the staff. Today it's about Compass itself. How it feels like a living, breathing thing. Always watching. There's a room at the end of all the camera feeds, no doubt, with people monitoring the comings and goings—but it still feels like those cameras are the eyes of some silent, unthinkable being.

Writing in the journal eases her, melts the tension that sits in the pit of her stomach all the time. It's strange, because the things she puts down are never pretty. Harsh emotions and cruel realities. You'd think they'd just rile her up . . . but it's more like popping a balloon to let all the bad air inside out, where it can dissipate, becoming less and less toxic with every passing breeze. She remembered once seeing a balloon rupture in slow motion. How it shredded and contracted around the air inside, which still held its shape until the tatters of rubber practically vanished. There's so little holding Adriana's bad air in. All it takes is the point of a pen to release it. And then she's free of it just a little. The thing is, there are so many damn balloons.

She squeezes her eyes shut tight against a push of tears. She's not the kind of girl who cries over things, no matter what. She's learned not to expect much from others—of course, her dad, the judge, the counselors she's seen, don't expect much from her. But then, you can't really disappoint when everyone already expects you to be a disappointment. So maybe Compass is where she's supposed to be.

That's a thought she's not ready to pop, so she closes the book and slips it under her mattress.

◆ ◆ ◆

Once a week, the girls have Self-Esteem group. Platitudes versus attitudes. Not a single girl in the room wants to be there, which could be said about most things at Compass, but Self-Esteem group is its own special circle of hell. Even though it's run by Jameara, who ranks high on the decency spectrum, it's still torturous, and she knows it.

"Girls, it's important for your futures that you not only see the glass half-full, but also full of something worthwhile," she pleads.

"*Half*-full of something worthwhile, you mean," Monessa deadpans, and shifts her slouch to something boneless. "Other half is nothing but air."

Finally, mercifully, it ends. If Adriana had to think of one more thing to "validate" herself, she would have screamed. She slips through the gang of girls in the doorway, leaving the meeting room. It's the free hour before lunch, and the auto-locks in the common areas are turned off. The girls can hang in their pods or the Rec Hub, or visit the library. They are constantly reminded that this is more freedom than other detention facilities ever give.

Adriana, her journal tucked inside the elastic waistband of her pants, goes to the library for privacy—what little she gets—instead of her room, where Bianca is likely to peer in and wonder what Adriana's up to, along with Monessa, who sticks to Bianca like a thorn on a rose.

But no one's going to look for her in the library. It's a sanctuary she found on the first day, although it's only open to them Monday, Wednesday, and Friday. Sometimes it's empty; other times, there are a few girls in there, all in their own private bubbles, not wanting to be bothered, just like Adriana. Communal isolation.

"Hello, Adriana!" Ms. Detrick is the librarian. She gets points for remembering Adriana's name right off the bat. Adriana flips her a wave and heads toward the back of the library. Like most spaces within Compass, the library has an open design. A few rows of bookshelves, not deep enough to get into any trouble, and a big space in the middle. No place to hide. But there is one spot that Adriana found. A little alcove in the back corner that leads to an emergency exit that's mostly out of view. Adriana plops down in the corner of the alcove. She may be creating some kind of fire hazard, blocking the emergency exit like that, but so far Ms. Detrick hasn't complained—and as Adriana's father always says, it's better to ask for forgiveness than permission. It's a philosophy that helped him to screw up his life, but also allowed him to redeem it. Wisdom is a double-edged sword.

Once seated, and mostly out of sight, she pulls out the journal. Lana bought it at a sorry little stationery shop at their local mall and wrapped it up as a gift. One of the few kindnesses Adriana's stepmother ever offered. Even so, it was probably bought at a discount.

She leafs through it, idly scanning her older entries about her stepmother, her father, her half brother, and the "friend" who landed her in juvie.

No, she didn't land me here. I did.

Like Alvarado said, in his gloating, self-satisfied way, it was Adriana's own stupid decisions that kicked her to this god-forsaken curb. But on the other hand, when the world slips you nothing but bad choices, how do you know which choice is the least-worse one?

"Adriana?"

Caught off guard, she looks up at the librarian. Quickly she closes her journal.

"Didn't mean to startle you," says Ms. Detrick. "It's almost lunchtime. You should get back to your room—you don't want to miss roll call."

Roll call! Adriana has no idea what happens if she's not there for lineup—but everything in this place is about punctuality and following orders. And for girls who regularly defy authority, no one ever seems to miss lineup—whatever the consequences of not being there to be counted, they must be bad.

Pins and needles in her legs. Adriana stamps her feet to wake them, and sees that she's the last girl in the library. Because it's such a short and direct walk to the girls' unit from the library—and because there is no shortage of cameras in that hallway—it's one of the few areas where the girls don't have to be escorted by guards. "And," Jameara told her, "it encourages responsibility. You and no one *but* you has to make sure you're lined up for roll call." It's one of Compass's many experiments in self-reliance. One that she's about to fail.

She hurries out just as the bell rings, sprints down the hall to the Rec Hub. If she's a second too late, all the doors will auto-lock, and she won't be able to get inside. She'll be caught out in the hallway and face the consequences of not getting with the program.

"Here comes Miss Zero'n," says Monessa as Adriana arrives, out of breath. "Lucky Bonivich ain't here yet to see you're late."

Adriana spares her a cutting glance, not caring if Monessa doesn't like it. "Zero'n" instead of Zarahn. It's one of the various annoying nicknames Monessa has been trying to foist on Adriana, but none of them are sticking.

Adriana doesn't have time to go to her room, because she can already hear Bonivich's approaching footsteps, and the sound of the doors all locking. She does her best to catch her breath, clasps her hands behind her back, and glances around to where Pip stands lined up nearly a head shorter than the rest of them. She's in Pod B, but she hangs more with Bianca, Monessa, and Jolene, who are in Adriana's pod.

"Let's go, ladies!" Bonivich strides in, checking that everyone's lined up in front of their pod doors. Once roll call is done, she turns and strides back to the front. "Fall in!"

"Delusions of a drill sergeant," murmurs Adriana.

Jolene giggles behind her and quickly crosses over to where Pip stands. Hands clasped behind their backs, the girls turn and walk out of the Hub, heading toward the cafeteria.

It's only when Adriana arrives in the cafeteria that she realizes her journal isn't in her waistband.

WORDS, AWOL

She tries not to panic. She tries not to let on in any way that something is wrong. She can't reveal a crack that anyone could jam a wedge into, splitting it wide.

After lunch, she tries to retrace her steps, but the hallway to the library is closed. When she's able to get back to her pod, she looks in her room, just in case by some incredible mercy, someone found it and returned it. No such luck.

She has no memory of having put it back in her waistband. Her last memory of her journal was closing it, and slipping the floppy pen insert in her shoe—then realizing she was going to be late for roll call . . .

. . . and she left it there! She left it on the floor for anyone to find. How could she have been so stupid? There were things she wrote in there that nobody should see. The wrong person gets ahold of it, and she'll have enemies here. Maybe a whole lot of them.

Would Ms. Detrick see it? Would she read it? Would she turn it over to Alvarado, only for it to end up on his desk again? The thought of it sickens her. The library is closed to the girls' side until the day after tomorrow. All that time to stress and fret about its fate.

Anxiety about her journal keeps her eyes open and staring at nothing for most of the night, leaving her exhausted in the morning. *Get through this,* she thinks. *I'll figure a way into the library.*

The morning seems to pass like a stream of miserable selfies. Flashes of semiconsciousness. Now she's in the shower. Now she's standing in front of her room for roll call. Now she's lined up for a breakfast she's not hungry for. She hopes that breakfast with the other girls can be a distraction—or at least that it can pass quickly like a screenshot, too, but suddenly time goes the way of Einstein and stretches for the maximum level of personal torture.

Still twitchy-anxious and distracted, she stands behind the chair Bianca has saved for her. And when every space is taken, they all sit down.

Monessa's clearly not happy that Bianca's been making room for Adriana right next to her, but Bianca couldn't care less. Adriana catches Pip's gaze moving between the two, then Pip gives Adriana an innocent smile. But somehow that smile doesn't seem reflected in Pip's dark eyes.

She watches everyone, thinks Adriana. But then, perhaps she needs to, to keep herself safe from the bigger, more volatile girls.

Adriana scoops up some eggs in her spork. They taste like moist crumpled paper.

Paper. Like my journal.

Damn—she can't keep it out of her mind for five seconds.

Monessa doesn't say two words the whole time, and although Bianca chats amiably with Adriana and the other girls, she says nothing to Monessa. Adriana isn't sure what to make of that, except maybe the two of them argued. Maybe about her. Monessa's jealousy is thick enough to paint the walls a nice puke green—but Bianca would just tell her to pick a better color. There's some satisfaction in Bianca's cold shoulder to Monessa, but Adriana also feels that can't end well for anyone.

Breakfast passes without incident, except Adriana catches Monessa's under-eyed stare, a promise that it isn't over between them.

Bring it, bitch, thinks Adriana, staring back.

And later that morning, she does.

History. The class right before free hour, and her chance to get into the library. Problem is, the boys will be there today. Can't go anyplace the boys are. But maybe she can get there the second the hour starts, before the boys arrive. Maybe Ms. Detrick will hold off the wolves until she has a chance to look for her journal—or even better, hand it to her at the door.

Snick, snick, snick.

On the classroom screen, their history teacher is droning, and Adriana can't focus enough to even know what it is she's droning about.

Snick, snick, snick.

What is that annoying sound? It's coming from right behind her, intruding on her stress bubble, getting on her nerves. Adriana glances around to find Monessa sitting at the desk behind her instead of in her assigned seat. Their classroom attendant and their talking-head teacher either don't notice or don't care. Slack in the rules? Why couldn't it be slack in Adriana's favor, instead of this?

Snick, snick, snick. The girl is cracking her knuckles, one right after the other. She does it over and over, like she has an endless amount of hands with an endless supply of knuckles. Adriana's frayed nerves jump at each crack of bone against bone.

Monessa meets Adriana's look; her lips curve in a smug smile.

"Miss Zarahn, please pay attention," says the teacher.

Heads turn Adriana's way and heat comes to her cheeks.

"Stop it!" she hisses at Monessa, and turns her attention back to the monitor. There's a beat of uncomfortable silence before the teacher resumes her lecture. Something about Victorian corsets, and how women's woes were dismissed by Victorian men as something called "vapors."

Thunk.

A vibration travels from underneath her chair up Adriana's spine.

Thunk. Monessa's kicking the leg of Adriana's chair.

Adriana draws upon the little patience she has, already thinned by lack of sleep. She doubles her concentration on the monitor, tries to pretend it's nothing.

Thunk-thunk. Pause. *Thunk.*

The vibration trembles through Adriana; her aggravation zips from low burn to flame. She jerks around and glares at Monessa. Enough already.

"What are you—ten?" she says through gritted teeth.

Monessa gives her the finger.

Anger flashes hot in Adriana, crowding out the drowsy fog in her head. She's up and out of her chair before realizing she's moved, before remembering Monessa is half a head taller and about twenty pounds heavier. Dimly she hears her name yelled from the monitor, but it's too late. She rears back her fist and whams Monessa right in the face.

Monessa rises out of her chair, shoving it aside. She grabs Adriana. The two of them grapple. Adriana loses her footing and falls with Monessa on top of her. Monessa presses her against the cold, hard floor. Trapped, Adriana tries to twist out from under the larger girl. Monessa's fist connects and pain blooms in Adriana's jaw. Her teeth slice across her lip and she tastes blood. Her world narrows to shouting girls, Monessa's weight, and an alarm bell blaring. With one hand, she grabs Monessa's hair and wrenches hard. With her other hand, she punches Monessa in the throat.

Suddenly she's free of Monessa's weight, and muscular arms are jerking her off the floor. Bonivich holds her, and another guard strong-arms Monessa into stillness. Adriana's face throbs, her elbow and hip hurt from striking the floor, and her heart beats like a racing rabbit.

She catches sight of Pip looking at her. And secretly giving Adriana a thumbs-up.

The fight with Monessa earns Adriana three days in isolation. Full confinement to her room for seventy-two hours—the juvie version of solitary. When her meals are delivered, and again when the tray is picked up, she has to stand facing the wall, with her hands plastered against it. The black eye and swollen lip Monessa gave her begin to heal and are less sore and puffy when she touches them. All the nurse gave her was ice, without even a dose of sympathy, since it was a fight, after all. It frustrates Adriana that Monessa's bruises will heal, too, and she won't get to see how bad they were.

Now her journal will remain AWOL for three more days. But Adriana will get back to the library. She'll find it. She has to. Maybe Ms. Detrick, who seems nice enough, has it locked up in the drawer behind the checkout counter. She hopes for that. She counts on it, because that's what gets her through these days.

Hours and hours of nothing to do but lie on the bed, her hands tucked behind her head, staring at the ceiling and listening to the comings and goings of the other girls.

Alone with her thoughts, she wonders how she's going to get through more than half a year in a place where no one around her can be trusted and where she can make enemies without even trying.

She survives the time without screaming and pulling out her hair. Finally the three days pass, and after breakfast alone in her room, Jameara comes to get her.

"You're going to see Alvarado," Jameara announces, and escorts her to his office, because it takes his stamp of approval in order for her to be a human being again.

Once Jameara leaves, Alvarado expresses his disappointment, and once more makes Adriana an accomplice in her own humiliation.

"A difficult few days, Ms. Zarahn."

She responds with a deadpan quip.

"For you or for me?"

He rumbles out the obligatory chuckle. Adriana takes a deep breath and silently sighs. This all seems so scripted. Inevitable. He must have this exact conversation with everyone upon release from isolation.

"Choices, Adriana," he lectures. "Whether you know it or not, you have a million to choose from, so why do you gravitate toward the ones that don't serve you?"

She wants to curse him out, break his nose, and watch the blood spill out over his walrus mustache. But that would just confirm what he's saying. At least she has the ability to control herself now, even if she didn't that day with Monessa.

He lectures on and on until she can't hear anything in his words but her name. Like a dog being scolded. *"Blah blah blah blah, Adriana. Blah blah blah, Adriana."* Her attention is on his cluttered desk. A stack of folders. An empty ashtray that must be wishful thinking, since he can't smoke here. A large coffee mug that holds down a crooked stack of papers. The mug says "#1 DAD." She muses that he must have bought it for himself to put on display, because she can't imagine he has kids—and even if he does, she can't imagine they'd feel such a sentiment. Her journal isn't anywhere among the detritus. She doesn't know if that's good or bad. And she can't ask. She doesn't want him to know that she lost it.

He picks up a pen in his thick fingers and clicks it a few times, holding it poised over her open file, as if threatening to write something, then changing his mind, over and over. He peers at her through his glasses. She wonders if the glasses, like the mug, are some sort of artificial accessory. Something to make him look more legit.

"Have you come to regret this particular choice?"

"You weren't there."

"Yes, but your teacher's camera caught the interchange, even if she didn't. The other girl was annoying you. She wanted you to blow up. You did. She won."

Adriana purses her lips, knowing that Alvarado's right and hating it.

"Did she get solitary too?"

"Does it matter?"

"It matters to me."

Alvarado clicks his pen again, then puts it down. "Yes, she did."

"Well, then, no one 'won.'"

"Yes," he says, "I suppose you're right. A lose-lose, all around. How might you have—"

"I could have told the room monitor," she says, anticipating the question. After all, she had plenty of time to prepare for this conversation, and to think about all the things she could have done that she didn't. "I could have ignored her. I could have asked for permission to go to the bathroom, and removed myself from the situation."

"Yes, you could have done all those things."

"But that would send a message that anyone could mess with me. And they would."

"Adriana, I don't think—"

"Yes, you do. And you know it's true. Even if you're not allowed to say it, you know it's true. In a place like this, the only way you get respect is to not take shit. So if it took time in isolation to do that, it was worth it."

Alvarado doesn't say anything for a while. He looks at her through those glasses that are probably just a prop. Then he picks up his pen, clicks it once, and scribbles something in her file. "If there's any truth in what you're saying, then that means we won't have a repeat performance. And if there is one, then everything you just said was, pardon my French, bullshit."

"That's not French," Adriana points out. "French would be *merde de taureau*, but no one actually says that." Not that she speaks much of it, but it helps to have a grandmother who's French Moroccan.

That makes Alvarado smile—but it's a condescending smile—as if he's silently saying, *Well, isn't she precious.*

"Noted," he says. "You're free to go."

◆ ◆ ◆

Officer Bonivich escorts her to her morning class. Monessa's already there. Her appointment with Alvarado must have come before Adriana's. Monessa doesn't mad-dog her. Doesn't even make eye contact. The mood in the room shifts as soon as Adriana enters. Is it just her imagination? No, it's real. Does it mean she's earned some respect? Only time will tell. Bianca offers her a slim grin. Pip gives her a little wave. Adriana's assigned a different seat, as far from Monessa as possible. Life finds a new rhythm of normal.

Then, as soon as class ends and free hour begins, Adriana heads for the library.

First stop, the corner where she was sitting. She doesn't expect to find it there, but she has to start somewhere. The corner's been cleaned, Nothing's out of place. She asks Ms. Detrick, certain that she must have it. This is her domain; she would have seen it. But the librarian just shakes her head, oblivious.

"Sorry, honey. Are you sure you left it here?"

Now Adriana begins to panic. She recalls that when there's a missing person, the first forty-eight hours are the most critical. After that, the chances of finding the person drop drastically. Her journal's been missing longer than that, and a sense of impending doom overcomes her, as if she's lost a piece of herself.

Logic! Think logically, Adriana!

There are really only a few possibilities. A) It was thrown out by a janitor. That would be terrible, but not the worst thing. B) It was found by someone else and tossed out for spite. That wouldn't be the worst possibility either. The worst possibility would be: C) It was found by one of the other girls, and they still have it. They're reading it. They're secretly sharing it with others and laughing. And waiting for the chance to use it against her.

Adriana feels her chest tighten at the thought. *Please . . . please let it be anything but that.* It would be the worst of all possible worlds.

But there is a fourth possibility.

That it's still here in the library. Somewhere.

She spends her entire free hour searching for it, ignoring the funny looks from other girls in their reading bubbles, wondering what she's up to. She has a gut feeling that it's futile. That it's either gone for good or will make an ugly appearance in someone else's hands at the worst possible time.

YOON AND ZINDEL

"What's the matter, Adriana?" Pip asks her at lunch. Pip got there early today—didn't show at roll call, but Bonivich didn't say boo. Pip already ate before everyone else, so now she's free to talk. Special dispensation for being so frail compared to the other girls, wonders Adriana, or something else?

"Nothing's the matter," says Adriana. "Good to be out of my room is all." She stands, the first of the other girls at the table, while Pip remains seated.

"You look like you just lost a friend," says Pip.

Adriana glances into Pip's dark eyes and back down at her lunch, appetite gone. Something about the way Pip looks at her as if she knows something Adriana doesn't. *Like she knows who has my journal.*

"Don't have any friends to lose," replies Adriana.

Pip frowns at that. "I thought I was your friend."

Adriana immediately feels bad. "You are, Pip. And thanks for saying that. It's just that being alone with your thoughts for that long . . . My head's not a good place to be these days, you know?"

Pip offers her a knowing smile, then whispers, "I was in isolation once."

"You?" Adriana can't imagine it.

"Yep. Hit a girl in the head with my lunch tray. She needed six stitches."

Adriana covers her mouth. Pip giggles.

"She really must have pissed you off." And all at once, Adriana starts to wonder why Pip is even here. But she doesn't want to ask. She doesn't want to rip the smile from Pip's face.

Do you know where my journal is, Pip? she wants to ask. Because she trusts Pip to tell the truth. Even if one of the other girls has it, she knows Pip will tell her if she knows. But Adriana doesn't ask.

The table fills and everyone else sits down with Pip. Conversations buzz around Adriana in the lunchroom. She nibbles at her grilled cheese sandwich, waiting for someone to say something and produce the journal. She sneaks looks at various groups of chattering girls. *Which one of you is waiting to ruin my life more than it's already been ruined?*

Lunch finishes without incident. Neither Bianca nor Monessa nor anyone else says anything to Adriana about the journal, but she doesn't let her guard down. If one of them has it, she has to be ready for whatever they're planning.

Nothing happens that afternoon or the next day. She's beginning to think it's a dead issue. That her journal is in some trash dump by now. Gone forever. Adriana goes back to the library during her free hour on Monday morning. She knows it's pointless to keep checking, but there's a voice in the back of her mind that says as long as she's still looking, it's not completely gone.

It's on her third pass around the bookshelves that she spots something.

Because it's not an eye-catching color, the only thing she has to go on to differentiate it from the other books is its spine. It would be the only book on the shelves with nothing written on its spine. And as she scans her eyes across a lower shelf, she sees it there, wedged in among the books. She tugs it out, relief washing over her—no, not just over her, through her, like wind through a ghost. In a moment she realizes that there's a method to the madness of its location. It's toward the very end of the fiction section, between Yoon and Zindel.

Someone shelved it alphabetically.

Which means they opened it and saw her name written on the inside cover. She wants to be grateful, but instead feels suspicious. Why didn't they give it to Ms. Detrick? Or Jameara? Or, God forbid, Alvarado? Is this person saying, *Your secret's safe with me,* or *I know who you are?*

But the bell rings, which means time to haul ass back to the girls' unit for the roll call. She'll have to contend with this later.

◆ ◆ ◆

"Who am I now?"
"Do I still exist?"

Good question, Adriana Z. It's like Jung says: We are what we choose to become. Compass runs on intel. We create it or we carry it. Trust no one. Everyone wears a mask. I do. You do. The pretty hide shadows. The strong hide weakness. A big-ass ugly mustache hides fake teeth. You know of whom I speak.

Adriana sits in the corner of her bed, staring at her journal, still not ready to believe what she sees. Wanting to will the words into nonexistence. Not only did someone read her journal—someone wrote in it. And not just on one page. It seems all of her entries warranted commentary from this intruder. This interloper.

"Crabgrass and grabass" I like that! The rhyme I mean. Made me laugh. Not that I don't like grabbing ass. Like that, too. But only by consent. Just that kind of guy.

So, it's a boy! She knew the cafeteria and library were shared with the boys' side—but there are always multiple locked doors between them. It's as if they exist in two different alternate-day universes. This guy, whoever he was, found her journal and had the absolute nerve to judge her.

59

If that story about how you wound up here is true, you rank high on the chump scale. Are you that gullible? Or are you just not too bright? I don't mean that in any offensive kind of way, I just want to know. Or maybe you knew all along that letting someone use you in the name of friendship would end bad for you. In that case you're just self-destructive. I can relate to that. Being a glutton for punishment. So which is it, Adriana Z? Naive, dim, or self-destructive?

Adriana is breathless with indignation. How *dare* he! She reads on, resenting his stinging words, curling her free hand into a fist, and wishing he was in striking distance instead of on the other side of their limited world.

That bit about Compass being a living thing. Slowly digesting us. Nice. But "pavement" and "enslavement" is a stretch. And I don't care who you are, you shouldn't be throwing a word like "enslavement" around like that.

Oh, so he thinks he's a fucking literary critic? She hurls the journal, and it flaps across the room like a shooed pigeon. Then she gets up to grab it and read more. Because maybe she *is* a glutton for punishment—but how dare he suggest it!

As for some of the other stuff. Poor you. You sound a bit self-absorbed, needy, and judgmental. Just sayin.

Maybe you're not, but that's how you come across. Might help to know that.

She slams the journal closed and shoves it under her mattress, hoping out of sight will be out of mind. She sits with her fists balled on her thighs, staring angrily at the wall. *Just let it be. Just let it be.*

But she can't. Who does he think he is?

She pulls out the journal, grabs her pen, and begins writing.

Wow, you're full of yourself! You don't know me! I'm not self-pitying, not self-absorbed, and definitely not needy! You don't know what I've been through and I don't need your commentary on my life. What—think you're some kind of philosopher? You're just an asshole shitting out pointless opinions. If I want half-witted amateur analysis, I'll go to Alvarado and his stupid walrus mustache, you arrogant jerk!

She thinks a moment and adds,

And fuck Jung—I didn't CHOOSE to become anything!

She slams the journal closed again and shoves it under her mattress once more. She jounces off the bed and paces the room, anxious and upset. He violated her privacy. And what annoys her most—what really ticks her off—is that her

61

response to him will never reach him . . . unless she does the unthinkable. Unless she returns the journal to that spot between Yoon and Zindel. And now she's truly, truly furious. Because she knows she's going to do it. And he must know it too.

SO, WHO'S CALCULATING NOW?

She has to wait until the girls have access to the library again. Then, as soon as she's released from class for her morning free hour, she makes a beeline for it.

"Always the first one in," says Ms. Detrick as Adriana enters the library. "Good to see you, Adriana."

She lets Ms. Detrick think her enthusiasm is for the library in general. She peruses the shelves, trying not to look conspicuous, until reaching the end of the fiction section, the last row, and finds the spot between Yoon and Zindel. If she knew the boy's name, she'd shelve it accordingly. She briefly considered leaving it under *A* for *asshole* but thought better of it. If he goes looking for it, the place he left it would be the first place he'll look. But she puts it in spine-first, so when he sees it's in backward, he'll know she has seen it and read it. She wonders if he'll even check for it. If maybe his sniping was a one-time thing, and he'll move on. She hopes not—but only so he can read the verbal slap she gave him.

What she really wishes is that she could hand him his ass in person. But the boys and girls are kept so separate, you'd never know there are boys there at all. Sometimes you'd hear the distant bounce of basketballs when they were out in the yard, or the echo of their voices when they were in the cafeteria, but that's it. And apparently there are a lot more boys than girls—which explains why the cafeteria is so much larger than what the girls need.

Adriana still isn't sure why she wants to share her journal with a boy she doesn't know and will never meet. She wonders if he'll apologize. She wonders if he'll just double down and trash-talk her back. She's not sure which she wants more, and that irritates her.

At the end of the hour, as Adriana prepares to go, Ms. Detrick stops her and offers her a book.

"I thought you might like reading this."

Adriana takes the book, *Anne Frank: the Diary of a Young Girl*, and glances at Ms. Detrick, eyebrows raised.

"I'm sure you've heard of it—but have you ever read it?"

"No," says Adriana, studying the cover. Four black-and-white photographs of a dark-haired girl frame the title. She smiles whimsically in one, shyly in another, looks with interest at something to the side in the third, and gazes thoughtfully down in the fourth. Something about the photos touch Adriana.

Each one captures a different piece of the girl's personality.

"Since you've lost your journal, I thought you might appreciate reading this one. Anne Frank was in a dire situation, yet she never lost her spirit and she never lost hope. It's my personal copy, so you keep it as long as you like."

"Um, okay," says Adriana, turning to leave. "Thanks, Ms. Detrick." She doesn't tell her that the lost journal isn't lost anymore. And anyway, the book will give her something to do other than lie on her bed and stare at the ceiling, wondering if the boy is going to answer her.

"Ms. Detrick?" she asks before she leaves. "I was just wondering . . . do a lot of boys come in here?"

"They have to do class assignments, so they show up sooner or later." Her expression goes from mild to that sly look adults get when they know you're fishing for something. "Why do you ask?"

"Just curious. Bet you see some of them all the time. Frequent flyers." She gives Ms. Detrick a grin that she hopes is disarming—but Ms. Detrick's expression turns stern. "Best you pay attention to your own classwork. Never mind the boys."

"Yes ma'am," replies Adriana. As much of an ally as Ms. Detrick seems to be, there are just some things she can't be party to. Because she gets to go home at night. She gets to actually *see* the person she's having a conversation with. Even if it's an angry one.

After lunch, but before class, Officer Bonivich comes for Adriana, telling her that Jameara wants to see her, and escorts her through various tunnels to the unit counselor's office in the administration building. Except to Adriana's surprise, Officer Bonivich doesn't stop at Jameara's office. They walk past it, and Officer Bonivich opens a featureless white door nearly invisible in the wall. It opens onto a short corridor. Adriana's anxiety kicks into high gear.

Where the hell is she taking me? Am I about to disappear like conspiracy theories say people do in these kinds of places?

Officer Bonivich glances at her. "Here we are," she says, and opens a set of narrow doors painted pale blue. Adriana steps into an octagonal room and takes a moment to orient herself. In this place of sad walls and few windows, a skylight lays a bright glow on the soft blue walls. There's a vase of flowers. Yes, the flowers are plastic, and the vase is almost certainly bolted down, but compared to the rest of Compass, this is luxury. Jameara sits on a small sofa that's somewhat less industrial than the furniture elsewhere in the facility.

"Adriana." Jameara greets her with a bright smile and waves her to an adjacent chair. "Sit down, please." Then she turns to the officer. "This'll only take a few minutes."

Bonivich nods and steps out of the blue room to wait in the hall. With the door closed, the room is completely devoid of sound and kind of creepy. Like this is where they interview candidates for mind-control experiments.

"Nice digs," Adriana says.

"This is one of the visitation rooms," Jameara explains. "I like to meet girls from the unit here when it's available. Offices are for people like Alvarado."

Adriana braces against the arms of the chair, not willing to trust Jameara until she knows what this is all about. "So . . . a room to trick families into thinking this is what it's like here?"

Jameara's smile flags only slightly. "It's so that families can enjoy their time together in a comfortable place."

"So what have I done to deserve this 'comfortable place' today?"

But Jameara doesn't answer the question just yet. "How're you doing, Adriana? I hope your room restriction wasn't too terrible." She folds her hands in her lap and leans forward a little, inviting Adriana's confidence.

She just wants an update, so chill.

"It was boring," says Adriana, releasing a breath, her tension fading. She settles more comfortably in the armchair. "But I suppose that's the whole point."

Jameara gives her a sympathetic tilt of the head. "Time-out can pack a punch when it's a long time-out."

Adriana senses Jameara has something to tell her, so rather than engaging in any more small talk, she leans back quietly, waiting for Jameara to spill it.

"I've got some good news for you." Jameara's smile sparkles with sincerity and Adriana feels a bright flare of anticipation. Has her time been shortened? Has the other girl finally confessed, and Adriana's getting out?

"What kind of good news?"

"I mentioned to you during intake that we assign chores

here. We feel having a job of some sort encourages responsibility."

"I guess," says Adriana, her anticipation sloughing away at Jameara's words. *Great. This isn't about getting out, it's about mopping floors.*

"Our librarian tells me you've taken an interest in our book collection during your free time. She's asked that you be assigned to the library—shelving books, cleaning up, and doing some light clerical work for her."

Hmm. Better than cleaning floors. Plus, it will give her a reason to monitor the comings and goings of her journal.

"Sounds good."

"Excellent," says Jameara. "During your morning free hour, then again from four to five, you'll help Ms. Detrick. That'll be every Monday, Wednesday, and Friday, when the girls' side has library access."

"Yeah, I know," says Adriana, then realizes that sounds snarky. "I mean, yeah, that's great. Thanks."

"No problem," says Jameara. "And another piece of good news. Your family has asked to visit. They're scheduled for Sunday."

"Next Sunday?" *Oh God.* She had forgotten about family visits.

"Yes, your mother called to set it. She sounds anxious to see you."

"She's my dad's wife, not my mother."

"All right, then," says Jameara, not even apologizing for the mistake. "Your stepmother, then."

Adriana has no interest in seeing Lana, and Jameara clearly reads that.

"You know, some kids here never get visits . . ."

Can I be one of them? Adriana wants to say. But instead asks the hard question.

"Will it just be her, or is my father coming?"

"I assume your dad's coming, but your stepmother didn't say."

Adriana *does* want to see her father. But is the hope that he'll show worth the pain if he doesn't? If she refused the visit, she'd probably regret it later. And if he *is* planning to come, then if she refuses the visit, he'll be disappointed in her, yet again.

Oh my God, Adriana. Decide! Go, or don't go! Either way, stop thinking about it.

"Fine," says Adriana. "I'm glad I get a visit." And when he doesn't show, she can be annoyed at him and relieved at the same time. "How long's the visit?" Adriana tries to remember what the informational booklet said. Fifteen minutes? Half an hour? Thirty minutes with Lana would be thirty minutes too long.

"Right now, twenty minutes. You can earn longer visits if you maintain good behavior," Jameara says, rising to fetch Officer Bonivich from the hall.

Adriana releases a breath. Only twenty minutes. She can manage that if her dad is there. But why does she want to see him anyway? He'll sit there with that disconnected look—probably not saying more than two words to her—and Lana will be chattering on about herself like she doesn't have an off switch, occasionally asking Adriana stupid questions and pretending like all this is normal. Those are going to be a torturous twenty minutes.

Leaving the visitation room with Bonivich, they encounter Mr. Morley, the warden. His official title is "Compass Director," but everyone knows what he really is. Morley looks even more stiff and stern in person than he does on TV during his daily State-of-Detention address. Bonivich gives him a sharp nod, all but saluting, and leads Adriana past the head honcho—who barely acknowledges Bonivich as he strides by.

While Bianca and Monessa don't share much about their personal lives, they're more than happy to talk about others—because gossip is its own currency, with an exchange rate that defies the various things-we-don't-talk-about rules of lockup.

At dinner, with all the usuals at the table, Bianca leans over to Adriana and points at an Asian girl sitting with other girls who Adriana doesn't yet know. "That over there is Lisa Wang. She took a fire ax to her boyfriend's car while he was doing the deed with her best friend in the back seat. They tried to get out while she was still swinging the ax, and the asshole lost a finger."

"Shoulda lost something else," mutters Monessa, to everyone's agreement.

Bianca points again, this time to a different table "And that girl with the pigtails—that's Maya Brun. She broke her youth pastor's arm. She said the guy was touching her inappropriately, but no one believed her. So she broke his other arm."

"I would have done the same," says Jolene.

"Don't you believe her," says Bianca. "Out of all of us, Jolene's the one who wouldn't hurt a fly."

Jolene looks a little insulted. "Well, maybe a fly." Then she gets up to bus her and Pip's trays.

Only after she's out of earshot, does Bianca whisper, "Jolene's story gets all the sad violins. She and her boyfriend had a shoplifting problem. They sent her here for four months; then, when her time was up, no one showed to get her. Social services went out to her place to find her parents were gone. No forwarding address, no relatives stepping up. So Jolene's here until either someone comes for her or she turns eighteen."

Adriana can only shake her head. "Can they do that? Just not come to take her home?"

"Are you kidding? It happens all the time," Monessa says. "Anyway, I think drugs are involved. Meth, heroin, or some other shit. Once you start dancing with *those* stars, you don't stop. People don't act like people anymore."

"She's still got her boyfriend, though," Pip offers. "Writes letters, and calls her once a week."

"Yeah," says Bianca, not impressed, "from Westbrook Men's Correctional. He was eighteen when they got caught, so he got sent to an adult prison. I don't think he's very good for her."

Adriana tries to reconcile the story with the Jolene she's come to know, and it's hard. "She seems tired sometimes, but she's always so positive . . ."

"Not always," says Pip. "She cries sometimes."

"She's like the opposite of *La Llorona*," says Bianca. "Instead of a ghost crying for her lost children, she crying for her lost parents."

That gives Adriana a shiver.

"I have her help me," says Pip. "Not just because I need it, but because maybe she does too."

Monessa nods. "We look out for our own here," she says—but the look in her eyes makes it clear that "our own" doesn't include Adriana. Monessa still sees her as an outsider threatening to upset the status quo.

Back in her room, Adriana tries to distract herself from thinking about fire axes, and arms she'd like to break, and parents who don't take you home from juvie, and the prospect of her own family's visit. What if her own family doesn't show to pick her up after her time at Compass? No, she can't think about things like that.

She sits on her bed, back against the cold cement wall, reading Anne Frank's diary. A tap on the door window draws her attention from the book. She looks up. Bianca waves at her through the narrow window, opens the door, and pokes her head in.

"Okay if I come in?"

Adriana closes the book and slides it under the mattress where she usually keeps her journal. Since they're not allowed to be in each other's rooms—and Bianca knows it—Adriana says, "I'll come out."

They sit in their pod's small living area. The other girls are in their rooms, which gives them a rare moment of privacy. Except, of course, for the camera in the corner.

"So, what's up?" Adriana asks as they sit on the small sofa.

"Same old."

She points to Bianca's ponytail of long braids. "Cute." It's a new style. She wonders who helped her do it. It makes her look even more elegant.

"So . . . what's your story, Adriana?"

Adriana's surprised Bianca's asking straight out. Against the code.

"Wrong place, wrong time," Adriana says. No sense being anything but vague. But Bianca waves her hand like swatting a fly. "Not *that* story. That's everybody's story. I mean who are you away from this place?"

Who am I? thinks Adriana. *Or who* was *I?* Because Compass really does feel like a bookmark between before and after.

Adriana shrugs. "I played field hockey but wasn't tough enough. I draw but not well enough. Some creepy agent dude said he liked my ears, and said I could be an ear model. But when I asked about the rest of my face, he just came back to my ears. So I guess I'm pretty but not pretty enough."

Bianca smirks. "So, your thing is 'not enough.'"

"I guess."

"Well, I think you're more than enough."

73

For a moment Adriana wonders if Bianca is flirting, but then realizes this is not about that. Bianca is just trying to do what friends do. Adriana appreciates it, but can't help but wonder if it's two parts calculated to one part sincere. Does Bianca have an endgame?

"Heard you're gonna be working in the library," says Bianca. "Plum job. Better than setting up the cafeteria like Monessa, or sweating in the laundry like Jolene."

Adriana shoots her a shocked look. "How'd you hear that? I just found out a minute ago."

"The walls have ears," says Bianca with a snap. "So . . . being that you're gonna be in the library and all . . . do you think you could do me a favor?" She fixes Adriana with wide eyes.

There it is. The endgame. Adriana's not surprised but a little disappointed. It would be nice if flattery didn't come with a request attached. But then on the other hand, it can't hurt to have someone like Bianca owe her. So, who's calculating now?

"Pleeeeeease?" says Bianca. "I hardly ever say please to anybody."

Adriana swallows a sigh of exasperation. "What do you need?"

Bianca studies her before she speaks. Like maybe she's reconsidering the ask. But then she finally says, "There's a book I . . . need, but don't want a record of it being checked out . . ."

"So, you want me to steal it?" says Adriana. Great. First day as a helper in the library and she'll be back in isolation. Plus, she'll lose her cushy job.

Doing a favor was how I ended up at Compass.

"No, not steal it," Bianca says. She even acts a little affronted, like Adriana's offended her. "Just borrowing it without checking out. I'll return it so no one will know it was ever missing. Kind of like private browsing but with hard copy."

Private browsing? What the hell is this book? Why would anything that needs to be "privately browsed" be in a detention center?

Adriana hesitates. It's not that she wants Bianca to beg . . . all right, yes, she does want Bianca to beg.

"Please, Adriana. I'll owe you a solid, okay? More than a solid."

"You'll owe me liquid and gas too."

"Ew, that's gross."

That makes Adriana laugh. "Fine. So what is this book?" she says, trying to sound less curious than she really is.

Bianca hands Adriana a piece of paper. An author's name and a number. A nonfiction book, then. Interesting.

"Thanks, Adriana. I won't forget this."

Adriana nods. No, she won't. Adriana won't let her.

SECRET DETRACTOR

During her formerly free hour before lunch, on the next day the girls have library access, Adriana goes straight to the library— where she probably would have gone anyway even without the new job. Ms. Detrick greets her cheerfully and sets her to shelving books.

Then, as soon as the librarian gets busy behind her desk, Adriana makes her way to the last shelf of the fiction section, where she left her journal, turned backward. With her heart full of butterflies that she tried to dismiss all morning, she stoops to see that the book is exactly where she left it. But it's not backward anymore!

"Adriana—you should take the trolley with you."

She turns to see Ms. Detrick standing by the book trolley.

"Don't just shelve one book at a time—take the whole trolley. And it will be easier for you if you organize them on the trolley first. Dewey decimal for nonfiction, alphabetical by author for fiction."

And although Adriana bristles that Ms. Detrick thinks she needs to explain that to her, all she says is "Yes, Ms. Detrick."

Adriana wants to go for the journal, but Ms. Detrick is all over her, analyzing her shelving technique and blathering on about everything from the history of libraries to the scourge of book mold. There's not a second that Adriana can grab the journal unnoticed. Even when Ms. Detrick goes back to her desk, she's still monitoring Adriana's every move.

Retrieve the journal or get the book Bianca wants? She's not gonna be able to do both right now. Maybe she'll have better luck when she returns at four p.m. Does she dare leave the journal with the boy's new notes and all her secrets for anyone to read? It's killing her not to see what he's written to her. Should she try for the journal now?

No, she can't. Ms. Detrick has a clear view of the fiction section from her desk. On the other hand, the nonfiction section is mostly out of the woman's view. Adriana's shoulders sag. Looks like it'll be easier to get Bianca's book now.

She continues shelving books, making sure all the books are perfectly flush, and wondering if that makes her too anal. By the call numbers, Adriana can tell the books she's reshelving are just down the row from the one Bianca wants.

Adriana consults the scrap of paper for author and number again, then scans the shelves till she finds it—and once she does, it feels like her eyes are bulging out of her head like some cartoon. It feels like a bomb just exploded in her brain.

She hears rustling from Ms. Detrick's desk, so she puts the book back, slightly misaligned, noting its exact location, so she can grab it before she leaves for lunch. She pulls the next-to-the-last book off the trolley and sets it neatly in place just as Ms. Detrick rounds the corner.

"Everything okay, Adriana?" Ms. Detrick glances at the trolley and smiles to see that it's empty. "You're a fast worker, dear."

Adriana's heart is pounding, but she manages a sunny smile, like the ones she used to give her mom. "Thank you, ma'am. Just about ready for my next task."

At the end of her shift, Adriana manages to slip Bianca's book into her waistband, and hide it beneath her bright yellow shirt, without Ms. Detrick seeing.

But just as she steps into the hallway, she hears, "It's not what you think."

Startled, Adriana slews around and finds Pip standing there.

"What's not what I think?" Adriana asks.

And Pip looks pointedly at the slight bulge at Adriana's waist. "That. It's not what you think." Then she strides off.

How did Pip know about the book Adriana lifted? She wasn't even in the library. And what the hell does she mean?

Overload. Adriana's brain shuts down.

Later, Adriana feels like her brain's still muddled as she sits in the yard during their outside hour, reading more of Anne Frank's doomed musings. Bianca sits down on the bench next to her. They are the only two in that corner.

"Hey," says Bianca. Then, glancing at the cluster of girls on the yard's other side and the bored guard at the door, she lowers her voice. "You get the book?"

"Yeah. Want it now?"

Bianca gives her an energetic nod. Since her back is to everyone, Adriana slips it from her waistband and pushes it into Bianca's hands. Noting, once more, the title, *So, You've Had a Baby: Next Steps to Being a Great Parent.*

Then Bianca shoves the book into her own waistband, where it bulges like a bun in the oven, instead of a book.

This is what Adriana can't get her brain around. Bianca has a kid? Or is having a kid? She opens her mouth to ask, but somehow the words don't come.

Bianca tilts her head. "You got a question for me?" Her voice drips with irony.

Adriana swallows. She can't go there. She just can't do it. So instead, she asks Bianca something else she's been curious about. Something that will shift the attention.

"Actually, I do," Adriana says. "You're pretty good friends with Pip, aren't you?"

"Uh . . . I guess," Bianca says, caught entirely off guard by the change of topic.

"She seems to have more . . . freedom than other girls here. And she knows stuff."

"Stuff?" Bianca's clearly playing stupid. "What do you mean?"

"Come on." Adriana exhales impatiently. "She knows stuff about us, but nobody knows anything about her. Like how come she's here? What could a girl like her have possibly done? She's kind of mysterious, y'know? She never talks about her family."

"Maybe she doesn't have one," says Bianca. "Maybe she's an orphan."

"If you don't know, just say so," Adriana says with a huff. "I just stole a book for you—the least you could do is be honest about this."

"Don't be like that," Bianca says, glancing around. "Look, I don't know anything. We all know a little about why each of us is here. McKenna got into a knife fight and Zharia steals things and Mysti lies about everything just to cause trouble."

"How do you know all that?" asks Adriana.

"You hear things, and you figure things out," says Bianca. "But no one has anything on Pip." Then she gets real quiet. "All I know is that girls who Pip likes seem to get lucky. And girls she doesn't? Let's just say things don't ever go their way."

But before Adriana can ask anything else, the guard sounds her whistle, and it's time to line up.

Whoa, let's both take a breath. You still ticked? Can we start over? Hi, my name is Arrogant Jerk. Funny that you got the initials right. For my first and middle names, anyway. AJ. I go by my middle name, though, on account of no one ever gets my first name right—so you can just call me "J." It can stand for "jerk" if you want it to.

So I made you blow up. I'll admit I kinda meant to.

I figured making you mad was a sure way of getting you to write back. So, no—I don't think you're stupid, and I don't think you're naive. The stuff you wrote proves you're neither of those things. You get a bead on situations like a sharpshooter. But you keep smacking yourself upside the head with your rifle butt. That's not a criticism, just an observation that I'm sure you made yourself. It doesn't take a moron like Alvarado to make that diagnosis.

Adriana grins in spite of her annoyance. Yes, he's right. She hates that he's right—that he knows her just by reading her private words. But then, isn't that the purpose of those words? To bleed yourself onto the page? If he knows her from those words, that means it worked.

She sits in her room now, reading blue-penciled words in a ragged scrawl. His handwriting isn't the best, so she has to take it slow. Sometimes he lapses into block lettering, which is much easier to read.

She managed to get the journal from the library during her afternoon shift but had to wait to read it until after dinner, when she had time back in her room.

Sounds like you explode easy. We got guys here about ready to explode. When they talk, and don't take this wrong, they sound like you. Are you about ready to explode? I'm not talking about just exploding in ink.

81

You don't want to be pulling that pin in real time at Compass. That'll get you solitary or worse.

Adriana wishes she'd had that advice before she lost her shit on Monessa. Not that it would have made any difference. When you explode, you explode.

And when I say worse than solitary, I mean honest and true worse. I've seen a lot of things in my years at Compass. Not all official. The bad actors aren't all kids. There's guards and staff you don't want to cross. I'm sure you've already figured out that Alvarado isn't your friend. And there's one cafeteria worker . . . Not Dorella—she's cool—but one of the other ones. I won't go into details, cuz maybe you just ate—but just make sure you're nice to the guy, because you never know what might end up in your food.

Anyway, if there's another girl that you absolutely have to unload on, for self-preservation or whatever, don't let them see you coming, and do it clear of cameras and other eyes. You're fierce—I can tell. Don't let anyone kill your fire.

J

Huh, thinks Adriana. *I've got fire.*

She flips to what she'd originally written back to him. Wow. She really flamed the page. Well, what did he expect? Even if he hadn't provoked her, she probably would have been just as mad. Writing in someone's journal like it's your own! And she didn't see an apology either.

Can we start over? That could be an apology, sort of. She can live with that. Her eyes flicker over his words again—*Hi, my name is Arrogant Jerk*—and she smiles. At least J's got a sense of humor.

She grabs her floppy pen insert, turns to a fresh page, and writes.

Fierce, huh? If I'm fierce it's because I have to be. But you've got the advantage here, J. I spilled myself out onto those pages that no one—certainly not you—was supposed to read. I'm over that, kind of, but the thing is, you know stuff about me, but I know nothing about you. Not even your name. All I get from you is criticism, half apologies, and advice that is dangerously close to mansplaining Compass to me.

You want to share this journal with me, fine—but you're gonna have to give me more. Some meat. And don't you dare take that in the direction I know you're thinking. Mind out of the gutter or I kick you to the curb. (Of course, if you're in the gutter then you're already at the curb, so less distance to kick.) Give me something real. Maybe even in verse, if you've got a mind to go there. I want you to impress me, J. Think you can? Guess we'll see.

A

83

There—short and sweet. Well maybe not so sweet, but push-back is to be expected. She puts the journal under her mattress, anticipating her next time in the library, when she can slip it in for J to find. How funny, she thinks. She's sharing her journal with a boy—a stranger—and suddenly she doesn't mind.

PART TWO

JON

A LITTLE ARMAGEDDON WITH LUNCH

Stupid newbie

Stooopid nooobie

Picking a fight with a bull

Thinks he's a matador

Gonna get gored

Crowd won't be bored

Stupid newbie

Odds are stacked

The crowd is packed, jacked

They want blood

Maybe gonna get it

Gate opens

Bull goes ballistic

Stupid newbie

Shit for brains
What were you thinking?
A deer in headlights
Standing there blinking
Now you can't save yourself
Someone's gotta do it for you
While my damn lunch gets cold
And the respect you now show me
Means you owe me
Some kind of life debt
Don't need it, don't want it
I'm no bank
Holding a note on your nuts
A lean on your spleen
Shoulda let you croak
Stupid newbie.
You're a joke.

From a plastic chair at the back wall of the cafeteria, Artorias Jonathon Kilgore—Jon to his friends—observes his domain. The bulge in his pants is nothing more than Adriana's journal. Today, he gets to sit before anyone else at his table, on account of he won a bet with a guard who thought he was stupid. Bet Jon couldn't recite the entire periodic table from memory. Not only in atomic order, but alphabetical order as well. Sucker.

He takes a few moments to scan the room for trouble before eating. Lunch Lady Dorella slops chili, mac 'n' cheese, and fries on plates, plus a few carrot sticks so they can say it's healthy. Kids in bright green shirts pass through the line grabbing their plates and find tables. There are three primary guards. Rush is the good cop, Wash is the asshole cop, and Garza, who's on cafeteria duty today, is new, so no one's sure which direction his learning curve will go—toward decent, or in a more turdly direction. He's the one who lost the bet. The fact that he's honoring Jon's win points toward decent. Garza stands near the door, trying to look more confident than he probably feels. Jon's seen guards come and go. Coin toss as to whether or not this guy will last.

Since Jon's been "detained" longer than anyone else at Compass, Jon is like an institution. He's got the best table, and a chair that only he gets to use. Not that it's a better chair, but it's *his* chair. It's the principle of the thing. His is the best spot for seeing everything and everyone. Who's about to explode. Who's about to die.

A dried-up kid who's been here nearly a year moves toward his table. Thinks because his skin is the exact same shade of black, they got more than that in common. They don't. The kid changes direction when Jon twitches his left eye. Good. There are already too many other yapping greenshirts in his circle, trying to curry favor from his dangerous self.

Other kids look over at him, grumbling, all jealous that he gets to be king for a day. Or at least for a meal. Finally some of his regulars arrive. The table fills. They sit in unison, then scarf food fast enough to be done before Jon, who likes to eat slow.

His attention lands on the newest kid, who's at the very back of the line. Simon, Cyrus, Sawyer—something like that. If Simon/Cyrus/Sawyer wants to survive his first day here, he'd best stop tapping timid-like on a bigger kid's back. Especially when that bigger kid is Knox, who doesn't take too well to that sort of thing. This new kid has been full of questions since he got here this morning, and Knox is clearly not in the mood to answer his stupid newbie questions. Knox has been simmering for days, looking for an excuse to go all Terminator.

Two tables over, Raz—Jon's right-hand man here at Compass— talks to Stripes—a guy in their pod tattooed with an invisible expiration date on his dented skull. But then Raz glances over to Knox, seeing the same potential problem Jon does. Jon nods in Raz's direction, indicating that Raz needs to defuse the Knox situation before it goes south. Raz is the voice of their dynamic duo. He has the gift of charming teachers, of swaying the warden into seeing reason. His charm works on everyone but Lunch Lady Dorella, who must have natural immunity, or maybe a vaccination against bullshit.

And so Raz heads for the impending disaster to talk Knox down from the proverbial ledge . . .

. . . but before he gets there, Knox drops his tray, grabs the new kid, and slams him against the wall, leaving the kid's toothpick legs dangling. Knox shakes him like a pit bull shakes a Chihuahua. Like he's fixing to break the kid's neck before flinging him away.

In an exasperated whoosh of a breath, Jon drops his fry and

heads for the fray. Knox can't be deflected by Raz's charm now—the dude's no longer a time bomb; he's a grenade. His pin's been pulled, and things are about to take shrapnel. Only someone like Jon can stop it. Someone with the rep and a scary history like his.

From the corner of his eye, Jon sees the new security guard hugging the side door, muttering into a walkie-talkie. The guy should take charge. Too late to call for backup now.

Jon steps up to Knox. The little kid's skinny legs are still kicking, his eyes bulging in stark terror.

"Knox." Jon puts a megaton of force into his voice. "Drop the kid."

If anything, Knox's fingers tighten and the kid thrashes harder, his face turning purple. Yeah, Knox is definitely in grenade mode.

Jon forces himself to show no expression. In the four times he's taken the big guy down, he's learned there's only one way to do it. The problem? Knox learns from past mistakes. Each time it's a little harder for Jon, because Knox can anticipate his moves. So Jon has had to learn to be increasingly unpredictable.

Jon's pretty sturdy. Not as massive as Knox but a head taller than most greenshirts; strong, and tougher than Monday meatballs. Kids at the table closest to the Knox detonation start to break for cover—because when the elephants begin to dance, it's time to leave the party—but they try to look cool while making scarce.

Everywhere in the cafeteria, kids are yelling, enjoying the

show. Some start chanting Jon's name, maybe hoping he'll recognize their voices and later draw them into his gravity well. Fat chance. He already has enough space trash in his orbit to crash and burn a continent.

When the new kid stops flailing and goes limp, Jon acts. He kicks Knox in the back of his knee. The big guy squalls, his kneecaps hit the linoleum floor, and he drops the small fry from his meaty hands like, you know, a fry. Guess Knox *hasn't* learned all that much from his previous run-ins with Jon.

Jon catches the new kid before he hits the ground. He took a junior lifeguard class before his mom got sick, so he scans the kid: pulse, breathing, and color—which is quickly fading back to normal—then he exhales in relief when the kid's eyes flutter open.

The roar in the cafeteria drops a few decibels, and Jon looks around, half expecting Knox to lumber to his feet in full nuclear mode. No, he's still on his knees, looking puzzled at the side door. Jon turns to see that the seasoned guard, Rush, is standing next to the useless rookie, smirking. Don't know why he's grinning like that when a kid could have gotten killed if Knox had really launched.

So as rookie Garza settles each table, telling them to finish eating, Rush approaches the battle zone in a slow lumber. They call him Rush because of his general lack of speed. And also because it's his name.

Jon hauls the kid to his feet, feeling a self-righteous mood lift his shoulders and narrow his eyes. Rush studies Knox, but

Knox is still petrified on his knees.

"What took you so long?" Jon demands. His mood buoys from the grunts of admiring greenshirts. When Officer Rush fixes an eye on him, Jon adds, "Sir."

Rush's attention shifts to the newbie. "You okay, kid?"

Jon admires the kid's pluck as he straightens his spine. "Yes, sir."

"You go unconscious?" Rush asks.

"Nah," Jon says before the kid can open his mouth. "He's tough. Right, kid?"

The newbie meets the expectation even while looking gray as a corpse. "I'm fine."

Garza manages to settle all the tables, and the cafeteria returns to its normal volume. Then Garza returns to Rush's side like a baby chick going back to Mama.

"Want me to take the kid to the infirmary?" Garza asks Rush.

For the kid's sake, Jon's gotta maintain control of this situation. He lowers his voice. "Don't do that to him. Not on his first day. Let the others see him shake it off. The nurse can check him after lunch."

Rush gives him an assessing look, so Jon adds another "sir."

Rush turns to the rookie. "Leave the kid, but take Knox to the director's office. He's spent enough time there, so he can tell you the way." Garza looks at Knox and blanches.

"Don't suppose you'd let him off with a heartfelt apology, sir," Jon suggests. "And a head-shrinking session with Alvarado." Knox is one of theirs, after all—and this might smooth things between him and Jon, considering the way Jon just unceremoniously castrated him.

Rush gives Jon a quizzical look, then turns his attention to Knox. "Stand up."

Knox gets to his feet, suddenly docile and tired-looking.

"First, apologize to Dorella," Rush says, his tone stern.

Knox turns to the lunch lady. "Sorry," he says in his heavy growl. "Didn't mean to scare you, ma'am."

She laughs at the very idea. Dorella's harder than a battering ram. Was here long before Jon entered detention. "Y'gotta bring a whole lot more than that to scare me."

"Now apologize to the kid," Rush orders. "Kid, what's your name?"

"Silas," he says, unconsciously leaning closer to Jon as Knox turns toward him.

"Sorry I swatted you for being such a fucking mosquito," Knox says.

"Try again," demands Rush. "You get no more chances."

Knox's gaze drifts to the floor as if all the air has left him. "Yeah. Sorry, Silas."

Rush takes one of Knox's fire hydrant–sized arms and mutters, "You'll spend the rest of lunch in your room. Time to say good night, Gracie," which Jon doesn't understand. Then he tells Jon, "Tell your unit advisor to take Silas to the infirmary after lunch. If he looks sick or vomits or coughs up a lung or something in the meantime, tell one of the staff."

"Yes, sir."

As they walk to Jon's table, Jon tells the kid, "If you gotta hurl, just do it. Older kids than you have chucked their chowder after facing off with Knox."

The kid gives him a shaky smile and looks a lot better.

When they get to the table, Jon, with a flick of his head, sends two of the other kids packing, so as to clear space for Silas and Raz. Then, once they're all seated, Jon settles a hand on the kid's shoulder. "This is Silas." He glances down the table at the rest of his people. "This kid survived Knox in berserker mode on his first day. Show him some respect."

Raz takes one of Jon's fries and considers the kid.

"Like most folks, I enjoy a little Armageddon with lunch," Jon tells Silas. "Try to keep it to Thursdays is all I'm asking. Gordy, get the little guy a burger."

Then Raz, fixing Jon with his signature grin, adds, "How about some of Jon's fries while you wait, little dude?"

Jon shrugs. They're cold anyway.

After lunch, Jon and Raz are escorted to an unexpected meeting with their unit advisor, a straggly gnome of a man named Luppino. Jon hopes not to sweat, as that'd stain Adriana's journal, which is still hidden in the waistband of Jon's pants. He sits comfortably in an uncomfortable chair. Raz, on the other hand, is twitchy and can't find a position. Luppino's office is a glass-enclosed cubicle in the boys' school pod. A fish tank. Of course, it's reinforced safety glass—as if to remind the kids here that they are fully expected to be violent enough to break regular glass. Garza, who escorted them, stands outside the door waiting for Luppino to show up, since he can't leave them alone.

"Psst," says Raz, in a whisper that's not at all a whisper. "Psst! Hey, hey!"

Raz is a small, manic furnace of a guy. Can't sit still even in peacetime. Raz wants to plan. Present a unified front for their unit advisor when he comes in. But Jon isn't biting. What happened in the cafeteria happened. Everybody saw that Raz and Jon were defusing, not instigating. Besides, Jon doesn't feel conspiratorial today. So he eases a little more away from Raz—because social distance isn't just for viruses.

"Psst! Psst!"

Raz doesn't take hints well.

"Not talking now," Jon says.

"But—"

"Not talking now."

Raz doesn't take clear statements well either. Theirs is a practiced dynamic. Jon is the zen to Raz's chaos. Together they are a universe in balance.

In the hallway outside, Luppino walks right on past, escorting Silas to his cell—his brand-spanking-new green sweatshirt already stretched and dirty from his wildlife encounter with Knox.

The little dude sees Jon through the glass, gives him a slight wave and a faint smile. Jon returns an indifferent one of his own. Or maybe it was his dangerous look since the kid goes flaccid, and he practically pastes himself to Luppino.

Meanwhile, Raz, unable to sit an instant longer, takes the opportunity to go through Luppino's top desk drawer in search of edible contraband, since Garza, still in the hallway, seems distracted by some shiny object. There's always something in Luppino's desk. Gum. Chips. Oreos. Luppino is addicted to the staff vending machine. Raz finds a roll of mints and bats them over to Jon, giving him first dibs.

Meanwhile, Ironside, Compass's educational tech master, rolls past and into the ops center across the hall—a room full of monitors and hardware specifically arranged to resemble a starship battle bridge.

Jon can't remember the technician's real name. Everyone calls him Ironside, because that's what's stenciled in gothic text on the back of his wheelchair. It's what he likes to go by. A reference to some old TV show about a kick-ass paraplegic detective. Definitely ahead of its time. Ironside's the puppet master of technology at Compass. With classrooms going all day in both the boys' and girls' wings of the education center, he monitors and streams instructors teaching about dead US presidents, methane lakes on Titan, the effects of Beethoven's hearing loss on his music, and other totally useless information.

Jon has been here long enough to see the complete transition from teachers who actually drove to Compass and stood in the classroom in a face-off with detainees, to live streams that could be from anywhere, including a bathroom (which Jon was convinced was the broadcast studio for his science teacher). Turns out that better teachers ensconced at a safe distance actually improved education on the boys' side. Jon isn't sure how it impacted the girls. He'll have to ask Adriana.

Of course, writing to the girl is like sending a message to one of those methane lakes on Titan—or even beyond the edge of the solar system, because it takes at least a day at the speed of light to get to her, and another day to get back. He supposes it's still faster than old-school letter writing, though.

Jon found the journal near the library's emergency exit and quickly realized what it was. At first he was just going to leave it there, but then he thought it might be better in his hands than in Raz's or someone else's. Anyone else's. And it wasn't like he was going to read it.

Except that he did.

How was he supposed to resist that?

And he liked what he read. But, of course, he couldn't leave it without comment. Then he shelved it in a place where only someone who was looking for it would find it. He maybe half expected her to write back to him, and yeah, he deserved the verbal reaming she gave him. It still makes him smile to think about it.

Raz, who's been pacing around the room, looking in all the places he's not supposed to, plops down in his chair when he sees Luppino coming back down the hall from his newbie mission. He sits at his desk across from them, looking exhausted even though the day's barely half over. Maybe not enough coffee this morning. Maybe too much booze last night. Who can tell?

"I'll make this brief," Luppino says, flipping back his shaggy hair. "Considering what happened during lunch, we feel Silas needs some help easing into Compass. You two have been assigned to be his buddies until he settles in."

Jon leans back in his chair just shy of the tipping point. He has no interest in babysitting this kid. But he says nothing. Instead he just glances at Raz, giving him silent permission to do what he does best. Raz'll get them out of this stupid assignment.

But instead Raz goes in an alternate but equally acceptable direction.

"Sure," Raz says cheerfully. Then his smile drops just the slightest bit. "I can see what's in it for you, sir, seeing that no one employed at this fine establishment wants to get fired—or worse, put on trial—for the gross negligence of letting a younger kid nearly get killed right underneath your noses," says Raz. "But what's in it for us, sir?"

Jon grunts with satisfaction as the negotiation begins. His grunts scare most juvies. Less intimidated, Luppino rubs a scruffy chin.

"Are you under the misapprehension that Compass Detention Center operates as a democracy, Mr. Barbosa?" he asks Raz.

Jon likes the word *misapprehension*. Lots of greenshirts and even Compass adults live in Misapprehension Land. Jon likes to think of himself and Raz as being the only ones at the detention center living in the Objective Reality Zone.

"No, sir," Raz says with a suave smile. "Compass operates as a meritocracy. Those who got merit get the rewards." After Luppino quirks an appreciative grin, Raz adds, "Jon and me don't ask much. We're the best you can assign the kid . . ."

Luppino rolls his eyes. "Spit it out, Barbosa. I died of old age somewhere between 'What's in it for us?' And 'Jon and me don't ask much.'"

About a mile ahead in his thoughts, Raz has to pause to figure out what Luppino means, then gives a courtesy laugh.

"Good one, sir. Truth be told, what Jon and me is asking for is something to help the kid. Right, Jon?"

Jon's got no idea what Raz is on about but narrows his eyes in an affirmative way. Luppino knows—everybody knows—that Raz is the mouth that clears the path before Jon and his considerable rep. Whatever Raz has in mind, Jon trusts he has both their interests at heart.

As Raz works his way toward closer mode, Jon's thoughts begin to stray. He wonders if Luppino knows anything about Adriana. Jameara, his counterpart on the girls' side, must know tons about her. Is there crosstalk between them? She and Luppino have to communicate regularly to be effective together, right? Any third-party information would be helpful. All Jon has is her name and a handful of words between them. And not all good words, either. He finds himself a little envious of the things that Luppino might know. Stupid to feel jealous of worn-out, frumpy Luppino. Stupid to feel anything because of a girl and her journal. Stupid to feel. Period.

"That could work," Raz says, ready to close whatever deal he's working. "Okay with you, Jon?"

Jon nods. Raz will tell him later what he's negotiated for

helping the kid through his first days in detention. And Jon will inform Raz that Raz gets full custody of this Silas kid. Because although Jon has plenty of time to waste, he's not wasting it on a newbie.

Luppino stands, so they do too.

"Take it easy on Silas. He's a bright kid but no street smarts. Probably won't be at Compass long, so let's make it a good experience for him, okay?"

"Sure thing," Raz says, just as the bell rings and the classroom doors open.

Jon steps from the cubicle, shifts the journal to a more secure position under his waistband, and links his hands behind him, wondering how you make incarceration a good experience.

10

THE TELEPORTATION TEAM

So is that your attempt at poetry? "Stupid newbie"? Best subject matter you could find? I'm pretty new, so am I a stooopid nooobie, too? Should I be offended? Well, I'm not. I won't give you the satisfaction ☺.

So was this real? Who's the stupid newbie? I know it's not you, since you already said you've been here a while. Did you really save his sorry ass, or was this all some hypothetical?

And did I really draw a happy face up above?

You should know that I'm not an emoji writer. Far from it. That smiley face was a freak accident. Like lightning hitting some poor slob through a window.

Leaving his wife a widow.

Sorry, I couldn't resist. False rhyme anyway.

And by the way, it's "lien," not "lean."

A

P.S. Too bad about your cold lunch. I'm all teary-eyed.

Yeah, the thing with the newbie really happened. Don't want to talk about it. Except to say I'm tired of having to step in and solve situations for our beloved management. They're as useless as a mop in the rain. Same rain, by the way, that left that poor woman a widow. But the thing is, she planned the whole thing. For the insurance. Installed a lightning rod on the roof leading right down to her cheating husband's favorite chair. Sizzled and served up to the tune of five hundred grand. Double indemnity; twice as nice. You see that movie? Double Indemnity? Real old. They got it in the library. As if Compass wants to give us an education on how to get away with the perfect crime. Except that they don't get away with it. Sorry for the spoiler.

P.S. Yeah, I know it's "lien," that was just a play on words, gurl. (And yeah, I know it's actually "girl," so shut up.)

Jon was never a newbie. Even when he was. He arrived at Compass like a storm cloud. Opaque and silent. Lightning flashing deep within, threatening to shoot it out with some biblical deluge, making widows like the one he and Adriana were inventing. All rumors, mostly, but it was enough to clear his way. To set him apart from anyone else who was new to Compass. You don't need to prove yourself when they're already afraid of you.

When he arrived, he was fourteen but looked older. Fourteen, but felt younger. Nobody knew that, though. Couldn't let them know it. Even now, nearly four years later, he can't let them know what goes on inside his heart and head. Not the other kids, not Alvarado, not even Raz, who knows him best. He wonders if he could say stuff to Adriana. Maybe if it was in disappearing ink. Some Harry Potter shit that vanishes after the person's read it, because the written word could always fall into the wrong hands. Like Adriana's fell into his. Only his were the right hands. Luckily.

Jon had once read how some buildings in Europe were built on the ruins of older cities, and those older cities were on top of ruins that dated back to the Romans. Compass is like that, although not on such a grand scale.

On the land where Compass stands, there used to be some sort of factory. Which got torn down to build a school. Which got repurposed and expanded into the detention center. And so the sprawling Compass complex has a big underground cavern that was dug out for whiskey smuggling during Prohibition, maybe a hundred years ago. At least that's the rumor. But rumors are plentiful and cheap at Compass. No telling if it's real until someone lays eyes on it, and even then, it's got to be someone trusted not to make shit up. Which is, like, nobody.

As it turns out, Jon gets to see it with his own eyes.

"Yeah, Moonshine Cavern's real," Rush tells Jon, Raz, and the other kids he escorts down into the bowels of Compass the next afternoon. "Mostly it's just used for the backup generators and storage for stuff that nobody wants and nobody remembers. But I guess someone finally remembered and decided something's gotta be done about it."

Enter: the Teleportation Team.

Every kid at Compass gets assigned a character-building chore, and the Teleportation Team is not the best job, but it's not the worst, either.

It was Raz who coined the name, because "We move stuff from one place to another like magic." It made Jon laugh and so the name stuck. Maybe the adults at Compass feel like stuff magically disappears and reappears someplace else—but the feeling is much different for Jon. Especially when his sore muscles attest to the general lack of teleportation technology.

Basically, the kids on the Teleportation Team are the heavy lifters. They move furniture from one administration office to another or dispose of crap nobody needs anymore or haul out boxes of files that are being sent to the shredder. Because of the nature of the work, it's mostly bigger kids, with the exception of Raz, who specifically asked for the detail.

"Why do you and your scrawny little ass want to do this?" Jon asked.

To which Raz responded, "I'm lean, not scrawny. There's a difference."

105

At first Jon assumed Raz signed up so that they could be working together—but then realized there was another reason. For the most part, nobody cared about little things that disappeared from forgotten cabinets and drawers—which meant there was a treasure trove of tradeable contraband. Enough that Raz could practically start a small business.

There are anywhere between five and ten kids on the Teleportation Team at any given time, depending on who's been released, who's sick, and who's in behavioral isolation. Today there are six. There's Jon, Raz, Gordy, and Stripes, who are all from Jon's pod. Then there's Bobby Blaze, who's in for arson, because sometimes you can't escape your name. Usually Knox is on the team, but he's still in isolation from his attack on Silas. Instead, they got a substitute from Boys' Building two. A kid named Culligan—a muscular, blond guy, who's ugly in a rare sort of way. The kind of face that you can't help but stare at like a freeway accident.

Rush leads them down to the tunnel that connects Boys' Buildings one and two. Jon's been down this way countless times. It's how you get to the yard and the admin building. He always thought the doorway that's halfway down the hall was the connector to the girls' building, but apparently not, because this is where Rush stops. He swipes his key card and pulls open the door to reveal a concrete stairwell descending into darkness.

"Uh . . . I don't like it down there," says Gordy, who's got the biggest heart in Compass, but mega developmental issues. "Can we go back?"

"Don't worry, Gordy," says Rush, "there's more light down at the bottom." Which clearly isn't true, but Gordy always takes what people say at face value.

At the first landing, the concrete steps turn to rusty steel, and then farther down they become stone. You can tell when you're passing into the era Compass was a school, then further back to when it was a factory.

"It's like time travel," Raz comments.

"Teleportation, and now time travel," says Stripes. "We're all about the future here."

Gordy chuckles. "Time travel—I get it," he says, "because the walls and stuff are, like, real old! But that ain't the future, Stripes, it's the past."

Culligan, who doesn't know Gordy, snorts at that—but Gordy doesn't seem to notice, so Jon lets it go.

At the very bottom, Rush opens a door that isn't even locked, and reveals to them Moonshine Cavern. The team steps in and gawks like they just walked into Willy Wonka's chocolate room, only nasty.

It's an expansive space—but not really a cavern, because the ceiling is low, with rough-hewn stone pillars holding up the world above. It feels more like the depths of a mine. As promised, the space is full of junk, all of which has clearly been here since long before any of them were born. Everything from ancient office furniture to piles of clothes to household appliances that are so out of date, they're barely recognizable. There's a rotting wooden door halfway off its hinges in the far back. Impossible to get to since there's mountains of stuff piled in front of it.

"It's dark back there," Gordy says, looking all worried at the far door, like maybe there's a vampire's lair back there. "Where do you think it goes?"

"Just more of the same," Rush says. "When all this is cleared out, I'm sure you'll be cleaning the next room too."

Stripes goes over to something that looks like a small upright coffin, only it's green, and has some circular deal on top. "What the hell is this?"

"Refrigerator," says Rush. "At least I think it is—it's before my time." The fact that anything can be before Rush's time boggles their minds.

"And we're supposed to move all this stuff out?" Jon asks.

"In stages," says Rush. Then he looks at his notes. "Today we're looking for desktop stuff."

"Like . . . computers?" asks Blaze.

"Don't be dumb," says Stripes. "This is all from before there were computers."

"Wow," says Gordy, cautiously poking around. "Before phones too?"

Jon picks up a black rotary phone like they have in old movies. "No—but back then they didn't fit in your pocket." His mom had one of those—a yellow one. Didn't work, but she kept it anyway, on account of it was the house phone from when she was little. She was sentimental that way.

"Can we, like, break stuff up?" Culligan asks. "Y'know, to

make it easier to get upstairs?"

"I doubt it," says Raz. Then he turns to Rush. "Where are we bringing it, the dumpsters or somewhere else?"

"Loading dock."

"Just as I thought." Then Raz turns back to the others. "My guess is the warden has a new side hustle. Prolly gonna take it all and sell it on eBay or something, because when crap gets old enough, suddenly it's not crap anymore."

Jon grins. "That'll put a crimp in *your* side hustle."

Raz leans closer. "Quiet about that."

"Hey," says Rush, "what happens to it isn't your business. Your job is just to get it up there."

Rush finds an old spindly-legged metal chair near the door—probably from before there even were plastic ones—and settles in to read his current get-rich-quick book.

They get to work, bringing things up to the first landing of the stairwell, which is as far as Rush will let them go unsupervised. Jon grabs an old manual typewriter that must be made of lead because it's a struggle to lift.

"Why is old stuff always so heavy?"

"I know, right?" says Raz. "It's the real reason why the *Titanic* sank." And then he adds, "Anyway, this is better than babysitting the newbie, right?"

The newbie. Talk about a sinking ship—the kid already feels like an anchor around Jon's neck. He just had to save the kid. No good deed goes unpunished.

Jon starts to wonder what Adriana would think of all this.

She'd probably get all metaphoric and stuff. *Our lives at Compass. Rusty and forgotten. Sinking slowly under its own weight to the depths of the earth.* It makes Jon smile, which makes Stripes suspicious, because suspicion is where Stripes lives.

"If you gotta grin like that, look somewhere else, because it's freaking me out."

Things go pretty well . . . until Gordy starts coughing. He's been getting over bronchitis and has been hacking into his elbow for days. The others are used to it, but the new guy on the team, Culligan, bristles.

"Dude, stop that!"

"I can't help it," says Gordy. "It's dusty down here."

"Just stay the hell out of my airspace."

Which is kind of difficult since they're all digging through the same pile of junk.

"I mean it! Stay the hell away from me!"

"Nurse said I'm not contagious on accounta I've been on penicillin for three days already," Gordy offers.

Which makes Stripes smirk. "Yeah, when he remembers to take them."

Which confuses Blaze. "I thought the nurse is supposed to watch you take meds."

"Yeah, well it tastes bad," says Gordy. "So I cheek it and spit it out after she's gone, then take the pill with dinner. That way I can hide it in the food and swallow it without gagging."

Culligan laughs at that. Not a friendly laugh. The kind of laugh that makes you want to punch a guy. "Huh. That's what they do with dogs," Culligan says. "You a dog? Maybe we should call you Fido. Woof woof."

That pings Jon into the red. "Hey! Don't you talk to him like that."

Suddenly Culligan puffs up like one of those frilled lizards, trying to look big and intimidating. Thing is, he's already big. Strong as an ox, maybe, but ugly as a moose.

"You think you can tell me what to do?" Culligan says.

Jon quickly assesses. Culligan's trying to be the alpha here. Problem is, he's not an alpha, and will never be. He's a henchman—although Jon's not sure whose henchman he is. If it comes down to a fight, Culligan has size, but Jon has agility.

"You make fun of my man Gordy, you gotta deal with me," Jon says, not backing down in the least.

"It's okay, Jonny, I don't mind," says Gordy, which just makes Jon even more pissed at Culligan.

Then, at the very moment it seems escalation is inevitable, Raz steps between them. "Hey," he says to Culligan, "I know you're filling in for Knox today, but if you want a permanent spot on the team, best to take it down before Rush notices. Just sayin'."

They all glance over at Rush—who is usually on the ball, but right now is dozing in the chair. Whatever he was reading hit him like anesthesia.

Culligan turns and spits, which is much less hygienic than Gordy coughing into his elbow. "Who says I even want a spot?" But clearly he does, because he steps off and goes back to work.

This turd is going to be a problem, thinks Jon. As if he already doesn't have enough turds on his plate.

Jon's day ends with an appointment with his lawyer, but without as much as a shower after his stint on the Teleportation Team to make him presentable.

Maritza Gottlieb, public defender extraordinaire, sits across from Jon in the RTMB, and bites into her baloney sandwich. Officially it's called the attorney-client conference room, but somewhere along the line people began calling it the Room That Means Business, then it got shortened to RTMB. Most kids don't even know what it stands for.

"Things okay, Jon?"

He shrugs. "Yeah, sure."

Jon jitters a leg and grips the conference table till his knuckles hurt, the wood cold in his sweaty hands. He's come to hate these meetings because they never bring good news. At best false hope. Gottlieb studies him, so he stills his leg and drops his hands to the chair. Gottlieb can't see him squeeze the edges.

He's distracted by Gottlieb's sandwich. She's a gaunt, pencils-in-her-bun public defender, who starts the day with a satchel stuffed with too many case folders and six quartered baloney sandwiches. She wolfs down a section every chance she gets. Jon has nothing against baloney. Gottlieb offered him a portion once, and he gagged at the first bite. He has a problem with what she does with the baloney. She puts it between slices of high-fiber bread, spreads it with wasabi mustard, and piles on alfalfa sprouts.

That's just wrong.

"You here because you got something new?" Jon asks. He's never big on small talk and beating around the bush—especially when it comes to Gottlieb. He doesn't want to have yet another conversation with a lawyer who probably has a cheat sheet just to remember who Jon is.

"Maybe," Gottlieb says.

"So, is this about my appeal?"

Gottlieb shakes her head. "Nah, still waiting for the wheels to turn. But I've been working the whole juvenile angle. Once you turn eighteen, in theory, you're shipped off to an adult male facility. That's just a few weeks away."

"Theory," Jon says. "Like the theory of gravity, right? Shit's real enough when you hit the pavement."

"Yes and no," says the lawyer, "because there might be a little quantum physics involved too. Quantum physics, you know what that is, right?"

"Yeah, I know," says Jon. And he also knows he shouldn't have used that stupid-ass gravity metaphor, because now Gottlieb's on it like a dog on butt.

"See, there've been issues with kids like you who graduate to an adult prison."

Jon has to chuckle at that. "Graduate, huh? What's the problem—not enough caps and gowns in the prison system?"

"Funny," says Gottlieb, but she doesn't laugh. "No, the

problem is hurling younger guys in with an older general population. A young guy like you, who goes in with some hope of eventually getting out, can end up institutionalized and hardened."

Jon can see that. It's why older guys who get released after serving their time end up doing stuff that gets them right back in. They want freedom, but prison becomes their comfort zone. In the adult penal system, you become what you see—you become what you *live*. Here at Compass, there are actually some people who see you as a kid who made a mistake, but still a kid. There are some people who genuinely care about you and hope you have a future. But the moment they see you as a man instead of a kid, all that hope gets transferred down to someone younger. The Silases of the world.

Jon has been trying to mentally prepare himself for the reality of prison, and although he puts up a good front—hard as nails on the outside—down in his soft places he's scared out of his mind.

"Anyway," says Gottlieb, "they're building a new correctional facility for prisoners twenty-five and under. Keep 'em out of the general population for a while. Won't be done for at least another year or two."

"So, what's your maybe?" John asks because none of what Gottlieb says sounds like good news to Jon at all.

Gottlieb leans just a little bit closer across the table, as if she's telling a secret. "It might be possible—emphasis on *might*—to keep you at Compass as long as your appeal is still pending, even after you turn eighteen."

"As long as my appeal is pending . . ."

Jon considers all of it and connects the dots. They're going to game the system by taking advantage of its own dysfunction.

"So . . . we don't push on the appeal," Jon says. "We let it keep getting delayed . . ."

"Exactly! We keep you out of sight and out of mind, stalling the courts without appearing to stall. Then I file a motion to keep you here at Compass until the new facility is ready."

"Will it work?"

Gottlieb shrugs. "That's why I said maybe. It all depends on the judge we get, how crowded the adult prisons are versus Compass, and on your own behavior here."

"That's a lot of 'depends,'" which, Jon notes, is also a brand of adult diapers. Appropriate because right now Jon feels like shitting himself.

Gottlieb sighs. "What you were convicted of, Jon . . . it was pretty cut-and-dried. The mercy of the court only goes so far, especially now you're older. Frankly, anything we get is better than the alternative."

Jon nods. Nothing about his trial had felt merciful; he can't imagine things being less so. He wonders what Adriana would think if she knew. He wonders if he has the nerve to tell her.

But best not to think about that. Better to focus on Gottlieb, and her lawyerly dance moves. In the end, this whole stalling gambit is a win-win for Gottlieb; she gets to take Jon's appeal off her crowded plate, while helping Jon at the same time. Jon wonders which motivates her more.

"Do what you gotta do," Jon says.

"And you as well," Gottlieb counters. "Best behavior, Jon."

"Right," Jon says. "Model prisoner."

NOWHERE TO HIDE

J,

Before I got sent here, I never thought about places like this and the kids in them. I guess I was like an ostrich, my head in the ground. I thought kids here weren't like me. They were somehow "other." But now I see how wrong I was. They're all girls exactly like me. Either they got dealt a bad hand, or they made a mistake that started dominoes falling, or they were so angry, they broke what they had. I think maybe I'm a combination of all three. But sometimes I still feel like that ostrich. Because there are still things here I don't want to see and I don't want to know. Does that make me terrible?

Adriana

P.S. How's the newbie?

Adriana,

You're not terrible. Maybe every once in a while you've got to be the ostrich to keep yourself sane. But remember, ostriches are powerful. Remember, they used to be dinosaurs!

The Newbie is okay. He's a good kid, I like him. But he doesn't belong here, and that makes me mad. Not mad at him though. I don't know how much I can do to keep him safe in this place. So many kids here are like wolves just looking for weakness. So I gotta be a grizzly and scare the wolves off. It's not always easy.

J

Jon's meeting with his lawyer sticks with him like a bad haircut. Tossing and turning with dreams of his appeal getting pushed back until he's old and withered, he wakes brain-fogged. He's a zombie as he joins the rest of the greenshirts in Boys' Rec Hub one, to go to the showers, then be escorted to the cafeteria. He and Raz have the new kid safely tucked between them. Silas has been switched into their pod to make monitoring him easy, to the despair of the kid who got switched out. A guy called Flots, who's pretty much just meat on a stick. Some muscle, but not much brain. That was the deal that Raz made with Luppino—switching Flots out. Because Flots is a general pain in the ass.

Lunch Lady Dorella nods when she sees Silas between Jon and Raz. She slops red sauce on their breakfast burritos. It'd take more than salsa to resuscitate those breakfast innards wrapped in a tortilla. If he weren't hungry, Jon would let this mummy rest in peace.

"Good to see you taking care of business, Jon," Dorella says, nodding toward Silas. She's got a voice full of gravel and yesterday's smoke. Jon feels Dorella's approval ease the weight of his bad dreams.

"Thanks, ma'am."

As she spoons canned fruit onto Silas's plate, Raz asks with a grin, "Good to see me too, Dori?"

"Like a hemorrhoid," she says. "And it's Dorella to you. Move along."

Jon's table is waiting for him to arrive so they can sit down. Stripes isn't at their table today. He's maintaining relationships elsewhere. Gordy's at his usual spot, but he looks worried. Gordy must think Silas is taking his place in Jon's entourage. He gets anxious about his status with Jon every week or so. He'll talk to Gordy, maybe on the way to class. Maybe try to get him to help with Silas, too, so he doesn't feel left out. Besides, the more others help out with Silas, the less Jon will have to do himself. Win-win.

Knox is sitting in a corner of a table of nobodies, in full-potato mode since the doc upped his medication. Should Jon say anything to Knox? Maybe not until his meds are stabilized.

Raz starts the morning's conversation. "While Luppino was talking to us yesterday, we missed a pop quiz and Myers electrocuted himself in science." He gulps down half his juice. "Life is good."

"Is he dead?" Silas's eyes go big as doorknobs.

"Nah. Didn't even knock him out. They sent him to the nurse, and she let him rest in the infirmary so he missed the rest of class. Got him a little scorch mark on his finger. He's crazy proud."

"They're gonna make us take that pop quiz, you know," Jon says. "Anyone tell you what was on it?"

"Was it magnetism? What were we doing before the kid almost got strangled by Knox?"

Silas winces.

Jon tries to remember. He's generally good at science, but that doesn't always mean he's tuned in. "Something about power. Like amps, volts, and watts, conductors—stuff like that. Would explain Myers."

"Myers can't explain Myers," Raz says. Which was a fair observation. "Anyway, it's all a blur, man."

Unlike Raz, Jon likes science. Not just because it's danger-ous but because there are cool things. Like how viruses attack a body, how sulphur stinks up a room worse than Stripes's farts, how ants eat a dead pig in a few hours, and how black holes swallow up whole planets.

Raz, on the other hand, is all about history, psychology, and governments. Which maybe helps Raz navigate his way through Compass, but Jon would rather watch mold grow on bread than spend an hour studying dead dictators in countries he'll never see.

Lately, Jon has taken an interest in philosophy, though. The art of thinking. And since so much time at Compass is spent stuck in your own thoughts, Jon figures it's worth learning to do properly.

"How about the library?" Jon asks. "Do we get time in the library this afternoon?"

Raz shoots him a look. Might be because he's been talking too much about the library. "I mean, Silas hasn't been there yet—we should introduce him to the place."

He won't use the kid to sneak the journal in there. No one knows he's got it. No one's seen him writing in it. And no one will.

He wonders how Adriana will respond to his latest entry. Will something he said make her mad again? The thought of that kinda makes him smile. Not that he likes making her mad, but he likes the way she pushes back. They both play hard, even if it is just words. He stops eating his burrito. What if she takes it and doesn't put it back? What if she's done with his sorry ass? What if she's moved on? A lot can happen in twenty-four hours. Will he care if she grabs her journal back and he never sees it again? Now he's mad for asking himself the question because he knows the answer.

Raz and Silas are staring at him. "What?" Jon wipes at his mouth. "I spill something on me?"

"For a second it's like you were the one who got magnetized." Raz shoves his empty plate away.

"Myers was electrocuted, not magnetized," Jon points out. "And not actually electrocuted, just shocked, 'cause electrocuted means zapped dead."

"What are you, freaking Webster? I know what it means."

"I wish my classes were the same as yours," Silas says, looking at the clock on the wall. They'll head for their classes in about twenty minutes.

Raz scoffs, but Jon maybe reads something in Silas that Raz missed.

"Anybody bothering you?" Jon asks. "'Cause we can take care of that for you."

Silas shakes his head. "Hardly anyone my age is at Compass. There's only ten kids in middle school here, including an older guy repeating eighth grade, and Gordy. They're letting me take some classes with the ninth graders, though, 'cause of my test scores."

Raz whistles. "Looks like we got a brainiac, Jon. Guess we won't need to check his homework."

"They got Silas helping me with math," Gordy puts in. "He's even better with numbers than you, Jon."

Jon nods at the bigger boy and switches his attention back to Silas. "You always been good in school?"

Silas grimaces. "Mostly. Since my mom died, I get moved a lot, so it's hard when a new school's behind me or ahead of me in a subject, or using a totally different book."

A little sparkle of something hits Jon in the chest. Less than electrocution, more than a Fourth of July sparkler.

So the kid lost his mother. Just like Jon.

It makes Jon think of his mom, who sometimes feels so far away in his memory, and other times it's like she's right there in the next room, so close he can smell her cooking. Jon wonders if it's like that for Silas too.

It's a rule of thumb that greenshirts don't ask each other what got them put into Compass. But Raz's thumbs have no rules.

"Why you go to so many schools?" he asks Silas. "Foster homes?"

"Yeah." He plays with the rice on his dish. "Social services moves me around a lot. Fifteen different homes since I was six."

Raz whistles again—softer and sadder this time. "That's tough. I don't blame you for doing something to get back at them, even if it got you put in here." Which was Raz's way of asking without asking.

Silas frowns. "I didn't do anything. They shut down my group home, and there wasn't any place for me to go. The social worker said I have to stay here until something comes up."

That makes Raz laugh. "Right. Hey, if you don't want to tell us the real reason you're here, that's cool."

"But . . . that *is* the reason . . ."

And Jon believes him. Because he's heard of stuff like this before. Even so, it's hard to believe that a screwed-up system could be *that* screwed-up. But it is. He knows it is. Some places have got laws to keep foster kids from being housed with juvenile offenders. Jon's not sure whether there's no such law here or it's just being ignored.

"Man, no one deserves that," says Jon. He finds himself getting angrier the more he thinks about it. Kid's mom dies, they move him through more homes than years he's lived, then load him into a bureaucratic catapult and launch him over the fence into a high-security detention center. All because they got no other place to dump him.

And then, on his first day here, he almost gets killed by Knox.

Jon sets down his fork before he weaponizes it. Around the table, everyone reacts to Silas's words with silence and is looking at their food or at Silas. Everyone but Gordy. Gordy's looking at Jon. His face reflects an agony of confusion. Like he just got told that not only ain't there a Santa Claus, but your grandma's Christmas cookies are made of kale.

"He don't belong here," Gordy says. "How can people be so mean?"

Gordy has always accepted that he belongs at Compass. His mental age isn't much older than a kindergartner's, so he believes what others tell him. But Jon knows that, like Silas, Gordy shouldn't be here. His brother was a drug dealer who got himself killed, and left Gordy with all the evidence they needed to put him away as an accomplice—which someone decided was better than any other option, since there were actual accomplices who saw Gordy as a loose end. But ask Gordy, and he'd say he was here because he let his brother get killed—and nothing was going to make him believe otherwise.

Heartbreaking. Just like every other story here.

Gordy's still waiting for an answer. Now Silas is looking at Jon, too, like maybe Jon's got one. Jon shakes his head. "People are what they are." A non-answer, but at least it shuts down the question. Jon thinks about his mom. He thinks about her doctor, and all that went down in his own life. "Besides, it's a waste of time trying to change stuff that already happened."

Now everyone's looking at him.

"You mean like fate?" Silas seems hungrier for answers than for his breakfast burrito.

Jon's science brain won't let that lie. "No such thing. We all got to answer to the laws of thermodynamics. It's all cause and effect. Maybe you don't make the cause, but sometimes you're stuck smack in the middle of the effect."

In the back of Jon's brain, he wonders why Raz is silent all this time. Then Raz pops in with, "The trick is to pay attention to all those causes and effects and cause some effects yourself."

Silas chews his lip. Gordy's gaze ping-pongs from Jon to Raz. "I don't wanna cause no effects on no one," Gordy says.

"Don't worry about it, Gordy," Jon assures him. "Raz and me can do all the causing and effecting. We got your back."

In history, the instructor drones on about views of criminal rights in the eighteenth century and tries to get a debate going over the idea of retribution versus restoration, and which is more important: punishment or making up for what you did. But that discussion's DOA, with not enough heart paddles in the world to revive it. Incarcerated kids don't want to talk about the nature of incarceration.

Even so, retribution sticks in Jon's brain because that's all he's known at Compass. He's here because he's paying for what he's done. Never mind what led up to it. There are always consequences to your actions, his mom used to say. Still holds no matter what made you act. But even so, a compass is supposed to help you find direction. So isn't *this* Compass the wrong tool for retribution?

Depends on what you want out of retribution. Payment meted out through years of your life? Or rehabilitation—so that the rest of your life in the outside world can be its own sort of payment. A testament to who you could become, instead of dwelling on who you were.

Testament. He likes the word. Becoming a thing that crumbles your crime to dust. But you don't get to be a testament unless you're given that second chance. Otherwise you become the opposite. You become a statistic.

So which would it be for Jon, then? They could rehabilitate you until you were squeaky clean, but still let you rot in detention. Then rot in prison once you age out. Does he deserve that? On good days the answer is no. On bad days, the answer is definitely. But in the end, it's not his decision to make anyway.

What did you do to land you here, J?

He almost looks around to see who said it—but the voice is in his head. It's how he imagines Adriana's voice to be, as if they're standing in the same room. As if they're face-to-face.

Nothing worth repeating, he'd say, keeping his attention fixed on her.

Her eyes are steady on him, even though he has no idea what color they might be. *Is it what you did? Or is it who you are? Is it a part of you?*

And he'd have to admit that, yes, it is a part of him. Because it made him everything he is today. He knows that's true, but he also knows that Compass has a hand in making monsters too. Jon wishes Adriana could have known him before his mother died. When he was innocent—or at least not guilty. The days before his deeds and detention turned him hard and scary.

If she knew, would she accept the terrible thing? Accept him?

Tell me, she whispers. *Because that's the only way you'll know for sure.*

Then he's back in class. Did he fall asleep? If he did, no one noticed. And though the instructor's voice is all leaden weight, he feels sky-high.

Did Adriana speak to him in a dream? Even though his head is ducked down like it always is in class, he feels that instead of being weighed down with punishment, he's restored and set free.

Their Spanish teacher calls in sick, which is a thing even remotely. Luppino gives them the good news, and rather than leaving them with the classroom attendant and no teacher, he tells the class that they'll have to spend the hour in the audio lab or the library. But they don't get to choose. Luppino divides them randomly. Or maybe not so randomly, as he separates the kids that are nitro from the ones that are glycerin. Rush takes half the class to the audio lab, and Wash takes the rest to the library. No one likes Wash much. Especially kids of color. It's not that Wash is racist, it's just that he's racist. Although Jon gets the feeling he's more of an equal-opportunity asshole. He sees every kid here as beneath him in one way or another. If he can't judge by race, he finds something else. Today he's lining up kids by height, just to be even more of a dickwad.

It's only by luck that Jon and Raz are in the library group. When they line up, hands clasped behind their backs as always, Raz flashes Jon a raised eyebrow, which Jon totally ignores, unable to tamp down his exuberance. The journal's still at his waist. He's itching to get it back to Adriana. It doesn't even bother him that Stripes takes an opportunity to shove Jon when Wash isn't looking, just because. He doesn't get a second chance, since Wash takes notice when he sees the line ripple.

"Stay in line," he warns, all gestapo-like. "Give me trouble, you get trouble back."

Once in the library, Jon arrows past Ms. Detrick to Adriana's spot on the fiction shelf. The journal's probably shades darker than it began, stained with days of his sweat. Then he stalls in the Z's.

Their former hiding place is gone.

Someone must have checked out *The Pigman* and *The Book Thief*—Zindel and Zusak. Last book on the shelf now is Yoon, *The Sun Is Also a Star*—and this star will shine a spotlight on the journal if he puts it there, because with no other Z's, it will be the last book on a half-empty shelf, in full view for anyone to see. He figures he could just slip it in nearby, close enough for Adriana to find, but that prolonged moment of thought is enough to make his luck wither and blow away.

Silas and Gordy are heading toward him, and appear ready

to cling to him like static, happy that they're all in the library together.

"Things suddenly got good," says Gordy, with whom it's always all or nothing. "Silas even put the math teacher in a good mood. Didn't give us homework. So the little dude's a hero."

"Yeah, for five minutes, at least," says Silas.

They glue themselves so tight on him, there's no way Jon can slip the journal into its hidey place, which isn't so hidey anymore. He smoothly switches direction to the science section, the two of them tailing him close as comet dust.

"Hey, Jon, could ya maybe help me find something on plant cycles?" Gordy asks. "I gotta do a report."

Jon obliges, if only to keep them from noticing the journal that's still in his hand. If he tries to slip it back into his waistband, that will draw their attention. *Why ya stealin' a book, Jon,* Gordy would ask, *when you just gotta check it out and get it for free?*

"Little dude can look low, I'll look high, and Gordy, you look in the middle," Jon says when they get to the science section. Gordy and Silas do as instructed, and as long as their eyes are on the shelves, he's safe. After another few moments of Jon's uncharacteristic interest in Gordy's homework, Silas stands up, holding a picture book on botany.

"I think this'll work."

Gordy grabs it from him and looks at the front and back cover. "I don't see nothing on plant cycles."

"It's in there," Jon assures him. "You just gotta crack it."

Gordy does, and it's like he wants to go through the whole book right there, page by page, so Jon says, "Better check it out before there's a line. Don't want to be late." And although it's just the beginning of the period, the thought of being late propels Gordy toward Ms. Detrick's desk. But Silas lingers. Jon tries not to be impatient with the kid.

"Do me a favor," says Jon. "Go grab me a book written by somebody whose last name starts with *H*."

"Uh . . . what kind of book?"

"Doesn't matter. My English teacher said I got to read a book by an *H* writer. She's having me go through the whole alphabet, and that's what I'm up to."

Silas, who's a quick study, sees that the nonfiction shelves all have Dewey decimal numbers and heads to the fiction section, which is organized alphabetically.

"And make sure it's not a stupid one!" Jon calls after him, so that he'll take his time before deciding.

There is, of course, no such assignment. But Silas doesn't know that. So while Gordy's checking out his book, and Silas is looking for a nonstupid *H* book, Jon sets to the task of placing Adriana's journal. But he realizes it's futile. If it's not where it's supposed to be, she won't know to look for it elsewhere. She'll just think he hasn't put it back yet.

"Hey," calls Silas. "I got two for you to choose from."

"Get a third," Jon tells him.

Then an idea hits him. So simple, so elegant, he has to smile. He reaches out to a nearby shelf, grabs a book, and puts the journal in its place. He glances at the book in his hand. *Basic Writings of Kant.*

It figures he reached for the philosophy shelf. The universe telling him he needs to think more. Or that he thinks too much. Or maybe that he needs to think better. Kant was an eye-for-an-eye kind of guy. Retribution instead of restoration. Definitely not a fun guy to have at a party.

"Whatcha got there?"

It's Raz, who snuck up in Jon's blind spot.

"Kant," Jon says.

"Why not?" Raz asks.

"No, fool, Immanuel Kant. The philosopher."

"Oh, right," Raz says, "that guy." Although clearly Raz has never heard of him. "Since when you got an interest in philosophy?"

"Since when do you care what I'm interested in?"

Just then Silas comes over with three books. Hopkins, Hinton, and Horowitz. Jon grabs the Hinton one, which is the thinnest, because if he has to fake reading a book, he might as well fake reading a short one.

As for Kant, it's not coming with him. Instead, it's going at the end of the fiction section. Right where the journal's supposed to be.

He can only hope that the girl in charge of shelving books doesn't see it before Adriana does.

SHARKS SEEKING MINNOWS

J,

The others might think you're a grizzly, but I know
the truth. You're more like a beagle. That's not an insult.
I love beagles. But careful, because if a beagle barks too
much at an ostrich, she'll kick its sorry ass to the moon
with those dinosaur feet!

I have to admit you had me scared, J. When I didn't
get my journal back right away, I thought you were done.
That I'd never get it back. Or worse, that you'd shown
it around to the other dudes for laughs. Sorry I thought
that. I should have trusted you. When I saw that Kant book
mis-shelved at the end of fiction, I thought, "What's this
guy playing at?" But then I got it! That was smooth, J.
Way to keep things away from prying eyes—because who's

gonna be looking at the nonfiction philosophy shelf. Or half shelf. Ah, who am I kidding. There's maybe a quarter shelf of philosophy in our library. Ten books, maybe. Too bad, because when mostly all we got is time to think, you'd think they'd give us books about thinking. Y'think?

I checked it out, BTW. The Kant book, I mean. Wondered why you chose Kant, when you could have picked any book, so I read it to see if maybe I could figure you out. Here's the dope:

1) My brain hurts.

2) Since Kant believes we can never truly know reality because we're limited by our senses, I cannot empirically prove my brain hurts.

3) He uses the word "empirically" a lot.

4) Kant would insist that you, J, should be punished for making my brain hurt. Because he really believes in punishment. Like, really. Like it's at the very core of civilization, which leads me to point five:

5) The dude's got issues. Or at least he did when he was alive a few hundred years ago. But was he ever really alive? Actually, never mind; that's another philosopher's issue.

6) If this is what you like to read, you take yourself way too seriously—and this is coming from a girl who knows she takes herself too seriously—and you're worse than me. Or, one might say, you're a man after my own heart. But let's leave my heart out of this.

7) With that in mind, the book I've switched out with the journal this time is one that's impossible to take seriously. All right, yes, it's about the end of the world—but it's a *funny* end of the world. So . . . don't panic, read the book, and get back to me, yeah?
Your friend in words,
Adriana

P.S. Spoiler alert! The answer is forty-two.

The exercise yard is cracked cement, a few rusty chin-up bars, and one sorry half basketball court with a bent hoop. The walls are either towering cement blocks or the brick butt-end of Boys' Building two—because it wouldn't do to have kid criminals visible from the interstate. There's only one side of the yard where the outside world can be seen beyond a chain-link fencing topped with razor wire, but there's nothing much to look at. Just forest and more forest. Occasionally a deer makes an appearance, as if to taunt the kids. Like the place is some sort of reverse zoo.

But today, the yard feels like freedom.

At least to Jon. Hearing back from Adriana makes his spirits soar in a way that scares him a little—because it shows him how little control he really has over his own emotions. He already knew that. Found that out the hardest way possible. But at least it's good emotions he's lost control of this time.

He left the journal in his room, under the mattress. They're supposed to check for contraband in all the rooms, but unless there are problems, they don't bother. He feels like it's burning a hole in that mattress, though. He wants to get back to it, but at the same time, doesn't want to write back to her too soon. He shouldn't play too eager. Still, he wants to read what she wrote again. That stuff about Kant having issues made him laugh. And maybe he'll go back and reread all her earlier stuff. The book she left for him is there in the room too. Not hidden, because he officially checked it out, so he's allowed to have it. The one thing he's worried about, though, is the blue pencil, which he's definitely not supposed to have. He lifted it weeks ago from the classroom art supplies by breaking it in two and sharpening the lower half, making it look like just a short pencil when it got counted. He usually keeps the upper half hidden in his room, but today it's on him, hidden in the fake little pocket he made in the waist of his pants by tearing a hole in two overlapping seams. It's not like he invented it—he learned the trick a long time ago from guys who were at Compass before him and are now long gone. It's the place where other guys hide things like cigarettes. The Powers That Be must know they do this, because pants keep coming back sewn up, but it's never mentioned. Maybe they think a little bit of disobedience works like a pressure valve for bigger disobedience. What worries Jon is that a pencil can be seen as a weapon, and if he's caught with it, he could get written up. They'd also check his room for more contraband. And this time they'd look under the mattress. He tries not to worry about it, because it's throwing ice on his good mood.

The boys get an hour in the yard several days a week, and two hours on Sunday. Some play a rough game of hoops, while others pace the line impatiently waiting their turn. There are guys who do body-weight exercises on and around the chin-up bars. The rest move in aimless tracks like sharks seeking minnows.

Wash is on yard duty today. When Rush is in charge, things are easy. Like the surface of a pond on a windless day. But today a storm brews. Maybe on another day, Jon would have noticed that brewing storm by now, but today his head is above those clouds.

Jon shoots hoops for ten minutes, then quits. Raz thinks it's fun to maneuver Jon around Stripes, because Stripes has no patience, and it's fun to see him pop. But Jon's heart isn't in it, and that throws the whole dynamic off. He walks off the court to Raz's protests, and instantly another kid on the sidelines takes his place.

Another reason he walks off the court is that Silas is hanging by himself at the fence. Some of the sharks seem to be massing near the little guy. Raz abandons the game, too, when he sees where Jon's heading.

The mass seems to sense the coming storm. Some move in another direction, seamless like they meant to go off that way all along, but three turn on them, thick browed, jaws clenched. Knox is one of the three, sullen and silent. Still heavily medicated by the look of him, but that only tamps down his belligerence; it doesn't quash it. No amount of chemicals can do that.

The biggest of the three, Viper, built like a missile, angles toward Jon. "Where you think you're going?"

"Dude." Raz takes a step away and spreads his hands. "You don't want to be messing with Jon."

Through the space between Knox and Viper, Jon sees Silas starting to move away from the fence, uncertain, like he can't figure where to go, but anywhere else is looking good.

Viper spits at the cracked concrete, missing Raz's shoe by an inch. He takes a long gander at Jon from head to toe. "So did you do it?"

"Do what? I did a lot of things. You gotta be more specific."

"The thing that got you in here."

Jon could laugh at that. Once a month or so, there's a new rumor about what Jon did. It floats for a while then drops limp like an old balloon—only to be replaced by another rumor. Jon suspects Raz has a hand in spreading them. It's all about keeping up Jon's mystique.

"Like I said," Jon tells Viper. "Gotta be more specific."

"The mall," Viper says. "They're saying you're the guy who blew up that H&M at the mall a few years back."

Now Jon can't hold back his laugh. What's Raz been telling people? "First of all, who *wouldn't* blow up an H&M? And secondly, you can't believe everything you hear."

"My cousin worked in that mall! She got a friend lost half her face. You think that's funny?"

No, Jon has to admit that it's not. He gets serious. "Sorry about your cousin's friend. But I had nothing to do with that."

"I don't believe you."

A rumble of voices starts up around them. This confrontation has become the center of attention. Jon glances to Silas, who looks scared. The kid's gonna have to learn not to look that way. Looking scared is not good for your health.

And neither is being in Viper's sights.

Viper moved from the third boys' building a few months ago when he about beat another kid to death. A kid older and bigger than him. He mostly stays away from Jon, as he has his own crew and his own places to be. Until today.

"You don't want to be doing this, man," Raz says to Viper, almost but not quite getting between him and Jon. "Wash'll see."

Viper flicks a glance to the yard's entrance, where Wash is otherwise occupied. Then Jon glances at the third ejaculate of this trio of scumbags, and realizes who it is. Culligan. Now Jon knows whose henchman Culligan is.

Then Silas screams, "Watch out!"

Something glints in Culligan's hand, and he lunges at Jon. Jon goes right, slams into Raz, and they both lose their footing and go down. Wash now jaunts toward the commotion—too little, too late. Jon rolls up into a fighting stance. Raz is still down, his elbow bleeding, and a scrape on his jaw where it hit cement.

"I'm okay," Raz says to no one in particular.

Knox, seeing the guard move in, puts his hands atop his skull, like he's surrendering. Nothing else about Knox looks like he's giving up—his feet bounce like a boxer's. As if his lower half doesn't know what his upper half is doing.

Rush hurries out into the yard, having been called by Wash, and takes charge. Both have hands on their Tasers as a warning.

"Easy does it, boys," Rush says. "Do we have a problem here?"

"That one's got a knife," Silas shouts. He points at Culligan, who growls low and slings a killing look at Silas.

"Is that right?" Rush moves closer to Culligan, but not within lunging distance. "Drop what's in your hand, son. Now."

Culligan lets the shiv fall. It's not a real knife, but just as deadly. Jon feels cold pulse through him, like a torrent of ice. Any slower, he would have been cut. Deep.

"You three on the ground," Rush says. Knox goes down immediately. Viper and Culligan curse but do as they're told. But both of them glance at Silas on their way down. And that infuriates Jon more than anything else that happened here. Because by pointing the finger at Culligan, that damn kid's made himself a target.

The next day, a guard escorts Jon to Alvarado's office. Not his normal scheduled psychological evaluation, which already happens more often than Jon would like. He hates getting his every thought dissected by a blunt knife.

The windowless room always smells of tobacco smoke and stale coffee. Does it bother no one that a shrink is addicted to smokes and caffeine?

Alvarado rises to give him a self-consciously firm hand-shake, and then he rounds his desk to sit next to Jon in one of the few comfortable chairs at Compass. A rug of orange and brown leaves lies beneath their feet, trying to make the place seem cozy—and failing.

The man smooths his mustache as he studies Jon. Adriana called it a walrus mustache in her journal. Jon ducks his head so Alvarado doesn't see his lip quirk.

"You understand why you're here this morning, Jon?"

"I'm figuring it's about what happened in the yard yesterday. Since I almost got stabbed, you gotta make sure I don't get PTSD."

"And that you didn't instigate it."

Jon puffs out some air. "That's right; blame the victim."

Alvarado raises his eyebrows that are nearly as bushy as the mustache, and just as shoe-polish brown. "You see yourself as a victim in all of this?"

"No! I was just—" But Jon realizes Alvarado has cornered him as he always does. It's like he gives Jon a brush to paint a picture, but only a single color to paint with. "Nothing. Never mind. I'm fine. No PTSD, not a victim. Are we done?"

Alvarado leans back in his chair. "I didn't call you in to talk about the incident. I heard that you had a meeting with your lawyer. That can always be stressful, so I thought you might want to talk about it."

Alvarado's always trying to get him to talk about the events that landed him at Compass. Alvarado knows—it's his job to know—but he still wants Jon to endlessly rehash his mom's death and all the bad choices he made after. And yeah, "bad choices" is an understatement. He knows that. Nothing Alvarado can possibly say or do will add to Jon's enlightenment on the matter.

So Jon clenches his jaw to keep from saying something that can sharpen Alvarado's blade.

The doctor doesn't seem to notice Jon clamping his mouth shut, so intent on what he's got to say, like a dog going after a meaty bone.

"Does your lawyer think your appeal will succeed?" Alvarado asks.

Jon shrugs and doesn't meet his eyes. "Client-attorney privilege," says Jon. "Can't say."

"Anything you tell your therapist is also privileged information. I can't tell anyone."

Which may be true, but Alvarado's not the kind of man who inspires trust. Which means he should have chosen a different profession, but too late for that now.

"Next time I see my lawyer, I'll ask her if I should talk to you about it." Which kicks the can farther down the road. Best he can ever do with Alvarado.

Kicking the can just makes it heavier and harder to kick the next time, his mother once said. *Not worth breaking your toes.*

Jon still feels his mom most everywhere he goes. Still hears her voice in his head. Not that she's a ghost. She's gone. He knows that for sure, but her words linger like an echo. Sometimes he thinks he feels her touch or the breath of her kissing him good night, but he's pretty sure that's just air from a vent.

He doesn't feel her in Alvarado's office. Never has. Weird, because he's sure she'd like to rag on the man's pile of papers and dog-eared books. She'd have liked the rug, though, because they had one like it back at their apartment.

Alvarado studies him, expectant, intentionally letting the silence become awkward, hoping Jon will feel a need to fill it. Which he does.

"Maybe instead of worrying about me, you should worry about that new kid."

"Which new kid?" Alvarado asks. "You mean Silas Coady?"

First time Jon heard the kid's last name. It annoys him that Alvarado knows more about the kid than Jon does. At least on paper.

"What about him?" Alvarado asks.

"The kid doesn't belong here. You'd better get him out of here before something bad happens to him."

Alvarado leans forward, suddenly interested. "Is that a threat, Jon? Are you threatening this boy?"

Jon's eyes go wide. "Wait—what? No!"

"He's already been attacked—were you behind that?"

"I was the one who stopped it!"

"Making yourself appear the hero."

"That's not why I did it!"

"Yet now you're threatening to hurt him."

"That's not what I said!"

Jon wants to jump up and smack the guy, but that won't go over well. Impulse control is already flagged as one of Jon's main problems. Certainly part of the reason he's here.

Alvarado takes a deep breath. "Jon, do you know what gaslighting is? It's saying or doing something, then denying it ever happened. Making the other person doubt their own memories—even their own sanity. It's about control. It's about manipulation." He stares Jon down. "I won't let you gaslight me, Jon."

Jon forces himself to be calm. New paintbrush, same paint. The only way to win is to not pick it up. "All I'm saying is that he's a foster kid, not a detainee. He doesn't have the kind of social skills that will keep him safe here. He could get hurt, or worse, if he stays at Compass." Jon fizzles out, not sure if he's said too much or too little.

Alvarado still studies him. Probably he's not buying it. Alvarado's not used to Jon speaking truth. Not that Jon lies to him—usually he just deflects. But all that aside, Alvarado's got to do something for Silas, right? Isn't that as much his job as vivisecting Jon's brain? Luppino basically put Jon and Raz in charge of Silas's protection—but it's not enough. Raz doesn't have the attention span, and Jon can't be there 24/7. He's gotta do things such as having pointless meetings like this one.

Alvarado looks at his watch. "I'd like you to return for a session in a few days. I'll arrange it with your unit counselor. Maybe we can talk about what happened in the yard yesterday. As well as this issue you're having with Silas."

Jon straightens because the psychiatrist's eyes have gone steely. Is the doc gonna ignore everything he just said? Jon gets up, sorry he even said anything.

"I don't want to hurt the kid," Jon mumbles.

To which Alvarado replies, "I never said you did."

THE MEERKAT

Wash silently escorts Jon to his pod, although even Wash's silence feels like a personal insult. Maybe it's just his body language. Like he's doing you a favor allowing you to exist. When they get to his pod and Wash locks the door behind him, Jon sees his five pod-mates hanging out in their little living room. The pod living room is always crowded, because there are more boys in each pod than there are supposed to be. A storage room got turned into a cell. And in one cell they somehow squeezed bunk beds. He hears the girls' building has empty bedrooms, yet the three boys' buildings are packed to the gills. Guess that proves that guys are worse than girls. Or girls are just better at getting away with shit.

The TV is on for background noise, but nobody's watching the bland, curated offerings. Silas studies on the couch, while Raz,

Stripes, and Gordy sit at the table, playing poker with Myers, who has fully recovered from his electrical event, and is back to his completely uninteresting, mostly invisible self. His full name is Michael Myers, like the comedian, or the horror movie slasher. Everyone thinks he probably tips the scale toward the latter, because he's quiet, like psychos usually are. Myers has to share the bunk-bed room with Gordy. Gordy doesn't mind the company, and nothing bothers Myers. Except maybe electricity.

The poker players share a bag of popcorn, only some of which actually ends up in their mouths, and they bet with felt chair footpads they've been stealing for months. The guys waste their time on the game, since A) felt footpads obviously have no value to anyone but the janitors who have to replace them, and B) the deck, which has been at Compass longer than Jon, has only forty-three cards. But since everyone knows which cards are missing, it's now a part of the strategy.

Gordy shouts, "Hey, Jonny," as if he's been gone a week instead of an hour. Jon gives a curt nod as Gordy flaps his cards at Jon, because Gordy will continue waving till Jon acknowledges him.

Stripes scratches at a narrow tattoo that runs from behind his ear to his collarbone and tilts his head at Raz. "You cheating?" No anger, just like he's making conversation.

Raz exhales. "It's your turn. Play."

Stripes has a paranoid streak a mile wide. He's convinced that everyone's always out to get him. Which makes Jon wonder why he plays poker, where everyone actually *is* out to get you.

Alvarado would probably say that persecution is his comfort zone, then would do something that made the guy even more paranoid. Damn Alvarado—Jon can still feel him inside his own head, and it's not pleasant.

Jon leans against the wall, observing the dynamic of the game. Myers has the biggest pile of little green felties but is quiet about it, so no one seems to notice. Guy's got the crucial survival skill of not being noticed. Stripes, with tats permanently furrowing his unibrow, keeps track of everyone's eyes and hand positions, but more out of habit than anything else. He's more like a dozing tiger today than an angry one.

"Deal you in?" Raz asks Jon.

"Nah, I'm good."

But Raz continues to study Jon, clearly sensing that something is off. Or maybe he just knows that seeing Alvarado always messes with his alignment.

"They gonna write you up for what happened in the yard?"

Jon frowns. Why'd he go there? He's about to say no, but then remembers how sure Alvarado is that Jon's behind every turning gear at Compass. So he hedges his answer the way Stripes always hedges his bets. "Who knows? Probably not."

Myers finishes dealing and looks at his cards.

"You cheatin'?" Stripes asks.

"Not today," Myers tells him.

Raz checks his cards but keeps his attention on Jon, not willing to let it go. "Why don't you know? What did Alvarado say?"

No way is Jon reporting on what happened in the walrus pit,

especially when he's still smarting about how their meeting went. Instead Jon collapses on the couch, as far from the poker game as he can get, and ignores the question.

Silas is bent over his homework, which he can only do mentally, since he's got nothing to write with. There's bits of popcorn around him, as the other kids have been flicking burnt kernels at him—because nothing's more annoying than someone studying when you're trying to goof off.

Why can't Alvarado see that Jon actually wants to help the kid? Is it so far-fetched to think Jon might want to do something for someone else? He squeezes the armrest till his knuckles turn white. The doctor's manipulating him like he always does, twisting everything Jon does into something it's not.

Adriana would get it. Even after his "stupid newbie" poem, she believed him when he wrote how he worried about the kid and wanted him to have a chance.

Yeah, because she doesn't know you.

Right. Funny thing about that, though, is that everyone here at Compass who *thinks* they know him has got him all wrong. Which means that Adriana, who doesn't know him at all, actually knows him better. Adriana would call that poetic irony or some shit.

He shuts out the card game, another distraction, especially with Raz now flicking popcorn at Myers, who just quietly won another hand. Myers takes it, like he takes most everything dished at him. Gordy's looking at Jon, probably hoping he'll maintain order now that the game's threatening to go south.

Gordy's not good with conflict—even if the conflict is only just looming. He's also got more empathy than he knows what to do with. Always feeling bad for anyone who doesn't get treated fair. Which is everyone.

Jon can't afford empathy right now. You don't survive in juvie by crying over every hurt mouse you find. Especially with a court case coming up. Especially when Alvarado thinks you're a sociopath threatening that mouse.

Silas pops up from the couch and crosses the room to grab a tissue. When he turns to come back, he glances at Stripes's cards. Then he gives Raz a passing grin.

Which causes Raz to push his pile of felties into the pot. "I'm all in," he says, smirking at Stripes.

Stripes narrows his eyes suspiciously, then notices Silas heading back toward the couch—and puts two and two together.

Jon knows what's coming before it happens. Like he's already watching it in instant replay.

Stripes leaps to his feet, popcorn and cards raining around him. "Cheater!" he roars at Raz. "You think I don't know the kid's spying for you?"

The tiger no longer sleeps.

Silas scuttles back to the couch. Like he expects Jon to protect him from his own stupidity. Stripes balls his hands into fists and looks from Raz to Silas as if he can't decide who to pound first.

Because this sometimes works, Jon launches from the couch and yells at Stripes. "Shut it down! You want the guards in here?" Because, unlike Knox, Stripes can control himself when he wants to.

Stripes hesitates, looks in the high corner of the room, and stretches a smile at the camera. All good, eye-in-the-sky. All copacetic. Thing is, the smile is hard to see when his ink makes him look perpetually angry.

Stripes turns to Jon. "The kid helped Raz cheat. You saw that, right?" He looks at Gordy and Myers. "He was rubbernecking my cards like a goddamn meerkat!"

And the thing is, Stripes is right. Maybe the kid didn't do it intentionally, but that grin screwed Stripes's bluff. Even so, Jon's got to talk Stripes down. "Not worth getting written up, man. Let it go."

Then they all hear the outer door open at the end of their hall. A guard's in the air lock.

"And that's the ball game," says Raz.

The outer door has to be completely closed and engaged before the guard can proceed to the inner door, and there's maybe twenty yards between them. The boys know they have fifteen seconds from the time the outer door opens until the guard arrives at the inner door and has eyes on the room.

The boys launch into action. It's what Jon calls "doing the roach." They scatter, all of them finding neutral positions. Yeah, whoever's manning the surveillance room can see it on the camera, but hopefully all the guard will see when he gets to the pod is six kids doing different things, all peaceful and quiet.

Jon grabs Silas's textbook and looks at it with great interest. Raz gathers together the cards. Stripes leans against the wall looking up at the TV, like suddenly *Dancing with the Stars* is riveting drama. Gordy sits with his chair turned sideways, looking at his knees like he's in time-out. And Myers does his best not-worth-noticing act.

Only Silas stands there like the last kid in musical chairs, not knowing what to do other than look nervous and guilty.

The inner door opens. Rush and Garza come into the space, take in the scene.

"All bucolic," says Rush. "Like a Norman Rockwell. Just the way I like it."

"I don't even know who that is," Raz says.

"Artist," says Jon. "Painted Thanksgiving dinners and rosy-cheeked white children."

"And the old guy with the pitchfork?" Stripes asks.

"Different artist, same idea," says Jon. "What can we do for you, Officers?"

Garza looks to Rush for guidance, and Rush looks at Silas, who stands there bug-eyed like he just saw an alien pop out of someone's chest.

"What's up with him?" Rush asks.

"Prolly just intimidated by your uniforms, sir," says Raz.

It makes Rush chuckle. It's always good when Rush chuckles. "Kid, don't play poker," he tells Silas. "You don't got the face."

"I wasn't," says Silas in earnest. "I was just doing my homework, I swear."

Rush takes another glance around. Then, satisfied they've disrupted anything that was about to go down, he turns to leave, allowing Garza to give their final word.

"You boys play nice now."

Weak. Someone's gotta school Garza in parting shots.

The inner door opens. The inner door closes. And the second it does, they breathe a communal sigh of relief. Although Stripes is no longer at a raging boil, that doesn't mean he's not simmering. He stalks over to Silas, getting in his face.

"I'm not done with you, Meerkat."

Then he storms into his room, pulling the door closed behind him hard.

In the tweaked silence that follows, Silas gives off a nervous laugh. "What's his problem?"

And Jon feels the fury that left Stripes suddenly leap into him.

"You got a death wish?" Jon yells, his voice both hoarse and loud. "Do you have any sense at all? First you get on Knox's nerves, then you finger the most dangerous guys at Compass—and now you piss off Stripes?" He tries lowering his voice, but the volume control must be broken. "Any one of them could kill you!"

Gordy stares at Jon, his mouth hanging open. He ducks his head when Jon tosses a glare in his direction.

"You don't have to yell at me," mumbles Silas.

But he does. He absolutely, positively does.

"You're a train wreck, and I'm not going off the rails with you!"

Jon knows his words are losing steam, because suddenly he's not sure who he's really yelling at. The kid for having no sense? Alvarado for believing the very worst of him? Or himself for being enough of a sucker to give a shit? He feels like one of those car airbags that explodes on impact.

And the look on the kid's face deflates him faster than a knife ripping into him.

"I just . . . I just . . ."

"Just shut up and go to your room," Jon says, and realizes a moment later that he sounds like a pissed-off parent. Which just annoys him more.

"Damn," mumbles Raz, once the kid is gone. "The Meerkat must have taken one of the cards. I can only find forty-two."

Back in his room with the door closed and the rest of the world shut out, Jon tries to get his mind off what just happened. What he did to the kid.

So? I blew up. Big deal. People blow up all the time. It doesn't mean a thing.

Except that maybe it does.

Except that maybe it is a big deal for a kid who, like Jon, has no one waiting for him on the outside.

But it's toothpaste out of the tube, as his mom would have said. Can't get it back in, so just let it dry, because it'll be easier to scrape up.

Jon's reading the book he checked out—the one Adriana wanted him to read. *The Hitchhiker's Guide to the Galaxy.* He found it shelved where the Kant book should have been. So mis-shelving is their new thing. The book keeps his mind occupied and gives him something to talk to Adriana about when he writes her back. He's going to have to come up with another book for their little shelving shell game. He has no idea what book it's going to be, but it makes him smile to think about. Whatever book he chooses, she'll check it out and read it. He'll have to choose wisely. Choose insightfully. She didn't seem all that thrilled with Kant.

In the book he's reading, there's some really, really bad alien poetry. It makes him laugh because it's even worse than his own attempt at poetry.

Stupid newbie.

He sighs, because it just brings him back around to thinking about Silas.

Then, as he's reading, he gets to the part about the number forty-two—"the spoiler," as Adriana had called it—and Jon laughs out loud. She knows what he'll find funny, even without knowing him. But is that so strange? Because there are things he knows about her without actually knowing her too. Like the ambivalence she feels about her family. Like the way she secretly dissects the relationships of the people around her. Like the way she manages to trust him in spite of all the time she's been burned by trust.

How do you fall for someone you've never met?

Wait—is that what's happening here? Is he falling for Adriana? He'll never see her, so what's the point? Still, the idea looms large. After all, does he need to see her when she's in every line of ink on those pages? He knows things that go beyond what his senses would be able to tell him. Things that Kant would call empirical.

She dots her *i*'s with little misshapen circles but not happy faces.

She crosses her *t*'s at an angle for no reason beyond a defiant freedom to do so.

And she writes in smooth, swooping letters that are almost like old-school cursive, so pleasing to the eye, he sometimes traces them with his fingertip.

I have to be careful with this.

Jon knows he can't reveal to Adriana that there might be some unexpected depth to his feelings about her. Depth is not his friend. Because right now his life is about walking on a frozen lake. If there's depth beneath the ice, best never to know it. Because once you know, that's when you plunge through. No, Jon's got to play it cool on all fronts, since Compass is temporary. At best, their little word game can only go on for a few months, so why set himself up for a world of pain? That's what his rational mind tells him. But there are times he wants his rational mind to take a flying leap.

He rereads the page he had just read before his mind started wandering and laughs again. Then he closes the book, wanting his evening to end in a moment of laughter that connects him to Adriana.

As he's getting ready for bed, he trips over his shoes, which tends to be a nightly occurrence, since he always kicks them off in the middle of the room. As he pushes them over to the corner, he notices something sticking out from the bottom of his left shoe. He turns it over to reveal the missing playing card. It wasn't taken by Silas, as Raz had accused; it was just stuck to the bottom of Jon's shoe.

He peels it off, then grins when he sees what card it is. The queen of hearts. And then something occurs to him . . . how many cards did Raz say were left?

Forty-two! Ha!

John knows that this is only coincidence, but there are plenty of people who'll tell you that there's no such thing as coincidence—and tonight John wants to believe that there are signs and wonders and what his mother would call "micromiracles." He wants to believe that there is a design behind that which seems random, a point behind things that seem pointless, and that when the world is absurd, it is intentionally so, just to make us laugh.

Jon has no idea what Adriana looks like, but in his mind she's now fixed as the queen of hearts—vaguely mournful, but with a bouquet of hope blossoming in her hand, longing for more than the cage of her card will allow.

14

THE BETTER ENEMY

So hitchhiking, huh? Hard to imagine a world where that was ever a thing. Putting up your thumb and getting into the car of whatever crazy-ass stranger stops. Always a chance you'll get a one-way trip out of this world—and I don't mean in a science fiction sort of way. More like a horror story, if you catch my meaning. But on the other hand, now we've got Uber, so that's different how? Anyway I think nowadays aliens would have themselves an app to get them off-world.

Sorry I'm rambling. It hasn't been the best week, so I'm just trying to hitchhike my thoughts to a different place. The newbie—Silas—keeps triggering the wrong kids, and I'm worried he's gonna get hurt. I can only protect him so much. Plus there's other stuff going on—but I'm not gonna waste your time complaining. I'll get over it. The book helped. So does writing to you.

So, yeah, Kant can be a douche. Lots of those classic philosophers were. Jung is better. Philosophical, but more psychological. More about what makes us tick, rather than studying the noise itself. He's all about rehabilitation and meeting people wherever their head is at—even when their heads are in batshit places.

Do you think there are people who can't be rehabilitated? Who did something so bad it can't be forgiven? Maybe don't answer that. Or even worse—how about people who can't be rehabilitated because they don't even care if they do wrong? They just keep doing it because they can. There are guys like that here. They think the world owes them something, and that no one else but them's got a right to exist. I'll bet it's easier on the girls' side. But then again, girls can be meaner than guys sometimes. I hope things are good for you over there.

So anyway, do you know how long you're gonna be at Compass? I only ask because I want to know how much space I should be taking up in the journal. Wouldn't want to fill it up too fast.

Not panicking,
J

◆ ◆ ◆

157

"You finish that English essay?" Raz asks. They're standing in the cafeteria line for dinner, Raz in front of him, and Silas in front of Raz.

"Ain't started yet." The paper's not due for two more days. Unlike Raz, Jon always waits for the last moment, 'cause anything can happen in the meantime. He could be remanded to an adult prison or the teacher could die, or Earth could be blown up by aliens who write bad poetry and eat greenshirts for snacks.

Raz doesn't get it. Juvie's not a realm to conquer; it's limbo. Detainees are suspended between intake and release, social workers and lawyers, probation and long sentences. Why get in a tizzy over one essay in limbo?

They hear Gordy, still honking from his lingering bronchitis somewhere behind them, and Stripes advising Gordy not to cough in the food line, since more kids are like Culligan about that sort of thing than not. If it was anyone but Gordy, Stripes would be ripping the guy a new one, too, for all that coughing.

In front of them, Silas is walking stiffly, like maybe he's trying to be as invisible as Myers, who's somewhere in line behind them. Silas hasn't looked at Jon or Stripes all day. Jon's not sure if the kid's angry or scared or hurt over what happened at the poker game yesterday. Probably all three.

Jon feels rotten about the whole thing. So maybe he didn't want a kid following him like a poodle. And maybe he wanted a kid as smart as Silas to show some sense—to be, you know, savvy about his surroundings and the dangers of a place like this. You'd think after almost getting strangled by Knox just for asking him a question, he'd learn a trick or two. But no—instead he makes enemies of Viper and Culligan. And on top of it, he pisses off Stripes. Was it wrong of Jon to get him to wise up? Probably. No one's ever accused Jon of having helpful instincts.

"The mac 'n' cheese looks like toxic waste," Raz says just as Silas is handed a plate of the stuff from Dorella. Silas throws a quick glance at Raz, then plunks the plate down on his tray almost defiantly and turns to go. *Good,* thinks Jon. *Grow yourself a layer of protective attitude.*

"I'll have the sloppy joe," says Raz.

Dorella turns to Raz, deadpans him a glare that looks just like the straight-lipped *meh* emoji. "Not happening, Mr. Barbosa" she says. "Thanks to your helpful analysis of our mac 'n' cheese, that's what you'll be getting for dinner." And she gives him a steaming plate of the stuff. Raz groans and bellyaches about it, but everyone knows you don't defy Dorella's edicts.

"What would you like, Jon?"

"Sloppy joe, ma'am. Extra fries if that's okay with you."

Silas is on his way to the tables with Raz behind. Jon figures lunch could be an opportunity to make things right with the kid. Maybe it's fate that Jon's gotta help Silas out. Maybe there's a higher reason that he and Raz got picked to wise up the little guy. Jon's mom would have said so. Maybe Adriana would think so too.

Didn't Adriana say she has a little brother? Maybe she could give Jon some tips on apologizing to a kid without actually having to say *I'm sorry.* Maybe she'd know when to help him and when to draw the line.

With his thoughts anywhere but in the moment, Jon bumps into Raz, who had suddenly, without warning, stopped short, and Jon's plate, with its glorious sloppy joe and double fries, flips and hits the floor, splattering both of them.

"What the hell, Raz?"

"Shit—sorry, man. Want me to get you another sandwich? Or you want my plate and I'll get a new one?" For a second, Jon wonders if Raz orchestrated the whole thing to get a sloppy joe of his own. But the line to the tables is stalled in front of them, so it was a legitimate stop-short. And maybe he was mooning about Adriana too much and not paying attention.

Jon cleans the worst of it while Wash mutters, "I should make you eat that off the floor." Then Wash reluctantly gives him permission to go back in line and get it replaced—and while another kid might have to go to the end of the line, the kids in front offer him cuts. Only one or two kids behind them complain, and not all that loudly. The perks of being an institution at an institution.

By the time he gets to his table, every spot is taken except his own, everyone impatiently waiting for Jon to arrive so they can sit down—because when Wash is on duty, he never lets anyone sit until the table is completely full. One more of his many little tortures. Jon brushes past Flotsam—the kid who got switched to another pod so Silas could be in theirs. Flots is sitting next to Silas. Lately he's been hanging with his new pod-mates at meals, probably hoping to bond as a matter of self-preservation. But apparently he doesn't want to lose his position in Jon's crew.

Poor Flots. Trying to straddle two worlds can only end badly.

The first five minutes of a meal is always the same. Silence as everyone does everything short of making love to their plate. Silas is about as far from Jon's seat as he can be, just as hyper-focused on his food as everyone else. The kid's inhaling his mac 'n' cheese like it's his last meal on earth. Well, at least he's still at the table, not seeking new allies somewhere else. But then, where else would he go? Like they say: "Better the enemy you know."

Jon wishes he was sitting closer to the kid, so maybe when everyone starts coming up for air, he could say something kind, to let the kid know Jon's not mad at him. Wasn't really him that Jon was mad at anyway. It was the whole situation.

Gordy's in his usual spot, partway down the table. He looks too worried to wave at Jon. His lips tremble halfway between a smile and a scream, like the big guy's riding a roller coaster and it's out of control. He's still scared about Jon's outburst yesterday. Jon never blew up in front of Gordy before. It's kind of shattered his world. But it still doesn't stop Gordy from eating.

Silas is the first of them to speak.

"I feel funny," he says. "Like . . . like something really bad's gonna happen . . ."

Next to him, Flots laughs. "Already did. You're here."

"It's a prem'nition," says Gordy. "My grandma had those. They're scary. 'Specially when they're true."

Silas pushes his plate away. Stripes is immediately on it.

"Hey, Meerkat—if you're not gonna eat that, you can give it to me. Least you could do after what you pulled last night."

Jon dips a fry into his sloppy joe sauce. The fact that Stripes is making his peace with Silas before he does ticks him off.

But before Silas can even respond, he starts choking and turning red.

"What's up with *him*?" says Myers, who sits across from him.

"It's the prem'nition!" wails Gordy, freaked beyond measure. "It's coming true!"

Jon gets up so fast, his chair skids backward, overturns. He hurries to Silas. Silas is no longer choking but instead gasping, and scrabbling at his throat like he can't breathe.

"He needs the Heimlich maneuver!" shouts Raz. "Anyone know how to do the Heimlich maneuver?"

Wash appears on the other side of Silas, muttering into his radio. Then he yells, "Everybody back!" Everyone listens except for Jon.

"It's the mac 'n' cheese!" someone at another table yells. "It's food poisoning!"

And the rumor ignites across the cafeteria.

"He can't breathe!" Jon shouts at Wash.

"I can see that!" Wash shouts back, doing nothing. "The nurse is on her way!"

But the infirmary is in the admin building. She might as well be coming from the other side of the world.

Silas's eyes roll back in his head, and he slumps in his chair. Jon catches him as he slips to the floor and lays him carefully in the aisle, unconscious. Stripes and Flots back up another two steps like they could catch what Silas has got. Now Silas is the center of the entire cafeteria's attention. No one's sitting. They're all standing, trying to get a look, while the rumors of food poisoning and anthrax and God knows what continue to spread.

Jon scowls at Wash. "Do something!"

Wash shifts from foot to foot. "Calm down. The nurse'll be here soon."

Jon knows CPR from his junior lifesaving class. Not that he has any skill in it, but he can't just stand there doing nothing. He kneels beside Silas.

"Maybe you should wait for the nurse," Wash says uneasily.

Jon ignores him while Raz asks, "You going to give him the Heimlich?"

Jon ignores Raz, too, and begins chest compressions. He has no idea if the kid's heart has stopped, but it's just what you do.

Rush arrives a moment later, with more wits about him than Wash. He grabs Silas's left wrist. There's a medical alert bracelet there. Jon hadn't noticed it before. There are other kids who have them for all kinds of allergies. Bee stings. Peanuts. Strawberries. You only have a bracelet for it if it's really bad.

Jon stops CPR, because maybe that's not what the kid needs. Silas's face seems to be swelling like a puffer fish now. His lips are getting all fat like an influencer with collagen injections.

"It's an allergic reaction," says Rush.

"What's he allergic to?" asks Raz.

Rush squints at the bracelet. "I don't have my glasses . . ."

"Penicillin!" shouts the nurse, out of breath as she races to Silas's side. She knows without having to look. Of course she knows—she just processed him a few days ago. She feels for Silas's pulse. "Is anyone here taking penicillin?" Then, seeing Gordy, she turns to him. Gordy's eyes widen, and he seems to physically shrink like a star before it goes nova.

"He got one of my pills?"

Then Rush looks at Silas's plate of half-eaten mac 'n' cheese, then at every face around the table. And Jon knows what he's thinking, because Jon's thinking it himself.

It was in his food. And it wasn't an accident.

Wash gets a grip on Jon and pulls him away from Silas. "Show's over, guys. Let the nurse do her job."

Feeling lightheaded, Jon moves away, becoming just another observer of the drama. More guards arrive with a gurney. The nurse jabs an EpiPen into Silas's thigh. He's lifted to the gurney and rolled away.

"He dead?" says Stripes. "I think he's already dead."

"Shut it!" growls Jon. "Shut it before I shut it for you."

Wash tries to get everyone to return to their dinners, but the room's not having it. Most still stand in groups spinning rumors. Some are looking at the cafeteria workers like they're spiking their food with rat poison.

Meanwhile, at Jon's table, Gordy has his head in his hands, crying. "It wasn't me," Gordy wails. "He saw it coming, but it wasn't me."

But Silas didn't see it coming. It wasn't a premonition, because the penicillin was already inside him. It was his body telling him that he was about to go into anaphylactic shock.

From something that's supposed to help people.

What kind of messed up world is it that you could die from something that can save someone else's life?

No. No, Jon will not even think the word. Just because they rolled the kid out unconscious doesn't mean he's dead. If he was dead, they wouldn't be rolling him so fast.

The exit of Silas's gurney is the trigger, and greenshirts start yelling about poisoned food. Some throw full trays at the kitchen, where the doors roll down fast with a metallic clang like a town battening down for a hurricane. Rush tries to take control, but no one hears him in the din. He shouts into his radio but maybe no one hears him at the other end either.

And in the chaos, Jon has the most selfish of thoughts.

I need to tell Adriana about this. He should be thinking about the kid. Instead he's thinking about Adriana.

Reflexively, he reaches down to his waist, where he hides the journal when he has it. But he doesn't have it now. Instead his hand slips into the little unofficial "pocket" he ripped between two overlapping seams in his waistband. And when he brings his hand back, there's white powder on his fingertips. At first he's confused. Thinks it's detergent or something that got caught in there. But then he tastes it. It's bitter. A very specific kind of bitter.

And when he looks up, he sees Raz watching him.

A beat, and Raz looks away, scratching his ear. "I didn't see nothing," Raz says.

"Raz, it's not what—"

"SHUT UP!" yells Raz. "I didn't see nothing, so just shut up!"

Then, with chaos and paranoia building, someone across the cafeteria puts a finger down their throat to make themselves vomit and succeeds. And that's when the next level of hell breaks loose. Kids yelling, throwing stuff, hurling themselves against the metal shutters of the food service area, like they're going to kill the cafeteria workers before they die themselves. A Klaxon sounds, the exit doors lock, and a strident voice blares over the loudspeakers.

"Lockdown. Lockdown. Lockdown. Compass Detention Center is in lockdown. Remain in your current position until directed by authorized personnel. We are in lockdown."

The message repeats four times. It takes that long for those attacking the kitchen doors and hurling food to stop. A phalanx of guards storms into the cafeteria.

And all Jon can think about is Adriana, because he can't bear to think about Silas. He wants to be away from all of this and disappear into that journal, because vanishing into those words, *her* words, is so much better than thinking about this, and what happens next.

Because Raz wasn't the only one who saw that incriminating powder on Jon's fingers. Not-so-invisible Myers was standing right there in plain sight, staring at him too.

PART THREE

PARALLEL DIMENSIONS

HOW DARE TIME MOVE SO SLOWLY?

Drunk and disorderly,
Since you ignored her, we
Spiral down with her
Into the ground.
You wept at her grave,
Then you slept at a rave,
And left me alone all night.
Child Protective
Said you're defective,
And took me away.
"I'll make it up to you,"
I hear you say,
But you delay,
Because your priority,

In spite of Authority,
Is drowning your grief
Boneless at the bar.
Because I am your skeleton,
Torn from you,
Leaving you spineless.
Just a worm at the bottom
Of your bottle
I sometimes want to throttle.

Then out of the blue,
You meet someone new,
Who gives you a reason
To be a man again.
Lana prevails,
All hair, and all nails,
And I'm back
Where I started,
Smack in the way
of your better day.
She doesn't hate me.
She doesn't like me.
She tolerates my presence.
But sees obsolescence.
The old family;
The leftover daughter,
Just water under a broken bridge.

Colter has displaced me,
Erased me,
A crib in your crib,
His bedroom now
All I get's a fold-out,
No warmth when it's cold out,
While you paint the mold out
In baby boy blue,
With spaceships and trucks.
You say a boy's room
Must have boy things,
Because in your eyes
The only gender fluid
Flows standing up.

And still, I'm your skeleton,
And still, you're spineless;
The mindless worm in the bottle.
Which means it's never really empty
As long as you're inside looking out.

A few days before the lockdown, Adriana gets her first visitation with her family.

She's dreading, dreading, dreading the letdown from not seeing her father there. From the very real possibility that it will be just Lana.

And Lana is the first person she sees when Officer Bonivich

opens the door to the visitation room, escorting Adriana in. Her heart misses a beat, hovering, prepared for a plunge . . . but it's not just Lana. Her father is there, and so is Colter.

Lana stands and tears up the moment she sees Adriana, which makes Adriana cast her eyes anywhere but toward Lana's. Instead, she takes in the room. Bright fluorescent light flattens the Sunday afternoon sunshine from the skylight. Little family groups occupy different areas of the large room. She hadn't noticed it the first time she was here, but a long shelf holds games and children's books along with teddy bears, dolls, and dump trucks so the detainees can play with their younger siblings and read them stories. Or maybe those are only brought in for visitation days.

Adriana moves toward her family. Her dad shifts in his chair, no doubt wishing he was anywhere but here. Three-year-old Colter has a death grip on Lana's leg, his eyes fixed on the intimidating Bonivich, not even seeing Adriana yet. Finally, when he does, he launches from the safety of his mother to his half sister.

"A-dana!" exclaims Colter, wrapping his arms around one of her legs.

"Hi, Colter." She leans down to give him a proper hug, and limps with him still clinging, toward her father and Lana.

"He misses you. We all miss you," says Lana.

Circumnavigating Colter and his claim on Adriana's left leg, Lana envelops Adriana in a tight hug as if she's Lana's long-lost child. *Or sister, considering how much younger she is than my dad.*

The flowery fragrance of Lana's perfume is suffocating. Adriana holds her breath and lets her arms dangle, not returning the hug.

Lana releases her and steps back, blinking to clear her wet eyes. Keeping her hands on Adriana's shoulders, she studies Adriana's face. "How are you?"

Adriana stares at Lana's blouse, which is demure and opaque as prescribed in the visitor's guidelines. "I'm good," she says.

"Are you sleeping? How's the food?"

Adriana shrugs. *The food is lousy and I'm awake half the night, but you're just asking 'cause you're supposed to, and you don't want the real answer anyway.*

She skates a glance at her dad, and, to avoid meeting her eye, he shifts his attention to Colter.

"Colter, give your sister some breathing room."

"Her leg *breathes*?" he says. Then he lets go, and gallops around a nearby table like, well, a colt. Lana, glancing worriedly at the guard, gently grabs him and sits, pulling him into her lap. He wriggles to get free but gives up when he realizes freedom is not an option. Not for him, not for Adriana.

He smiles at her. "Can I have a yellow shirt like yours?"

The very suggestion makes Lana flinch. Colter is the only one of them who genuinely wants to be here. She's no inmate in his eyes. And she truly misses him. Adriana used to play with him to distract herself while trying to live with a family she didn't recognize.

Adriana drags a chair next to her dad and sits. She looks quietly at him until finally he reaches out a hand and squeezes her shoulder. "Hey, princess," he says, barely looking at her.

"Hi, Dad." He never calls her princess. Just another layer of awkwardness painted on the moment. So she decides to let the paint dry a little, and turns her attention once more to the rest of the room.

That's when she spots Monessa with an uncharacteristically sweet expression on her face. She's bottle-feeding someone's baby. Adriana can't help but stare at her in shock. Monessa must have seen Adriana enter but is pretending Adriana doesn't exist. Adriana's attention skids to an older woman—Monessa's mother? Where's the baby's mother? In the restroom?

Wait.

No way.

Monessa has a baby?

There's not enough spandex in the world to wrap her mind around this.

And suddenly she makes the connection! Bianca secretly wanting that book on newborns. *It's not what you think,* Pip had said. It wasn't for Bianca—it was for Monessa! Does anyone else know that Monessa has a baby? Or is it just Bianca and Pip? Pip seems to know a little bit about everything going on at Compass. Maybe more than a little bit.

She immediately thinks of Jon. She has to tell Jon about this new revelation! Does he get visitors? she wonders. Is the boys' visitation room anything like this? Or do just the girls get pastels and picture books?

She should go over to Monessa. Say something. But

Monessa's so focused on her baby, maybe she doesn't even know that Adriana's there after all. Instinctively, Adriana knows whatever happens in the visiting room stays in the visiting room. She shouldn't say anything. She probably shouldn't be looking at them either. But the alternative is looking at her own family.

"I got Spider-Man shoes," says Colter, kicking his feet.

Adriana smiles at him. "They're really cool, Colter."

Lana sighs. "Twenty minutes isn't enough time," she says.

Time for what? Adriana wonders. To stare at each other and search for things to say?

She places a yellow block on the table, sets a blue one on top. "Let's see how high we can go," she says to Colter, and hands him a red block. Colter takes it and places it very carefully on the blue one. He looks expectantly at Adriana.

"Your turn, A-dana. This one!" He gives her a purple block.

Adriana laughs. "All right. You can be the architect."

"Ar-ka-tek," Colter says, marking the word in his memory. *Little brothers are the best. Does J have a little brother too? Or maybe a little sister?* He'd be a good big brother. He's free with advice with her, so maybe he got that from having younger siblings. She puts another block on the tower and her heart warms, thinking about J with his family.

Her dad taps his pocket for the third time that Adriana has noticed—nervously sensing the absence of his phone. No technology to hide behind here. He looks at Lana. "I locked the car doors, right?"

Lana sighs. "We're at a detention center—security's everywhere. I'm sure it's fine."

Adriana frowns, taking the thought to its obvious conclusion. "Yeah. And anyone who'd steal it is already on the inside, right?"

That makes Lana squirm a bit. Adriana feels both guilty and triumphant at the same time.

"Have you made friends?" asks Lana.

She thinks about Pip and Bianca. Can she really call them friends? They are girls she hangs out with, and they hang out with her.

But on the other hand, there's J.

She wonders what would happen if she told them about him. Not that she would, but what if she did?

I met a boy.

What do you mean you met a boy? There are boys?

Of course there are boys.

In with the girls?

Oh yeah. They're in with us all the time.

She smirks thinking about that conversation. But Lana must take the smirk to mean something else. Like maybe Adriana is making fun of her.

Lana's cheeks turn pink. "Well, at least are the other girls nice?"

Her dad clears his throat. "Don't be rude—answer your—" Then he catches himself. "Answer Lana."

Was he going to say "your mother"?

"This isn't the kind of place where you make 'friends,' okay?"

Trying to release the rising tension, Lana summons another of her big, fake smiles. "The visitor's guide says we can buy you something from the vending machine. What would you like, baby?"

Did Lana really just call her "baby"?

Adriana glances across the room at the vending machine and sees her favorite barbecue chips. No way is she asking Lana for them. She is *not* Lana's baby.

"I'm good."

And when her dad's glower reaches her, Adriana hands Colter more blocks and, oozing sarcasm, says to Lana, "But thanks for asking, sweetie pie."

Her father grunts his disapproval, heaves himself up, and buys the potato chips, dropping the bag on the table. She's actually surprised he knows which ones she likes.

"Eat 'em, don't eat 'em. I don't care."

"*I'll* eat 'em," says Colter, but looks to his mother for permission, having sensed the unsettling undercurrent.

"We'll share them," says Adriana. Lana nods at Colter, who opens them. Adriana doesn't take any, letting Colter have them all. Her father notices and is not amused.

Thanks a lot, Lana. Once more you've ruined things between my dad and me.

Adriana glances at the clock on the wall. Six minutes to go. How dare time move so slowly?

A foul smell wafts from the direction of Monessa and her

baby. A diaper needs changing. Adriana selfishly wants to see Monessa do it, just to see her get baby shit on her hands. Does that make her evil? J wouldn't think so.

"They had a lot of rules coming in here," her dad says. "They searched us. Even your little brother."

"Sorry," says Adriana.

Colter comes over to her, climbs into her lap, and yawns, leaning his head on her chest. "It's okay. They got a magic wand." In a moment, he's dozing in her arms.

"Not blaming you," her father says. "It's just that there's a lot of rules."

Adriana's not sure what to say. What did he expect? If they don't trust the detainees, are they going to trust the families they came from?

"We can't wait until you're home again, Adriana. It'll go fast, you'll see . . ." Lana's eyes plead for her to . . . what? Pretend that she's overjoyed that they're visiting? Pretend she's not ashamed for Colter to see her like this? Pretend that it's okay for Lana to replace her mom?

Never gonna happen.

Her father stands. "We should go," he says. "Time's almost up."

Adriana glances toward the door and sees Officer Bonivich step through. *Perfect.* She's not the only one watching the clock.

"I'm fine," she says to her parents, standing and handing Colter to Lana. "Don't feel like you're obligated to visit all the time."

Distress crosses Lana's face, but her father gives an abrupt nod, as if that's his thought too.

After saying goodbye to her father and Lana and giving Colter a kiss on the top of his head, Adriana follows Bonivich down the hall that leads back to the girls' building. A feeling like she's lost something, something precious that she might not find again, washes over her. She falls back a step so Bonivich won't notice and dashes the threat of tears away from her eyes.

She remembers a little girl she once saw running after her mother, a look of desperation on her face. Heartbruised, Adriana wants to race back to her dad just like that little girl and apologize a million times until everything is okay between them. But it's going to take more than words to fix how wrong things are.

GHOSTS TO US

Adriana,

That *poem* about your father hits hard. Harsh what went down. Sounds like he's a broken man still putting his pieces together. Not that it excuses him for any of it. Parents aren't superheroes. And we can't ever forgive them for that, I guess. But somehow we gotta learn to live with them in their various states.

Reminds me of a science teacher on the outside that had us imagine ourselves as a superhero who could actually change states—solid to liquid to gas—at will. I told her that was weak, and that I wanted to be that fourth state—plasma. Radiant matter—like lightning. It makes up Earth's ionosphere, the interior of the sun, and stars. No one messes with plasma.

I like getting to know who you are, Adriana. The truth of you. It feels like the stuff of stars. Maybe you and me together, we could ignite. Maybe WE could be invincible like plasma.

J

Adriana's room seems even more confining than usual; its walls press against her awareness. So opposite of how she feels when she reads J's words. Sitting cross-legged on her bed, she reads J's latest entry again, and imagines the claustrophobic space around her expanding until it includes both of them.

The library is busy. Girls search for books to complete their classwork. The usuals try to disappear into their private reading bubbles but are having a hard time of it today, since there are so many non-usuals there. Ms. Detrick works at her desk, keeping an eye on the girls, and rising now and then to check out or check in books. Bianca, Monessa, and Jolene sit at a table near the one window. Adriana wants to join the girls at the table, but she's got a whole cart of books to deal with.

Sunshine falls through the bars crosshatching the window, laying stripes across the table. As if they needed a reminder from the sun itself where they are. Just a few days ago, Jolene was going on about how her family was definitely coming to get her on Sunday. Family, not parents—as if to Jolene the idea of "parents" is so far away from her reality, she can't say the word. Instead she just has this vague vision of a big blobby family that's coming to envelop her, absorb her, and roll away with her, letting her dissolve into it forever. But the blob didn't come. It never comes. It's probably never going to. Adriana makes a mental note that she should write about it, and then feels guilty that she's taking Jolene's misery as inspiration.

Monessa looks sadder than she's ever seen her. No, not sadder. Stonier. Monessa hides her emotions behind a concrete façade, like a dam. Seeing her baby and then having to walk away must have left those waters behind the dam high.

Adriana looks at the shelves. She hasn't written back to J yet. She wants to, but she doesn't want to give him empty small talk. She wants him to have something substantial from her. The book J mis-shelved this time was *I'll Give You the Sun*. Quite a promise—and it made sense, since he was talking about plasma and the stuff inside stars. Now she feels pressure to find the perfect book to displace when she next shelves the journal. But it's a good kind of pressure. Like trying to solve a riddle.

"Hey, what's with you?" asks Bianca. "Why you just standing there like that, looking like someone ate your dessert?"

Adriana tries to clear her head and the emotional billboard that is her face, then takes a moment to sit with Bianca and the other girls. "Just tired is all."

Tension still simmers between Adriana and Monessa, but both keep their distance.

"Adriana!" calls Ms. Detrick. "No socializing while you're working."

"Yes, Ms. Detrick."

"Give that woman a whip!" says Bianca beneath her breath, and the other girls snicker.

Adriana shrugs an apology for being antisocial and gets back to work. Then, back in the nonfiction section, she happens to glance out the window and sees a string of boys coming out of one of their buildings into the yard. Like the library and the cafeteria, the yard is a shared space, but by the time the girls get there, any signs of the boys have been erased. This is the first time Adriana is actually seeing some of them. And she wonders if J is among this group. Her heart flutters a bit thinking about it. Pressing a hand against the sun-warmed glass, Adriana peers through the frame of bars. Her curiosity blooms, and her interest in J deepens. Even though he's no more to her than words in blue pencil on the page of her journal, the idea that he is both close and far makes her want to close the gap.

"It's like they're in an alternate dimension."

The voice makes Adriana jolt just a bit. She turns to see Pip next to her, looking out toward the boys too. Her approach, as always, was stealthy.

"I hear there are more of them than us," Adriana says.

"Four times more boys than girls here," says Pip. "But they're shadows to us, and we're shadows to them."

Then Pip looks at her—really looks. Deeply. Suddenly Adriana

183

feels unguarded. Vulnerable. Like Pip can totally read her mind and knows exactly what's going on. Adriana knows that can't be true . . . but clearly Pip suspects something, because she says, "The library would be a great place to leave a message for a boy you knew on the outside."

"I don't know any boys on the outside," says Adriana, flustered. "I mean no boys on the outside that are inside. Here. Now."

Pip giggles at Adriana's awkwardness. "I know what you meant." Then she shrugs. "But if you do need a message passed, let me know."

And she turns to walk away, like what she said wasn't a big thing at all.

Adriana should let her go, but instead she stops Pip and says, "What about getting information about a boy?"

Pip turns back and smiles. "What kind of information?"

"Anything. Everything. Whatever you can find out."

"Got a name?"

And that's where it all falls apart.

"I just have his first and middle initials."

Pip shrugs. "Get me a name and we'll talk." Then she strides off like it's nothing.

More and more, Pip seems like the tip of some mysterious iceberg. Pip the tip. But maybe that's not a bad thing. Because like Bianca said, people Pip likes tend to have fortune shine on them. And Pip likes Adriana. She begins to wonder if telling Pip about the journal might be worth the risk. But what would be the point if Adriana doesn't even know his name?

And then something occurs to her. Something she could kick herself for not thinking of before.

The books are all shelved. The hour's up. The other girls have left. But she still has a five-minute window before the doors lock her out and she misses the pre-dinner lineup. Ms. Detrick would be getting her out the door right about now, but she's on an aggravating phone call with a book supplier.

"How many times do I have to tell you? This is a *detention* center! The students can't pick up the books—you need to deliver them *here!*"

Adriana stands at the checkout desk, at the computer. Logging in new books and materials for the library is one of her tasks, so it's not a red flag if Ms. Detrick sees her here—but in ordinary circumstances, she'd check on what Adriana is doing.

"*Detention* center—not *convention* center! Is there anyone else there I can speak to?"

Adriana is definitely the last thing on the woman's mind at the moment.

She opens the checkout menu. Checked-out books are organized alphabetically by the person's name. She doesn't know J's true name, but she knows the last book he checked out. The one she left for him! *The Hitchhiker's Guide!* She searches for the book's checkout history and smiles.

Gotcha!

She closes the window and reopens Ms. Detrick's screen just

as Ms. Detrick hangs up on the imbecile she was talking to and releases a grunt that is her quiet version of a primal scream.

"Ms. Detrick, I'd better be going, or I'll be late for lineup."

She sighs. "Sorry, Adriana. I got caught up. See you in a couple of days!"

As Adriana exits into the hallway, she sees Bonivich already marching toward the girls' wing for roll call. "Cutting it close today, Adriana."

"I had work to do," says Adriana with a shrug. "Shouldn't a productive member of society take pride in a job well done?"

"Yeah, yeah," mutters Bonivich.

Although Bonivich doesn't notice, Adriana is all smiles for the walk back to the girls' building. Because the boy with the blue pencil now has a name.

Artorias Jonathon Kilgore.

"Lockdown. Lockdown. Lockdown. Compass Detention Center is in lockdown. Remain in your current position until directed by authorized personnel. We are in lockdown."

It's the following evening. A Klaxon alarm blares so loud, it could induce cardiac arrest in someone older. For Adriana, it makes her heart pound heavily a few times in irritated defiance, and sends an adrenaline rush that makes her ears hot and her toes tingle.

The other girls show little more than annoyance.

It's movie night. One evening a month, the girls are brought to the Ed Center's multipurpose room, which has a theater-sized screen, to watch an inoffensive, nontriggering (in other words, boring) movie. Even so, the girls look forward to it, because it's something different.

But tonight, the alarm goes off ten minutes into the movie, whooping like maybe nukes are falling from the sky.

"What's happening?" Adriana asks.

"Didn't you hear? Lockdown," says Bianca. "Worst timing ever."

"All right, girls, you know the drill," says Bonivich, who's quickly joined by two more guards. "Hands on your heads, and line up against the wall."

"So what happened?" asks Monessa.

"Nothing you need to know," replies Bonivich. Which means Bonivich probably doesn't know yet either.

"Must be pretty bad," Adriana whispers to Bianca as they're marched back to the girls' wing.

"Quiet, Zarahn!" snaps Bonivich. "No talking during lockdown."

And then something amazing happens!

A line of boys, hands on their heads as well, passes in the other direction—heading from the cafeteria—because the boys were at dinner when the alarm went off. Whatever happened, it must have happened during the boys' dinner.

"Ah, shit," says Bonivich as she sees the guards leading the boys down the hall toward them. "No eye contact!" orders Bonivich. "I catch anyone looking, you'll be in isolation for a week!"

It's an empty threat, but they get the idea. Still, that doesn't mean they don't sneak looks at these green-shirted aliens from an alternate dimension.

One of them is Artorias Jonathon Kilgore, thinks Adriana. And although she felt sure she'd be able to pick him out, she has no idea which one he is. Maybe he's not here. Maybe he's in a different group.

Or maybe he's the reason for the lockdown.

Did something happen to him?

Did he do something?

She knows it's completely irrational to worry—there are a million possible reasons for lockdown, and with the tempers that rage in a place like this, fights are breaking out all the time. Like the one she had with Monessa. But that didn't bring a lockdown. This had to be something big.

Everyone's locked into their pods, but mercifully not sealed in their rooms. Adriana has to wait this out with Bianca, Jolene, and Monessa.

"It's always something stupid the boys did," Monessa complains. "I don't see why we have to go into lockdown with them."

Bonivich comes back an hour into lockdown, to give them the bare bones of what happened.

"Riot in the cafeteria," she says. "A kid got rushed to the hospital. Par for the course."

Adriana wonders what course that could possibly be par for.

"What was his name?" Adriana asks.

Bonivich glares like Adriana just hurled an insult. "How

the hell should I know? Get to bed. Lockdown'll be over by morning."

With nothing else to do, Adriana pulls out the Anne Frank book—which she had forgotten about—from under her mattress and flips to where she left off reading. Anne's family has moved into the Annex with another family, and everybody is getting on each other's nerves. But despite being in constant lockdown, unable to go outside or even look out a window, Anne keeps a sunny spirit, pouring her thoughts and feelings into the diary. *Just like me,* thinks Adriana. Except Adriana's sharing her journal. Not really *her* journal anymore. It's J's too. Not J. But Jonathon. Jonny. Jon. *It's our journal now.*

Adriana wonders what he's doing during lockdown. Is he thinking about her? Waiting for her to write back? *Or maybe he's the kid in the hospital.* No! She has to stop thinking that way. Instead, she imagines his voice telling her how silly she is for thinking that. What does his voice sound like? At first it was just some anonymous guy voice—but the more of his responses she reads, the more she hears the timbre of a voice inside her head.

Stop it! You're never going to see him, never going to hear his voice. He'll never be more than blue pencil on the pages of your journal. Maybe so . . . but just thinking about it makes Adriana feel less lonely.

IS, NOT WAS

The boys are marched to their pods straight from the cafeteria riot, passing a line of girls that most of them are too freaked to even look at.

Wash closes the door to Jon's pod with a solid finality that doors only seem to have during lockdown. And once the door is closed, Jon's pod-mates all do the roach, scattering in their small common room. Like no one feels allegiance to anyone but themselves, and they need a four-foot square of landscape to feel safe.

Trust has flown out the window. Only suspicion remains.

Jon feels Silas's absence more keenly now that there are only five in the room. The kid had a compelling presence whether pestering them with questions or dampening the air with his hurt silence.

Has a compelling presence. No way is Silas past tense. He can't be.

On the heels of that thought, Stripes asks, his overloud hoarse voice strangely subdued, "You think he's dead?"

"He was alive when they carted him off," Jon says before anyone can offer a less hopeful opinion. "And those EpiPen things do miracles. It's got to have worked." He tries spreading affirmation in nods to the skeptical Stripes, snuffling Gordy, frowning Raz, but his gaze snags on Myers. Jon grits his teeth. Myers saw the damning white powder on Jon. Has he told anyone what he *thinks* he knows? Will he tell anyone?

Someone tried to frame Jon. That's the one thing he's sure of. Is that person in the room right now? Gordy was taking penicillin, but he hasn't got a mean bone in his body. Did someone trick him into giving up a pill? Possible, since Gordy trusts even those who don't deserve it.

If it was one of his pod-mates, the most likely suspect would be Stripes. But it seems like a move too nasty even for him. Unless he didn't get how serious an allergy Silas had. HAS. Silas HAS.

As if he's plucking Jon's thoughts right from his head, Gordy chokes out, "Who'd wanna kill Silas? He wouldn't even squish a bug."

Myers turns away—Jon reads it as a conspicuous attempt not to meet Jon's eye.

Raz rouses himself and says, "Gordy, we don't know anything yet. And anyway, it could have been an accident. Right, Jon?"

"Yeah," says Jon. "An accident."

But Raz glances at Jon just a little too long.

Gordy wipes his streaming eyes on his sleeve. "An accident,

huh? Like maybe the penicillin was on my fingers from before, and I touched his fork."

"Yeah, something like that," says Raz.

Gordy shakes his head. "But I didn't touch his fork . . ."

Jon settles on the couch. Everyone seems to take this as a signal to settle as well. Gordy sits a cushion away from him. Stripes takes a seat uneasily at the game table. Only Raz moves restlessly around the room now, while Myers still leans against the wall, as far from Jon as possible.

"Yeah, who says it's something intentional?" says Raz, trying way too hard to sell it. "Maybe a sick cafeteria worker dropped their meds in the mac 'n' cheese. Somebody barfed, right?"

"Yeah—first one guy, and then a bunch more," adds Gordy, "because he saw the first guy barf."

"Or maybe it wasn't just from seeing the first guy. Maybe they all got sick from it."

Gordy snuffles, then coughs so hard, Myers flinches. "You know I gotta mix it in my food, Jonny—can't get it down elseways. But none of it fell into Silas's food, I promise. Besides, I take it at breakfast, not dinner."

"No one thinks you did it, Gordy," Jon says, trying to calm him down.

"How come we didn't know Silas was allergic to penicillin, hah?" says Stripes. "They should've warned us. We have a guy taking penicillin and a guy deathly allergic to the stuff practically in the same room."

"Yeah," says Myers. "Someone screwed up for sure." It's his

first offering in the conversation. Jon can't help but feel the double meaning in his words.

"The kid had a medical alert bracelet," Raz says. "Anyone can see it."

"Yeah, but who looks?" says Stripes.

Who? thinks Jon. *Someone who wanted to hurt him and pawn it off on someone else.*

Jon turns to Stripes. "You were pretty mad at him at the poker game. You even threatened him."

Stripes rounds on him. "I wasn't the only one who threatened him. You railed on him but good. We all saw it."

The guilt over that, and never making it right with Silas, robs Jon of breath. Then Raz jumps in with, "Who says it's one of us? Might be someone like Flots who maybe thinks getting rid of the Meerkat will get his spot back with us."

Gordy starts snuffling again. "We even gave Silas a nickname. He was one of us."

"Is!" insists Jon. "Not was."

Raz squeezes Gordy's shoulder on one of his paces behind the couch. "It'll be okay, Gordy. Whatever happens, it'll be okay."

Jon can't help but look at Myers, who's still leaning against the wall, thinking his thoughts and not sharing them.

Raz might be trying to protect Jon—but he must be thinking the same thing Myers is: Jon did it. Which means Raz is in damage control mode, trying to shift the others' attention away from Jon. He can't help but think that Raz is pissing into the wind. He doesn't know that Myers saw the powder on Jon, too, and will probably tell someone the second he gets the chance.

Jon's used to blame. Sometimes Raz and he dream up stories to tell the other greenshirts to keep Jon's reputation fierce. And Raz sells it like no other. Lying is his superpower. He could sell you aliens landing in the exercise yard, just because he feels like it—and you'd buy it like a shitty used car, because he's just that good. So when bad stuff happens, Raz always floats that it was Jon, and Jon doesn't deny it. But he only does that when Jon has a solid alibi for the adults, clearing him of blame. Raz is good at knowing when to spin things. He knows you shouldn't go overboard accepting consequences for something you didn't do. Credit, but not the consequences.

Maybe once he gets the journal back, he'll explain to Adriana how to create a reputation in Compass, Raz-style. Nah—she'll just say he's mansplaining. She's sharp—if she wants the protective shell of a strong reputation, she'll figure that out on her own. Probably already has. But maybe he should tell her not to believe anything she hears about him—because once she knows who he is and starts tuning into the rumors, it could shatter the thin glass of their sort-of relationship into a million bits.

Raz tries peering out the little window in the door. "Hey." He pounds on the door. "Wash! Come on, man. Tell us something."

But it's useless. Wash isn't even in the long air lock between their pod and the rest of the building, and Raz's shouting isn't going to make it all the way down that hall and through the second door.

"Yo, Raz," Jon says. "Even if he was right there, you know he can't open the door or even talk to you in lockdown. Not till he gets an all clear."

Raz slaps the door so hard it must sting bad, then slides down the wall like he's surrendering.

Stripes suddenly launches from his chair and slams into his room. Tension must have gotten to him. They hear him practically bouncing off the walls in the room, flushing the toilet over and over. Mostly he's got his OCD under control, but it comes back when he's stressed.

That seems to give the rest of them leave to go—like how the first person leaving a lousy party begins a sudden race for the door, until it's just Jon and Raz in the common room.

Jon sits on the sofa armrest to see Raz better. To maybe get a bead on what he's thinking. "Raz, I need you to understand something."

But Raz doesn't look at him. "Maybe I don't want to," he says. "Maybe you shouldn't say anything."

"What you saw—that powder—it wasn't what it looked like."

Finally Raz looks at him. "It wasn't penicillin?"

Jon sighs. "I think it was. But I didn't put it there. I reached into the seam—you know, where I keep stuff—and it was there. Which means someone put it there, even before I got dressed this morning, and is trying to frame me."

Raz looks at him, considering. After the silence stretches his nerves to a screaming point, Jon asks, "Do you believe me?"

Raz slowly nods. "I think I do—and not just because you say so. Remember when you dropped your tray and had to go back to get another lunch? And just after you got to the table, Silas says he doesn't feel good—so you didn't have time to spike his mac 'n' cheese.'"

Jon's shoulders drop, like he's suddenly releasing a week's worth of tension.

"I knew it couldn't be you," Raz says.

"You didn't seem so sure a second ago."

Raz shrugs a bit awkwardly. "I don't know . . . maybe I was starting to believe the stories I make up about you."

"They're good stories."

"The best. But the thing is, I know you really like the Meerkat, so it doesn't make sense that you'd try to hurt him. I figured, if you did it, it was to push them to get him out of Compass and into a real home."

"I wouldn't have done that by poisoning him."

For a moment Silas's face flashes in Jon's mind. Not like he usually is—but his face when he was hauled off on the gurney. All puffy and purple. Eyes rolled back. Did the monster who did this know it could kill him?

And Raz, reading it in Jon's face, says, "If he dies, it's murder."

Jon squeezes his eyes shut, wishing Raz hadn't said it. Like if it's never said, then it won't be true.

"Sorry," says Raz. "He might be okay, but we should plan for the worst."

Jon nods, realizing Raz is right. They're on the same page now. It never occurred to Jon how much he needed Raz to be on the same page. He always kind of felt it was Raz who needed *him*. But it works both ways. And for a moment, he considers telling Raz about Adriana and the journal. Would Raz think it was weak to fall for a girl Jon doesn't even know?

No, he can't think about that now. Jon wrangles his thoughts back to the problem at hand. "I wiped the powder out of the seam the second I got back here," Jon tells Raz, but Raz shakes his head.

"There'll still be traces—don't you ever watch TV? Forensics and all that. How'd they even get the stuff in there anyway?"

Jon shakes his head. "I don't know—but however they did it, they planned it real good."

"So who do you think it was?"

"At first I thought Knox—he'd poison someone in a heartbeat. But like I said, this took cold planning. Knox might beat someone to death if he redlines, but he doesn't plan shit in advance.

"Viper might," suggests Raz. "After what happened in the yard, he's had it out for the kid."

"And for me—so this would be two birds with one stone," says Jon. "But Viper wouldn't get his hands dirty—guy thinks of himself as a warlord. He'd have someone do it for him."

"Culligan!"

Jon nods. "That's what I'm thinking."

Then Raz gasps. "He was with us down in Moonshine Cavern! When Gordy was talking about cheeking his pills."

"That's right!" says Jon, having forgotten that conversation. It's all falling into place. Culligan got one of Gordy's pills. Which means Gordy probably knows he's missing one, but maybe was afraid to say. Something else Culligan would be counting on.

"He'll be pointing the finger at you fast, otherwise the frame won't take," Raz says. And once they find that powder on you, you're screwed. No one'll believe your story."

"And on top of it, they'd have Myers to back it up." He'd definitely sing to admin about how he saw the stuff on Jon's hand.

"Myers?"

Jon doesn't even want to get into it. "Got to get these pants to the laundry," Jon says.

"No pickup till tomorrow," Raz says. "You're screwed if they search you today."

And just then, they hear the far door open. Footsteps march toward the inner door.

Jon feels panic coming on, but then he hears Adriana's voice—or at least how he imagines her voice to be.

Don't panic.

The world's about to blow up, but all you gotta do is stick up your thumb, and someone'll rescue you.

Today that someone is Raz.

"Switch pants with me," Raz says.

Jon gapes at him. "Huh?"

Raz beams. "Best solution. Culligan will finger you, not me. So they'll check your stuff, not mine. If you're wearing my pants, you're clean."

Fifteen seconds. That's how long it takes the guards to get to the inner door, and Jon and Raz have already wasted half of that talking. "Hurry up!" says Raz.

That rouses Jon. He peels off his pants and kicks them over to Raz. It takes him longer to pull on Raz's pants, as Raz is smaller than Jon. Tight and high. Flood pants, his mom would have called them.

They manage it just in time.

A shadow passes the peek window in the pod door, and then the door opens. Rush steps into the room. Stripes, Gordy, and Myers swarm from their rooms like wasps rather than roaches. And Jon feels a pit open in his stomach, because he knows, he knows, he knows the news isn't good. He knows they're here to tell him that Silas is dead.

Rush doesn't keep them in suspense. He doesn't mince words. Gets right to the point.

"Silas is going to be okay."

Jon feels relief wash over him and someone behind him inhales noisily. Never has he been so thrilled to not have a shred of actual intuition.

"It was touch-and-go for a while, but he's over the hump," Rush says. "It was an allergic reaction, but I guess you already figured that out."

"I'm sorry," says Gordy, his eyes filling with tears of relief. "It wasn't me, but I'm sorry."

Rush nods, knowing Gordy well enough to know it's from the heart. Then he turns to the rest of them.

"Each of you will be interviewed for the incident report.

Jon, they want you first."

Then Raz jumps in front of him. "Why Jon? He wasn't even near the kid when it happened."

"All I know is that they want him first," says Rush. "The rest of you will be talking to Alvarado for counseling . . ."

Then Rush looks at Jon, purses his lips, and says, "But Jon's going straight up to Director Morley."

IMPEACHABLE

Most greenshirts only see Director Morley on-screen, when he gives State-of-Detention reports. You're in bad trouble if you actually get called to see him. It means you're about to be dumped into a deeper hole than the one you're already in. Maybe one of those holes that has no end.

Jon's been to his office eight times in the last three years.

Once Rush and Jon have exited the pod, Rush stops him, and, muttering an apology under his breath, handcuffs him.

"Didn't want the others to see this," Rush says. It's the only kindness he can offer under the circumstances. Jon's never been handcuffed before when being brought to see Morley. This is how he knows he's the prime suspect in Silas's attempted murder. Does this mean he's the only one?

They make their way down to the tunnel that runs beneath

the complex, past the door that leads to Moonshine Cavern far below, then continue onward to the administration building.

As they move up the stairs, and through the outer offices, barely anyone turns their head. They're used to seeing detainees being escorted to the administrative elite. Not everyone gets all the way up to Morley. You have to be substantial to see the warden. Before today, Jon always saw that as a badge of honor. Today it fills him with dread.

On his way to Morley's office, Jon sees a female guard leading a female detainee away. Someone else who just had an audience with the director. Jon averts his eyes, as does she. Only after she's passed does Jon wonder if it could have been Adriana. He turns back to get a glimpse of her, but she and the guard have already turned the corner. He didn't even register what she looked like. If he hadn't averted his eyes, would he have known? Would there have been something in her eyes that shouted to him all the words she'd written? Could it have been her? His rational mind says the chances are slim, but his heart wants to believe that it was.

They reach Morley's office.

"He's ready for you," says his assistant, sitting in a glorified cubicle outside Morley's door. You'd think the assistant of the most important man at Compass would get their own outer sanctum before reaching the inner sanctum.

Streamlined in an Italian silk suit and a rust-colored tie, Director Morley sits at a desk with a fancy pen next to his left hand and his notes in a script that is all slants and loops.

Behind him, photographs of Morley with politicians and celebrities line the wall.

Rush frees one of Jon's hands and locks it to the arm of the chair when Jon sits down, leaving the other hand free. Not that being shackled to a heavy chair in a high-security facility with a guard standing at the door leaves him free to do more than scratch his nose.

Jon tries to ignore his handcuffed hand, as well as the overly tight pants, and keeps his attention fixed on Morley's face. Or more accurately, his neck. Morley's got a flap of skin, kind of like that thing on a turkey. The wattle. It's like he used to be fat, and lost a ton of weight, but his skin never got the memo. It kind of flaps back and forth like a hypnotist's pendulum. But looking at that is better than looking at his eyes, since they're as dead as a barracuda's.

Morley clears his throat and moves the pen off his notes. "Artorias Jonathon Kilgore. Not the first time you've been in my office." He taps a thick folder next to his notepad. "You've quite the record for a juvenile detainee."

Jon clears his throat and ignores Rush tensing behind him. "Yes, sir. But you know I was exonerated of all the Compass stuff. And it wasn't me that did this thing to Silas. I was . . ." He gulps as the director raises his head and fixes a fish-eye stare on him.

"Mr. Kilgore, you are not to speak until you're given leave to speak. Understand?"

Jon nods. He shouldn't have said anything. Usually he

wouldn't have—he'd wait to see what they had on him, but he's riled, and that's not good for an interrogation. What with lockdown and no chance yet to interview Myers, Jon can't figure why they'd be so sure it was him. Did Culligan say something to a guard on the way back to his building?

Jon has those previous eight visits with the director—experience with the man's manipulations—that'll help him deflect anything Morley throws at him.

The director has a computer off to the side that shows a freeze-frame of Jon talking to Knox, who's holding Silas high off the floor. The kid looks small and scared in his overlarge greens his first day at Compass.

Jon knows he should be paying attention to Morley, but the colors on the screen hypnotize him. When did security get color cameras? Do liquor stores and gas stations have color cameras now? He usually doesn't care what happens outside Compass. Except when changes leak in, like splashy colored security screens.

"Care to explain this, Mr. Kilgore?"

Jon has no time to chase the confusion off his face. Why are they bringing this up now?

"This is your time to speak," the director says dryly.

As he describes the incident with Knox, Jon keeps his voice cool, like he's giving a class report. He focuses on Morley's turkey wattle, keeps calm, and delivers just the facts. After he finishes, Morley's barracuda eyes don't blink, which totally unnerves Jon. Fish eyes and a turkey neck. Like Admiral

Ackbar, that fish-headed guy in *Return of the Jedi. "It's a trap!"*

The director asks, steel in his voice, "So you didn't order the attack on the boy?"

Jon gapes at him. "Did I *what?* Sir, the video shows that Knox went berserk because Silas was poking him, asking too many questions. I was the one who took Knox down. Stopped him from strangling the kid. Sir."

Where the hell did they get the idea that Jon had ordered the attack on Silas? Who was spinning this garbage? Talk about fake news . . .

Maybe Jon is going to have an even harder time clearing himself than he supposed.

Next, Morley dials in another video. Jon's stomach twists when he sees himself looming over Silas, and the kid's shrinking back like he's expecting to be hit. This time the picture is a grainy black and white, and Jon's back is to the camera. They must save the good cameras for the public areas rather than pods. It's after the poker game and before the guards came in to break things up.

He tries some subterfuge. Squinting at the screen and pasting a perplexed look on his face, Jon looks at the director and back at the screen. "Is that supposed to be me?"

"Of course it's you. You don't remember threatening the boy?" A snide, impatient note creeps into Morley's voice.

Jon tries a casual shrug, causing Raz's pants to ride up. "Hard to tell Stripes and me from the back. Sir. He, Stripes, I mean, was pissed after the game 'cause he thought Raz and Silas were cheating. I had a little talk with Silas afterward about not ticking off detainees. You know Mr. Luppino assigned me to be Silas's mentor? If that's me, then it's me mentoring him, sir."

Jon tries to adjust his pinching pants with his free hand when Morley shoots an unreadable look at Rush. Feeling his scalp prickle with sweat, Jon waits for Rush to call him a liar. Surprisingly, the guard says nothing.

Moving on, the director selects another freeze-frame. It's the cafeteria barely hours ago. Jon tenses, expecting the director to run the video. He's not sure he wants to see Silas swell and turn purple again. Instead, they all look at Jon in the line of greenshirts, a few feet away from Silas, frozen in time before everything went down.

"Is this where you dropped the penicillin into that young man's lunch?"

Instead of fury over the accusation, Jon feels irked that the director doesn't seem to even know Silas's name.

"No, sir." Jon doesn't try keeping the sarcasm from his voice. "This is where I bumped into Raz, dropped my lunch tray, and had to go back for another lunch. You can hit play and see for yourself."

This time, Jon manages to stare at the director without looking away. He's startled when the director breaks first and glances again at Rush.

Morley says reluctantly, "There was a problem with the video. This was the last shot taken in the cafeteria today. Our technical staff is looking into it."

Jon's shaken. Without waiting for permission to speak, he says, "So you've got no video of me dropping my lunch, going back to the lunch line for another one? Which means you have no video of whoever put the drug into *Silas's* mac 'n' cheese? Or me performing CPR on him? Or the nurse jabbing him with the EpiPen? Are you kidding me?"

"Silence, Mr. Kilgore," the director thunders. It takes a moment before they both get their breath back. But they hear Rush breathe in nearly a whistle.

With a flash of petulance on Morley's chiseled features, he says, "A staff member with an unimpeachable reputation reports that you threatened the boy."

Jon frowns. Is the director talking about one of the guards? Maybe a teacher? Who would lie about something like that? Certainly not someone "unimpeachable."

And then it becomes crystal clear.

"In spite of what you might think, doctor-patient privilege does not protect you when you make threats against another detainee, Mr. Kilgore."

Alvarado! It was Alvarado, that damn weasel of a walrus. Jon opens his mouth to refute it, but Rush clears his throat in warning. Right. He has to have permission to speak. But not just that—if it's his word against Alvarado's, Alvarado wins. Of course they're gonna believe a hack shrink who hears what he wants to hear.

Maybe he should stop talking to Morley. That's what his lawyer would say he should do. Can he wait till they interview other witnesses? Enough people saw what happened that he's sure to be what his lawyer calls "exonerated." And not just by detainees but trustworthy, *unimpeachable* sources like Lunch Lady Dorella, and the nurse.

But on the other hand, they'll also hear from Culligan, and probably Myers, pointing the finger directly at him. Then Morley will say Jon was just doing CPR and pretending to care in order to cast suspicion off himself.

He squirms with doubt. If the director wants a quick conviction, he's got Jon's court case before detention and Alvarado's "expert" opinion. That'll railroad Jon into an arrest for attempted murder. Even Raz would find it hard to defend Jon against the fake stuff piling up against him.

If Viper did kill that video feed, maybe he can also manipulate everything else. He could scare other kids into lying about having seen Jon—since most detainees are afraid of Viper and his crew. Unless Silas knows who dropped the powder in his mac 'n' cheese and is willing to say, then Jon is royally screwed. But how could Silas know? If he'd known, he wouldn't have eaten it.

Silas himself would know Jon wouldn't do it, right? Silas knows Jon cares, even if he has a funny way of showing it.

But there's no proof beyond word of mouth.

Except . . .

Except, maybe there is.

Maybe there are *words*.

But not word of mouth.

Because Adriana knows Jon couldn't have done this.

Jon's written to her all about his time with the kid, his sympathy for him, his stepping up to protect the kid. It's all recorded right there in the journal.

"Mr. Kilgore?" Morley says, his tone so icy Jon knows he's said Jon's name more than once before Jon heard him.

"There's proof that I'm innocent." Jon's so confident that he's on the verge of grinning.

"Really?" Morley manages to inject a cargo of contempt in that one word. "Well, by all means, do share with us this proof."

He's about to spill everything about the journal. Because that's proof enough, isn't it?

Except . . .

Except maybe not.

Because those words.

They might be his words.

But they don't belong to him.

They're Adriana's.

And just like that, it all falls apart like a house of cards missing the queen of hearts. Adriana's privacy, their friendship, everything intimate, every fight, every word that screams *I could be falling in love with you*, everything lies naked in front of Morley and his crew of uncivil servants who'll treat Adriana's journal like porn.

He can't do that to her. Even to save himself, he won't betray her.

"Cat got your tongue, Mr. Kilgore?" The director has thawed

209

enough for more sarcasm.

Jon resurrects his confident smirk again. At least on the outside. "I don't need today's cafeteria video. I have my own trustworthy, *unimpeachable* sources. Security Officer Wash was there for the whole thing, Lunch Lady Dorella will remember that I had to return for a second lunch, and the nurse will remember me performing CPR on Silas. Silas Coady—that's his name, 'cause I think you might have forgotten. Anyway, I think my three adult eyewitnesses will stand against the Walrus's— um—Dr. Alvarado's half-baked opinions."

After he finishes speaking, he grips the armrests, something roaring in his ears that stops him from hearing the conversation between Morley and Rush. He feels sick that he almost betrayed Adriana, almost ended whatever it is they have together. Is he really that selfish, that scared of what Compass can do to him?

Something Rush says forces him to stop beating himself up and listen to their conversation.

". . . too soon to resolve the issue, sir. May I suggest you allow security to do a thorough investigation? My opinion is that a rush to judgment could be bad for all of us. It's also my opinion that Silas would have died without Jon's intervention."

Morley goes from sarcastic to surly in a heartbeat. "How long before I get the report? The police are here. I have calls from the media and from Child Protective Services asking how a foster child under our care has been attacked not once, but twice!"

"Shouldn't be long," Rush says.

"It can't be soon enough," Morley says, his wattle waddling, then points a stiff finger at Jon. "And keep your eyes on this one. My money's still on him."

Rush steps forward to squeeze Jon's shoulder in a warning not to talk back—but Jon has lost interest in defending himself with Morley. Rush has his back. For now, that'll have to be enough.

He tries to thank Rush on their return to Jon's pod, but Rush cuts him off.

"It's my job."

So Jon says nothing, still cradling that warm feeling of having Rush in his court. Adriana will believe him too. Rush may have known him longer, but Adriana knows him better.

Rush pauses outside the pod door. "You know who to watch out for, right?"

Jon understands him. If Silas can be attacked, Jon's in danger too. "Yes, sir." Since Rush is still hesitating, Jon asks, "May I see Silas? I mean when he's well enough."

"Maybe. After he's back from the hospital. If he wants to see you."

That sets Jon back, but he nods. The kid may be done with Compass. Done with Jon. Maybe this will spur the state to get him a decent home. Maybe even before Jon can say goodbye. Sadness ripples through him.

He catches Rush staring at the bottom of Jon's pants—and the way the hems end a good distance above his ankles. Neither of them says a thing about it.

Rush lets him back into an empty pod. The rest of the guys must still be up with Alvarado, waiting their turn to be grilled. The therapist is probably taking notes on everything they say, hoping to find more evidence of Jon's evil ways.

Jon starts to smolder. Alvarado tried to get him charged with attempted murder. What an asshole.

How long will they keep them in lockdown? Till Silas wakes and tells his story? It may be days before he or Adriana gets to the library so they can share what's happening.

He wants to tell her about what the Walrus has done now. Maybe he'll skip the part about him almost telling about the journal. He made the right decision in the end, and that's what counts, right?

He wonders if the girls know any of what happened. And what if Adriana's thinking he's the one that was rushed to the hospital? Maybe she's worried about him, all anxious, thinking he might be hurt, and fighting to stay alive.

Jon's a little spooked about how happy that makes him.

ON TRAIN WRECKS

It's the morning after lockdown. Yet even though things seem back to normal, they're not. Maybe they are for everyone else, but not for Adriana. Not until she's absolutely sure that J is okay. No, not J. He has a name now. Jonathan. Jon.

She's in art class. Girls' art class is held only ninety minutes every other week. Unlike the other sterile classrooms, this room has murals on the walls and old paintings by dead artists thumbtacked to the ceiling tiles, as not to mess with the murals. There's also an actual physical teacher present, instead of a talking head on a TV screen—and she actually lets them choose their own seats.

Bianca sits by her lonesome at the opposite end of the room. When Adriana tried to follow there, Bianca stopped her.

"Art's a private thing," Bianca said, and told Adriana she

doesn't let anyone near her when she creates. After all the rebuffs and betrayals in Adriana's life, you'd think this tiny rejection wouldn't arrow to her core, but it does. She drops into a chair near the exit and watches girls fill up the chairs between her and Bianca. Monessa keeps to herself as well, not bothering to antagonize Adriana today, not even by giving her a cold shoulder. Monessa's attitude today is neutral, which is annoying in its own way. The only girl unintentionally drawing attention to herself today is Jolene, who's all red-eyed and sniffly because her ever-absent family burst her fantasy bubble once more.

Feeling itchy, Adriana glances back to the open door where a guard stands. Someone Adriana hasn't seen before. A special art guard? Someone who'll make sure none of the priceless pieces they create get stolen? Or maybe it's something to do with the riot yesterday. Rent-a-cops to enforce the peace. Security theater. Like they have at airports. Stern military wannabes policing all those dangerous liquids.

Pip sits next to Adriana in the last empty chair in the room. After a moment, Pip leans close to Adriana. "You give any more thought to my offer?" she asks.

Adriana glances at Pip, her throat feeling dry. "Your offer?" she whispers. She knows what Pip's asking, but somehow it feels dangerous to be beholden to Pip and her eyes that see everything. Better to feign ignorance and let Pip do all the work.

Pip's baby face shines innocently. "You wanted information on a boy, didn't you?"

Yes, yes, yes, she does.

"Sort of," says Adriana. Maybe she can find out by going at it sideways. The less she seems to care, the better. Adriana glances at the clock behind her.

"Hey, what was up with the lockdown, anyway?" Adriana feels itchy again.

"Why do you think that I know?"

"Because you do," says Adriana.

To that, Pip smiles. Maybe flattered by the fact that Adriana thinks Pip knows things. Which she does.

"A boy was poisoned," says Pip.

Adriana sucks in a breath and the words spew out of her. "Who? Did he die? How can you get poisoned in juvie?"

A click of heels in the hallway, and the door opens. The teacher has arrived. No more talking among themselves.

A glint lights Pip's eyes. "You want me to find all that out for you?"

Adriana takes a deep breath as the art instructor breezes in, an unnecessary scarf in the over-warm room waving in the air behind her like a banner. "Sit up, me lovelies. Time to get in touch with our muses! Time to paint eternity from our very souls!"

Adriana knows that favors do not come for free, and Pip will exact a price, but to hell with it. She has to know.

"His name is Artorias Jonathon Kilgore," Adriana whispers to Pip. "I want to know everything you can find out about him."

That afternoon, during her book-shelving hour, Adriana catches Monessa in the library. She's not a regular. Maybe she's doing research for a project. Or maybe she's looking for another baby-mama book. Adriana shelves books at the end of the same aisle, pretending she doesn't see Monessa, the same way Monessa pretends she doesn't see Adriana. Finally Adriana decides to break the ice, because someone has to.

"It's Dewey," she says. And off Monessa's dead-eyed stare, she adds, "Dewey decimal. You have to know the call number of the book you're looking for. Only fiction is shelved alphabetically."

"I know what Dewey is," Monessa snaps. "And I didn't ask for your help."

Adriana notes the area that Monessa is browsing. Yep: 306—relationship and family.

"If you're looking for another baby book, there aren't any. I checked."

Monessa gives her a wall of body attitude. "Why would you check?"

Adriana thinks about her answer and decides that honesty is called for, even if it won't be appreciated. Besides, Adriana's too tired and too over it to do the bush-beating dance.

"I saw you with your baby the other day," Adriana says.

Same flat stare from Monessa. "So?" she says. "I saw you there too. So?"

"You were good with her," offers Adriana.

Monessa snorts bitterly at that. "Well, how good could I be if I'm stuck in here?"

"I just meant—"

"I know what you meant, and I don't need pity, especially from you!" Then she frowns, going into herself for a beat. "My mom can take care of her. She's a better mother anyway. Won't screw my girl up."

Oh, like she didn't screw you up?

Nope, not gonna say that.

"I can get Ms. Detrick to order some books for you. She doesn't have to know who we're ordering them for."

Monessa shakes her head. "Who says I need a book anyway? Maybe I'm just waiting for the damn bell to ring."

And that's when Adriana realizes. She wasn't really looking for a book. The only reason Monessa came down this aisle is because Adriana is here. Because she wants to talk to someone who saw her with her baby. Even if it's just trash talk.

"How old will she be when you get out?" Adriana asks.

"Twenty months." The fact that Monessa knows it down to the month says a lot.

She's not just counting the days for herself—she's counting for her daughter and knows how many days of her daughter's life she'll miss.

"So you'll be home in time for her second birthday," Adriana says, trying to do the glass half-full thing. "You'll get to teach her how to blow out the candles."

That makes Monessa smile, but only for a fraction of a second. Then the hint of a tear gets bitch-slapped by fresh attitude. The old Monessa returns with a vengeance.

"The only reason Bianca likes you is because you're new," she says. "You won't always be new."

She turns on her heel to go, clearly determined to have the last word. But she stops. And without looking back says, "Neshama. My girl's name is Neshama."

"It's a pretty name."

"No," says Monessa. "It's a *strong* name."

"That too."

Then Monessa walks away, still not turning back even for a parting glare.

"It was a kid named Silas," Pip says. "He's new here. And he's alive."

They're out in the yard, during their "vitamin D hour" of indirect sunshine—more indirect than usual, since the sun hasn't made an appearance through the clouds in days.

So it wasn't Jon. Of course it wasn't. It was silly of her to think that, out of all the boys in Compass, it was him. Still there's a flood of relief in knowing for certain it wasn't.

She knows Pip reads the relief in her. Should Adriana care that she's telegraphing her emotions? Probably. But who is she kidding? She's been telegraphing her emotions about Jon even before she told Pip his name.

Pip continues, "Silas hangs with that boy you asked about. Artorias Jonathon Kilgore. They're in the same pod."

Adriana's heart leaps. Silas. Of course—that's the newbie kid Jon wrote about.

Pip gives her a knowing look. "You're sure Jon Kilgore is your guy?"

Adriana nods.

Pip shakes her head and sighs. "You're not gonna like this," she says. "But everything points to Jon Kilgore being the poisoner. Not only that—he's got a really bad rep, been accused of everything short of murder here in detention. They say that's what got him into Compass in the first place. Killing someone. Or killing a bunch of people. Something about a hospital, or a mall. Might all be rumors, but whatever it is, he's been here a long time, and most other kids are scared of him."

"Jon wouldn't kill anybody," she blurts. His words on the page are more real to Adriana than rumors. He's got a dreamy bent, a philosophical take on things. The boy with the blue pencil doesn't kill. Period. There is no room for any other reality in Adriana's world.

Pip laughs. "You're so clueless, Adriana," she says, but kindly.

Her bottomless eyes scratch at Adriana's soul. Adriana tilts her head, her hair swinging forward to hide what Pip might see on her face. Maybe Pip's making it up, just to see how Adriana reacts. But why? No, Pip is telling the truth—or at least the truth as she knows it. Which means she doesn't know everything.

"Some guys are just train wrecks," says Pip. "And some are train wrecks hauling nuclear waste. You don't wanna be anywhere near someone like that when they go off the rails."

"Thanks, Pip," she says, not feeling thankful for the advice at all.

"Girls!" says the teacher with way too much enthusiasm. "Let's center ourselves and let our muses do the talking now."

Adriana tries to focus on the lesson, but that's not happening today. There are no complementary colors in her soul today. But as she broods over the watercolor wasteland before her, it occurs to her that she's going about this all wrong. There's someone who *does* know the truth. Someone who won't just give her rumors. If she has the nerve to ask for it.

J . . . There's something I have to confess. Don't get mad at me. But I did some digging and I found out who you are. Well, maybe not who you are, because I already know that from the things you write to me. But now I also know your name.

If that makes you mad, I'm sorry—but you shouldn't be. You've known my name from the start, and you even know why I'm at Compass. So, can you blame me for wanting to know a little more about you?

The thing is, there's a lot of baggage attached to your name. Rumors. Stories. And I know most of them can't be true. Maybe none of them are true—because the person you are in all that gossip doesn't fit with the person who writes to me. That's the person I know. The person I trust. The person I believe.

So I'm going to ask you a question . . .

MORE LIKE A MONGOOSE

When lockdown lifts, Jon expects to feel a whoosh of relief, but it's as if his own personal lockdown follows him like a rain cloud.

Everything has changed. Even days after Silas's poisoning, no one's speaking to Jon. Other greenshirts freeze or slide away if he gets too close. Even Raz is different. He speaks to Jon, but in a non-Raz way: fake, full of the politician friendliness he uses on others, like he's trying to sell you on his charm and a used car that may or may not be stolen. It reminds Jon of when his mom was talking to him at the end, assuring him everything was gonna be all right, when she knew for a fact that it wasn't.

Gordy's the only one who treats Jon like he used to. Now that they know Silas is going to be okay, Gordy seems to have forgotten about the poisoning and Jon's rage at Silas after the poker game. Gordy reminds him of how his mom described God: full of forgiveness and forgetting of past sins. Gordy and Raz are the only ones now sitting at Jon's table. The fair-weather friends and hangers-on have all disappeared—but Raz doesn't stay long. Now he's always got someone else to talk to, something he's gotta see.

Silas is back at Compass but still in the infirmary, so Jon's the one helping Gordy with math and reading. Rumors are flying that Silas is permanently damaged or that they've found him a foster home or that he'll be moved to another facility to protect him against Jon's life-threatening self. Jon's not sure what to believe. A good friend would wish him a safe place outside Compass. Jon just wishes he could see Silas again. To see if he's really okay. To say he's sorry—and to make sure that Silas knows it wasn't Jon who did this to him.

Even Adriana isn't speaking to him. At least it feels that way. He's gone to the library twice since lockdown lifted, and her journal hasn't materialized. He almost asked Ms. Detrick about Adriana, but that would only lead to trouble for them. Not that it matters for him—how much worse can it get? Well, it'd be worse if Adriana never writes to him again. And sometimes it feels like he's gonna explode with all the things he's gotta tell her.

Today's different as he meets with his lawyer. Gottlieb greets him by talking about him in third person, like he's not there, muttering, "Tells me he'll be a model prisoner and then fights in the yard and gets called to the director's office for poisoning a kid. Thinks that's best behavior? And he expects me to save him after all that?"

Still, she seems to believe Jon when he says he didn't spike Silas's food. But it's her job to believe Jon. Or to pretend to. She seems aggravated even after reading that Jon's kinda-sorta CPR may have saved Silas's life. Apparently saving someone's life doesn't count when you're also accused of having tried to end it.

"Bad timing," Gottlieb says. "This is bound to come up when the court evaluates whether you get to stay at Compass or get shipped off to an adult prison once you turn eighteen." Then she sighs. "It might even affect your appeal."

Jon doesn't want to think about that. He hasn't allowed himself to hope—or so he thought, but the very idea that something as stupid as a false accusation could destroy his chances at ever seeing freedom? It makes him feel uncomfortably vulnerable. Maybe he had some hope after all, because now he feels it hitting the pavement with no parachute.

Today Gottlieb's sandwich is salami with avocado—which is wrong on more levels than baloney and sprouts. It makes Jon want to cry. But he realizes that an unnatural sandwich is not what's giving him that feeling.

"How can this hurt my chances at anything? They didn't bring charges—because they can't prove anything, because I didn't do it!" He clenches his chair so tight, he may leave permanent dents.

Gottlieb puts down her garlicky sandwich oozing green avocado and looks at Jon. "I know the law says you're innocent until proven guilty. But once you've been found guilty of one thing, it's easy to see you as guilty of everything."

"That's not fair!"

"I never said it was. The law is our best attempt to fix the screwed-up way the world works. But it's not always successful."

Rather than a guard waiting just outside the door, it's Luppino, the unit counselor, waiting for Jon—although a guard who Jon doesn't know lingers a few yards away, at a respectful distance, to afford Luppino and Jon a semblance of privacy.

"Hello, Jon," Luppino says. "I hope things went well with your attorney."

Jon shrugs. "Things go like they go."

"Indeed they do. Walk with me."

Luppino being there to escort Jon isn't necessarily a bad thing, but it's not a good thing either. It's a weird thing. Like having your principal show up to escort you back to class from the bathroom.

Jon tries not to loom over Luppino, who looks even more scraggly and shrunken than usual. *No need to make him feel threatened.* But then again, Luppino is beyond being fazed by anything. Jon could be eight feet tall and Luppino wouldn't care.

"Where's Erasmus Barbosa?" Luppino asks the security guard, ignoring the polite distance between them. Jon's attention sharpens. So he isn't the only one Luppino wants to see—he wants to see Raz too.

"He had an appointment with Dr. Alvarado."

Luppino rolls his eyes as if the universe continues to block his reasonable requests at every junction, then says something under his breath, something rude and profoundly snarky about Alvarado.

Jon's rarely shocked, but he does a double take at Luppino's words. So the boys' unit counselor doesn't like the Compass psychiatrist? Are staff allowed to even have personal opinions about each other? Kids have 'em, but it never occurred to him that the staff might not always be in lockstep with each other. Jon always saw Luppino as a paper-shuffling little gnome. But if they share a dislike of Alvarado, that raises Luppino's status in Jon's eyes. Now he's Papa Smurf at the very least.

Jon paces beside Luppino, dragging a bit, dreading the possibility that they might be headed for the director's office.

"Silas has asked to see you," Luppino says.

Jon releases a breath he didn't realize he was holding. "I'd like to see him too, sir."

Luppino meditates on that for a moment "The kid may have a death wish. How many times has he been attacked in your presence, Mr. Kilgore? Three times?"

Jon swallows. "Only twice. Sir." Which makes Luppino scoff—and rightly so, because it's two times too many. "Neither of them were my fault, sir."

"Even so, I find it worrisome—"

"—I would never hurt Silas, sir. I stopped others from hurting him."

"Let me finish," Luppino says. "I find it worrisome because someone may be trying to mess with you by messing with him—and might continue to." Then he sighs, in clear exasperation. "There are others who have entirely different 'theories' on the matter, but I've seen firsthand how protective you are of Silas—and he corroborates that. He likes you, and he's a smart kid. I trust his instincts on this."

"Thank you, sir."

Of course, from what Jon's seen of Silas's instincts, it only proves the kid has bad judgment. No way is Jon gonna say that to Luppino, though.

"When's Silas coming back to the unit?"

Luppino doesn't answer. Instead he says, "I have an errand to run; you'll have to come with me." Then, to Jon's surprise, he takes Jon into the infirmary.

Luppino's errand is bogus—Jon can see the only reason he's here is to bring Jon to see Silas. It makes Jon a bit suspicious. Good deeds from the staff are few and far between. But maybe being hard and jaded is more work than being human. Because Luppino says, "You got five minutes with him." Then Luppino leaves him with Silas but waits just outside the door.

Jon walks slowly to Silas's bed—one of six in the room, but just a few of them are occupied. Jon's only been to the infirmary a few times, to treat minor wounds from fights, and for vaccinations and things—but he's never been to where the sick juvies are kept. There's a kid to his right who's asleep, and a kid to his left who's moaning and fingering a scab on his jaw, scooting farther under the sheets as if Jon's presence scares him.

Silas is in the bed closest to the window, which looks out on a wall, so what's the point? The kid looks half his size, and he was puny to begin with. His color's off, like he's lost blood along with the weight.

Jon approaches Silas, and his eyes, which looked a hundred years old at first, rejuvenate quickly once he sees that it's Jon. There are no chairs, so Jon sits gingerly on the edge of the bed, hoping the motion doesn't hurt the kid. He glances at the infirmary door. Luppino is waiting. Eavesdropping, but that's okay, because anything that's said will just reinforce Jon's innocence.

Silas struggles to sit up, so Jon props the pillow behind his back. Just that small amount of exertion seems to tire the kid.

"Gotta talk to you about my poisoning."

"I didn't do it, Silas."

Silas manages a pained smile. "I know that. I trust you."

That takes away Jon's breath. The last few days before the poisoning hadn't seemed full of trustworthy actions on Jon's part.

Silas takes a shaky breath. "The police questioned me. You know? I told them you weren't anywhere near me when it happened, and couldn't have gotten to my plate, 'cause that's the truth."

The kid trusting him and standing up for him when nearly no one else at Compass does—not even Raz—almost makes him cry. Almost.

Jon says, "Luppino thinks it's not about you—it's about me.

227

I think maybe it's both. Kind of a two-birds-with-one-stone kind of thing."

"You think Knox? You think Viper? Because that's what I'm thinking—and I said so, but no one's jumping on it. Alvarado says they can't make accusations without evidence—and any evidence they have points to you."

It reminds Jon of what Luppino said. How others have their "theories." Well, a theory isn't evidence, as much as Alvarado might want it to be.

"Whoever did it probably didn't think it would mess you up as bad as it did. Might have scared them. Might be the end of it."

"Maybe for me," Silas says, "but if it's you they're really after, this won't stop them. It kinda worries me."

That flummoxes Jon. It's been a long time since anyone has worried about him. He uses his gentlest voice, like he'd used with his mom at her sickest. "Don't worry, Silas, I can take care of myself. Been doing it forever."

"Yeah, I know," Silas says. "And maybe you don't call me that anymore. Maybe you and the guys can call me Meerkat."

It surprises Jon. "You like that?"

"I like having a nickname," he says. "It means I got a place here."

Jon smiles. "All right, Meerkat. That's fine with me!" And then something occurs to him. "But, come to think of it, *Mongoose* might be better—on account of mongooses kill snakes."

That makes Silas laugh. "When I'm ready to take on Viper, I'll let you know!"

A few minutes later, Jon exits the infirmary with Luppino, the guard following silently behind them. John can't help but feel a rush of affection for Silas. He looked like death warmed over, but he was more worried about Jon than about himself. The Meerkat's got a big heart.

"Since your class is half-finished," says Luppino, "I'm taking you to the library till it's time for your next class. Think you can stop yourself from starting a riot there?"

"No, sir. I mean yes, sir. No riot, sir."

"Jeez, you don't have to call me sir all the time."

Jon smirks. "Copy that, Papa Smurf."

Luppino grimaces. "On second thought, sir is just fine."

Once he's in the library, it takes everything in him to tamp down the jubilation he feels. The journal's got to be there. Adriana wouldn't keep him waiting this long. This day that started so awful just keeps getting better.

Ms. Detrick is at her desk and gives him a nod. Jon loiters near a newly acquired astronomy book, then, as soon as no one's paying attention to him, he wanders to the last place the journal was. This time there's a fiction book mis-shelved there, so he grabs it and heads for the fiction books. The new hidey spot is in the A's. He gets lightheaded when he sees the journal sitting where the mis-shelved book should be. Making sure no one sees him, he pulls the journal from the shelf, not even considering that the title of the book Adriana chose to mis-shelve was *Thirteen Reasons Why*.

. . . So I'm going to ask you a question.

I know I have no right to ask this question, but I'm going to anyway. And I don't need a whole lot of reasons why—just one will do.

If you don't want to answer, I'll understand, but I hope you will.

I want to ask you . . . no . . . I need to ask you . . . What did you do that landed you at Compass, Jon?

Jon's torment has taken on a new shade. He lies in his bed awake, wishing he could sleep, and wishing it could be dreamless, because no good will come of his dreams tonight. Right now, he feels nothing but distance from everyone and everything.

Silas is back in his room. Everyone in the pod walked on eggshells around him when Wash brought him in. Myers glanced at Jon but said nothing. *I know you did it,* that glance said, *but it's not my problem.* If he had told anyone about the powder that had been planted on Jon, Silas wouldn't be back in their pod, and Jon would probably have been charged. Or maybe he had told, and the case against Jon is quietly being built. Maybe Alvarado and the director are letting things stand to give Jon a false sense of security.

Or maybe Jon's just being paranoid.

But Jon's mind is less on that than it is on Adriana, who had to go and ask the big question.

He should have known this was coming when he saw the book she chose to mis-shelve. None of the books they've been choosing have been random. Like Adriana said, she didn't need a bunch of reasons—just one. But it wasn't as simple as that. He read Adriana's entry right there in the aisle. He couldn't stop himself. He had waited too long to hear from her. He read it twice. Then slipped the journal into his waistband and did his best not to think about it through class, and dinner, and the awkward, stilted talk of Raz, who left the table after a few minutes; Silas, who was trying to pretend like his poisoning never happened; and Gordy, who, when he couldn't think of something new to talk about just repeated the same basic conversation.

And now Jon's in his room, trying to figure out what to do.

He feels his frustration—powerful but diffuse—spread across the entirety of Compass like a layer of dust that no amount of scrubbing can clean. She asked the Big Question—which means he's about to lose her.

He supposes he could lie to her and say he didn't do anything—that he was framed the same way she was. Wrong place, wrong time, wrong friends. But their little relationship, if you could even call it one, is based on truth. He won't profane that by lying.

He has no choice; he's got to find a way of putting all of it into words in a way he never has before. Not just the events—he's gone over the events with lawyers and social workers too many times to count. What he needs is to give her the deeper truth.

So he grabs his pencil, turns to the next blank page, and prepares to be up for the entire night.

Adriana,

You're right. I'm mad that you asked. But I'm not mad at you. I'm mad that the lies about me made it all the way across to the girls' side. I'm mad that someone spread them far and wide enough to make it to your ears. I guess the reason why I didn't tell you my name was because I know you're smart, and once you knew my name, you'd go out and find all you could about me.

And there's a lot to find out.

It's true that I got a fierce reputation. But it's cultivated. Like some nasty-ass garden of pain. A rep is power here at Compass—but more than that, the rumors and made-up stuff throws everyone off the track from what's real. I'd rather have people believe shit like I'm a terrorist, or a slasher, or a deep-cover spy than to know the truth. Because the truth is worse. At least it is to me.

So all the stuff you heard? That's just a smoke screen.

But why should you believe that? Why should you believe it if I don't give you the truth?

And so I will.

Maybe you'll hate me, and maybe you won't. And maybe you'll break off and never want me anywhere near your journal ever again. I could say I don't care. But that would be a lie. I do care. But I'll tell you the truth anyway.

A BRIEF HISTORY OF JON

It started with my mom.

She got sick. Real sick. Like the kind of sick you don't always come back from. I denied it at first. No one wants to believe their mother might die. And at first, she wasn't looking so sick. Just tired. Worn down. Like she was working even harder than usual, that's all. But there were times I could tell she was in pain, and pretty soon I had to accept how sick she really was.

But there was hope. Not magical hope, but real scientific hope. See, maybe I'm not a genius, but I know my way around Google. When I found out the name of what she had, I did some deep-dive research. Like the kind I never do in school, because grades aren't life-and-death. But this was literally that.

233

I found out a lot about her disease. I became an expert. I coulda gone to med school on the stuff I learned. I knew what her chances were (not great). I knew what the treatments were (not many). And I knew how the treatments worked (not well).

But . . .

There was a new treatment that people were getting. Its results were good. People who had been given a death sentence were going into full remission. Not everybody, but a lot of people. What they call "a statistically significant amount."

My mom was NOT receiving that treatment. She told me it was all right, that her doctor knew what he was doing, and was doing the best he could. But I showed her what I found, and I remember the look on her face.

Anguish.

Like looking in a window full of fancy jewelry and knowing none of those diamonds are ever gonna be yours. But that look got replaced by pride—pride in me for finding it and showing her that sparkling window.

She takes me in with her to her next appointment. She wants me there since I did the research. She asks her doctor about it—and why isn't she getting this new second-generation immunotherapy. Why she had to find out about it from her thirteen-year-old son.

And his face takes on that identical anguish I saw

in my mom; the difference is, he's standing inside the
jewelry store, looking out, not looking in. He would give
her the treatment, he says—he tells us he even tried
to get it approved twice—but both times her insurance
denied it. And no one but people with their own
diamond mine can pay for it out of pocket. Plenty of
those, I'm sure, but not where I come from.

"Nothing I can do," says the doctor.

But, see, I don't know how any of this works other
than how it's not working for my mom. And yeah, now
I get that insurance sucks like a safety net made out
of cobwebs—but, see, I'm only thirteen when I'm in that
room. People think there's four years between thirteen
and seventeen, but that's not true—because there's a
million years between me then and me now.

"Fuck the insurance," I tell him, and my mom gets all
up in my business about my language, but I don't care.
"Give her the treatment anyway," I say. "Charge
it to someone else. Or better yet, don't charge it to
anyone at all. Make it like a clerical error. That stuff
happens, right?"

"I can't do that," he says, all apologetic.

"You can!" I yell at him, "but you won't!" because
I'm a million years young, and I don't get that this guy
doesn't make the Rules of Healing. All I see is that he
has the power to save my mom, and he's not using it.

So that's what I take out of that meeting, because

I need a face on my momma's misery, even if it's the wrong face. As far as my idiot brain is concerned, he's the one who's condemning my mother to death.

That was the beginning of a deep dive I didn't even know I was taking.

So I watch as my mom becomes sicker and sicker, and her hair falls out from the radiation and chemo, even though we know it's not doing the job. It's extending her life, maybe, but not saving it.

But then things change.

"I'm getting a new treatment, baby," she tells me.

And sure enough, she stops getting sick from the chemo. And she's happier, and her hair even starts growing back. I figure the doctor finally did start giving her the good treatment.

I stop worrying. For a while.

But about a month later, I suspect something's not right. Because she starts getting weaker. And she's further away in her eyes. And she starts talking to me about Aunt Tanika and how I shouldn't give her any trouble. And I ask why would I give her trouble, and why are we even talking about Aunt Tanika? But she just says again, "Don't give her any trouble," and makes me promise.

That's when I find out the truth. Because I check out her medications, and then look them up. These new meds . . . they're not about curing her. They're about making her comfortable. Any life-saving treatment has stopped. These medications are just painkillers. And in my head, it's all that doctor's fault. He stopped treating her, and was now just helping her die quiet.

I confront my mom, tell her what I know, and she says it was her choice—and, yeah, maybe it was—but I tell her she shouldn't have to make that choice. Not when there's a treatment that could save her.

So she dies. My mom dies. She dies. It's a Tuesday. A fucking sunny Tuesday. And it's sunny and bright at her funeral, too, and that makes me furious, because in the movies it's always raining, and everyone's got those big black umbrellas, and it's like the universe itself is crying instead of shining happy daylight with a blue sky and tweeting birds that mock everyone's misery.

It was the day of the funeral that the poison filled my thoughts. That doctor. That bastard! He could have saved her life, but he didn't. And all I could think about was how he'd be going home every single night, eating and drinking and laughing and living his life while my mom was cold in the ground because of him. And yeah, I know it was the cancer, and yeah, I know it wasn't him, it was the fucked-up medical system that refused to pay for the treatment—but like I said, I'm just a kid, and I'm thinking with my pain, and his was the only face I had for the system. And someone had to pay.

So a week after the funeral, I go to his office

building. But I don't go to his office. Instead I go down to the parking garage, under the building. I know when his office closes, because I know my mom's appointments were always at the end of the day, since she worked. Or at least she did as long as she could.

There are three parking levels, so I don't catch him the first day I go, or the second. But on the third day, I'm waiting all the way down on parking level three, and there he is, getting out of the elevator. I follow him to his car. A Mercedes. I knew it would be a Mercedes, or a Lexus, or a Tesla.

Just as he's about to open his car door, I go up to him. And yeah, I'm just a kid, but I'm really big for my age. And in my eyes the doctor was a stupid fat little man who ruined my life. Never mind that he healed people— probably a lot of people. That just made me angrier.

"Dr. Tesch?" I say.

"Yes?" he says.

"You killed my mother," I say.

And still, he doesn't remember my face. Doesn't know who I am. Like I'm just one of a hundred kids whose mother he killed.

So I grab him by the lapels of his fancy jacket, and I push him against his car and the alarm goes off, but I don't care. I grab him again, and push him up against the concrete wall. "You killed my mother!" I say again, getting right in his face.

He starts blubbering that he'll give me his wallet. I tell him I don't want his wallet. He tells me he'll give me his car keys. I don't want his car keys. Then what do you want? he asks.

And deep down, I know what I want. I want to hurt him. Bad. I want him to feel some of the pain, some of the misery that my mom felt. To make him hurt the way she hurt. The way I hurt.

But I can't. Because I'm not that guy.

Even though every fiber of my being wants to go off on him, I can't bring myself to hit him. Can't make myself hurt him. The most I can do is scare the shit out of him. Which I do. And I do it much too well.

"I WANT TO HEAR YOU SAY IT!" I scream, holding him against that wall. "I WANT TO HEAR YOU SAY THAT YOU KILLED HER!"

But he doesn't say it. He just gasps, and it makes me even angrier that he won't admit it. But even if he does admit it, I know I won't be any more satisfied, and that just makes me madder—and that must show in my eyes, because he gets even more scared.

Then he gasps again like someone drowning, and I think for a moment, maybe I can be that guy. Maybe I can hurt him. And it's like my thought becomes its own reality. Because suddenly he goes down, as if I did. As if my thoughts were a fist in his face.

He's on the ground now, grimacing. And he clutches

239

at his chest. And the grimace gets worse. It gets tight like a Halloween horror face. Then he goes limp. Totally limp. And his eyes stay open, but I know something's really wrong, because they're not open like he's looking. They're open like there's no one home.

For a stupid instant I think he's playing dead. Then I realize maybe he's not playing. And I get scared. So I start doing CPR, like I did for Silas when he had his allergy attack. But I'm all hopped up on adrenaline, and I pump much too hard, and I hear ribs crack. And it's creepy, and it's terrible, and I'm only thirteen even though I look older, and suddenly I feel even younger, and I'm crying, and the scraping of bones in his chest, and his eyes—his open empty eyes—I can't take it anymore, so I run. Someone comes out of the elevator. Some woman. I run past her, skipping the elevator, I go up the stairs, and I'm one level up when I hear her scream, because she's found the body of the doctor who let my mother die, and I get out of the building and I leave fingerprints on the glass door, and the guard sees me and yells "Hey!" But I am gone, running all the way home.

Aunt Tanika is there, because she's been staying with me since the funeral, helping pack up all my stuff, most of which she's going to get rid of, and the rest she's going to stuff in her car and drive with me all the way back to Philadelphia tomorrow. But that's a tomorrow

I don't think is coming. I hear her in the kitchen, and don't even say hello. I go to the bathroom, wash my hands over and over, as if I could literally wash my hands of what happened. Then I lock myself in my room.

And I wait.

And I wait.

And before midnight, the police come. It took a few hours for them to figure it out, but they come, just like I knew they would.

There's more after that. A lot more. But, long story short, I got tried as an adult for murder. Yeah, it was a heart attack that killed him, but I made that heart attack happen. They said I beat him and broke his ribs first—that was me trying to give the poor guy CPR. No one believed that. And it was worse, because I had planned it, and because the district attorney believed I went there fully intending to kill him, which I didn't intend at all, but it was my word against the word of a dead doctor, who talked louder than words, so whoever came up with "dead men tell no tales" didn't know what the fuck they were talking about.

Second-degree murder. Twenty years. Ten with good behavior. And yeah, I've got all the remorse in the world, but remorse don't change a thing. I'm not getting out any time soon, Adriana.

I have an appeal coming up, and my lawyer thinks I have a shot . . . but it's been "coming up" for years, and will probably be coming up for a whole lot more years. So I'll be at Compass until I'm eighteen, and then go off to someplace worse.

There it is. The Story of Me. Bet you're sorry you asked. But you did. And I told you. So you'll have to deal with it. Or don't deal with it, I don't care. Except that I do.

Jon

The deed is done. It can't be undone. The journal is wedged where *A Brief History of Time* should be. Which, among other things, is about black holes. Like the kind Jon feels he's hurled himself into.

He's working Moonshine Cavern now. Can't get out of it. Can't curl up into a ball and disappear into a singularity. Such things aren't allowed at Compass.

No matter how much they pull out of Moonshine Cavern, it doesn't seem to make the slightest dent. Maybe because most of the time they're just moving crap to get to other crap that Morley wants.

Today's assignment is specific: lamps. The lamps they're looking for are old, heavy, cast-iron things. Some look useless, but others seem to have some value. Like the ones with green-glass shades. Treasures mixed in among the trash.

Jon's mind isn't on the work. How could it be? It's on the journal that's still sitting in the library, waiting for tomorrow, when

Adriana will find it. There will be no opportunity for Jon to get it back before she does. Now it's nothing but a time bomb. Tick, tick, tick.

What the hell was he thinking? Spilling everything to Adriana? How could he have done that? Yeah, she asked for the truth, but she didn't ask to be beaten over the head with it. Hitting someone like that, truth or not, is just as wrong. Wrong as hitting them for real. But once he started, it all flowed out of him. There was no way to stop that river of pain. And now that flood is probably going to wash Adriana away. Flush her out of his life as if she had never been there. How could he have been so stupid?

"Get the hell out of the way if you're not gonna work, asshole."

"Hey!" Rush bellows at Culligan. "None of that kind of talk!"

Culligan just grunts and saunters off.

Jon wants to slam him—but that would only get Jon in trouble, not Culligan. Words get a reprimand, fists get solitary.

"And Kilgore," says Rush, "maybe you should focus, and get your head out of the clouds."

"Sewer's more like it," snipes Culligan.

"Hey!" yells Rush, a little louder this time. "What did I say?"

Through all of this, Raz says nothing. Doesn't engage. Doesn't even watch. Even Gordy cautiously eyes the exchange, but Raz just scavenges for lamps, like he doesn't hear.

Jon tries to put Culligan—and Adriana—out of his mind, but he fails on both counts. His irritation at Culligan, his rage at himself, and his grief at losing Adriana—which he's certain he's done—is all he can see. Emotions spin into a tornado so full of flying shrapnel, he can't function. And before he knows it, he's knocked one of those green-glass lamps off the junk stack, where it hits the ground, shattering.

"Ooh, that's bad," says Gordy, wringing his hands as he looks down at the broken lamp. "That was a good one too."

"Kilgore!" bellows Rush. "What's your problem today?"

This time Culligan doesn't say anything—because with Rush it's always three strikes, and Culligan's already down two.

"It's just a freaking lamp," says Jon, and kneels down to clean it up.

Gordy joins him, picking up the pieces.

"It's my mess, Gordy—you don't have to clean it."

But Gordy insists . . . because there's something else he wants to talk about.

"So, I've been thinking about that old mystery door in the back," he whispers. "What if it leads to a place even deeper than this, with even older stuff? I mean it's an old door, right? So it's gotta lead somewhere old." Then he gasps. "Hey—what if it's like a dungeon or something, with skeletons 'n' shit?" As he says it, he seems just as excited as he is horrified by the prospect.

Jon doesn't want to shatter Gordy's fantasy. "Well, if we keep pulling stuff out of the cavern, we'll eventually reach the door and find out."

Again that horrified/excited look from Gordy. Jon smiles. There are so many times he wishes he could see the world like Gordy does. With wonder. Back in less sensitive days, they used to call a guy like Gordy a man-child. As if there wasn't any value to innocence lasting a lifetime.

They finish picking up the broken pieces of green glass and drop them into a trash bin by the stairs.

"Be more careful next time," admonishes Rush from his chair, flipping a page in the book he's reading. Today it's *Live Rich, Die Broke*. But for Rush, it's more like live broke, then just die. Poor guy.

Through all of this, Raz still says nothing, and it ticks Jon off just enough to push Adriana and the journal out of first position in his mind. At least for a few seconds. Jon returns to work, pulling out stuff from the junk stack beside Raz. Raz doesn't even say hey. Finally Jon has to say something.

"How long you gonna treat me like this?"

"Don't know what you're talking about."

"The hell you don't." Jon lets that sit.

Until Raz finally says, "Maybe I don't like that I had to save your ass and risk my own."

Jon thinks back to the pants switch. "I thanked you for that. Didn't I thank you for that?"

"And maybe I don't know what's going on in your head anymore."

"You never did."

"Yeah, I see that now."

Jon doesn't want this to be an argument, so he takes a different tack. "Raz . . . we've always been tight. I might not have shown it—but that meant something to me."

Raz scoffs at that. "See, this is what I'm talking about. Since when have you been all touchy-feely?"

"I'm not! And if you tell anyone I am, I'll beat the shit out of you."

That makes Raz smile—but only slimly. "Listen . . . I gotta think about myself," he says. "My future, you know? You didn't poison the Meerkat. Fine, I believe you. But guilt by association, right? As long as they think it's you, I'm screwed too."

"The truth'll come out."

"You don't know that. Even if you didn't do it, you might go down—and you know how it is—a ship sinks, it pulls down everyone around it."

"So now I'm a sinking ship?"

"I don't know. Are you?"

That's the first time Raz makes eye contact. Jon wants to be angry at the question . . . but he realizes he can't. Because the answer he wants to give isn't the truth. The truth is . . .

"I don't know."

"Well," says Raz, "just in case, I'm puttin' on my own life vest first."

"HEY!" yells Rush. "This isn't a social club!"

Jon walks away from Raz and tries to give his attention to digging out lamps, but he doesn't even know where his head is at anymore. No, that's not true, he does. It's in orbit around Adriana. At least until tomorrow, when she boots him into the icy cold of interstellar space.

22

CAMERA OBSCURA

Adriana holds the journal in her hands, knuckles going white. She can do nothing but stare at the wall.

She's in her room. It's nearly dinnertime. Just a few minutes until Bonivich gathers the girls and marches them to the cafeteria. But she needs more than just a few minutes to process this.

Adriana forced herself to wait until she got back to her room before reading what Jon had written. She's glad she waited— because being a basket case in one of the public areas wouldn't have gone over well. Everyone would want to know why Adriana's brain was spilling out of her ears, leaving splotches of gray matter on the floor.

The first thing Adriana feels is shame.

Not shame at Jon—but at herself for asking the question in

the first place and forcing him to tell her. And also shame at her own self-centeredness. She has endlessly raged about her problems and the unfairness of her life. But her issues with her father? Her resentment of Lana? Even her temporary incarceration here at Compass—all those things pale in comparison to what Jon has experienced. Funny how things in your own life feel so huge until you're slapped upside of your own perspective.

What Jon did—stalking that doctor, confronting him the way he did, might have been wrong, but it was also human. If Adriana's mother had died like that—would Adriana have acted the same? Would she have wanted to take out her anger on the doctor—because he was the face of a broken system that doled out salvation to the highest bidder? And no, violence is never the answer—but that's easy to say when you're calm and in control. When your dark emotions take the wheel away from reason, you lose traction quickly. You fly from your life's path, and all that's left is gravity and the ground below.

Jon hit that ground with terminal velocity. And although he wasn't there to kill the man, the man died. If the doctor hadn't had a heart attack, Jon would have been charged with assault—and since the worst he did was push him against a wall, it might not even have been battery. He maybe would have gotten off, because it was a crime of passion. The depth of Jon's grief would have *meant* something to the court. But once someone dies, sympathy dies with it.

And he was right to be worried about Adriana's reaction. Someone else might close the book on him—literally—and break off all communication. Easy enough to do. Someone else might take Pip's advice, agreeing that Jon's life is a train wreck best to be avoided.

But that's not the person Adriana is. Rather than pushing her away, this display of raw, painful truth makes her want to reach through every layer of concrete between them to hold him. To tell him with the soothing tone of her voice, not just the lilt of her written words, that she understands. That she sees him. Hears him. Loves him.

Imagine that. She loves him!

All they share is a handful of written exchanges, and yet she feels she knows him more deeply than anyone else in her life. What's more, she feels he knows her too.

It makes her think of how, back in fifth grade, she was given an assignment to create a pinhole camera. A camera obscura, the teacher called it. Just a sealed shoebox with a tiny hole at one end, and a sheet of photo-sensitive paper on the other, in the darkness of the box. That pinprick let in just the tiniest amount of light, and yet it was enough to paint a picture of the entire scene in front of the box on that sheet of paper.

Adriana's journal—*their* journal—is that camera obscura: a tiny window into each other's souls that somehow allows them to see everything.

Adriana closes the journal and presses it to her chest. In that moment the entire world shifts. It's so powerful for Adriana that she could swear the ground itself is moving beneath her feet—an earthquake that only she can feel. This, she realizes, is what it feels like to have your world rocked.

And she knows without question—without any shadow of any doubt—that she and Jon are going to meet. She doesn't know how, but they will. Adriana will make it happen with the sheer force of her will.

Even if she has to dig through every wall between them with her bare hands.

PART FOUR

NO WALLS BETWEEN US

23

ALIGNMENT

"You, girl, are out of your mind!"

Adriana knew Bianca would say something like that. It's the next day. There are four of them at the lunch table today: Bianca, Jolene, Monessa, and Adriana. Pip isn't around. She seems to be the only one able to escape Compass's mandatory schedule.

"Meeting up with a boy—where the hell do you think you are?" Bianca laughs. "Some fancy-ass cruise, making out with boys you don't even know while your parents get drunk?"

"Ooh that sounds fun!" says Jolene.

Monessa smirks. "I don't think making out is what she has in mind."

Adriana's already beginning to regret this—especially because Monessa is with them—but if Adriana's going to find a way to make this happen, she's going to need a whole lot of people on board. So she told them about the journal. Didn't *show* it to them, because she doesn't want any of them to read it. She didn't even tell them how they pass the journal, because if they knew that, they might start looking for it in the library. And she didn't tell them why Jon's really at Compass. That's going to stay between her and Jon.

"I just want to meet him," Adriana says. "That's all."

"Right," sneers Monessa. "And he wants to 'meat' you."

That makes Jolene snicker, then look off wistfully. "My boyfriend was too old for Compass," she says. "Otherwise he'd be here too, and I could go with you. It'd be a secret double date!"

"Can we please just focus?" says Adriana.

Bianca smiles and pats Adriana's hand. "Girl, honestly, I've never seen focus like you got right now. Which must mean you're really dead set on this . . ."

Monessa slouches. "You got the dead part right."

Adriana knows better than to confront Monessa, because that's just what she wants. When it comes to Adriana, she doesn't know anything but confrontation.

"She's right, you know," says Bianca, which is not what Adriana wants to hear. "The guards got Tasers and pepper spray—and after that riot, they are just itching to use them."

That sobers things up a bit. Adriana glances over to Bonivich, who stands at her post by the door, wearing a perpetual frown. It must hurt to frown that much. Or maybe your face adapts.

"Has anyone ever seen Bonivich tase someone?" Adriana asks.

"Yeah, she tased a bitch," Monessa says, shoveling a forkful of pasta. "No hesitation. Girl went down and broke her nose. Point is, you get caught in the wrong place, and there's no telling what they'll do."

"I'm not scared."

"Then this fork's got more brains than you." Monessa considers her fork a moment more and points it at Adriana like a wand. "Maybe I'll just report you to Jameara. No, not Jameara! Alvarado!" Monessa's face lights up with a nasty look of delight that's thicker than the spaghetti sauce on her mouth.

The thought of getting hauled to Alvarado to talk about Jon is more horrifying to Adriana than any of the weapons on Bonivich's belt.

"No one's going to do that," says Bianca, tossing Monessa a glare, "but maybe you ought to let this sit. Give it a few days and maybe you'll feel differently."

"I don't want to feel differently," insists Adriana.

Bianca shakes her head. "But it's impossible! Never in the history of Compass has a boy met secretly with a girl."

"How would you know, if it was secret?" Jolene asks. Which is a very good point.

"The only place this is gonna happen is in your dreams," says Monessa.

And this time Adriana takes the bait. "For once, will you not be so negative?"

Surprisingly, Monessa doesn't go on the offensive; she just inhabits her slouch more fully. "I'm not negative, I'm real, and if you're not real, you end up like . . ." She involuntarily tosses a look to Jolene. Luckily Jolene doesn't catch it. "Well, let's just say you end up with a whole world of disappointment. And disappointment can kill you just like a knife. Only it's more painful."

The look on her face tells Adriana that Monessa has known disappointment intimately. But there was also a different look on her face when she held her baby—which means Monessa knows joy and hope, too, even if she's afraid to show it here.

So Adriana lets Monessa be, but Bianca fires back at her instead. "If you're not gonna help, Monessa, then why don't you just stay out of it?"

"Because I'm sitting here, and it got thrown in my face, just like you!" Then she backs off a bit. "And besides, I didn't say I wasn't gonna help—I just said it was stupid and pointless."

"Well, Adriana's gonna need a plan," says Bianca. "All we got now are a bunch of flapping lips."

And then Jolene says what they've all been thinking. "You know who Adriana needs to talk to, don't you?"

Yes, Adriana knows.

The girls are never supposed to be in other girls' pods. You have your pod-mates, for better or worse. And everyone else, you get to see in the Rec Hub, or in class, or at meals, or at places like the library. The philosophy behind it is that it's supposed to simulate the feel of a family—but Adriana suspects that's bullshit, and it was just the way Compass was built. If the architects had made every room accessible only by Batpole, then they would say it was intentionally designed "to foster a sense of playful adventure." (Of course, Monessa would say it was to teach them all to be pole dancers.)

But Pip is in her room today, in Pod B, too sick to attend class or come to lunch, so Adriana has to appeal to the kindness of others, which is in short supply at Compass. As it turns out, special allowances are made when it comes to Pip. Allowances enough to bend rules that are supposedly too rigid to bend.

"I know Pip likes you, and she'll be glad you're paying her a visit," says Jameara, who escorts Adriana there herself, "but aren't you supposed to be in the library now?"

"I told Ms. Detrick I needed the period off for personal reasons."

That makes Jameara laugh. "You know you're trusted when you can get away with saying something like that."

"So Pip—what's she sick with?"

Jameara takes a moment to think of how to answer. "Pip has asthma and a weak heart. So when she gets sick, we take it very seriously. This time it's just a cold, but it's hit her hard."

Jameara unlocks the outer door to Pod B, then when the outer door seals, they stroll down to the inner door, Jameara opening it to the pod. "I'll give you your privacy," she says, then points to the green button on the wall. "Buzz when you're ready to go."

Adriana enters Pip's room to find Pip sitting up in bed playing with a Nintendo Switch—which aren't allowed at Compass, but Pip's universe is like a trip through hyperspace: a bubble that exists outside the rules of the known universe.

Beneath the hem of Pip's trousers, her bare feet are thin and narrow with short, skinny toes. She looks vulnerable, which she must hate. Or maybe she doesn't hate it—because looking weak and vulnerable is good camouflage when you're not.

Pip looks up from her game. Her nose is red, eyes bloodshot, but otherwise she seems okay. "I was wondering when you'd show up," Pip says.

That almost makes Adriana gasp. She only just spoke, with the girls in the cafeteria a short time ago and none of them has been back here yet.

"How did you know I was coming?"

Pip looks at her for a moment and then breathes a phlegmy sigh. "I'll let you in on a secret," she says, and pats the bed for Adriana to sit next to her, which she does. Then Pip whispers, "I *didn't* know. But sometimes pretending that you do gives you an advantage."

Adriana smiles. Pip didn't have to tell her that—she could have just stayed mysterious and kept Adriana off balance.

"So, you here to keep me company? Or maybe you're trying to catch my cold so you can stay in your room a few days." Then she smiles. "Or maybe there's something you want."

Adriana decides not to beat around the bush. "You're right, Pip. I want your help."

"Wait—don't tell me—you need me to get a message to that boy!"

"No," Adriana says, then comes clean. "I already got messages to him—and him to me. A whole lot of them, actually."

It catches Pip by surprise. She coughs a bit, then clears her throat. "Wow, I knew you were smart, but I didn't know you were *that* smart."

Adriana explains to Pip how it happened. How it was just an accident that she had left the journal in the library, and that Jon was the one who found it and started the conversation.

"Even so," says Pip, "you figured out how to keep it going without anyone finding out. Not even me! That takes skill! So who else knows?"

"I just told Bianca, Monessa, and Jolene."

Pip nods and considers it. "Bianca will be good with it. She'll secretly resent you because she'll wish it was her journal and not yours, but she won't stand in your way. Monessa won't tell anyone, but she'll find little ways to use it against you. And Jolene? She'll blab it to everyone unless I get to her first and tell her not to."

Pip has, of course, hit the nail on the head with all three of them. Adriana's amazed. "How do you *do* that? How do you get people so well that you know exactly what they'll do?"

Pip shrugs like it's nothing. "I watch and I listen, that's all. My parents always said I was a great judge of character."

"First time I ever heard you talk about your parents."

"They're not in the picture," Pip says. Adriana thinks that might be all she'll say about it, but she throws Adriana a little bone. "Yeah, they were chased away by medical bills. They realized I'd get better care as a ward of the state than with them. So, really, they did me a favor." Adriana can't help but notice

259

how Pip speaks about it without bitterness or judgment or even sadness—as if abandoning her was nothing more than a mutually beneficial transaction. Adriana wants to press for more but knows she shouldn't.

"If you already have a line to the boy, what do you need me for?" Pip asks.

Adriana takes a deep breath. Probably deep enough to catch Pip's cold, but she doesn't care. "I need you . . . because I want to meet him."

To Pip's credit, she doesn't laugh, doesn't dismiss it out of hand the way Bianca and Monessa did. Instead she thinks about it. She thinks about it for a good long time.

"So, I had a friend once," she finally says, "who was all into astrology—which I think is BS, but hey, when you got no clothesline to hang your life on, it does the job. Anyway she used to get all excited about planets aligning. Of course, they all won't line up for like 400 billion years—but having six of them align happens once every hundred years. It's rare, but it does happen. So what you're asking? That's like getting planets to align. It's possible, but it's once-in-a-hundred-years kind of possible."

"But still, it's doable, right?"

"There are things and people that'll need to be tweaked. Maybe they'll tweak and maybe they won't." Then she smiles wide. "But it'll be fun to try!"

BREAK TO US

Jon. I've been trying to write to you, but somehow words aren't enough. At least not my regular words. So I wrote them as a song. A ballad. I'd call it a power ballad, but we don't have much power here at Compass. I don't have a melody. Maybe you can add that. So here it goes . . .

The things you say scare me,
The things you say dare me,
To see you in new ways
I haven't before.

The things you've done shock me,
But still they won't block me,
From breaking down every last door,
'Cause you've shaken me down to the core,

I'll break out,
I'll break through
All these walls,
Break to you!
All the barriers keeping us lonely will fall
I'll reach out
And take hold,
You'll be strong,
I'll be bold
Till there's no walls between us at all.

Till there's no walls between us,
    Just love to redeem us,
        No, nothing and no one
            Between us at all.

You've lost all that's dear to you,
Still, I am here for you
Ear to the cinder-block wall, I can hear
How your words bridge the distance
Your heartbeat's insistence,
On finding me when I am lost

I don't care what this feeling might cost

    You'll break out,
    You'll break free
    From your chains

Break to me!
All the barriers keeping us lonely will fall,
I will meet you halfway
Between night
And the day
Where there's no walls between us at all

Where there's no walls between us,
　　　Just love to redeem us
　　　　　No, nothing and no one
　　　　　　between us at all.

　　　They can't tell us we'll never find it
　　　They're too jaded and narrow-minded
　　　We will meet in that place
　　　Eye to eye, face-to-face
　　　And our light's gonna leave them blinded!

We're victorious!
Broke the rules,
Broke to us!
All the barriers keeping us lonely are gone,
Let's reach out
And take hold,
We'll be strong,
We'll be bold
Till it's just Adriana and Jon.
　　　Now it's just Adriana and Jon

Lying on his hard bed. His cell door is open in case Silas needs him. Feeling shockingly breathless, as if the door to his escape capsule has opened in the vacuum of space. Jon's fingers are bloodless gripping Adriana's journal. She's gone headlong into lyrical poetry in response to his biggest secret, his most awful sin, flaying his life and heart open to her. And what is it she says in the journal entry?

She wants to break to him.

She wants him to break to her.

What?

Can that mean what he thinks it means? Is she just being metaphoric? Giving voice to a fantasy? He reads it again. No, the message is clear. She wants to find a way to meet. Not just in words but in action.

Is she crazy? After what he's done, how come she's not running as far from him as she can? And it'd be so easy. All she's gotta do is *not* shelve her journal in the library. That'd call whatever they had quits. The end. Finished.

As maybe it should.

But instead, she's gonna risk everything to meet him. If she gets caught, they could move her to another detention center. Or worse—they could use it as a reason to keep her incarcerated longer.

Why?

Because . . . his fingers keep brushing the words over and over. Afraid to believe them, but wanting to the bottom of his soul to believe them. Praying that her words don't disappear.

Because she loves him.

The thought of what those words mean makes him want to dance in his cell. Makes him want to stop time, because nothing's ever going to feel this good again. Makes him as scared as when his mom lay dying. As scared as when the doctor had the heart attack. As scared as the day he entered Compass. But a different kind of scared. Jon has never skydived and doubts he ever will, but this must be like the feeling before you step out of the airplane and let the physics of the universe take over. Trusting that those laws will hold—at least long enough for your parachute to fill with air, and bring you from terminal velocity to a smooth, safe landing.

She loves him.

Doesn't she know that people who care about him die of cancer or get poisoned?

Doesn't she understand that he'll probably be remanded to an adult prison soon? That he might rot there for years and years? That his only remaining relative—his aunt Taníka—bailed once he was convicted and hasn't been to see him since? Why would Adriana want to board a ship that's already sinking, like Raz said it was? You don't buy a ticket for the *Titanic* after it's already struck the damn iceberg.

Yet she loves him. Somehow that shines a light on all the dark places inside and outside him. The longing, the yearning sweeps over him like a rising wave, giving him buoyancy and drowning everything else.

He must see her. Even if it ensures him losing his case in court. No matter what the consequences, he must see her.

Because he loves her too.

"Jon?"

Hearing Silas's voice and seeing him lean hesitantly against the doorframe, Jon slips the journal behind his pillow and goes out to meet Silas in the pod living room, glad to see he looks like his old self.

"Are you . . . crying?"

"Hell, no," Jon tells him, wiping wetness from his eyes he didn't even know was there. "Got some dust in my eye is all. You need something, Meerkat?

They sit at the table. Silas looks around to make sure the others are occupied in their rooms and hopefully not listening in.

"You think any more about who spiked my lunch?"

Jon shakes his head. "Everyone thinks I did it. Hard for me to get any intel when they've already decided the case. Raz says he's on my side, but he's mostly shut up about it. Like even discussing it is just gonna make things worse."

Silas sighs. "They keep telling me that it must have been an accident and I shouldn't worry about it happening again, but I don't think anyone believes that." Then he pauses. "If it was just a one-off retaliation against me, that's one thing . . . but if it's you who's the real target, how can we not worry? What if they hurt Gordy next and try to pin *that* on you?"

It chills Jon to think that Gordy could be more collateral damage in all this—but he likes that Meerkat said *we*, like they're in this together. Like Adriana, Silas makes him feel less alone.

"Whether or not it's about me, they could still go after you again, Meerkat. Maybe just a different way."

The kid shrugs. "I've got my eyes open now. Hypervigilant. I wanna catch this guy."

Jon smiles. "Hypervigilant. You ever get beaten up for being a human fucking dictionary, Meerkat?"

"Only surreptitiously," he says.

Jon mimes flicking a booger at him, and it makes the Meerkat laugh.

Silas's casual courage amazes Jon. He almost died, and yet he's more concerned about Jon than himself. Can Jon risk the kid or Gordy because of him? And then something occurs to him. What if whoever's framing Jon finds out about him and Adriana? Will they go after her? It's too painful to think about, so he tries to tuck it away, but it's not tucking too well.

"Any of the adults on your side?" Silas asks.

"The director is convinced I poisoned you, and so is Alvarado. Luppino still has an open mind, and I guess Rush too. Maybe Ms. Detrick, since she kind of smiled at me today."

"Don't forget the nurse—she told me you tried CPR—and the lunch lady."

"Yeah," says Jon. "If you ask me, Dorella should be running the place—she gets everyone and everything here."

Even with those possible additions, it's sad that Team Jon is so small.

"I've got an appointment with Dr. Alvarado tomorrow," says Silas, "so I can ask him why he's so dead set it's you. If Rush or Luppino escort me there, I can ask them too. But I doubt the nurse or Dorella knows what's going on in the investigation."

Jon grimaces at the thought of the Meerkat doing detective work on his own. 'Cause what if the wrong people find out he's pushing on this? "Don't you think you should focus on getting out of this place?"

The Meerkat misses the point entirely and his face lights up. "That's a great idea. I can set up meetings with my social worker saying I'm in danger and what are they doing to find out who poisoned me. She might know something too. Perfect!"

Perfect is definitely not the right word. If only he could find a safe place to stash the kid. And Gordy. And Adriana. Just hide them down in Moonshine Cavern until this whole thing blows over.

Moonshine Cavern.

His heart misses a beat then pounds so hard it's almost painful.

"Jon?"

"Sorry, you say something?"

"No, but it looked like you went off to Mars for a second."

Jon has to take a moment to sift through his thoughts, because suddenly there's so much there.

"Farther than that, Meerkat," he says with a grin. "Farther than that."

25

NO IMPOSSIBLE NOW

Adriana . . .

I can't write you a song. Not because I don't want
to, but because I'm no good at it. The best I can do
is to say that you make me feel stuff. Which is saying
a lot. Because for the longest time, I haven't felt
anything.

I love you for that.

I love you for a whole lot of things. For writing
back to me when I messed with your journal that first
time. For being smart, for being funny. For being brave
enough to ask the hard question, and then not throwing
me away when I gave you the hard answer. I love you
for not pretending to be anything. And that makes you
everything. Or at least everything that matters to me.

Meeting you . . . yeah, I'd say that's impossible—but
so what? We've already managed the impossible, so let's
manage one more impossible thing. I believe we can find
a way.

And I know the place.

It's secret, but it's not so secret. It's mysterious, but
not so mysterious once you know the truth about it. It
shouldn't exist, and yet it does—and I'm beginning to
think that the only reason it exists is for us.

Meet me in Moonshine Cavern, Adriana. I picked
the place, now you pick the time.

Love,

Jon

"It seems like you're adjusting well, Adriana," says Alvarado. "I'm proud of you!"

What the hell is there to be proud of, you damned smiling walrus?

"Thank you, sir."

It's another one of Adriana's mandatory therapy sessions. Alvarado's desk is disorganized as usual, but his eyes are as focused as ever. She hates the way he looks you right in the eye. She wonders if it's part of his training, or if he read about extreme eye contact in some self-help book. *How to Lose Friends and Intimidate Others.*

She tries to be in the moment, because until Alvarado feels he has her undivided attention, he's going to torment her with questions and head games. But all she can think about is Jon and his latest journal entry. Adriana is overjoyed by what he wrote! She has no idea what or where Moonshine Cavern is, but that doesn't matter. Pip will know, or at least she'll find out. The important thing is that Jon is in!

"Where are your thoughts at today, Adriana?"

"Right here," she says, trying to sell the lie.

Alvarado brings up his hands and taps his fingertips together as he leans back in his chair, rocking slightly. It's a very self-satisfied gesture. Like he's thinking, but only thinking about himself and how good he is at his job.

"I get the feeling your time here is going to be very beneficial to you, Adriana," he says.

"Beneficial how?" She can think of nothing about seven months of incarceration that will benefit her.

Then Alvarado grins like he has a secret. "Let me show you something." He taps a bit on his laptop and casts his screen up to the TV on the wall, so they can both see. At first Adriana's not sure what she's looking at—and once she realizes, her heart crashes. It's a surveillance video taken in the library. A high, distorted wide angle that catches everything. Adriana watches herself slip the journal onto a shelf.

Did she say her heart crashed? No, this was more than a crash. This was an impact with the velocity of an asteroid wiping out all life on Earth. This is an extinction-level event.

"Sir, I can explain—"

But then he taps on his computer some more. "Always hard to find the moment you're looking for on these surveillance videos." Then he scrubs forward. Adriana watches herself scoot around the library in fast motion. Flashes of other girls coming and going.

"It's coming up—bear with me."

Adriana's forgotten to breathe. She takes a long slow breath, trying not to gasp. Could it be that he didn't know what he was seeing? That he completely missed her shelving the journal? It was right there before his eyes. How could he not see it?

Because the Walrus sees only what he wants to see, Adriana realizes. *He sees only what he's looking for. The things that fit the conclusions he's already made.*

"Ah, here we are!"

The video slows down to normal speed. Adriana's in frame again, but this time someone's with her. Monessa. This was when Adriana spoke to her about her baby.

"Monessa Williams is the girl you fought with, isn't that right?"

"Y-yes . . ." Adriana's still out of breath but tries her best to hide it.

"Part of my job is to monitor interactions among the detainees. There's no sound on this camera, but body language says more than words sometimes. Look at the two of you!"

So you spy on people's private moments? What the hell is wrong with you?

"We were just talking."

"Exactly! You're having a civil conversation with a girl who was your enemy just a few weeks ago! That's growth, Adriana!

Honest-to-goodness, bona fide growth!"

"Well . . . life is too short for enemies, right?"

"I couldn't have said it better myself!"

Adriana smiles. This could have gone very differently if Alvarado was actually as good at his job as he thinks he is. But this man sees everything and yet sees nothing.

"Now that you're in a routine and have found how you fit here at Compass, I think your time here is going to fly!" Then he stands up, indicating their session is over, and holds out his hand for her to shake. Which she does.

"Thank you, Dr. Alvarado."

Yes, thank you for being so unbelievably, undeniably, monumentally clueless.

So Jon and I are going to make this happen, she thinks as she's led back to the girls' unit. *Now comes the hard part.* It's one thing to say, "Let's do this," and another thing to actually make it happen. But Jon's right; there's no impossible now. In fact, it feels like their meeting is destined to happen. As if all the doors will unlock themselves before them. Adriana knows that's magical thinking. But so what? Maybe there are some kinds of magic in the world. Not Harry Potter wand-waving stuff, but common, everyday magical things that most people are too busy and too stressed to even notice. That kind of magic is all around Adriana now. Around both her and Jon.

26

HOW MONSTERS ARE MADE

It's like Jon's never been out to the yard before. Not this yard. Because the entire world looks different. Feels different. The trees beyond the fence are greener. The sounds from the basketball court are like a syncopated musical beat. Is this what love is, he wonders, or is he just out of his mind? Or both. He feels like if he jumped, he would fly over the fence. But he wouldn't do that even if he could. He wants to be here, where Adriana is.

He reminds himself that he still needs to be in yellow-alert mode. He can't let this feeling pull his guard down. So he goes to lean against the north wall where no one can sneak up behind him, far enough from the pickup game to have time to react if someone hurtles toward him from that direction. A good place to be alone in a crowd, even though right now, for the first time in a long time, he doesn't feel so alone.

Gordy and Silas aren't here—Silas is inside, tutoring Gordy in math, so he doesn't need to watch out for them. Raz is talking to some greenshirts at the far corner of the yard. Jon knows he's going to need Raz's help to meet Adriana—the guy has a gift for planning and subterfuge. Jon had meant to use their rec time for bringing him into the loop—but the thought exhausts him. Problem is, Raz is still avoiding him. Jon knows that can't last forever—Raz feeds off Jon's notoriety. They both know it. Jon's going to have to mend that fence sooner than later.

Jon's attention flicks around the yard, ninja style, wary of any possible threats. He targets the usual suspects. Like Viper and Culligan, who snicker while loitering at the foul line, occasionally glancing at him. Like Stripes, who plays some painful punching game with Flots. Like Knox, circling the yard, his eyes so glassy they may shatter. All seems well. Except for the fact that all of them toss Jon quick, secret glances. Surreptitious glances. Like maybe they're planning something.

Or maybe they're just wondering why the hell he's just standing there like he's no longer a part of their universe.

Because he isn't. And it makes him smile. Which probably makes him look weirder. But he doesn't care.

He wonders what Adriana does when she's out here. Shoot hoops and shuffle around like the boys do? Make friends and plot against enemies? Or is it different here for girls? But more importantly, can the yard come into play for Jon and Adriana's meeting? The yard has few options for escape; only the one tunnel door—which means the girls must come out through that tunnel too. But what doorway brings them to the tunnel? He grits his teeth. He needs to get a map of the underground areas and accessways. Can Adriana ask one of her girls about that? It sounds like one of them got pretty good intel on Jon. Maybe that girl could get a map.

Jon sighs. He isn't bringing much to the party. He's going to have to tell some of the other guys about this, because he won't be able to do it alone.

Wash and another guard stand planted in the yard's designated strategic position near the door. He flicks them a second look when he notices activity at the tunnel door. Someone opens it from the inside and talks to Wash. Then Wash turns to Jon, points at him, then signals Jon to come over, stern look on his face. Jon trots toward him, wondering what now.

"You know it's rude to point in some cultures," Jon says.

"Yeah, well this ain't that culture." He notices Wash puts a hand on his Taser. An unspoken threat. Wash is on the side of the vast majority who believe in Jon the Poisoner and probably in Jon the Serial Killer.

Wash clears his throat twice before saying, "Director Morley wants to see you."

Jon feels his stomach clench. Has the director gotten wind of him trying to get to Adriana? Has one of the other girls betrayed her? Panic washes over him. Did someone find her journal in the library?

"Morley wants to see me?" Jon croaks. "Why?"

Wash sketches a scant look at the messenger standing in

the shadows, another guard Jon doesn't recognize. The sudden addition of guards feels like a steamroller tipping sideways, affecting everyone in the way.

"The director says now. Assume position. I'm taking you."

Automatically Jon links his wrists behind him. He casts a quick look back at the yard, wishing he had someone there he could trust. Wondering who's watching him being taken away, and what rumors might be started because of it.

"Move it, Kilgore," Wash barks.

Jon feels like he's heading for an execution. If the director chops his head off and dumps his body in the forest, not a single greenshirt will know. Jon tries to imagine Morley as an executioner, and it just makes Jon laugh. Turkey-neck wouldn't even be able to heft the ax without falling over.

As they walk through the tunnel beneath Boys' Building two, they pass the door that leads to the old stairwell going down to Moonshine Cavern. How many times has he been down there working the Teleportation Team? Four? Five? Suddenly he wishes he'd studied the space down there more. Were there other entrances? Floor grates? Ceiling vents? There's the old broken mystery door at the far back, but where does it lead?

"Eyes front," Wash says. "Keep moving."

A bit farther down the tunnel, there's another door. Jon doesn't know where that one goes. He's never wondered, because he's never cared. Since the girls have to come this way to get to the yard, maybe that door connects to a tunnel leading to the girls' building. But it's not like he can ask Wash without the man getting suspicious.

One more door, and the smell alone—or lack thereof—would tell Jon that they were in the administration building, if he didn't already know. The admin building might be the key to their access, and security might be lighter too. Jon tries to make a mental note of everything he sees that might help him and Adriana.

Finally they arrive at Morley's office, where his assistant asks them to wait near her cubicle, then smiles at Jon and gestures at her candy jar. His eyes almost well up at her kindness—but since Wash almost goes apeshit at Jon's hands being anywhere but safely gripped behind him, he politely declines, grateful for the particles of compassion that occasionally show up within Compass's walls.

Now that he's just standing there waiting, his mind goes to bad places. *Did Myers rat me out?* Jon wonders. *Did he tell the Director he saw the powder on my hands?* No, it's not Myers's MO to snitch. It's his MO to pass through Compass like a ghost, leaving not even a whisper to stir his passage. Still, Morley wouldn't drag Jon here unless he had a good reason. He certainly hasn't been summoned for the Inmate of the Year award.

Maybe they caught the real culprit, and Morley's gonna apologize.

Ha! Shelve that under fantasy.

The director's door opens, a clerk exits, and Morley waves them in, unsmiling, wattle flapping. Jon freezes just inside the office. If Wash hadn't given Jon a wide berth, the guard might have crashed into him. Instead, he gives Jon an ungentle shove so he stumbles the last few steps inside.

There's a pair of green pants lying not so neatly on Morley's otherwise spotless desk. The faintest hint of white powder is visible around the waistband seam. Jon wiped it out—but clearly not well enough.

Too late to put on a poker face. Guilt spills from him—even if it's false guilt—and he can't keep his shoulders from slumping in defeat.

The director doesn't invite Jon to sit down. Jon wishes he had, because his legs are shaking.

"You think I'm stupid, Kilgore? You think no one noticed how ill-fitting your pants were when you were hauled up here last time? And did you think I didn't know that you boys hide forbidden items in the seams?"

In the barrage of words, Jon sticks on the pants being too short for him. He didn't think Morley had noticed.

A pompous note swells Morley's voice. "I had laundry services search your pod's bin." The director flicks a pant leg with a fastidious finger. "It took a few days for the test results on the powder to come back. Do I need to tell you what it said?

Again, Jon fights mightily to hide his reaction.

"So?" says Jon, "you don't know they're mine."

"Serial number," Morley says. "All clothing has serial numbers on their label, and who they were assigned to."

Somewhere inside Jon, a heavy boulder begins a long slow fall.

"Shit."

"So you admit they're yours."

"You already know they're mine—why do I have to say it?"

Then a nasty, victorious grin fills Morley's face. "You fool," he says. "There are no serial numbers."

And there it is. Jon just incriminated himself. There's no path to innocence now. Any court will convict him of poisoning Silas. And they'll try him as an adult. Again.

He glances up to see speculation warring with triumph on the director's face. Not so much warring as if settling a bet. Jon can't imagine what the man might be plotting now.

"Officer?" the director says, taking a seat at his desk with a flourish, as if playing to a studio audience. "Wait outside while I discuss Mr. Kilgore's situation with him. I'll let you know when your presence is required."

Wash looks relieved to be excused. Rush would never leave him alone with the director. Especially uncuffed. There's a rule against it, he's sure.

As the door closes behind Wash, the director looks at Jon, that speculative look growing a little bit hungry. Maybe Jon doesn't want to know what that's about. Maybe he doesn't want to be left alone with the director.

"Sit down, Jon." The director leans back in his fancy chair, while Jon sits on the uncomfortable chair across the desk.

"Have you ever heard the expression 'One hand washes the other'?"

Jon can't think of anything to say to that but "You sent Wash outside."

Morley chuckles. "This can go one of two ways," Morley says. "You get officially charged with attempted murder. That, on top of your existing murder conviction, and you'll be a very old man before you see the light of day, if at all. Or—"

"Or what, sir?"

"Does it matter, Jon?"

"Excuse me, sir?"

"Does it matter what I ask you to do? Because whatever it is, you'll do it, won't you? Because nothing can be worse than the alternative."

Jon looks at the incriminating pants on the table. And he knows Morley is right. Whatever the ask, Jon will do it. And there's nothing more humiliating than knowing he'll say yes even before knowing what he's agreeing to.

"What do you want me to do, sir?"

Morley nods. "Compliance. Good, Jon. That's what we like to hear." He rocks a bit in his chair, considering. He takes his time, savoring his dominance. Finally, he speaks.

"Right now, what I need is a man in the trenches. Someone who can do things within the Compass population that I can't do. Someone who can be my touchstone when I need something done."

All that sounds foggy to Jon, but whatever Morley means, it's not happening in this room at this moment. That should be a relief, but Jon can't help but feel like whatever Morley is asking could be a whole lot worse.

"Cameras don't tell me the things I need to know to keep

order here. I need someone who can give me intel. The names of troublemakers, letting me know when and how rules are being broken."

Be a snitch. He's making me his jailhouse snitch.

It's one thing Jon's never done. That breaks the sacred code of the incarcerated. It'd destroy what little honor he has left.

"But even more important than that, Jon . . . what I need is someone not afraid to take action. And clearly you have no compunction about all nature of actions."

"I . . . don't follow, sir."

"All right, then—let me give you an example. Let's just say I have an inmate who's known for unexpected bouts of violence, one who could kill a much younger kid in an instant. Let's call him Inmate X."

He's talking about Knox. Why's he talking about Knox?

"My inside man would be someone who could turn that inmate's violence on, and then turn it off, because he's done so in the past."

Jon feels the director's pointed look but refuses to meet the man's gaze, refuses to give away what he's thinking. He needs time to understand his own chaotic thoughts.

"My inside man would be able to send Inmate X into a rage that's violent enough to make sure he's pulled from Compass and relegated to a psychiatric institution where he belongs. And, voilà, a dangerous element is neutralized, and everybody's happy."

"Everybody but Inmate X."

"The greater good, Jon. The greater good."

Jon manages a grunt that's neither yes nor no. The director clears his throat, now sounding displeased. "Are we on the same page, Jon?"

"Your inside man would get, um, forgiveness for . . . for stuff he's been accused of . . . in exchange for doing you favors?"

Morley's brows lower. "Not forgiveness. Let's call it a delay of consequences."

Which means Morley could hold those consequences over Jon indefinitely. Asking endless favors of any nature until he leaves Compass. From this moment on, Jon would be Morley's bitch.

This is how monsters are made, Jon realizes. Do enough dirty work for seedy people, and you become the thing that you do. Jon never saw himself as a bottom-feeder, but Morley is now pressing his face deep into the fetid funk.

Maybe something of what's going on in his head flashes on his face, because Morley shoots him a patronizing smile. "Of course, there's always option A, Jon."

A dive into dishonor to save himself from a second conviction. His throat seizes.

Knowing Morley's still waiting for an answer, he manages a nod. Let the director decide what it means.

"Very good," says Morley. "Do this well, and it can follow you to your next institution."

Morley thinks that's a plus, but to Jon, it's the stuff of horror. Damnation of the worst kind.

Morley leaps up and goes to the door, calling for Wash to enter. Still frozen to his chair, Jon closes his eyes and tries to push it all away. Morley didn't touch him—but there are many ways to be violated. Right now, Jon feels like he's been ripped open and an arm has been shoved up inside him. He's been turned into a hand puppet, and he's never felt so filthy.

But then he finds a light deep in the muck of his thoughts. It can't chase the darkness away, but still, it's there, consistent, unyielding. It's Adriana. Morley can take his dignity and his pride, but he can't take her from him. And he knows it's crazy, but he can't help but feel that, like Adriana said, their lights will ignite and be blinding, chasing away all this darkness if they meet.

No . . . not if they meet. *When* they meet.

Because for them, there is no option B.

27

WORTHY OF ATTENTION

Adriana,

Screws got a way of turning whether you want them to or not. Things are getting tighter on my end. Don't want to go into details, but I'm worried, and I never worry. Seeing you is all I think about now. I know it's not cool for a guy to admit something like that, but to hell with what's cool and what's not. I got a face I wear for everyone else, but I don't have to wear it with you.

This WILL happen. I know it. But we're going to have to work to make it work. I got friends on this side that can help if I ask them. The Meerkat—which is what we call Silas now—and my buddy Raz, if he ever gets over himself. And maybe a few more who want to get in my good graces. I'll work on this end, you work on yours, and maybe . . . no, definitely . . . we'll get to each other.

Love,
Jon

At the free hour Pip, Bianca, and Monessa hang out in a corner of the Rec Hub with Adriana, quietly plotting.

"The more we talk about this, the more I realize it's gonna take a lot of kids on both sides to make this happen," Adriana says.

"The more there are, the harder it'll be," Pip points out, "because the whole thing is only as good as the weakest link—and that can be anybody."

To make it fly, they would have to trick a guard—maybe two. Adriana would probably have to squeeze and shimmy into places that weren't meant for squeezing and shimmying, and avoid cameras that are practically impossible to avoid.

"This is like an old-school caper," says Bianca, with a squeal of joy. "Like trying to steal the Hope Diamond."

"More like the Hopeless Diamond," snarks Monessa.

But hopeless or not, as the days wear on, it all begins to take shape. And wonder of wonders, it looks like it might actually happen!

"I'm feeling a little scared now," Adriana admits to Pip one day.

Pip's gaze goes cool. "If you don't want to do it, I'm not wasting my time."

Startled by Pip's sudden chill, Adriana crushes her anxiety. If she's going to see Jon, she needs Pip to point the way.

"I'm all in." She holds up her hand in a fist of solidarity. "We'll make it work. Easy peasy."

Jon,

I know there's a risk to keeping this journal going back and forth, but I need it to. It's like breathing. Like I'll die if I stop. I get the feeling it's that way for you too. But don't worry, we don't have to say anything deep, or meaningful—because, in truth it's all meaningful to me. Every word you write—even the absolutely annoying ones—feels like some kind of treasure. Is that stupid? I know it's stupid, but I don't care. I read your words over and over, until I hear your voice. It's a made-up voice, I know, but still, it's yours.

Sometimes when I'm passing a window, and I can hear the boys out in the yard, I try to pick your voice out from the crowd. Is it this deep one? Or that high-pitched one? Probably neither. It's probably that rich one in the middle. Baritone, they call it. Like a crooning saxophone, smooth as chocolate. It's maddening not knowing which voice is yours, but I guess I'll have to be satisfied with your voice in my head, until I can hear it for real.

Love,
Adriana

What few things that can stir Jon's heart these days rarely do so in a good way. But reading Adriana's words—and the idea of actually meeting her—leaves him breathless every time. It's like he's become addicted to the adrenaline rush of just thinking about her. He's never known such a thing before. Sure, there were girls he'd liked. Their faces, their bodies, their personalities. It was always a combination of those things, though. He has to admit there are times when a girl's body is the dominant feature in his mind, but that's just being a guy. Sure, it might be looks that grab your attention, but it's what's inside that holds you. Looks are kind of like a book cover. So, then, what if that book is a journal—a big leather-bound unknown?

Perhaps that's why his feelings for Adriana are so strong—because it's all about the pages in between, and not the cover. Who she IS—not what she looks or sounds like. Not the way she walks or the way she smiles, but the essence of her very being. That kind of love is beyond powerful. It could kill a person—probably has. But what a way to go!

So, all Jon has to do is figure out how to get to Moonshine Cavern without anyone on staff knowing. Right. That'll be as hard as a full-fledged Alcatraz break. Without cold water and sharks, of course—but Morley is just as bad.

Suddenly it seems Morley is everywhere. In the hallways giving tours of the facility to VIPs, in the observation window overlooking the cafeteria, looking down on the yard from his office. And each time Jon sees him, it feels like the man's eyes are on him.

You have an assignment, those eyes say. *Take care of business or face the consequences.*

How much time does Jon have until Morley implicates him with the "evidence" he has? Clearly the man plays a long game, but how long is long?

And while Jon is no friend of Knox, conspiring to have him committed makes Jon feel filthy. He knows where Morley wants to send Knox: Belle Vista—better known as *Hell* Vista—the high-security psychiatric hospital for the most violent, most disturbed juvenile offenders. The type of people they used to call criminally insane.

Instead of thinking about that, he thinks about the conspiracy he truly *does* want to be a part of. The one that will bring him to Adriana.

But something like that doesn't just happen. It's not even about planning—planning's the easy part. It's more like a feat of engineering. It will take accomplices . . .

"I think you're crazy," Silas says, "but I like it!"

The Meerkat is the first person Jon dares to confide in about the journal and his plan to meet Adriana. Well, not a plan, because it's still nothing but wishful thinking. But isn't that the first step to something real? Jon keeps finding himself high on imagining that he can make it happen with the sheer power of his will. But in the end, he always comes down, and realizes that wishing won't make it so. This will take action. He's just not sure what action yet.

"Keep your voice down," he says to Silas. "Just because no one's listening doesn't mean no one's listening."

They're in their pod's little living room. Stripes is sitting on the sofa watching TV but dozing with his eyes half-closed. Raz and Myers are off in their rooms, doing whatever it is they do when they're alone, and Gordy is out at a session with Alvarado. He'll come back like someone rang his bell real hard.

Silas leans in close and whispers—which is even more conspicuous than talking out loud, but Stripes's back is to them, and if he has eyes in the back of his head, they're closed too. "First thing you'll need is a reliable map of Compass," the Meerkat says. "I can help with that. I'm good spatially."

"Yeah, I agree you're a space case."

Silas ignores the jab. "I'll draw it up and leave question marks for doors and spaces we're not sure about. I'll also mark the locations of all the cameras."

Then Jon starts to get uncomfortable. "I don't want to get you in trouble for this."

The Meerkat shrugs. "It's just a map. I can say it's for an RPG or something." Then he adds "A role-playing game."

Jon raps him on the arm. "I know what an RPG is," he says, "but if you tell anyone I do, I'll kick your ass."

That makes the Meerkat giggle, which makes him seem a whole lot younger, which makes Jon worry even more about getting him into trouble.

There are so many moving parts going in all different directions for this to work, it makes Jon's head spin. And if anyone—*anyone*—who isn't a true ally gets wind of this, it'll be over before it starts. But it can't just be him and the Meerkat. And he knows he can't bring Gordy in, because as good-natured and loyal as Gordy is, he's a sieve when it comes to information. Raz could help, but how can Jon trust a guy who no longer trusts *him*?

When Jon actually does get help, it comes from a couple of unlikely sources.

"Why so glum?"

Dorella doesn't talk to most kids, other than to say, "Meat or fish?" or stuff like that—but she does, on occasion, talk to Jon.

"Glum? I don't know. Maybe because people think I poisoned a kid? Maybe because the director wants to put me on a leash? Maybe because I'm gonna turn eighteen soon, and there's a penitentiary with my name on it?"

"Pouting's not gonna change all that."

"I'm not pouting, I'm just . . . I'm just . . ."

"Pouting," says Dorella. And yeah, she's right.

"Hey!" someone shouts. "Who's holding up the line?"

"Come back another time," says Dorella. "We'll talk."

And so, at dinner that night, rather than pushing forward with everyone else like pups at a teat, Jon hangs back, waiting until everyone else has gotten their plates.

When he arrives at the warming trays, Dorella takes her time scooping out his food.

"Still feeling like the world's beating the crap out of you?"

"Yeah, mostly."

"Well, you're right, it is," Dorella says. "And it's going to keep doing it. But that doesn't mean you gotta lie down and take it."

That makes Jon cough out a rueful chuckle. "Compass doesn't exactly encourage fighting the Powers That Be."

Dorella shrugs. "You just gotta fight smart, that's all. With your head, not your hands."

Jon nods. It's not like he hasn't heard all that before, but somehow it resonates more when Dorella says it. And maybe because she's resonating today, Jon dares to ask her a question.

"So . . . ," says Jon, "what do you know about a girl named Adriana? Last initial Z."

"Adriana Zarahn? What about her?"

So now he has her last name. Score! "Nothing special—just whatever you can tell me."

"How do *you* know about her?"

Jon tries to shrug it off. "Maybe I knew her outside."

"No, you didn't. What—are you tapping messages to each other through the wall in Morse code?"

"Something like that."

Dorella considers him for a moment. Then realizes she never finished filling his plate. She spoons on some string beans. Then she says, "She's . . . worthy of attention."

A stamp of approval from Dorella means something. But then, Jon already knew that.

"You think *I'm* worthy of attention?" he asks.

"Sometimes. When you're not being a prick."

That makes Jon laugh. Then he leans closer. "What if I said I want to meet her?"

"Then I'd say, 'Have some lobster tail,' because you're more likely to get served that for dinner than ever get to see Adriana Zarahn."

"We're getting lobster tail?"

Dorella shakes her head. "Does all sarcasm die of oxygen deprivation in that head of yours?"

Then Jon smiles, all sly and slippery. "Thing is . . . you *could* smuggle me in some lobster if you really wanted to, couldn't you?"

"Your point?"

"That it's not impossible. It just takes motivation."

"I was wrong," Dorella says. "It's not oxygen deprivation— you got so much oxygen you're giddy. Better be careful before your head pops like a balloon."

Jon mimes his head exploding, and Dorella gives him his tray.

"Beef stew. Now get the hell out. My shift is almost over."

A few mornings later, Jon is approached in the showers—which is something you definitely don't want to happen, unless you actually do, but Jon definitely doesn't.

Of all people, it's Myers, and mercifully he has a towel on, but Jon doesn't. He's covered in lather, just about to get at his armpits, when he sees Myers standing there, like he's got no better place to be. Jon does a full-body flinch.

"Holy shit, Myers—back the hell off! I'm washin' here!"

Myers takes a single step back. "We gotta talk," he says.

"In the freakin' shower?"

"It's loud on account of the water, and there are no cameras."

Jon grabs his towel and wraps it around his waist, shielding his junk from whatever the hell this is, but leaves the water running. The thing is, Myers never has anything to say to anyone, so this is wildly off-brand for him. Jon is as curious as he is annoyed.

"I got a message for you," Myers says.

Jon's mind automatically goes to dark places. He figures it's got to be some threat from Viper, Culligan, or Knox, and that somehow they cornered Myers and turned him into their messenger.

But then Myers says, "It's from my contact on the girls' side."

Jon nearly drops the towel. "Contact? You got a contact?"

"Yeah. She says your meeting with Ariella is on. Pip'll coordinate there, I'll coordinate here."

Jon can't think of anything else to say but "It's Adriana, not Ariella."

"Whatever."

Jon could almost laugh. Myers, who has all the personality of a hole in the wall, actually *is* a hole in the wall—to the girls' side! It's mind-boggling!

"How long have you had a contact?" Jon has to ask.

Myers shrugs. "How long have I been here?"

Then he walks off like it's nothing.

◆ ◆ ◆

"Do you trust him?" Silas asks later, when they've got a moment out of anyone's earshot.

"Except for you, I don't trust anyone," Jon tells him. "But this won't happen without some help."

Silas nods. "A kid like Myers won't risk his neck without something in return. Ask him what he's getting out of this. If he doesn't say, or even if he hedges, don't trust him."

Jon smiles. "You're wising up," he says. "You may actually survive out there in the world, Meerkat!"

"What you guys whispering about?" Gordy asks, descending on them out of nowhere.

"Nothing," Jon says, a little flustered, which makes Gordy frown.

The thing is, Jon wants to let Gordy in on this. Mainly because Gordy always sees things going on around him, but not involving him. He's like the proverbial boulder in a river. A lonely thing to be. Jon doesn't want to leave Gordy out, but the guy is easily tricked into telling things he doesn't want to tell.

So Jon says, "Hey, Gordy, by the way, when's your birthday?"

"Next month. Why?"

"No reason."

To which Gordy begins to grin, and walks away.

Jon turns to Silas. "So now he'll think whatever we're planning is some birthday surprise."

"Nice. But there's gonna have to be one, then," Silas points out, "or he'll be really disappointed."

"One thing at a time," Jon tells him. "One thing at a time."

Myers starts shuttling tidbits of information back and forth between the girls' and boys' units. Jon has no idea how he's doing it, and Myers doesn't give away his secrets, of which, Jon realizes, he has many. But he knows Silas is right. You get nothing for nothing. So Myers has got to have some hidden agenda. Rather than trying to guess, Jon just asks him flat out, like the Meerkat said. It goes counter to Jon's sense of subtle intrigue, but maybe the straightforward, clear-light-of-day approach might be best. So, at a quiet moment in their pod, when everyone else is doing their own thing, Jon pulls him aside.

"Myers . . . why are you doing this for me?"

Jon knows the answer he expects. Myers'll say *you'll owe me one* or something like that. A favor for Jon now would mean a favor for him later. Or maybe Myers just wants to be in Jon's good graces. After all, he's never been part of Jon's inner circle.

But instead of any of those reasons, Myers simply says, "Practice."

"Practice? What's that supposed to mean?"

Then Myers gets all philosophical and metaphoric—which surprises Jon, because he didn't think the kid had anything going on in his head at all. "The way I see it, the future is a lock you've got to pick," Myers says, "because no one's going to give you a key."

And when Jon doesn't get it right away, Myers tells him something he can't unhear.

"Last year I dug up some dirt on my principal. Wasn't hard.

Then I blackmailed him to give me AP test answers, which I then sold online. But I forgot one detail, and the answers were traced back to his computer—and to me. It was one of the strikes that landed me here." Myers shakes his head thinking about it. "Practice," he says again. "If I had more practice, I would have done it right. And this thing you're doing, Jon, is just the kind of operation that'll sharpen my life skills. Getting you there, and getting you back without anyone at Compass knowing? That's like acing life's AP exam."

All at once Jon realizes that Myers isn't looking for short-term gain—he's seeing dozens of moves ahead. Which means, of all the kids here, Myers might be the true criminal mastermind. He's the kind of guy who could someday be quietly running corporations from behind the scenes . . . because of the "practice" he got in places like this. Which means that Jon is a test subject to him. Myers wants this to succeed just to prove to himself that it can. That's probably the coldest but purest motive of any of them.

"Myers, you scare me."

"Good," he says, and silently strolls to his room.

The next day at lunch something happens. Something strange, and a bit surreal.

Things are pretty typical in the cafeteria. Impatient, hungry kids waiting in line, sneering at the crap that gets dumped on their plates, resenting the fact that no matter how awful it is, they're still hungry for it. Today's choices are chicken and meatloaf. Jon's going to ask for the meatloaf, but Dorella serves him chicken before he can ask. He rolls with it—because Dorella knows what foods to avoid on any given day.

"Feeling any better about things?" she asks him.

Jon shrugs. "No better, no worse. Life is life."

"Well, better than the alternative. Next!"

Jon takes his tray to his usual table. It's just him, the Meerkat, and Gordy, since the others are still in line, and mercifully Rush gives them permission to sit without having to wait for a full table. Jon's head is somewhere else, pushing a fork around his peas, when Gordy says, "What the hell is that?"

"What the hell is what?"

Gordy points at Jon's tray. "That. Don't look like chicken. Looks more like pigs' knuckles or something."

Jon stares at the fleshy thing on his plate, all smothered in cream sauce. Gordy's right. It's not chicken. Not even close.

"What the hell is it?" Gordy asks again.

Jon smiles. "It's lobster tail, Gordy."

Dorella never says specifically that she's going to help. She just ignores him when he tries to talk to her about it, clearly not willing to take part in any planning. But she says things off-handedly that make it clear she's an ally.

"Almost out of rice," she says when serving him one day. "Getting more is a pain in the ass, since the bags are so big, and the storage is downstairs." She points to a door in back of the kitchen. "There's a door downstairs in food storage that opens into the tunnel between Boys' Buildings one and two. We use it when we have big loads that we need to take up the elevator in admin. But that's too much trouble for a bag of rice."

Jon takes his tray. "Thanks, Dorella," Jon says.

"Don't have to thank me. Serving you slop is my job."

So now Jon knows that the unmarked door in the tunnel doesn't lead to the girls' building; it leads to food storage! And it can be accessed from the kitchen. He gives the info to the Meerkat, who adds it to the map he's building of Compass.

Dorella might not be willing to participate, but Jon suspects she'll be willing to leave certain doors unlocked and look the wrong way at the right time.

And all of a sudden, wishful thinking is starting to look suspiciously like a plan!

28

SOMETHING ABOUT A BOY

Adriana,

My voice is no saxophone, but you're right, it's not high, and it's not low, it's somewhere between. Not all that smooth—it's a little bit raspy. What you might get if you crossed a snare drum with a . . . what . . . with a cello? Or maybe a harmonica, 'cause it's kinda bluesy too. But your voice—I'm sure it's a whole symphony, but one with a beat. Like if Mozart kicked it up to hip-hop. That's you.

I think you're wrong about the voices just being in our heads, though. Because there's more to a voice than tone. There's rhythm, and rhythm gets right into the page. That's the heartbeat of a voice—and I know yours, Adriana. Even with eyes and ears closed, I'd know it anywhere.

Love,

Jon

P.S. This is already feeling bigger than either you or me. Like it's this thing we're building that's going out of control—but not in a bad way.

For instance, there's this guy in my pod. Like the most boring dude in the world. Never does anything, never says anything worth remembering. Turns out he's like a supervillain in training. Like we're gonna see him in a Bond movie trying to take over the world! This boring guy! But he's your friend's contact here—and he's like the glue holding stuff together. I'm getting excited, Adriana. Are you?

In line behind Bonivich to the cafeteria each day, Adriana pays close attention to the route. It's already a groove in her mind, but it's easy to miss things that become so familiar you stop noticing, especially since Compass is a maze, what with all the tunnels and hallways. So she counts the steps everywhere she goes. Notes the positions of the cameras. The number of steps up and down stairwells. She does it over and over until she could get anywhere blindfolded.

The tunnel floor from the girls' wing to the cafeteria is concrete, as are the walls. Lamps cast enough light to see your feet, and still darkness seems to hang in the tunnel like a fog. One air lock, then another. They pass the Compass laundry room, where Jolene and several other girls spend their shifts dealing with the heat and humidity like an industrial sweatshop. She notices for the first time another door a few yards down from the Compass laundry room. "Authorized Access Only." As if any of the doors allow unauthorized access. Where does that door go? She's never seen anyone go through it.

So focused is she on that door that she doesn't notice Jameara coming up to her.

"Adriana, I need to have a word with you." Jameara notices Adriana noticing the door.

Adriana quickly shifts her attention away from it. "Now? I'll miss breakfast."

"This is important."

"Is this about another visit with my family?"

"No. It's about something I heard that has me a little bit concerned."

By now the last of the girls have gone through the air lock that leads to the cafeteria. It's only Jameara and Adriana in the tunnel now. Them, and whoever is watching on the other end of the cameras.

"What have you heard?" Adriana asks.

"Something about a boy."

It's like Adriana is suddenly impaled by an iron spike. But she doesn't let it show. At least she hopes it doesn't show.

"No idea what you're talking about."

"Adriana . . . I know you know the rules at Compass," says Jameara. "But I just want to remind you that there's no direct contact allowed with the boys' side. No exceptions."

"Yeah, I know. Why would you think I had anything to do with the boys?"

"Let's just say I have a source."

"Well, maybe your 'source' is just trying to stir up trouble. Maybe your source is a goddamn liar."

But Adriana's outburst only makes Jameara calmer. "I'm only looking out for your best interests, Adriana. Maybe you're right and it's just an unfounded rumor. But I have to warn you that if you're somehow involved with one of the boys, the administration will find out, and I won't be able to protect you from the consequences."

"Who was it? I want to know who it was, so I can rip them a new one!"

Adriana is furious, but she can't let her fury be visible to the cameras or be heard by the guards. And since Jameara is there during breakfast and lunch, watching Adriana like a hawk, she has to sit on it all day. She doesn't talk about it until dinner, as her crew sits in their usual spots. It's toward the end of Bonivich's shift, so she's less alert, and Jameara has gone home for the day.

"How do you know it was one of us?" says Bianca.

"Jameara has a source. What else could that mean?"

Pip is somber. "I have a lot of girls who agreed to help. It could be any of them, and all it takes is one to shut the whole thing down."

The idea of shutting it down sends Adriana spiraling. "We can't let that happen!"

"Not up to you," says Monessa. "It's up to all of us." Monessa casts her eyes to the side as she speaks. It's not like she can't meet Adriana's gaze, but more like she's defying it. More like she's saying Adriana doesn't deserve eye contact.

"It was you!" hisses Adriana. "I know it!"

Monessa raises her hackles, prepared for a fight. "Don't you be accusing me, bitch!"

"Just admit it!"

"If I double-crossed you, I would be doing it to your face, not going behind your back. But now I wish it *was* me, because this whole dreamy love thing of yours is bullshit!"

"STOP!" yells Jolene. "Just stop." Then she takes a deep breath and lets it out. "It was me."

That catches everyone by surprise. "Jolene? You told Jameara?"

"I didn't mean to," Jolene pleads. "I was talking to her about the letters I get. You know—from my boyfriend. Jameara says it's good that I have someone—but since he's in prison, she says maybe when I get out, I can meet someone who's not locked up. Someone who's a 'better influence.' And that just made me mad."

"So you squealed on Adriana?" says Bianca. "Jolene, that's cold."

"That's not how it happened! I was getting worked up, and I just said, 'I wish my boyfriend was here, like Adriana's.'"

Silence. Then, of course, Monessa's the first to break it.

"Jolene, Jolene, Jolene, Joleeeen," croons Monessa, then gives a bitter, rueful laugh. "Talk about screwing the pooch! Can't unring *that* bell!"

"I knew it the second I said it. She tried to get more out of me, but I just kept saying I didn't want to talk about it."

Adriana wants to be furious at Jolene. Wants to call her every name in the book, but Jolene is already so hapless, Adriana doesn't have the heart to rip into her. But she's not going to tell her it's all right either.

"We've gotta kill this," Pip declares. "Break off contact with the boys, and forget this ever happened."

"No!" insists Adriana. "We can still make it work."

"How?" says Pip. "With Jameara all up in our business, how do we do anything?"

And then Monessa says, "I'll tell her it was me."

Adriana turns to her. "What do you mean?"

Monessa shrugs. "I'll tell her that I made up the story. She knows I don't like you. I'll tell Jameara I made it up to get you in trouble, and to torment Jolene. Two birds with one stone." Monessa thinks about it and nods. "Yeah, I can sell it. I've done shit like that before."

"It's gonna get you into trouble, 'Nessa," Bianca points out.

Again, Monessa shrugs. "I'll lose a couple of privileges for a couple of days. Maybe get lectured by Alvarado. I'll live."

They all consider it. Finally Pip says, "I'll still need to break off with my contact on the boys' side for a while. Just to be safe."

Adriana releases a shuddering breath of relief. Monessa just salvaged the whole operation.

"Monessa, I'm sorry I accused you," Adriana says.

"You better be sorry," Monessa replies. Then she adds, "But if I was you, I'd accuse me too."

◆ ◆ ◆

Adriana's journal isn't showing up, and Jon doesn't know why. It's tearing him apart, because his time is running out. That's the only thing he knows for sure. Because Morley's lit a fuse on his life, and he knows it's burning short. It's been over a week since he gave Jon his sleazy mission of misery. No telling how much patience the man has left. No telling how long till Morley detonates Jon's life and has him arrested for poisoning a kid he'd never lay a finger on.

And it's not even a matter of finding the guilty party anymore. Morley doesn't care. It's not even a blip on his radar. All he cares about is who he can extort. For all Jon knows, Morley did it himself, just to get Jon on a leash. Would the man do that? Or is he just an opportunistic shit who saw a way to use the Meerkat's suffering for his own personal benefit? Got to be the latter. But honestly, the world's so upside down, nothing seems out of the question anymore.

Jon's connection to Adriana is the only thing keeping him from spinning off into oblivion. And he knows she must never find out what he's about to do. Because yes, she might forgive him, but he'll never be able to look her in the face—and he wants to look her in the face. His whole life is leading up to seeing her face.

So she can't know what he's going to do to Knox.

He plans it all out before it happens, running it through his mind over and over.

He's going to catch Knox late in the afternoon, when he's coming down from his morning meds, and he's as cranky as a pit bull just itching to do something that'll get it euthanized.

He'll kick Knox behind the knee, like he did when he got him to drop Silas—but this time not hard enough to make Knox fall. He'll do it just hard enough to piss him off. It'll seem like a miscalculation on Jon's part, but it'll be a calculated miscalculation. Knox'll turn on him, already on the verge. Nucleic boiling: that's what it's called. Just little bubbles before the kettle starts to scream.

Then Jon will deny that it was him, even though it was obvious that it was, and it'll escalate. Next Jon will suggest that Knox and Culligan got a thing going, because he knows that Knox is a homophobic prick, so that will turn up the heat.

And when Knox starts shoving Jon around, which he will, Jon will deliver the nail into Knox's mental coffin.

Keep your paws off me, you inbred piece of shit.

Because you can't use the I-word with Knox. It's worse than any other word. Because it's true. Because his momma's also his sister, and he's full of all the messed-up mindfuck that goes with that. Some guys at Compass know it, and some don't—but it's an unspoken rule that stuff like that stays unspoken.

But Jon will speak it, making the kettle scream as Knox boils over.

And so, it's no surprise to Jon that when he puts his plan into action the following day, it goes exactly the way he thought it would. Moment to moment, beat by beat. Like clockwork. Like he had actually been seeing the future when he planned it.

It takes Rush, Wash, Garza, and a fourth guard Jon doesn't even know to restrain Knox—because when Knox really blows, he's got the strength of ten. They have to tase him, and still it's not enough. He bites Wash's hand like that aforementioned pit bull, drawing blood, but finally they get him under control and haul him away.

By that point Jon's not watching. He can't. Because he can't stand the fact that he destroyed Knox so that Morley wouldn't destroy Jon.

In the end, Morley gets what he wants. Knox gets sent to Hell Vista—although no one tells the boys directly because no one talks about boys who leave Compass, unless they win the Nobel Prize or something, which hasn't happened, but Luppino swears it could someday.

But even without official word, everyone knows Knox's fate—and everyone knows that Jon was responsible, and that only adds to his fierce reputation. But he doesn't want it to. His rep once meant something to him, but not anymore. If he could, he'd be as invisible as Myers now, because if he was, he could slip between the cracks in the walls all the way to Adriana, and every terrible thing he's ever done would be washed away. Even this.

And still the journal isn't back, and Myers's contact has gone all quiet.

I bought us some time, he wants to tell Adriana. *Don't ask me how, and don't ask me why I needed to. Just know that I did. But it's not forever, so if we're gonna do this, it's gotta be sooner than later. Not just because I can't wait, but because this place can't wait. The walls are squeezing me like that damn trash compactor on the Death Star. We have to pull the trigger on this while there's still one to pull.*

And it occurs to Jon that the Death Star trash compactor was on the detention level, wasn't it? Some things never change.

29

THE OSTRICH AND THE BEAGLE

Jon—So I wrote this story for Colter, my three-year-old half brother. Take a close look and tell me what you think.

> On May forty-seventh,
> Apollo Eleventh the beagle
> Set out for the moon.
> "Oh, the shine of the moon,"
> Apollo did croon,
> "This journey cannot come too soon."
>
> Sitting back on his haunches,
> The catapult launches,
> And into the heavens he soars.

His friends are ecstatic,
You could call them fanatic,
The meerkat, and the wild boar.

For his comrades all knew
This was a rendezvous,
With the ostrich who lived far away.
They said she was flightless,
But rocketed bright,
Less a few random feathers that day.

At half past Jupiter,
The walrus was stupider,
Than a Thanksgiving turkey in June.
He said, "That's preposterous,
A beagle and ost-er-ich
Trying to get to the moon."

Once the beagle had landed
The launch crew disbanded
And Apollo rose up from the dust
What did he lay eyes on,
On that far horizon?
The ostrich, completely nonplussed.

On that lunar surface,
They stuck to their purpose

Talking of things so profound
Then a little bit later,
In a cavernous crater,
They moonwalked around and around.

"Has something transpired?"
So rudely inquired
The clueless old Walrus and Turkey.
They tried to find out
What the fuss was about,
But the truth, to this day, remains murky.

Jon's thrilled when the journal finally turns up in the library, but when he first reads the entry, it's a huge WTF. It's such a weird disconnect from everything that has been going back and forth between himself and Adriana. It's the missing pages torn from the journal that make it all click. Someone has ripped out every page with incriminating evidence about their planned meeting. At first Jon thinks that someone else has gotten to it. Then he realizes that Adriana must have done it herself. But why?

Because maybe someone—some adult—is on to them? Or maybe just suspicious. So, she ripped out those pages to cover their asses!

Which means that this dumb little story is a code.

Anyone else who reads it would just dismiss it. But embedded in there is everything Jon needs to know.

Like "the *shine* of the *moon*" and "the *cavern*ous crater." Moonshine Cavern.

And all the animals—including the time he and Adriana bantered about her being an ostrich and him being more like a beagle than a bear!

Once he knew it was code, the rest started to fall into place.

"The forty-seventh of May would be June seventeenth, right?" Jon asked Myers, who was clearly the boar/bore.

"Sounds right," he said. I haven't heard from Pip about it. Maybe they decided getting the message through this way was safer than through Pip."

"But when on June seventeenth?"

It was Silas who figured that one out. "Half past Jupiter," he said. "Jupiter is the fifth planet. I think it means five thirty."

"In the morning?" says Jon.

"No—it's gotta be evening," says Myers. "It might be quiet at five thirty a.m., but that's a problem, because there won't be any chaos to cover it. Any activity that early in the morning will trigger a shitstorm. So they've gotta mean five thirty in the evening, when there's tons of things going on. Cameras full of kids moving around, guards occupied."

"Then six thirty would be better," says Jon. "The boys are finishing up dinner—the girls are moving around their pods and Rec Hub, and the guard shifts are getting ready to change."

"So," says the Meerkat, "that would be half past Saturn—funny, because that's also a Saturday, so the code has a double meaning—but we still don't know how we're gonna get you there."

And then a voice from behind them says, "Leave that to me."

It's Raz—who has clearly been eavesdropping on the entire

conversation. Jon feels guilty and worried at the same time.

"You don't even know what the hell we're talking about," says Jon.

"No, I don't—and I'm deeply offended, Jon, deeply offended."

Jon knows it was a bit of a betrayal to leave Raz out—but Raz shouldn't be surprised, considering how standoffish he's been.

"Maybe I just don't want to get you in trouble, Raz."

"S'what I live for," he says, and with a smile claps Jon on the shoulder. And just like that the tension between them is gone. "So . . . there's somewhere you want to get. And I take it you don't want no one to know."

"Yeah, pretty much."

Raz nods, considers it, then says, "I'll help make it happen. So . . . where do you need to be?"

Adriana,

. . . Uh . . . yeah . . . Don't know what to say. I see you ripped a few pages out, so I guess you tried several versions that were bad (or, should I say, even worse than the poem you actually wrote). I get that. Ripping pages out, I mean. Some things just aren't meant for human eyes, right?

Thing is, your logic kinda falls apart. I mean, a beagle is like a pet—it wouldn't be in a zoo, like an ostrich. And a meerkat and boar only go together if there's a lion involved—but that'd be too Disney. I do agree, though, that the walrus is a pretty stupid creature. So's the turkey, so you definitely got that right. Also those are a lot of big words to hurl at a three-year-old. Transpired. Inquired. And nonplussed? Really? I had to look that one up.

Don't know whether you want my opinion, or my support, so . . .

. . . I'll meet you halfway.

In other words, kudos for the effort. But don't quit your day job.

Sincerely,
Jon

P.S. Very important! It should be half past Saturn. (Cuz it fits with the pattern!)

There's a date. There's a time. All Adriana needs now is a method for this madness.

"This is really gonna happen," Bianca says, practically squealing with delight, when their group of conspirators is assembled in the girls' Rec Hub. Adriana, Bianca, Jolene, Monessa, and, of course, Pip, who's the grease in the gears of this clockwork. Jolene tries hard to regain everyone's trust after her slip to Jameara. And although Adriana still doesn't entirely trust Monessa, Bianca does. The fact that those two are acting like besties again makes Adriana more comfortable about it—because if Monessa screws up or sabotages this in any way, she'll lose Bianca's friendship. It's strong motivation for Monessa to do right by Adriana. She already lost rec privileges for two days, since taking the rap for spreading rumors about Adriana.

"You owe me," Monessa keeps saying. "Both you and Jolene." Adriana worries about how she'll want that score settled.

"From now until this happens, we can't be making waves," Pip tells them. "We have to do everything the way we always do, or we'll draw attention."

"What if making waves is what we always do?" asks Monessa.

"Just don't make any *new* waves," Adriana tells her.

Monessa considers it and shrugs. "Yeah, I can do that."

"We have two weeks," Pip reminds them. "That's plenty of time to make this happen."

Hard to believe that it's only two weeks standing between her and Jon. Well, that, and a whole lot of walls. Two weeks feels like forever as far as Adriana is concerned, and yet not nearly enough time to pull it off.

"We're gonna need a plan on both ends," says Pip. "Getting you there is only half of it. We're going to have to get you back."

Bianca nods. "Pip's right. One-way trip is only good if you're tryin' to break out. Not if you wanna end up back where you started."

Adriana shrugs. "I don't care about getting back."

Monessa scoffs at that, like it's all her own personal joke. "Yes, you do," she says. "Your ass gets caught where it's not supposed to be, and the clamp comes down on all of us."

"And," adds Pip, "it won't just be three days of isolation for you—more time'll get tacked onto your sentence."

Jolene gasps at the thought. "Can they do that?"

Pip turns to Adriana. "Do you want to find out?"

Adriana's silence is their answer.

"Right," says Pip. "So it's settled—we're going to need a two-way plan. Who's got ideas?"

When Jon was six, his mom took him to see a barbershop quartet, because her grandpa sang in one when she was a girl. Four guys of various ages and ethnicities wore matching red-striped jackets with white pants and sang old-fashioned music without a band or orchestra—because they didn't need one. They sounded like a human pipe organ. It was interesting for the first five minutes, then Jon was all about the ice cream his mom had promised once it was done. But it must have left an impression, because he remembered it—and thought about it whenever he was in a group that had to work together. No matter how hard it might seem, all it required was finding the right harmonies.

In their matching green uniforms, the four boys sitting at a game table in the boys' Rec Hub might be a barbershop quartet, but if one voice was off . . . it'd be curtains, like the old-timey gangsters used to say.

Meeting in the Hub is less conspicuous than in their little pod living room, since there's enough background activity to mask what they're doing. Plus, not everyone's from Jon's pod. Flots is involved now. His part is unclear, but he's loving the opportunity to be back in Jon's inner circle.

Raz, even though he's in on it, manages to find tasks that allow him to keep his distance. Maybe as a personal security measure. Right now, he's engaging with Wash, to keep him from being too curious about what's going on at the table. Bullshitting and distracting. Sleight of hand—that's Raz's forte. When he gets out, he oughta try to be a magician.

Jon looks up to the observation window. Every community place at Compass has one. Morley's not there. He's like a dragon who's feasted. Jon served him up Knox, and he's satisfied. For the time being. Viper isn't happy that his left wing has been clipped off. Now he's just got Culligan. And any glance at Jon is filled with daggers. Do they suspect Jon was working for Morley? If they find that out—if *anyone* finds that out, he's as good as dead. Nobody likes a snitch. Jon doesn't like a snitch. But Morley left him no choice. He only hopes Morley's done with him. But he doubts it.

Jon, Silas, Myers, and Flots sit with a board game between them: Ticket to Ride. But rather than a train map of the US, they're all looking at the map of Compass that Silas has drawn. He's gotten every detail, including positions of cameras, and the level of security clearance needed on different doors.

Myers points to various spots around the map. "All exits to the outside have multiple levels of security—such as air locks, guard stations, and metal detectors that'll probably flag the iron in your blood."

"Yeah, but Jon's not trying to break out," says Flots.

"Let me finish," says Myers, all business. "So that's exits.

And as you know, there are air locks to get in or out of the dormitories too."

"Yeah," says Silas, pointing at the marked doors in and out of the dorm pods and Rec Hubs. "Anyone without a level-A passkey has to be buzzed in from the security office—and only guards have those."

"Your point?" Jon asks Myers.

Myers waves his hand over the center of the map. "My point is that all the stuff in between has barely any security at all. The cafeteria, classrooms, library—just regular doors, and even when they're locked, they're not alarmed, because who cares if someone's going from the classroom to the library? The only areas they really have to control are the outside exits and the dorms."

"But there are cameras," Jon points out.

"The cameras are our friends."

"How?" Jon asks.

And Myers smiles. It may be the first time Jon—or anyone else, for that matter—has seen Myers smile. "Because people put too much trust in their own eyes."

Then Raz comes up to them. "Lose the map and roll some dice—Wash is making the rounds."

Sure enough, Wash is sauntering around the room, sticking his nose in everyone's business.

"This game don't have dice," says Flots.

But they get the idea. Silas folds up the map, and they all put little plastic trains on the game board. The game looks in full swing when Wash arrives.

"So who's winning?" Wash asks.

Everyone looks at one another like cars that got to a four-way stop simultaneously.

"I am," Flots finally says.

"Huh," says Wash. "The winner among losers. Good for you, Flots."

Jon's gotta bite his tongue to curb his own back talk. Wash can't even say something nice without saying something shitty too.

"Game's not over," says Silas. And, as the only one who actually knows how to play, he lays down three yellow cards and builds a three-sectioned train, making the game look legit.

"Hurry it up," says Wash. "You're hitting the showers in five, then back to your pods."

Wash saunters off, and they pretend to play for another couple of minutes. Raz watches, like he's actually interested in the nonexistent game.

"Y'know, I've been thinking," he says. "We find enough cash, Wash can prolly be bought. Then we'd have a guard on our side."

No one says anything for a second. Just look at one another. Jon glances over at Wash, sauntering around like the lone rooster in a henhouse. He's got his hand an inch from his Taser, like he's a gunslinger ready for his quick draw and just hoping for an excuse.

"Nope," says Jon. "Not worth the risk."

Raz is disappointed but doesn't push it. "Okay. Just a thought." Then everyone clears the board of trains and puts the game away.

It's as they're getting ready to line up that Myers takes Jon aside.

"You know he's not your friend, right?"

"Who, Wash? Yeah, tell me something I don't know."

"No," says Myers, in his quiet, stealthy way. "I mean Raz."

Jon shakes his head. "We may have our moments, but Raz has been solid from day one. It's thanks to him people leave me alone. He built my rep."

"You think that helps you? All it does is give him power. Makes him the lion tamer."

Jon shrugs. "So? That makes me the lion."

"Yes," agrees Myers. "But at the end of the day, it's the lion that stays in the cage."

TAKE A DEEP BREATH

Jon,

I want you to remember that no matter what happens, or doesn't happen, there's going to be a time after Compass. And even if you bounce from Compass to another place like it, there will be a time after that too. I know this feels like forever, but it's not. Just remember that. There's another side to every wall.

Adriana,

Yes, there's an "after" for you—and I know it's coming sooner than later. But for me, it's not a sure thing. Appeals take forever, and mostly don't amount to a damn thing. How can I even think about the day I get free, when I can't even imagine who I'll be then?

*I could be some sorry, shuffle-footed middle-aged dude,
with no prospects. Why would I even want to think
about that? I'd rather think about you.*

Adriana finds ticking off the days unbearable. Just over a week until her insane rendezvous with Jon. It's all she can think about—and there's a buzz now among the girls. Not just in her pod, but all the girls. Adriana has no idea how many of them know, but Pip does. Or at least Adriana hopes she does. Adriana has come to imagine Pip with a finger in every pie and an eye in every corner. Of course, Pip can't know everything, but it's comforting to imagine she does.

As for the machinations of the break, it has to be assembled like a fine watch. Items put in place, screws loosened and light bulbs unscrewed in key places; staff members outwitted; secret spaces in the ceilings and behind walls that must be accessed; and binding it all together, a script of perfectly timed, perfectly coordinated movements as choreographed as a ballet. She has no idea what's going on with the boys, and how they're moving mountains to get Jon to Moonshine Cavern next Saturday night, but it must be just as tricky.

And every instant, something threatens to give them away.

"This is so much fun!" Bianca bursts out randomly after discussing the plan—but it's at the absolute wrong moment. They're heading toward lunch in the main corridor, and Alvarado just happens to be passing in the other direction and hears Bianca's outburst. It draws his complete attention.

"So good to see you in high spirits, Bianca," he says. "What fun are you talking about, pray tell?"

And Bianca freezes, doing her finest impersonation of a deer in headlights. Adriana practically sees the red flags unfurling from the walls like banners.

It's Monessa who saves the moment.

"She's being sarcastic, Dr. Alvarado," she says. And just because she's Monessa, she adds, "All those degrees, and you still can't read sarcasm?"

He gives her a Cheshire grin that raises his walrus mustache into the letter *M*. "We might shrink heads, as they say, but we don't read minds, Monessa." Then he strides past, crisis averted.

"You have to be more careful," Adriana scolds Bianca in a loud whisper—but Pip is more level-headed about it.

"It's okay, Adriana—good moods don't cause problems. In fact, they might actually put the staff off guard, you know? False sense of security."

With less than a week to go, Adriana is so wrapped up in the planning that she's caught completely off guard herself when Jameara comes at the end of lunch on Sunday to collect her for a family visit.

"Did you forget?" Jameara asks, clocking her surprise.

"No, of course not," Adriana tells her. "I just thought it was later." Yeah, she totally forgot.

Jameara walks her to the visitation room with typical

Jameara conversation—asking her how she likes working at the library, and telling her how happy Ms. Detrick is with her performance. She says nothing about her previous accusation that Adriana was getting together with a boy. What's in the past is in the past. Or so Jameara thinks.

"I'm sure Ms. Detrick will be a nice reference for you for future employers," Jameara says.

Adriana wonders how a reference from a librarian at a juvenile detention center can do anything but scare potential employers away.

The visitation room is crowded today, or at least as crowded as they allow it: six families talking, playing games, and trying to make the most of their time together. Sitting patiently at a small table with two chairs is Lana, who stands and waves when she sees Adriana.

Just Lana?

"Hi, honey," she says. "Colter has a fever, so your dad stayed home with him. I hope you're not too disappointed."

It's very telling that her father chose to stay home, instead of coming to see his only daughter and letting Lana watch Colter. But you know what? That's okay. Like Jon said, her father's a broken man still putting the pieces together. In fact, Adriana isn't even annoyed by Lana today. She actually finds herself a little bit glad to see her. Lana makes the effort. She doesn't have to, but she does. That says something, right?

"You're looking good," Lana says.

"Yeah, the portions are small, so . . ."

"No, that's not what I mean. It's your eyes. They look . . . happy."

Is that so unusual? Adriana wonders. *Maybe it's because I'm in love.* Adriana actually laughs out loud at the thought, imagining how that might go over with Lana.

Lana smiles. "It's good to see you happy like this, Adriana. And it's just good to see you."

They chat for the whole twenty minutes—and even though their talk is just about ordinary, middling things, for once it doesn't feel forced or stilted.

"Just a few more months, and you come home," Lana reminds her. "I have a feeling that things are going to be so much better for you when you get out."

Maybe, thinks Adriana. But right now, that's the distant future. Right now, she can't think beyond next Saturday.

Jon,

You're right—let's not think about the future. And we're done dwelling on the past too. Let's just talk about now. Now isn't perfect, but it's what we've got. That, and the moon and the stars and the planets. Especially Saturn . . .

So let's take a deep breath . . . and here we go . . .

PART FIVE

THE BREAK

THE IRRESISTIBLE FORCE OF GRAVITY

SILAS: FIVE DAYS AND COUNTING

Silas knows that foiling cameras in a detention center is a tall order. Most security systems are designed by former hackers who have gone legit—so the only way to beat them is to be a better hacker. While Silas knows his way around a computer, he's not arrogant enough to think he can take Compass's security head-on. He knows he's going to have to come at it sideways. Find a weak link. And weak links are always of the human variety.

"You're not supposed to be here," says Ironside, the tech guru who runs Ops. Silas has just stepped out of a meeting with Luppino across the hall. He intentionally left Luppino's door open.

"I know, Mr. Schendorf, but I was hoping I might get assigned to you."

"There are no assignments in Ops." Then the man turns

his wheelchair just a fraction of a degree toward his console—
enough to indicate the conversation is over.

But Silas holds his ground at the threshold, speaking loudly.
Or at least loudly enough for Luppino to hear across the hall.

"I know there are no *official* assignments—but see, tech is my
thing, and it's the one thing we don't get to do here. No phones,
no games, nothing. And the computers we *do* get to use are like
a hundred years old, and aren't good for anything."

Ironside gives him a not-my-problem glare. "Well, maybe
you shoulda thought of that before you did whatever it was that
landed you here."

"I didn't *do* anything, Mr. Schendorf."

Ironside chuckles at that. "Yeah, yeah, everyone here's innocent."

"But in Silas's case it's true," says Luppino. At last! Luppino
to the rescue! "Silas is CPS overflow."

That gives Ironside pause for thought. "What, so Child Protective Services just dumps him here?"

Luppino sighs. "It's not an optimal situation."

Ironside rotates his chair a bit, opening his stance. It's amazing how a tiny shift in position can make the man more friendly
than closed off. "Jeez, sorry, kid. Real sorry."

Silas turns his attention to Luppino. "I don't have a debt to
society, Mr. Luppino, but everyone here has a chore except for
me. Why can't I get assigned to something I want to do?"

"Isn't there anything he can do for you, Ray?" asks Luppino,
"It's just an hour, a few times a week."

Schendorf looks around the space full of servers and wires. In the corner are some gutted computers and a teetering pile of overstuffed folders. Definitely a fire hazard.

"That stack of old files needs to be keyed in," suggests Schendorf.

"I can do that!"

"Fine. But I'm not babysitting. And the second I don't have anything for him to do, I dump him in your office."

"Fair enough," says Luppino.

"Thank you, Mr. Schendorf!"

"You're welcome, kid. And call me Ironside—everyone does."

By the second day, Ironside has warmed up to Silas, and they're talking RPGs and Xbox cheats. By day three, Silas gets his own low-security login. And by day four, when Ironside is in the bathroom, Silas upgrades his access and creates a secret login name that gives himself full system administrator privileges.

GIRLS' SHOWER DETAIL: FOUR DAYS AND COUNTING

Mysti and Marisol have shower detail. They work as a team, even when they're doing stuff that isn't exactly legit. Such as unscrewing the vent above the third shower stall. It's not easy—the screws are mostly rusted, and they don't have a screwdriver, just a dime that's been filed down on two edges, so it kind of looks like a mini *Millennium Falcon*. But in the end, it does the job.

Marisol does the unscrewing, then stands below, boosting Mysti up into the vent, then keeping watch. It has to be Mysti in the vent, because she's the smaller of the two—and you never know how much weight an air duct can take. Even Mysti might rupture the thing and go crashing through the ceiling. There'd be no walking *that* back.

"What you're doing is a proof of concept," Pip told her. Mysti doesn't know all the details—only that it's about a girl who's trying to meet a boy. Pip had her at *boy*, because Mysti is a hopeless romantic. She's more than happy to be a conduit for true love. Or at least crawl through love's conduit.

Mysti's quick to discover two things about air ducts: A) they are nowhere near as spacious as they appear in the movies when people climb through them, and B) they're nowhere near as clean, either. The dust caked in there is as thick as dryer lint. So thick that it doesn't just make you sneeze, it makes you gag. Mysti feels like a chimney sweep from *Mary Poppins* times, using her body instead of a brush.

The map she was shown was correct; after three vents, she comes to a junction. A left turn, and two vents later, she finds herself looking down on the laundry room. Of course, that vent is still screwed shut from the other side—but that's not Mysti's concern. Her job is just to make sure that this leg of the journey is even possible.

Getting back to the showers, however, is its own challenge. There's no turning around in the narrow vent, so she has to shimmy backward all the way.

"Hurry up!" she hears Marisol calling. "We're almost out of time!"

Finally, she negotiates the turn at the junction, and reverse-shimmies her way back to where she started. Although Marisol helps her, lowering herself out of the vent is scarier than climbing into it. Finally, she comes out, with a shower of dust bunnies that are evolving into higher forms of life—possibly carnivorous.

"Ugh! Yuck," says Marisol, trying to brush the bunnies off Mysti with limited success. "So you made it?"

"Obviously. C'mon, let's finish cleaning the showers before they wonder why it's taking us so long."

Although Pip didn't tell them who their "proof of concept" was for, they're excited nonetheless. Sneaking through the vents of Compass? What isn't to love?

THE LIBRARY: THREE DAYS AND COUNTING

Melanie Detrick loves her job. Books can sometimes be the only respite from Compass that these kids have, and she sees it as her mission to help them with that particular sort of escape. But there are days when she wonders what these kids are thinking.

"Ms. Detrick, you need to look at this . . ."

She doesn't like the sound of Adriana's voice. What fresh hell could this be? A dead animal in the stacks? Another leak, ruining an entire case of books? When Melanie arrives in the fiction section with Adriana, she sees Bianca Viera, beaming with pride as she stands before a section of books that looks much prettier than it should.

"Bianca, what did you do?"

"I did what should have been done a long time ago," Bianca explains. "I arranged the fiction section by color! See how nice it looks?"

"You can't do that! How will anyone find anything?"

Bianca drops her shoulders in exasperation. "You're missing the point, Ms. Detrick. This is how it's done these days—just look at TikTok!"

"Those are people's *personal* libraries, Bianca, not lending libraries."

Bianca shrugs. "This is the only library I got."

Melanie takes one more look at the shelves and shakes her head. "They've all got to be put back."

Bianca is horrified. "Seriously? After all the work I put in?"

Then Adriana steps in. "I'll do it, Ms. Detrick."

But Melanie stops her. "No, Adriana, this shouldn't be your responsibility." Then she glances back at the checkout counter to see none other than Monessa Williams standing there, behind the counter. The girls know they're not supposed to go around to that side—but Monessa has never met a rule she didn't break.

"Hey! What are you doing back there?"

Monessa shrugs like it's nothing. "Checking a book out. Since there's no one here to do it, I'm doing it myself."

"Just wait, I'll be there in a minute."

"Well, hurry up—I ain't got all day. You wanna move these books or not?"

Melanie blows a tuft of hair out of her face. "Bianca, this is all on you. Alphabetical by author's last name. Get to it!"

"Some thanks I get for trying to be helpful!"

Melanie Detrick gets back to the counter and checks out Monessa's book. As for the single piece of official Compass stationery that Monessa pinched from a drawer while the librarian was distracted, no one will miss it.

BOYS' LAUNDRY DETAIL: TWO DAYS AND COUNTING

"Just what the hell are you doing up there?"

Matthew Mallett, a kid with more ideas than his brain has room for, stands on top of one of the industrial dryers with a handful of wet shirts. He looks down at Rush, who's toward the end of his shift and on his last nerve.

"I was gonna hang these shirts on the vent, on accounta we already started all the dryers, and these got left out—so I figured—"

"Do us all a favor, Mallett, and don't figure," says Rush. "Figuring is not on your list of personal skills."

"But they'll dry good here on accounta the airflow from the vent!"

"I got your airflow right here," says another kid, and rips a fart of biblical proportions, eliciting groans from around the room.

Rush sighs and takes a healthy step away. "Retirement can't come soon enough."

"We love you, too, Rush," says one of the other kids on laundry duty.

Rush turns back to Mallet, who's still standing on the dryer, trying to hang the shirts. "Just get down from there before you break your neck and I gotta fill out an accident report."

"Fine," says Mallett. "But don't blame me if these shirts get all moldy 'n' shit."

"May moldy shirts be the worst of your problems."

Mallett comes down, holding the wet shirts in his right hand . . . and hiding screws from the laundry room vent in his left.

PIP: ONE DAY AND COUNTING

On the way back from the last class of the day, Pip brings up the rear. It's clear to everyone she's having a bad day, coughing and wheezing and struggling to breathe. Usually Jolene hangs back with her when she's having trouble, matching her pace, keeping her company—but not today.

Unlike the boys, the girls don't have a guard bringing up the rear of every line. They think there's less aggression among the girls. Not true. The aggression is there, just much more subtle.

So Pip is by herself, falling far behind the rest of the line.

No one sees her slip and fall on the freshly waxed floor. But they hear her scream of pain echoing down the corridor. Up ahead some of the girls turn back and break formation to hurry toward her, but Bonivich yells at them to freeze in place, and marches back to Pip, already on her radio, calling for assistance.

Crying, her face red with embarrassment, Pip struggles to get up, but grimaces and wails again. "I think it's my ankle."

Bonivich kneels, tries to calm her down, but comfort is not

336

the woman's strong point. "Don't move," she tells Pip. "The nurse is on her way."

Approaching footsteps. The nurse and an aide hurry down the hallway. Girls begin to gather, and Bonivich warns them back into line.

"I think I'm okay," says Pip.

"Are you sure?" says the nurse. "Do you need your inhaler?"

"No," insists Pip. "It's my ankle, not my lungs."

The nurse and aide grab her gingerly and try to lift her, and although Pip is light, she's in an awkward position for lifting—so the nurse turns to Bonivich. "Scarlet, some help here?"

"Your name's Scarlet? Seriously?" says Pip.

"Don't start," Bonivich grumbles as she helps lift Pip to her feet.

With the three women around her, Pip puts weight on her ankle, takes a step, then puts more weight on it. Walking gingerly, she makes her way to the other girls, and the girls in line begin applauding, like she's a soccer player getting up after an injury on the field.

"I'm good now," Pip tells the three women. "Thanks."

Bonivich returns to the front of the line, getting back to the business of being a guard. As for the nurse and aide, they head back the way they came, the aide never noticing that Pip has swiped her security badge.

CAFETERIA: 6:00 P.M., DAY OF

"You know what you have to do," Myers whispers to half a dozen kids in the cafeteria. Just a handful of operatives. Wouldn't do to get any more involved. In his unobserved, quiet way, Myers handpicked kids for this particular aspect of the plan. Kids without much creativity or a desire to impress. Kids like him— because boisterous types and overachievers are not welcome in this gig.

"So, why are we doing this, anyway?" one of them asks.

"Tell you later." Meaning he's not gonna tell them at all. If they hear from other sources, that's fine, but he's got to be Teflon to these kids. Nothing that can stick to him from all of this.

"We don't need anything major," Myers tells them. "Just be your normal piggy, slobby selves."

No one takes offense to that. Maybe because the kids he chose are well-known slobs, and, if not proud of it, then at least resigned.

Six kids, at random spots around the crowded cafeteria. Throughout dinner they do their damage: a dumped plate here, a spilled drink there. Chili splattered next to the trash, instead of inside it. And one masterful kid who decided it was his job to spread the others' messes by walking in them and tracking them all over the floor. None of it drew the guards, though— because it was stealth slobbery.

When it's time to line up, the mess is one step short of epic.

Wash looks at it and shakes his head. "Youse are all a bunch of animals," he grumbles. "Cleanup team's gonna be here half the night."

Which is precisely the point.

◆ ◆ ◆

338

Kid's name is Crow. Known to those who know him, nonexistent to those who don't. Just like everyone else at Compass. One claim to fame: his hook shot. Can't do a layup or free throw for shit. But that hook shot—he sinks it every time, nothing but net. Except there's no net, just naked hoop. Compass denies them the satisfaction of a swish. Another one of its small cruelties.

But today's mission has nothing to do with the basketball court. Today's field of play is the cafeteria bathroom. Crow's mission is odd, and specific. He has no idea why he's gotta do it; all he knows is that it's needed. And that it's for Jon Kilgore—a guy he both admires and fears. He's never been in Jon's circle, always at least two degrees away. Not even sure Jon knows his name. But maybe now he will.

At six twenty, just as dinner's winding down, Crow goes to the bathroom. The big kid everyone calls Flots stands there, guarding the bathroom door. Conspicuously inconspicuous.

"You the guy?" Flots asks.

"I'm the guy," Crow says.

"Then get the hell in there."

Crow slips into the bathroom and finds the little package wedged up underneath the second sink, just like it's supposed to be. He's dying to know the big picture of all this, but he's not going to, because "All information is on a need-to-know basis," Myers told him. Want-to-know doesn't count.

In the cafeteria, the boys are starting to line up to be led back to the dorms. But then the bathroom door opens, and in

339

walks the man himself. Jon Kilgore. Serial killer, or terrorist, or whatever the hell he is.

"Hi, Jon. I'm Crow."

"Solid name," Jon says. "You all set?"

"Yeah."

"Then do what you gotta do."

Crow looks in the bag, pulls out a device that he's not supposed to have. Not because it's particularly dangerous, but because they're not supposed to have anything that has even the slightest potential for being a weapon.

"Sit on the john so I don't have to reach," says Crow. "This'll just take a sec."

6:25 P.M.

Toombs hates the fact that Compass doesn't leave room for self-expression. Everyone wears the same lime-green shirts and beige pants. The same no-name shoes. And there are no baseball caps, because things can be hidden in them. And besides, caps can signal gang affiliations—if not by color (since everything's freaking green), then by how you wear them.

But they can't control what he does with his body. That's why Toombs shaves his head. Not every seventeen-year-old can rock a chrome, but Toombs doesn't only rock it, he owns it. He's Black, so they let him do it. White guys with shaved heads means a whole other thing. Forbidden at Compass. Sometimes when Toombs is feeling particularly bold, he'll look at those wannabe skinheads and run a hand over his clean-shaven head, just to piss them off.

Today he's not entirely clean-shaven. They let him do that only once a week, and it's been four days, so he's got a faint dark fuzz. He can always tell the day of the week by the feel of his head.

Ulices Toombs has got a critical part in today's event. He doesn't really know the details—all he knows for sure is that it's fucking with Compass, and anything that does that is his kind of extracurricular activity.

He was chosen because of his assigned job at Compass, and because he bears a passing resemblance to Jon Kilgore, and because of his hair, or lack thereof. Toombs is on the cafeteria cleanup team. He's one of five kids who hang back when everyone else has left, and spends as long as it takes to clean up the messes everyone else leaves behind. On a good day it takes half an hour. On a bad day a whole lot longer.

At exactly 6:25, he heads for the cafeteria bathroom.

"You the guy?" Flots asks as he approaches.

"I'm the guy," he says, and Flots steps aside and lets him in.

When Toombs steps into the bathroom, the first thing he sees is another Black kid with a shaved head looking back at him. A kid whose head isn't normally shaved.

"That you, Kilgore?"

"Was," Kilgore says. "Now that honor belongs to you."

Another kid in there is gathering clumps of shorn hair from the floor and setting them on the sink next to electric hair clippers that have already done their job. Then the kid grabs a roll of double-stick tape.

"Hold still," says the kid with the tape, and starts applying it, strip by strip to Toombs's head until it forms a sticky shell. Toombs knows it's gonna hurt like hell when he's gotta peel it off, but that's a problem for later. Once his head's all taped up, the kid starts pressing clumps of shorn curls to it. Kilgore's shorn curls. Some stick, some fall off, but he keeps on going until all the tape is covered.

Toombs glances in the mirror. It doesn't look very good at all. Looks like a bunch of hair taped to his head. But when he squints, it almost looks real.

"You sure this is gonna work?"

"Of course it is," Kilgore says. "Crow's a goddamn artist."

6:27 P.M.

Malachi Soule stands in line but keeps an eye on the bathroom. Flots, who has been standing in front of the bathroom door all this time, has just been ordered into line by Wash, who's bringing up the back of the line today, with Rush at the front.

Malachi waits and watches. Any second Rush and Wash will start marching them back to the dorms—but before that can happen, a kid comes out of the bathroom with—wait—what the hell is going on with his hair? Not Mal's problem. All he knows is that he's supposed to create a distraction the second that kid comes out of the bathroom.

So Mal turns to the dude beside him in line, kicks his legs out from under him, and knocks him to the ground. Blaze—the

342

kid on the ground—is not in on this, which is good, because his reaction is authentic. He yells and makes a commotion, which draws Wash over.

"What the hell is going on here?"

"He tripped me!" Blaze says.

"It was an accident," says Mal.

"Like hell it was!" yells Blaze.

"Enough! This ends now!" says Wash, and although Blaze isn't happy, he lets it go.

By the time Wash is done with them, Rush has begun the march to the dorms, and the bad-hair kid is just another walking stiff in line. Wash does the count as they go by—every kid except for the ones on cleanup duty—but he's not looking at faces, and just because he's counting heads doesn't mean he's noticing much about them. For all Wash cares, it could be the king of England going by, as long as the count is right.

GIRLS' SHOWERS: 6:28 P.M.

Mysti and Marisol are in the showers again, doing their regular cleanup. Finally the door opens and a girl steps in. Although Pip didn't tell them who it would be, Mysti recognizes her.

"You're Adriana, right?"

Adriana shrugs. "Yep, that's me!"

Mysti nods and wonders which boy she's trying to meet—but knows better than to ask. Pip will tell them later.

"This way," Marisol says, and the two lead Adriana to the third shower stall, and the vent up above, which they've already

343

unscrewed again with their pocket *Millennium Falcon*.

Together, they give Adriana a boost up to the vent. Adriana's a bit bigger than Mysti, and Mysti hopes she won't get stuck in the narrow duct. That would be bad on *so* many levels.

"Hey," says Mysti with a smile, before Adriana disappears into the vent. "You should thank me—I cleaned out all the dust for you!"

GIRLS' LAUNDRY DETAIL: 6:36 P.M.

Jolene doesn't mind laundry duty. Yeah, it's monotonous, and the laundry room is annoyingly hot and humid, but it's better than some of the other chores. She'd rather do this than clean bathrooms, because, contrary to popular opinion, girls can be every bit as gross as guys. Especially when it's someone else's job to clean up after you.

Jolene can't pretend she's not nervous. After having almost ruined this whole thing already, she doesn't want to be responsible for it going wrong now. All three of the girls on laundry duty are in on it too.

There's no supervision on laundry detail, but they are under surveillance. Bonivich, or any number of guards, are just a camera's glance away.

Saturdays are sheets and towels. The boys wash and dry earlier in the day, then the girls fold and deliver. Most other detention centers have linens done by professional services, but not Compass. Compass prides itself on complete self-sufficiency. And besides, it's probably cheaper to have the kids

344

do it. It's always about money.

Adriana shows at 6:36—a few minutes later than she's supposed to. Jolene hears her first. A creaking in the ceiling above them, then Adriana's face appears behind the grate of the vent. Jolene knew this was coming, but still, it nearly gives her a heart attack, because now this is real. Now it's all up to her and the other girls on laundry detail.

"Sabrina," calls Jolene, her voice way too shaky. "Can you help me fold this sheet?"

"Yes, Jolene," says Sabrina. "Yes, I will help you fold that sheet."

Jolene rolls her eyes. Sabrina isn't winning any Oscars for her performance today. Jolene knows that the camera has a mic, but she also suspects whoever's on surveillance duty has to punch in, in order to listen—otherwise every cam in Compass would be blasting at the surveillance guards constantly. So it's important not to give them a reason to want to listen—because if whoever's on the other side of that camera starts wondering why the girls are acting like there's an elephant in the room, all eyes and ears will be on them.

Sabrina and Jolene position themselves on their marks and stretch the sheet out, first horizontally, then turn it vertical . . .

. . . which just happens to block the camera's view of the vent.

And behind the sheet, the third girl, Letty, pushes a bin full of unfolded sheets beneath the opening.

While Sabrina and Jolene make a big show of trying to shake the sheet smooth, Adriana punches the unscrewed vent screen

345

loose, and it falls into the bin. Letty quickly removes it, and Adriana drops down into the bin of sheets with such force that it snaps off one of the bin's wheels, and it shoots across the room.

Sabrina flinches and very nearly drops the sheet.

"Hold still!" says Jolene. "Now fold it in half."

"Which should I do?" asks Sabrina in a near panic. "Hold still or fold it in half?"

Meanwhile, behind them, Adriana climbs out of the bin.

"First hold still. Then fold it in half."

They wait for a beat, then in unison, they fold the sheet over, making sure it's still hiding the bin from the camera. Initially Adriana had suggested that they hide her in the bin, and wheel her to the next stop on her journey, but Jolene knew that was a nonstarter; the clean laundry bins are always checked by a guard before they even get out the door—although they're looking for contraband, not stowaways. Their best bet will be to hide Adriana in the laundry room until everyone leaves. And so, still obscured by the partially folded sheet, Letty helps Adriana into one of the empty dryers, closing the door, but not enough for it to latch.

Jolene heaves a sigh of relief that looks an awful lot like a sigh of exasperation. "You know what? Just drop the sheet," she tells Sabrina. "I'll take it from here."

"Okay, I'll drop the sheet so you can take it from here," repeats Sabrina, like a self-conscious robot—but forgets to actually tell her fingers to let go. So Jolene tugs the sheet out of Sabrina's hands, and it flutters down, making Jolene feel like a magician

346

revealing that the elephant behind the sheet has disappeared. If there was an audience, they'd be cheering.

KITCHEN: 6:36 P.M.

Dorella shuts down the warming trays as the boys head back to their dorms, revealing more crap left behind on the cafeteria floor than usual. She sighs. Not her problem. Whatever malfeasance occurs on the other side of the service counter, it's someone else's concern—although she worries the boys will be ridden too hard about it. Rush is okay, but some of these other guards are nothing but bullies with permission.

She'd like to say her day is over, but it won't be until she and the two other food service workers have cleaned up the kitchen. That's not a job they allow kids to do. Food prep surfaces and food handling has to be done by staff. It's a health code thing. It doesn't help being short staffed as they always are. Half the time Dorella has to work twelve-hour shifts. Breakfast, lunch, and dinner. Sometimes she feels as incarcerated as the kids she serves. Maybe that's why she gets along with some of them so well.

Out in the cafeteria, cafeteria-duty boys work picking up trash, cleaning tables, and mopping the floor. Officer Garza waits for them out in the hallway, wanting no part of it. As long as they don't start ripping each other's faces off, he's happy to sit in the hallway playing phone games or whatever the hell else these guys do when there are no heads to crack.

No, Dorella does not have a high opinion of detention

347

guards. She dated one once. Big mistake. So, yeah, she's a little bit biased.

Dorella drains the hot water from beneath the warming trays, then picks up the half-full pans, assessing what should be done with the remains of dinner. Some of it will go into the trash, some of it gets recycled into tomorrow's meals. It's all predetermined by a set menu—but Dorella can overrule it if the day's dregs are too miserable to save. While she works with the leftovers, her two coworkers steam clean the stainless steel food prep counter. The hiss is always so loud, Dorella's sure it's killed the high end of her hearing. Then, when she looks up, she sees Ulices Toombs, with his big old shaved head, coming into the kitchen from the cafeteria.

"You're not supposed to be here, Toombs," she tells him. "Get back to cleaning the Cafeteria."

He comes into the light, and Dorella realizes this isn't Toombs at all—but can't yet get a bead on who it is. He comes close enough to speak quietly and still be heard over the screeching pressure cleaners.

"It's not Toombs, Dorella—it's me."

It takes a moment for her to recognize him beneath the unexpectedly shaved head. Jon Kilgore. But his eyes aren't their usual shade of cool. Today his expression is a cocktail that's one part determination, one part excitement, and two parts utter panic.

"Jon? What are you—" and she catches herself, realizing what's going on. So this is it; this is his play for Adriana. She has no idea what they've planned and doesn't want to know. Frankly she's amazed that he's made it this far.

So, should she let this happen? She could end it now if she wanted to. Call in the guard and shut the whole thing down—probably better for everyone in the long run. But these kids don't have the luxury of long runs. All they've got is one moment after another after another. Why shouldn't they grab a good one when it might be the only decent moment they'll have for the foreseeable future? And besides, the assholes running Compass don't pay her enough to blow the whistle on a kid like Jon Kilgore.

"Dorella, I need your help. You know what I'm talking about."

Yes, she does. She already gave him that big old lobster tail, hinting she'd help. Cost her too. She glances at her coworkers, who are both facing the other way, deafened by their work, oblivious to the intrigue going on behind their backs. Then one of them glances in their direction—but Dorella's quick. She knows exactly what to say.

"Toombs," she says, "do me a favor—go down to food storage and bring up a bag of rice."

Her coworker hears that and turns away, probably grateful that she didn't send him. Those damn bags are heavy.

COMPASS SURVEILLANCE CENTER: 6:38 P.M.

At any given time, there are two guards on duty in the surveillance room. With over seventy cameras to monitor, it would take more than two to have eyes on every nook and cranny of

Compass, but that's not needed, because it's a smart system. Only critical cameras are constantly monitored: high-traffic areas, as well as all entrances and egresses from the facility. The rest are motion sensitive, only coming on if something moves within their field of vision.

Monitoring surveillance is like being an anesthesiologist. Ninety-nine percent boredom, one percent absolute panic. But luckily, it's been mostly boredom since last month's lockdown. Not that anyone's complaining.

The guards on surveillance duty today are Officers Pam Ko and Filip Fragoso, who eat dinner while monitoring the many screens before them. The boys are marching back to the dorms. The girls are lining up for their evening roll call. All typical. Although Ko and Fragoso are trained to keep their eyes on the screens at all times, it's kind of like driving on an empty highway. When there's nothing out of the ordinary to see, you can multitask.

"You want half this meatball?" Ko says. She holds half of a cold Subway sandwich up to Fragoso. "It's too much for me."

"Since when has a foot-long been too much for you?" Fragoso says.

"Hey, watch it," says Ko, "or I'll nail your ass for harassment."

Fragoso begins to stutter and bluster. "No . . . I didn't—that's not what I meant," he blurts." I wasn't suggesting—"

Ko cracks up at Fragoso's reaction. "Just watch the Boy Scout squirm!" she says. "You're like an ant under a magnifying glass—I swear, it's too easy!"

"You're evil, Pam."

"Don't I know it!"

Suddenly an alert pops up on the main screen, while on a secondary screen, an image labeled "Boys' Tunnel #1" comes on. An indicator light says there's movement, but the image shows nothing. Just a tunnel with four doors.

"Someone down there?" asks Ko.

"Doesn't look like it," says Fragoso.

The indicator light still blinks, suggesting that something's moving in the tunnel—but it doesn't register on camera. Just four closed doors and an empty corridor.

"Maybe it's a rat," suggests Ko, but Fragoso shakes his head.

"If it was a rat, we'd see it."

"So maybe a bug on the sensor."

"Maybe . . . but . . ."

Fragoso can't help but feel there's something off about this, but he can't put his finger on it. "Maybe we should send someone down there."

"Just wait a bit," says Ko.

They both watch the empty hallway for a few seconds, until the motion light stops blinking and the camera goes off.

"You see? Just a spider or something."

"Or a glitch," says Fragoso.

"Fine—you want to complain to Schendorf tomorrow, be my guest." But they both know they're not going to do that. Because Ironside takes every complaint as a personal attack. Neither of them needs the grief.

Of course, if Fragoso were to take a few more moments to think about it, he might realize that there were more doors than there should have been and that they weren't looking at Boys' Tunnel #1 at all—they were seeing the lower administrative hallway. Which means someone in Ops with administrative access switched the feeds. A herd of cattle could be stampeding down Boys' Tunnel #1, and they wouldn't know it.

"So do you want this sandwich or not?" Ko asks. Fragoso finally takes it.

ADRIANA

The dryer is still hot. Stifling. As if Adriana wasn't sweating enough, now she's going to be a literal hot mess by the time she gets to Jon. So much for first impressions.

But the important thing is that she *will* get to him! She's more than halfway there now! It's 6:40, and Bonivich comes to collect the laundry crew right on schedule.

"Let's go, ladies, you should have been ready to roll by now."

They finish packing the bins with sheets and towels—but before rolling them out, they have to switch out the bin with the broken wheel.

"Couldn't you have taken care of that already?" complains Bonivich. "Let's move it!"

Bonivich is right there. If she turns to the dryer, she'll see Adriana on the other side of the glass, like someone looking in from a portal in space. All she can do is hope the woman's back stays turned. Adriana's head is pounding from the heat, so she starts counting to keep her thoughts focused, and her heart from racing. She can withstand this. She *has* to withstand it. Ten seconds. Twenty. Thirty. A full minute. It's only a stroke of luck that Bonivich doesn't turn her way while the broken bin is switched out.

Finally, the girls are done, and Bonivich escorts them out and turns off all the lights. Adriana hears the laundry room door close. Darkness. She waits another ten seconds, then kicks the glass dryer door.

It doesn't open.

She kicks harder. Still, nothing.

She has a moment of panic thinking that the door did latch after all, and that she'll die of heat stroke in here. She leans back, getting better leverage, and kicks again. This time the door gives, swinging wide open and letting in a rush of cooler air.

She climbs out of the dryer into the dark room. It's not just dark, it's pitch-black—because one of the girls unscrewed the bulb in the exit sign. It's critical that the room be absolutely lightless, because according to Pip, the motion sensor in the laundry room isn't infrared. In a room that's always hot, a heat sensor would be useless, so the one in there is old-school, relying on light. But even the tiniest bit will be enough to activate it.

Part of Jolene's job was to clear a path for Adriana to the door, so she can make her way through the dark without obstacles. Adriana orients herself and begins to move slowly through the darkness, her hands in front of her—but just a few steps out, she reaches to her waist to find the ID card—the one Pip swiped from the nurse's aide—is not there.

No no no no!

But she settles herself. She panicked in the dryer. She will not let that happen again. She doesn't have the luxury. She holds still in the darkness, running the last few minutes through her mind. She had it tucked in her bra when she was in the vent— she checked. So it's got to be here somewhere.

Unless it fell out in the bin, got transferred with the sheets, and is long gone.

Turning slowly, she makes her way back to the dryer and reaches inside. Fearing the worst, expecting the worst, and finding—

The ID badge. It's there inside the dryer drum.

She has to suck in a deep breath of relief. How stupid to come this far and fail because she lost the key card. Adriana turns and resumes her journey across the dark laundry room. It feels like forever. It feels like she's crossing the distance between galaxies. Until finally she reaches a wall. She slides her hands to the left until finding the edge of the door, and slowly side-shuffles to the knob.

The instant she opens the door, there'll be light pouring in from the hallway, and that will activate the camera. But the camera is positioned above the door—so as long as she gets out quickly enough, and gets that door closed, the guards on surveillance won't see her—they might not even see the door closing—just a dark room. They may send someone to check why

354

the room is so dark, but by then, she'll be long gone.

As for the cameras in the hallway, the boys worked some magic with them, but couldn't do it for the laundry room camera without raising a red flag. So, in theory, once she's out of the laundry room, all should be good.

In a silent count of three, she opens the door, darts into the hallway, and closes it quickly behind her. Instinctively she looks to the hallway camera that's right there across the hall, looking right at her. Its red light is blinking to show it registers her motion . . . but the "on" light never illuminates. Jon's friends totally confused those cameras!

To the right, a few yards down the hallway, there's a locked door she's seen before. It's the only locked door she has to face. The only one that requires a key card to open—and although it says "Authorized Access Only," it's really just a low-security door. Meaning that the nurse's aide's ID badge should be able to open it. *Should.* Of course, if the aide reported it missing and it was deactivated, that would be that. How horrible it would be to come this far and be stopped by a bad key.

She holds her breath, swipes the card . . .

. . . and miraculously the door unlatches without the slightest bit of drama.

Inside is a musty, narrow, concrete accessway filled with blue and white PVC electrical conduits, hot and cold water pipes dripping condensation, and a dark red sewer pipe. This is the stuff behind walls. Compass's circulatory system. Its bowels. She remembers the poem she wrote about Compass being a

355

living entity. If it is, does it feel her moving through its guts? Is it malevolent, she wonders, or is it indifferent? Or is its personality defined by those who inhabit it? Those who run it?

The utility accessway feels forlorn and forgotten. Nobody comes in here but the facility engineer, and probably only when there's a problem. She suspects most of the staff at Compass don't even know this place exists—but Pip knew.

About twenty yards along, there's a catwalk that leads to a ladder that goes down a hatch into darkness, where the concrete gives way to the brick of an old foundation. A structure that was here before Compass was built. While everything else in the utility accessway is marked with either a sign, symbol, or warning, nothing marks that ladder down into darkness. Pip certainly never went down there—but according to the map that the boys cobbled together, this exact spot should be right above the far end of Moonshine Cavern. And the cavern has a back door.

But what if it doesn't lead there? What if it leads to nowhere? Or worse, what if it's some rat-infested pit?

Adriana hasn't come this far to be scared off by the unknown. Trying not to overthink it, she descends the ladder into darkness to find whatever she'll find.

JON

Whatever Silas did in Ops with the cameras, it must have worked, because when he stepped out from food storage into Boys' Tunnel #1, the cameras didn't come on. Now he stands at the door to the old pre-Compass stairwell that leads down to Moonshine Cavern. He can't believe he's here! That he made it this far! So many things could have gone wrong along the way—but when the universe is on your side, anything is possible, and the universe is clearly on his and Adriana's side tonight.

Just one final door.

It's not a high-security door, but it still has a lock and a sensor. Everything comes down to Raz now. His critical part in all of this. This final door is the true test of Raz's loyalty—because he's the one who rigged it.

"I got a trick," Raz told Jon. "It's the trick that landed me in Compass to begin with—well, that and the stuff I took—but it works like a charm when you don't get caught."

The trick involved a steel wool scouring pad that Raz had picked out of the kitchen trash when none of the cafeteria workers were looking.

"I'll shove the steel wool into the door jamb when we go down to work in the cavern," Raz had told him the week before. "So when the door closes, the lock won't engage—but the steel wool will complete the sensor circuit. All you'll have to do is jiggle the handle, and the door will open. They'll get an alert in the surveillance room—but get the door closed quick enough, and they'll think it's just another glitch—especially if the cameras don't show nothing."

Turns out that Raz came through! Because it barely takes any jiggling at all to open that door. Jon pulls it closed quick and descends the old stairwell, feeling like his heart is rising into his Adam's apple.

And here he is. Standing in Moonshine Cavern. Alone.

But maybe he's not alone.

He takes a deep breath and turns on the lights.

32

WHERE YOU END, AND WHERE I BEGIN

If the walls of Compass could put words to paper, Moonshine Cavern would spill out volumes tonight. Each piece of cracked, aged concrete, each pillar holding up the world above, every eroded brick and each layer of mortar between them; all of it is poised as if waiting for this night from the moment the foundation was laid.

A boy and a girl stand on opposite sides of the cavern; a mountain of debris piled between them is the only obstacle left keeping them apart.

"Adriana?"

"Jon? Is that you?"

"I don't know. I don't feel like myself all of a sudden."

"I know what you mean."

"I can hear you, but I can't see you."

"It's dark on this side, but your eyes will adjust."

"You're by the mystery door."

"The what?"

"Just what we call it."

"There's all this stuff between us."

"Yeah, filing cabinets and desks."

"I'll start moving it."

"It's too heavy."

"You're right, it won't budge."

"To hell with it. I'm climbing over it."

"Be careful, Jon."

"Today's not about being careful."

"Can that desk hold your weight?"

"It will, whether it wants to or not."

"Watch that filing cabinet—it's rusted through."

"I see it."

"You're almost there! Grab my hand."

"Just one more step, and—"

"There . . ."

"There . . . That wasn't so hard."

"So why is your heart beating so fast?"

"You can feel that?"

"I think I could feel it from across the room."

"You're still holding my hand."

"It's so warm."

"Yours is so soft."

"Guess what, Jon?

"What?"

"We're here. We made it."

"Damn if we didn't!"

"So . . . am I what you imagined?"

"You're everything and more, Adriana. Am I what you imagined?"

"Yes. But I did think you'd have more hair."

"Ha! I did till twenty minutes ago."

"You're tall."

"You're proportional."

"Is that the best you can say?"

"Hey—proportional is important. Proportion is beauty. The Vitruvian Man. The Golden ratio."

"You're a strange boy, Jon Kilgore."

"In a good way?"

"In the best way."

"Mmmm."

"What are you looking at?"

"Your eyes."

"What about them?"

"It's like I look into them, and I can see clear around the world and back again."

"I could say that about yours."

"Let's go around the world, and stay right here."

"I'd like that."

"Shhh . . . do you hear that, Adriana?"

"I don't hear anything."

"Exactly. Because the world has gone away."

        "And it won't come back until we want it to."

"I never want it to."

        "Come closer, Jon."

"Can't get any closer."

        "Yes, you can."

"Any closer, I'll be on your other side."

        "Why are you smiling?"

"Imagining what it'd be like to pass through you."

        "Like a ghost?"

"We're mostly empty space. There are worlds between every atom."

        "You and your science talk."

"Quantum physics says we could exist in the same space."

        "So, then, we could be ourselves . . . and each other at the same time."

"I'd like that. To be inside each other that way."

        "Just that way?"

"Maybe that's what all the rest is trying to get at."

        "That feels so true."

"Wanting to dissolve,"

        "To disappear,"

"Until I don't know"

"Where you end"

"And where I begin."

"Knowing what you're going to say"

"Before I say it."

"Not just finishing"

"Each other's sentences,"

"But finishing"

"Each other's"

"Thoughts."

"Until our words"

"All our words"

"Are gone."

"And there's nothing but"

"My hands through your hair"

"My palms against your scalp"

"My breath in your ear"

"My fingers along your spine."

"My heartbeat in your chest"

"Are you going to kiss me?"

"I thought I already was."

33

A FINAL KISS ...

Officer Calhoun, who works the girls' night shift, comes on at seven and expects a quiet evening. The girls rarely give her trouble, but when they do it's a doozy.

Tonight, there are problems right off the bat, because when it's time to move the girls from the Rec Hub to their pods, the count comes up one short.

"Everyone line up," she says. "Let me count again." She really doesn't want to have to do a full roll call like they do before meals, but she will if she has to.

She figures it's her own error, but when she counts them all, she still comes up one short.

"Did one of the girls get out today?" she asks. They're supposed to let her know when that happens. Usually they do, but a bureaucracy is only as good as its least competent cog.

The girls look to each other.

"No, ma'am," says one of them.

"Oh," exclaims Bianca. "It's Adriana—she's in the library."

"What the hell is she doing there?"

Bianca shrugs. "Something to do with inventory."

"Yeah," confirms Monessa. "Ms. Detrick called for her right after dinner."

"She can't do that without clearing it with security!" Calhoun tells her, exasperated.

"Wait," says Monessa, "I have the note here."

Then she produces a handwritten letter on official Compass stationery. Sure enough, it requests the assistance of Adriana Zarahn from 6:30 until 7:30, at which time the guard on duty is requested to pick her up at the library.

"Why is this letter with you?"

"I was supposed to give it to Officer Bonivich before she left," says Monessa, "but I forgot."

"You forgot."

The girl shrugs. "Happens."

Officer Calhoun folds the note and slips it into her pocket. That librarian is gonna get a piece of her mind. "Okay, off to your pods—lights out in an hour."

Whatever spell stopped time and kept the world away, it ends the moment Adriana reminds Jon of the time and says they have to leave.

Jon would have stayed there in Moonshine Cavern with her

365

forever. He almost believed that the staff wouldn't come looking. That they had somehow escaped the known universe and found themselves in an unknown one, with just enough room for the two of them. And, who knows, maybe all traces of that other, awful place would be washed away.

Turns out Jon only paid lip service to being practical, because today he's the dreamer, and it takes Adriana to bring them back to Earth.

"We have to get back," she tells him. "Too many people will get in trouble if we don't."

She's right, as much as he hates to admit it. A lot of other kids put their necks on the line for the two of them. Which means that one hour is all they're ever going to get.

They both have plans for getting back. Jon's is simple: go back the way he came, and rejoin the cleanup crew in the kitchen—they know not to be done before seven thirty. He'll play the part of Toombs, keeping his head down, and spend the night in Toombs's pod, enduring whatever funk he'll have to endure in the guy's room. Then in the morning, he'll switch places with Toombs when they hit the showers, and no one will be the wiser. This is all assuming the guards can't tell one Black kid from another—but, considering who's on duty today, that's kind of a given. The only thing to explain, then, will be Jon's shaved head—but if he makes it that far without getting caught, it will be gravy.

Jon doesn't know Adriana's plan—but if either of their plans has any chance of working, they have to get moving.

They both whisper, "I love you," not because they have to whisper in Moonshine Cavern, but because whispering somehow makes it even more true. A final kiss, and Adriana leaves. Jon catches a glimpse of her climbing a ladder in the darkness of the other side of the doorway and just like that, she's gone.

Once Jon's alone, he takes a deep breath, squeezing in a moment to remember this, locking it all into his memory, so he can come back here in his mind any time he wants to. Then he turns and begins the climb over all the old junk to the other side of the cavern.

But his head must still be too deep in the clouds, because he steps on that old, rusted filing cabinet, and his foot goes right through. A sharp edge tears through his pant leg and cuts into his calf.

Shit shit shit!

He pulls his leg out, but the damage has already been done. The cut is deep enough to need stitches, and blood is already running down to his ankle.

He realizes he can't go to the infirmary tonight, because it will completely blow his cover. He might pass for Toombs in a group of greenshirts, but not if he's the focus of anyone's attention. No, he's going to have to deal with this himself. But he can tell he's going to leave a trail of blood wherever he goes. This is not what he needed. It's proof that the magic is over, and the universe, which had moved mountains for him and Adriana, is already calling in its marker, demanding payback.

Jon makes it to the other side of the cavern, but the moment he does, he realizes that a cut on his leg is the least of his problems.

Because he's not the only one there.

Adriana sits in the hallway just outside the library. Her soul still tingles, her heart still dances.

"What are you doing out here?" Officer Calhoun asks when she arrives.

"You were supposed to be here at seven thirty—you're ten minutes late," Adriana says. "Ms. Detrick had to leave, so she locked up the library, since I'm not allowed to be in there alone."

"You're not allowed to be out here alone either!" says Calhoun. "And you know I have to get the girls into their pods at seven thirty, so this is the soonest I could be here. Who does this librarian think she is?"

"Please don't be hard on her," Adriana pleads. "I don't want to get her into trouble." Because if Calhoun does raise a stink, and it comes out that Ms. Detrick wasn't even here at all this evening, it could mean trouble for Adriana. But even if it does, she doesn't care. No matter what happens now, it will have been worth it!

"C'mon," grumbles Calhoun, "let's go."

Calhoun gets on her radio as they march. "On the move," she says. Adriana can only hear Calhoun's side of the conversation, but she can fill in the blanks. "Heading back to girls' pod C from the Education wing. . . . What do you mean you don't have a visual? . . . Well, that's not my problem—somebody needs to talk to Schendorf. . . . Yeah, I know, but somebody's gotta do it. . . ."

Adriana feels so light on her feet, she bounces. She hopes Calhoun doesn't notice, but she does.

"What are you so happy about?"

"Nothing," says Adriana. "I just love books!"

Finally, they're back at Adriana's pod. Calhoun opens the door. It's quiet. All the girls are in their rooms. "Have a good night," Calhoun says.

It couldn't get better! Adriana wants to say, but instead just says, "You, too, Officer."

Calhoun leaves, locking the door. Adriana listens to her receding footsteps, and then hears the outer door open and close as Calhoun exits. That's when her pod-mates come out of their rooms, all smiles and anticipation.

"Tell!" insists Bianca. "Everything! Don't leave a single thing out."

And Adriana is more than happy to oblige.

Jon's first thought, when he sees two silhouetted figures standing in Moonshine Cavern, is that it must be guards, having figured out that something's up. Maybe Dorella's kitchen crew got suspicious and squealed. Or maybe someone looked at Toombs too closely. All these things pass through Jon's mind in the fraction of a second it takes for him to see how they're dressed. These aren't guards at all. They're greenshirts. Big ones. And he knows both of them.

"Well, lookie here! It's the man of the hour."

"Huh. More like the moron of the hour."

It's Viper and Culligan.

"Great place to be alone, ain't it?" says Viper. "Can't get bothered, can't get heard. You can scream as loud as you want, and no one'll know."

Jon knows he can take Culligan. But Viper and Culligan together? Two against one? That'd be tougher.

"I . . . I don't want any trouble," Jon says. "I just want to get back."

Viper shakes his head. "Ain't gonna happen, Kilgore."

"Huh. *Kill* and *gore*," says Culligan. "Two things we're gonna see tonight!"

"We got a score to settle for our buddy Knox," says Viper.

And then Jon realizes there's someone else there. A third conspirator, slight of build, and hiding in the shadows, nearly invisible.

Invisible . . .

Myers! Of course it's Myers! How could Jon have trusted him? But the voice that comes out when he speaks . . . it doesn't sound like Myers at all.

"Too much talk," that voice says. "Do what you're here to do."

Jon knows who it is. But part of his mind doesn't want to connect the dots.

"Fists and feet only," says the ringleader. "You got that? No shivs."

"We didn't use no shivs," says Culligan. "He was bleeding already."

Finally Jon accepts the truth of this, as painful as it is.

"Raz?"

Raz steps out of the shadows to face him. "Sorry, Jon," he says, without anything close to sorrow in his voice. "Sometimes shit has to happen."

Jon feels his entire soul begin a long, slow fall.

"My boys'll do what they're gonna do," says Raz. "Better for you if you don't resist."

"Your boys? Since when are these assholes your boys? And how the hell did you even get here?" After all the hoops Jon had to jump through to make it this far, how could the three of them just waltz right in? And then Jon realizes . . . "Wash . . ."

Raz smiles. "I told you Wash could be bought. And after we got clear of the dorms, and into the tunnel, the same camera tricks that worked for you worked just as well for us."

"Can we do this already?" says Viper, his hands balled into mallet-sized fists.

Raz nods. "Lay into him," Raz says. "Give him everything you got."

Despite Raz's warning to just let it happen, Jon's not gonna just stand there and take it.

"Let's get on with it," he says, and raises his fists like Mr. Velasco taught him in his middle school boxing class.

But Viper just laughs, and Culligan, taking all his cues from Viper, laughs as well. They both roar toward him, Culligan in the lead, probably trying to impress Viper—but Culligan is the lesser fighter. He swings and misses, allowing Jon a chance to throw a punch; a glancing blow off Culligan's cheek. Damn, not a solid enough connection. Then Culligan swings again, and this time, the punch connects. It rocks Jon on his heels, and he jerks right into Viper's fist, which sends him to the ground.

He feels a trickle of blood from his mouth, and his lips start going numb. He wipes at the blood as he tries to scramble to his feet—but they don't let him, because this is not a fair fight. As if two against one isn't one-sided enough, now it's two against one on the ground.

Now they kneel and pummel him, until finally Jon's able to draw himself away and get to his feet, but the second he does, something new enters the battle.

A metal pole from the debris connects with Jon's head.

He doesn't even know who swung it, but there's a crack of pain, he sees bright zigzags of light, and the floor and ceiling seem to switch places. In an instant he's down again, this time knowing it'll be a long time till he gets up. His head feels like it's going to explode, or maybe it already has.

"I said hands and feet only!" yells Raz.

"You're no fucking fun," says Viper.

Jon hears the pole clatter to the ground, and now his brain is so scrambled, he can't even protect himself as they start kicking. Culligan starts it, grunting with each swing of his foot. Jon's gut. His chest. He feels cracking. Maybe it's a rib. Maybe it's a bunch of ribs. Now Viper joins in, his kicks even more brutal. Jon rolls over, and now the kicks land on his back. His spine. His kidneys. The pain is so intense, he thinks he's going to black out, but he doesn't.

Viper isn't satisfied to lay waste to his body—because there's a solitary, perfectly placed kick to his face. His left eye flashes those zigzags again, and its vision seems to go blue then gray then gone. Jon reaches out, manages to grab Viper's foot, keeping it from delivering another blow to his face.

"That's good enough," says Raz. "You can stop now."

But Viper takes the chance to deliver one more kick to Jon's side that's worse than all the others. He feels something inside rupture like a water balloon, and he knows it's bad. Real bad.

"There," says Viper, satisfied. "*Now* we're done."

Jon's pain is pinned in the red, and now with it comes pressure. So much pressure inside his guts, inside his chest, inside his head, like he's fixing to burst.

And through his good eye, he sees Raz bending down to inspect the damage.

"Sucks to be you right now, huh, Jon?"

Jon pulls in a shallow breath, just enough for him to say, "Why, Raz?"

Raz shrugs. "Same reason I poisoned the Meerkat and fingered you," he says. "Course, it wasn't s'posed to be that bad, but it all worked out, didn't it?" Then he gets a little closer, whispering into Jon's swelling ear. "See, I made you a reputation, so I could ride it. But I traded up. Got myself a better horse. Hell, might even be a whole stable if things play out right. See, Jon, there's a bigger game going on that you don't even see. Guess you're too blinded by love."

"You . . . you won't get away with this."

Raz stands, brushing off his hands. "What you don't get is that I already did. I got away with it before you even came down here. It was written in the stars, Jon. Written in the stars."

Jon finally feels his consciousness slipping away, but holds on to it just long enough to see Raz head up the stairs with the other two, leaving Jon alone, broken, and bleeding his life into the thirsty concrete.

34

BEYOND ALL WORDS

For the next few days, Adriana is blissfully unaware of the rumblings. In the library, she dreams through her shift, barely bothered that her journal hasn't reappeared on the shelf. She's glad that she isn't the one who has to ink words after being face-to-face, after that magical time in Moonshine Cavern, where their hearts beat millimeters apart, matching rhythms, as close as possible to beating as one. Jon's wish came true; they were plasma. All states at once. How do you weave words together after that? There are some things that exist in a place beyond all words.

Adriana goes over to the checkout desk, where a cart of books waits to be shelved, but before she wheels it off, Ms. Detrick stops her, and, heaving a noticeably heavy sigh, grabs a book from the "reserved" shelf behind her.

"You can shelve this one, too, Adriana," she says, her voice troubled. "I had ordered it for a boy who's . . . who's no longer here."

Which normally wouldn't be a red flag at all—kids are coming and going from Compass on a daily basis. Adriana doesn't pay it much mind . . . until she looks at the book in her hands. A shiny black cover: comets, planets, and stars juxtaposed against atoms, and the expanse of space between them.

It's a book on quantum physics.

Adriana takes a deep breath, and, to combat the spike of foreboding, she immediately floods her thoughts with all the random coincidences she's ever experienced. All those times when it seemed like one thing, but it was something else entirely, and she had laughed at herself for being so silly.

Can't be Jon. Can't be Jon. Can't be Jon.

But as she looks at the depths of space on that cover, she can't help but feel she's lingering at the brink of some event horizon, seconds from plummeting into a shaft of absolute darkness.

"What do you mean, no longer here?" she asks Ms. Detrick, clutching the book a little too tightly.

Ms. Detrick sighs again. Her sighs are always her tell. An indication that there's a much longer story that she's not going to share. "It's not your concern, honey. You can get back to shelving."

She feels herself shaking, feels her heartbeat pounding at the base of her neck.

Get yourself together. Act natural. Tease it out of her. She wants to talk about it just as much as she doesn't, so work this until she talks.

Adriana swallows, and casually puts the book on the cart, even though her hand is afraid to let it go.

Ms. Detrick's face shows more lines than usual. Worry lines. Her attention seems to be on paper inventory lists, but clearly it's not.

"Ma'am?" Adriana says as lightly as she can. "Who is this boy? Did this boy get sent home? Or maybe somewhere else? Because we could still get the book to him . . ."

Ms. Detrick looks up at her, a little bit flustered, and maybe a little bit angry. "Adriana, I said drop it, and get back to work."

"I will, ma'am, but I can't help but wonder . . . should the girls be concerned? Is it another poisoning like that boy who got poisoned the last time?"

Ms. Detrick's gaze shoots right to Adriana's eyes. "How did you even know about . . . ?" Then she closes her eyes, takes a deep, cleansing breath, and opens them again, back in control. "Never mind," she says. "There's nothing more to say on the matter."

"Yes, ma'am, but—"

Then a voice from behind her.

"Damn, girl, why are you gnawing on Ms. Detrick like some dog on a shoe?" says Monessa, coming up to them. "Back off and let the woman be."

"I'm just asking her about—"

"I heard what you're asking her, and Ms. Detrick's got enough headaches without adding you to the stack. C'mon I'll help you

377

shelve these books." And she pulls the cart away.

Adriana turns to Ms. Detrick, but she's already given her attention to another girl who's checking out a happy pink book with a meet-cute couple on the cover. Whatever that book is, Adriana hates it and will hate it forever.

When she catches up with Monessa, she's already shelving books. "Maybe I can do this better than you," she says. "Maybe I can boot you out and get your job."

"I think something happened on the boys' side," Adriana says, to which Monessa gets even more prickly than usual.

"So what? There's always stuff going down with the boys. Kids are always getting beaten up, so stop flapping your lips about it and wasting my time."

"Wait . . . somebody got beat up?"

Monessa freezes, book in hand. "I didn't say that . . . I mean, yeah, I did say it, but I'm just assuming, okay? It's just assuming."

Then Monessa's face takes on that clamped look she gets when her mind goes into its personal lockdown. It's her tell that nothing more is coming out, or going in.

Adriana finishes her afternoon library shift late and has to be escorted back to the Rec Hub. She tries to pump Bonivich about the boy who was maybe beaten. The one who no longer exists at Compass. The guard is even more tight-lipped than Ms. Detrick, either ignoring Adriana's questions or staring her down.

Something bad has happened. Bonivich will occasionally go silent, but now she seems in fortress mode. If a boy's been hurt or poisoned again, maybe they're blaming security.

Bonivich pauses before swiping her badge at an air lock. "Don't be spreading rumors on things you know nothing about. Hear?" Then she opens the door, then the next, then the next, saying nothing more.

Her friends are in the Rec Hub, but not talking. Or maybe they stopped talking when they saw Adriana brought in.

"A boy's no longer here in juvie. Anyone know who or why?" she asks.

Monessa shifts her attention to her algebra book, her shoulders hunched in something that looks like guilt. Or like she wants to throw the book. Jolene just bounces her knee. Bianca looks at Pip. Pip narrows her eyes. "Who says we know anything?"

What's going on here? Why are they acting like bad actors in a high school play?

"Maybe it's just another allergic thing," suggests Jolene. "Maybe it's nothing. Maybe better if you forget it."

There it is again. Jolene stares at the baseboard as if it's got all the answers. She doesn't believe what she's saying, like she's been told what to say. Her words are wooden.

Adriana feels her anger rise. These are supposed to be her friends or at least her crew at Compass. And they're lying to her. Ignoring Bonivich's order, she dives into rumor-mongering of the worst kind. "Ms. Detrick says a boy is gone from Compass. Monessa slipped that someone got beaten. I think it might be Jon. Are any of you gonna tell me that it's not?"

Jolene walks off like a wraith slipping away.

Monessa frowns at her algebra book.

Bianca finally says, "There are lots of boys here." Which sounds like an intentional non-answer to her question.

So Adriana turns to Pip. "Pip, you got something to say, you'd better say it now."

Pip says nothing. Shows nothing in her face. Just avoids Adriana's stare. "I'll look into it, okay?"

Adriana's face heats up. How long are they gonna keep this up?

Lowering her voice, she says in venom-laced words, "I want someone to tell me the truth. Now."

It's not Pip who speaks. It's not Jolene, who has forced herself into someone else's conversation across the Hub, and it's not Bianca, who's staring off like there's something interesting on the far wall.

It's Monessa who drops her algebra book, stands up, and gets so close Adriana can smell the mustard on her breath.

"You want the truth? Fine, I'll tell you. We was hoping to know more before we said anything, but since you gotta know now, here it is."

"Monessa, don't!" says Bianca. But Pip gives Monessa a nod.

"Jon never made it back to his pod," Monessa says. "One of the guards—Wash, I think it was—found him beaten to a pulp in Moonshine Cavern the next morning. It's all fuzzy after that, but Detrick is right. Wherever he is, he's not at Compass."

KANT'S JUSTICE

Jon slips in and out of consciousness, but mostly out. There are brief moments of semiclarity, where he rises close enough to the surface to see someone in blue tending to him.

Not a greenshirt is all he has the strength to think before he slips into the darkness again. Although it's not really darkness— it's more like the featureless gray of an overcast dawn. This must be what it feels like—or doesn't feel like—to not exist.

Time takes a flying leap into nowhere.

A slack string of loose moments of awareness. Each time he pulls something out of the gray.

I'm in the infirmary. No, this is more than that. It's a hospital.

There's something in his mouth. Something blocking his throat. He feels like he'll gag, but he doesn't. He feels like he's choking, but he doesn't. Because he's still breathing. But not really. Something is breathing *for* him. Air hisses in and out in a steady, mindless rhythm like the ticking of a clock.

Intubation. That's what this is. His mother was intubated at the end. So does he have cancer like her? Is that what's going on here?

Too many questions for his mind to handle. He submerges back down into the gray.

The next time, the pain rouses him. It was dull throbbing before, but it's grown sharper. It's in his face, it's in his skull, it's in his side and in his back. It seems everything in his body screams. It pins all his senses—he can hear it like an alarm blaring in his head. And it helps him to remember what happened. He was attacked somewhere. Some place where he wasn't supposed to be, but *had* to be. He was there for a reason—an *important* reason . . .

Adriana!

But before he can put any more of it together, a nurse appears and injects something into his IV. It instantly quells the pain, and any hope of coherent thought, submerging him back into the featureless gray void, where there's no time at all.

When he next opens his eyes, there's someone at the door, talking in hushed whispers with a nurse. Same nurse? Different nurse? He has no idea. Jon can't focus well enough to see who the visitor is, other than that it's a man. He uses every last bit of his will to turn his head slightly to get a better view. Only now does he realize that he's only seeing through one eye. The other is bandaged. Finally, the nurse and the man move closer, and one look at his face—even out of focus—and he knows who it is.

Alvarado.

"Good to see you're awake."

Of all the people from Compass, why did it have to be Alvarado? Because this is his job, that's why. To see to the psychological and emotional well-being of those in Compass's care. Too little, too late, all considered.

"I'm so sorry that this had to happen, Jon." Alvarado pauses, like he's expecting Jon to respond. It's not like Jon can hold a conversation with a tube down his throat. He can't even vary the speed of his breathing. It's a constant, steady pulse as air is pumped in and out of his lungs. It makes him wonder if he can breathe on his own. He wiggles his fingers and toes, confirming he still can. Whatever other damage he has, his spinal cord is still intact. That's something, at least.

The nurse steps out to see to other patients, and Alvarado pulls up a chair, sitting down, and answers questions that Jon can't ask.

"You're at Mercy General," Alvarado says. "You were attacked by unknown assailants. A lot of internal bleeding. Subdural hematoma—they had to relieve pressure on your brain. You've lost your spleen and your left kidney. Still not sure about your right eye—it's too soon to tell."

This is way too much for Jon to take, but he swallows it as best he can. Now he knows the answer to his second-most urgent

383

question. But he doubts he'll get an answer to his most urgent one. The one about Adriana. Is she okay? Was she attacked too? It's all still fuzzy, but he does seem to recall that she left before this happened. Before . . .

Viper!

Culligan!

And . . . and . . .

And Raz.

The memory of Raz's betrayal makes everything inside him hurt anew.

"You've been here for five days. After surgery, you developed a blood infection. It's still touch and go." He taps one of the hanging bags dripping into his IV. "Antibiotics," says Alvarado. "But there are so many antibiotic-resistant bugs these days . . ." He sighs. "The news could be better, Jon. I'm sorry."

Maybe honesty isn't the best policy, thinks Jon. Maybe there are some things he doesn't have to know.

Alvarado looks back, checking the door. It's still just the two of them. Then he turns to Jon and leans just the tiniest bit closer.

"I'm so sorry this had to happen to you, Jon," he says again. But this time he adds, "But it *did* have to happen. You understand that, don't you?"

And suddenly, even in his fog, Jon realizes that something is very wrong here. Alvarado did not come to pay him a social visit, or even to check up on him. The man has intentions that Jon hasn't even begun to consider.

"It had to happen, Jon, because there needs to be justice in the world. Just a little bit, to make the world bearable."

Jon tries to reach for the nurse's call button—there's always one of those, right? But Alvarado sees his hand searching the bed for it and finds it first, moving it out of Jon's reach. "Let's not have anyone interrupt our time together."

Alvarado's mustache twitches slightly. It looks like two dark waterfalls spilling off either side of his upper lip. John always thought it looked comical. He never realized how menacing it could be.

"Simon Tesch. Does that name mean anything to you?"

Yes, it does. Of course it does. How could Jon ever forget the name? Not just Simon Tesch. *Doctor* Simon Tesch.

"He died even before he could get to a hospital room like this. Died of a heart attack that *you* caused."

The helplessness that Jon feels is overwhelming. He just wants to lose consciousness again to escape this. But he feels his heart beating faster, adrenaline flooding him, keeping him awake and alert as if to spite him.

"I knew him, Jon. You didn't know that, did you? Of course you didn't—how could you? But he was a good man. And Simon had a family. A grieving wife, and two sons who now have to grow up fatherless because of you, Jon. Because of you."

Jon knows all this—and his remorse is real. But Alvarado doesn't care about remorse, does he? Despite his job at Compass, here is a man who ascribes to Kant's point of view, not Jung's. Rehabilitation and restoration are meaningless. The only accepted response to a crime is retribution. Punishment in equal measure to the offense.

And all at once, Jon knows the truth.

Alvarado had Raz in his pocket. He had Raz in his pocket all along. That's why Raz poisoned Silas. To frame Jon. To make sure Jon never got out. And when that wasn't enough, Alvarado had Raz stage the beating. What did Alvarado offer him? What made it worth betraying Jon? Or maybe it didn't take much at all.

"It's unlikely you'll survive, what with the infection and all the internal bleeding," Alvarado says, with cool matter-of-factness. "But on the off chance that you do, you won't say anything to anyone about our conversation today. You'll keep this between you and me." He leans a little closer. "First, because no one will believe the word of a young man of your dubious reputation. But more importantly . . . if you say anything, I won't just destroy you. I'll destroy everyone you care about."

Jon wants to reach up and grab the man, but he can't. He doesn't have the strength. He can't even make a noise beyond the hiss of the ventilator.

"Think about it, Jon. Think about my position at Compass. With a stroke of a pen, think of what I can do to Gordy. Or to Silas." And then he leans even closer. "Or to Adriana."

Jon squirms. In spite of every bone aching, he squirms, and Alvarado seems to enjoy it. *Of course Alvarado knows about Adriana!* With Raz as his spy, he must know everything! And he's not bluffing. With the power he has at Compass, Alvarado can define not just everyone's present, but their future as well.

"Nod so I know you understand me, Jon."

The tiniest nod is all Jon can manage.

"Good," says Alvarado. "Of course it might not even matter. If you don't survive, the problem takes care of itself, doesn't it? And justice will finally be served." Alvarado leans back in his chair, so self-satisfied. "Either way, you won't be coming back to Compass. And either way, you'll be exactly where you belong."

Jon closes his eyes, hoping this is over. Hoping that Alvarado will leave and never come back. But once his eyes close, an image fills his mind. A horrible one. It's his own funeral. But that's not the horrible part. The horrible part is that Alvarado is the only one attending.

"I can see you're struggling, Jon. But I can help you," Alvarado says. "I can help you think about the suffering you've caused." And then he lays his hand on the left side of Jon's abdomen. The bandaged side. And he begins to press down against the stitches—against the spot where his spleen has been cut from his body. In that moment Alvarado goes from being a walrus to a shark taking a bite out of his side, because the pain is excruciating.

Maybe I do deserve this, Jon thinks. *Maybe Kant is right.*

And so he fills his mind with the only antidote to the pain. A single image, because now he has an image.

Adriana. Adriana. Adriana.

He holds on to her, until he feels himself disappearing fully and completely into the pain, becoming Kant's justice.

36

THE SPACE BETWEEN

Silas is on edge. Everyone's on edge. Everyone on the boys' side wants to talk about it, but no one does. Raz is whispering stuff, though. He's whispering that somehow Viper got wind of the plan to break Jon to Adriana, and then Viper piggybacked his own agenda. Silas figures it's just rumors, though, until the guards come to haul Viper away for good. Word is that he's been transferred to Hell Vista. It's where Knox went. Now Viper's there too.

And now, just a few days after Jon's disappearance and a day after Viper's removal, Silas is called into Luppino's office. Their unit counselor always gives off vibes of wishing he was back in bed, but today, the man looks even more exhausted than usual.

"As I'm sure you know, Silas . . . Jon Kilgore is no longer at Compass."

"Yeah, I noticed," he says. Understatement of the year. Luppino must know where he is, and what happened to him. Back when he was a newbie, Silas would have asked right off the bat, wearing his concern there on his sleeve. But he knows better now. The things you feel can be used to manipulate you. Control you. Silas can't act like he cares as much as he does. He's got to present an attitude that says, *I don't give two shits, but maybe I give one.*

Silas leans back in his chair, the way he's seen Jon do, when he's playing cool. "So, anyone know what happened? Because you guys disappeared him real quick."

Luppino takes in Silas's one-shit-not-two aura, then says, "I'm not supposed to be telling you this, but there was a security breach on the night in question."

"Sounds serious."

"It was," says Luppino. "It *is*. Apparently, someone hacked into the system, and rerouted several camera feeds."

Silas plays it level and disaffected. "That really must have pissed off Ironside."

Luppino interlaces his fingers on the desk between them. "Mr. Schendorf has been let go."

"Let go?"

"He was fired. Because it was his responsibility to make sure these kinds of things never happen, and he failed."

Silas swallows and resists the urge to look down, because that will telegraph way too much. He never thought Ironside could get in trouble for it.

"How does it make you feel that he was fired, Silas?"

How does he feel? The guilt is just about oozing out of his pores, but he fights it and forces a shrug. "Sucks for him," says Silas. "I liked him, so I guess I feel bad. I'll miss him."

Luppino nods. "We all will. But there's something that caught my attention about all this, Silas. A kind of a riddle. I'm hoping you can help me out with it."

"Okay, sure."

"It's the hacker's handle. The screen name he used to get into the system. It's *ImpededRokParty*. Does that mean anything to you?"

Again, Silas forces a shrug. "No, not really. Sounds like the name of a band."

Luppino gives a mirthless chuckle. "Yes, I suppose it does. It didn't mean anything to me either. Not until I started to look a bit more closely."

Then he hands Silas a piece of paper with the screen name written out in big block letters.

IMPEDEDROKPARTY

And he gives Silas a pen.

"Do me a favor, Silas, and cross out every other letter. Beginning with the *I*."

Silas hesitates. But he knows he has to do it. Slowly, meticulously he crosses out the *I* . . . *P* . . . *D* . . . *D* . . . *O* . . . *P* . . . *R* . . . and finally *Y*.

✶M✖E✖E✖R✖K✖A✖T✖

"Could you please read what's left when you take away the spaces between?"

390

"I don't want to."

"I'm sure you don't. But read it anyway."

Silas doesn't do it. Luppino waits, like he has all the patience in the world.

"Meerkat," Silas finally says. "It spells meerkat."

Luppino nods and leans back a bit in his chair. "Silas. I'd like you to tell me your involvement with this."

Silas doesn't answer right away. It's all he can do to stop from sweating or maybe even vomiting all over Luppino's desk. That'd go over well, wouldn't it? He supposes he can stonewall. Deny, deny, deny. Say someone else is trying to frame him. But what good would that do? Luppino would know he's lying. Damn. He thought he was being clever with that screen name. Serves him right for flaunting any smarts he thought he had.

Silas crosses his arms and looks at Luppino, dropping all pretenses. "Tell me what you know, Mr. Luppino, and I'll tell you if it's right."

The man shakes his head. "Not the way this works."

But Silas holds his ground. "Yes, it is the way it works. Because otherwise, I won't say a thing, I'll lawyer up, and this gets real ugly." Then he keeps his eyes locked on Luppino, staring the man down. It goes on longer than Silas thinks it's possible to stare at someone like that. Then finally Luppino looks away, his shoulders slump, and for the rest of his life, Silas Coady will remember that he played chicken with his Compass unit counselor and won.

"No need to escalate this," Luppino says. "That won't help

anyone." Then he spills what the staff has been able to cobble together. "We know that the camera feeds were switched. We know that Jon switched places with another boy. We know he went down to the sub-basement."

"Okay," says Silas. "Is that it?"

"We believe he had planned to escape. But Clive Buchanan—the boy you call Viper—was down there, waiting to ambush him. Payback for a grudge."

Silas nods, neither confirming nor denying the theory. If they think Jon was trying to escape, maybe that's okay. Because then it leaves Adriana and her friends out of it.

"My question to you is this," Luppino says. "Were you pressured into helping Jon? Or were you pressured into helping Viper?"

Not the question he was expecting.

"Who says I was pressured?"

"It looks better for you if you were, Silas."

Finally, Silas can't play cool anymore. He's got to ask his own question. The one that's been screaming in his head since the moment he got here. "If Jon got beaten up, then you've got to know how he is. So how is he? *Where* is he?"

"Please answer the question."

"Not until you tell me."

Luppino is silent for a moment. And then, just as it seems they're about to lapse into another game of chicken, he says, "He's in intensive care, son. Critical condition. He's clinging to life, but only by the barest thread. I wish I had better news. I'm sorry."

Silas closes his eyes. Once again, he feels like he might throw up, but he keeps his stomach, and everything in it, exactly where it should be. When he opens his eyes, he's like steel.

"Viper can rot in Hell Vista. I wasn't working for him—I'd never lift a finger to help Viper, no matter what he threatened to do to me. But I *was* helping Jon. Not because he pressured me to, but because I wanted to. I'm not sorry I tried to help him. And I'd do it again."

Luppino gives him a solemn nod. "Understood."

"So . . . what's Director Morley going to do with me?"

"Morley?" Luppino scoffs at the mention of the director's name. "Morley's not doing anything to you. He's not good with puzzles. In fact, he can't even puzzle his own way out of this whole situation. As it stands, *I'm* the only one who figured out the screen name, so I'm the only one who knows of your involvement." Then Luppino hesitates, and actually offers Silas a slim smile. "As far as I'm concerned, it can stay that way."

And although Silas is relieved, he has to ask.

"And what about Jon? If he lives, what happens to him?"

But rather than responding, Luppino slaps a folder down on his desk, and says, "I'm pleased to tell you that you're being placed with a foster family."

Which is good news—news that stuns him—but it still doesn't answer his question. "I'm glad you found me a home . . . but what about Jon?"

"Mr. and Mrs. Sobel are a good match for you. They don't make fostering a business, and seem sincere, according to the social worker."

"You're not answering me."

"You're leaving before lunch. Rush will be here shortly, to help you collect your things."

It would be so easy for Silas to get caught up in the whirlwind of a sudden new life, but his own rising spirits just make him angry. Because he's not ready for his spirits to rise. Not when Jon's fate is still a mystery.

"Stop ignoring me!" yells Silas. "Stop treating me like I'm not even here!"

"You never *should* have been here, Silas," Luppino says. "The fact that you fell in with the wrong element wasn't your fault—it was ours. And I'm sorry."

Silas tries to ask again, but this time he can't even get the words out of his mouth, because too many are trying to come out at once.

"My best advice to you, son, is to leave this all behind," says Luppino. "Start your new life, and forget you were ever at Compass."

And now, as much as he's tried to hold himself together, Silas's tears begin to flow. Because forgetting Compass means forgetting Jon. How could he ever forget Jon? How could he ever want to?

Word comes down the following Tuesday. Because all terrible things happen on a Tuesday, according to Gordy. 9/11, the stock market crash. Elvis dying.

Gordy is inconsolable. Bawling so loud it echoes everywhere;

people in other parts of Compass don't even know where it's coming from. They invent stories about ghosts in the walls.

"I don't wanna eat! I don't wanna sleep! I don't wanna do anything ever again," Gordy wails.

Raz takes it upon himself to comfort him, like Jon used to do. "You'll be okay, Gordy," Raz assures him. "We're all gonna be okay."

Raz is the big man now. He's got Culligan at his beck and call, claiming to have rehabilitated him from Viper's goon into a fine, upstanding associate. Now it's Raz's table that everyone wants to sit at. His inner circle is the one other greenshirts wish they were in.

Everyone's affected after word comes down, although Gordy's the only one bawling. Some are quiet and subdued. Others are angry and take it out on each other in various ways. Of course, there's no one on staff who will confirm it. That's just the way things are at Compass. There's like a whole industrial vacuum system that sweeps everything bad that happens under the rug.

But it has to be true. Because why else would Ironside be fired? And why else would Morley be forced to resign? Morley getting the boot is the only good part if it—but the good can't come close to outweighing the bad.

"I can't believe it," wails Gordy over and over. "I can't believe that Jon's dead."

But everyone knows it's true. Because Raz says so. And why would Raz lie?

◆ ◆ ◆

Word reaches Pip after lunch, but she keeps it to herself until after dinner, when the girls have their free evening hour in the Rec Hub. She goes over to Adriana, who's sitting by herself on a couch, reading something by that science guy, Neil deGrasse Tyson. Not really her brand, but then, maybe it is now. It makes this all the more difficult.

Pip sits with her on the low-slung sofa, then takes her hand. Adriana's already looking at her funny, wondering what this is all about.

"My contact on the boys' side gave me some news."

"What kind of news?"

"Not the good kind."

Adriana turns away, seeming to force her attention back to her book and steeling her jaw. "I don't want to hear it."

"I know. But you should. Because I want you to hear it from me."

Adriana has been living on pins and needles all week. How could the best day of her life be followed by the worst ones? There's nothing worse than not knowing. But now Adriana realizes that maybe there is. Hope might be a knife poised over your heart, but knowing plunges it straight in.

Pip doesn't even say it. She doesn't have to; the words are right there in her eyes.

"When?" Adriana asks.

"I don't know," Pip says. "My contact said one of the other boys who was tight with Jon got word slipped to him by someone on staff."

Adriana's tears have started, but it's barely a trickle compared to the deluge she knows is coming. She finds herself getting mad at Pip. She knows not to shoot the messenger, but sometimes you just can't help it.

"That's all you've got?" snaps Adriana. "A guy who knows a guy who heard from another guy?"

"Sometimes trickle-down is the best we get."

Other girls are there now, beginning to cluster around them like antibodies around a wound—and Adriana realizes that Pip told them first. Bianca sits on Adriana's other side, grabbing her arm tight like Adriana might fall off the couch. Monessa kneels in front of her, putting a gentle hand on Adriana's knee, awkward with compassion, but trying anyway.

"Sucks, right?" Monessa says. "But I'm glad we did what we did for the two of you. I'm glad you got to be with him." Her eyes are glassy-wet. Adriana has never seen Monessa cry, but it looks like she's going to.

Adriana turns her gaze to the book that now lies there, cast aside, and it makes her hurt even more. *There's infinite space between atoms,* Jon told her. So maybe part of him has passed into her. And maybe she can hold it there. And maybe someday she'll find him again in that infinitely grand space between infinitely small things.

But not today. Not right now. Because right now, she feels like crawling back up into that air vent and hiding there until she wastes away into nothing. Dying between the walls of this awful place and letting it digest her.

"We're here for you," says Bianca. "We're all here."

"For as long as you need us to be," says Jolene. "None of us are going anywhere."

"Speak for yourself," says Monessa. And in spite of everything, Adriana has to laugh at that. Until Pip introduces something new into this bitter equation. She reaches behind her to pull something out.

"My contact on the boys' side got this from Jon's room before they cleared it out." And she presents Adriana with her own journal. "Can't vouch for the boys, but I didn't read it," Pip says. "'Cause I'm not like that."

Adriana grips the journal, then can't stop herself from turning to the last entry. It's her own words. After that, just page after empty page, each one a dagger left to rust in her heart.

Now the floodgates finally open, and Adriana begins sobbing like it's the end of the world. Because it is. It absolutely is.

37

DISCHARGE

Adriana sits across from Alvarado for the last time. She couldn't be happier that she will never have to see this man again.

"Well, Adriana, it looks like you've made it through your time here with minimal damage."

Damage? There wouldn't be any damage if he did what he was supposed to do, and actually took care of the kids at Compass. Some people here are genuine. Jameara. Ms. Detrick. Dorella—even Bonivich, in her own uptight way. Others are just cogs picking up a paycheck. But there are also some like Alvarado: bastards who see Compass as their own personal realm. A realm that, after seven long months, she's leaving.

"Yeah, no damage," she regurgitates. *Except for falling in love with a boy who got disappeared.* She can't help but think that it never would have happened if she and Jon had never connected

399

over the journal. The other girls keep telling her that it's not her fault. Easy to say, but not so easy to feel.

Alvarado shuffles papers from Adriana's file around his desk and flicks at his mustache. Adriana wonders what microscopic treasures have just been ejected into the air.

"Your grades have been respectable, and your behavior, for the most part, has been good, if not exemplary." He closes her folder and looks at her with a practiced smile that is so insincere, she just wants to punch it off his face. "So how does it feel to be going home?"

What a stupid question, she wants to say. But instead, she just says, "Good. I'll miss my friends. At least the ones that are still here."

"Well, as you know, the girls love to receive letters, so you can always write. Although in my experience, girls who've been here tend to leave their Compass friends behind."

"Are we done here, Dr. Alvarado? Because my family's already waiting downstairs."

"You'll need to stay with me until Jameara comes to pick you up. Even though you've completed your time here, you're technically still with us until you cross through the last security door." Then he goes quiet, letting the silence become awkward. It's his favorite trick—wielding silence to make you feel uncomfortable.

"As long as we still have this time, is there anything else you'd like to share that might help bring closure to your time here?"

Adriana could say no and just let it be. But if it's closure he wants, then Adriana decides that's what he's gonna get. "Yeah, I'll share," she begins. "You probably already know this, but people here don't like you. And I don't just mean the kids. The staff doesn't like you either. Also, you're not very good at your job."

Alvarado maintains his smile—that mask of professional congeniality. "I can see that it makes you feel good to demean me. You may want to look at that."

"You always want me to speak the truth, and for once I'm not scared to anymore—so, yeah, it does feels good. By the way, word is the new director doesn't like you either. Which means you'll probably be looking for a job pretty soon." Then Adriana leans just a little bit closer. "And I hope that you don't find one."

Still, his face shows nothing but his pleasant half smile. But she does see his mustache twitch just the tiniest bit. Which reminds her—"Oh, and everyone laughs at your mustache too."

Then Alvarado takes a deep breath, and says very slowly, "You know, Miss Zarahn . . . there are things I'm aware of that could keep you here at Compass . . . if I choose to share them."

Adriana knows that this thinly veiled threat is meant to frighten her. Intimidate her. But it doesn't, because she also knows it's not true. Even if he knows all about her shimmying through air vents and meeting up with Jon, all he can do is spout accusations, dredging up a situation that the new Compass administration wants to get rid of in the worst way. It won't be good for Alvarado if he makes waves. Whatever he knows, or doesn't know, he won't say a thing.

Adriana stands up, if only to look down on him. "You have no power over me anymore," she says. "And I hope that someday you get a radioactive dose of the mindfuck you put us through."

"Careful," he warns, in almost a growl. "Be careful of the enemies you make and the bridges you burn, Adriana. Because the same poor choices that landed you here once could land you here again."

"Yeah, bad pennies keep coming back, don't they?" she says. "Never know when you're gonna be across the desk from one."

Just then, Jameara knocks on the door, and without waiting, barges right in. "Is everything wrapped up, Dr. Alvarado? Because we're on a schedule."

"Yes," he says. "Yes, I believe we're done." He stands to face her. "Goodbye, Adriana," he says, with his professional I-care-a-lot mask back on his face. "I wish you only the best in all your future endeavors."

But he doesn't reach out his hand to shake, because he knows Adriana won't take it.

Jameara leads Adriana out of the administrative offices and takes her to say goodbye to the other girls before the girls head off to lunch. Jameara explains that this is a routine unique to Compass. Having the girls see one of their own in civilian clothes and saying goodbye gives them hope.

Over the past few months there's been a lot of turnover. More than half the population. New girls of various temperaments show up to replace the ones who leave. The new girls treat Adriana like an old-timer. She doesn't feel like one, but she doesn't feel "new" either. Compass hasn't broken her . . . but the things that happened here—the *thing* that happened—has left her . . . dented. But then, dents can always be pounded out.

Jolene left six weeks ago. They finally found a blood relative to take her in.

"My grandma's sister—so my great-aunt," Jolene told them. "I never even met her, but she has room—and she has mobility issues, being old and all—so having me there is a win-win."

Monessa left a few weeks later with a "see ya" instead of a goodbye. From the little window in the Rec Hub, Adriana and Bianca watched her walk with her mother to a car in the parking lot, holding her baby girl in her arms. Her mom helped Monessa put the baby in the car seat, and they were gone.

Bianca, who's already been gathering new girls into her orbit, still has four months at Compass. She never told Adriana what had gotten her such a long sentence, and even now, Adriana doesn't want to insult her by asking.

"I'm sure we'll run into each other years from now," Bianca says, having no delusions about keeping in touch, "and we'll have a fancy-ass lunch on your expense account—because you're gonna have one, girl. A big one!"

And then there's Pip—who seems to have no expiration date on her time here. It's almost as if she's here by choice—and the strings she pulls have grown like roots into the very structure of the system, wending their way into its systemic breakage. But then, maybe she just wants people to think that. Maybe she'll leave just like everyone else when her time here is up.

"I'll miss you, Adriana," Pip says as Adriana gives her a gentle hug. "You made life interesting." Then she whispers into Adriana's ear. "None of us will ever forget . . ."

Adriana feels her heart wince a bit. None of them have spoken for months about what happened. Adriana just hurt too much, and all the girls knew it—and since their participation had never come to light, Adriana supposed there was a bit of self-preservation at work too. It never happened. Except that it did.

"Love you, Pip."

That makes Pip pull away from the hug. "Same," she says. "Do good out there, Adriana."

Jameara seems impatient to get Adriana out the door, but Adriana has one more stop she wants to make, and Jameara allows it.

It's the boys' day in the library, but that doesn't matter now that Adriana's a free woman. Jameara walks her straight in. Some boys sitting at the tables look up at Adriana with piqued interest, then look away, probably worried that their interest will get them into trouble. Adriana wonders if any of these boys helped Jon get to Moonshine Cavern that night. Or if any of them helped betray him.

Ms. Detrick smiles when she sees her, comes out from behind the checkout desk, and although physical contact from staff is discouraged, she gives Adriana a hug anyway. "Who will I ever find to replace you here?" Ms. Detrick says.

"No one can hold a candle to you."

Jameara smiles at that. "You've left good impressions here," Jameara says. "That's something to be proud of."

"Tell Alvarado," Adriana says. "On second thought, don't."

That makes both of them laugh. Even the guard, who's hanging out at the door, smirks. "I'm glad you stopped by," Ms. Detrick says. "I have something for you." She reaches into a drawer and pulls out an envelope. It has Adriana's name written on it, in extremely careful lettering, to make sure it couldn't possibly be misread. "This came in an outer envelope that was addressed to me," Ms. Detrick says.

"Odd . . . ," says Jameara.

Adriana takes the envelope. *No, it's not odd,* thinks Adriana. *Not if you suspect all the mail that comes for kids at Compass gets read before it arrives.*

"Do you know where it came from?" Adriana asks.

"I checked—no return address." Then she fishes through the drawer to find the envelope it came in. "Postmark is from West-brook Township. That's about an hour from here."

"Hmm," says Jameara. "Interesting . . ."

Ms. Detrick and Jameara wait, as if Adriana is going to open it right there. Well, they'll have to live with their curiosity, because she slips it into her pocket unopened, happy that she has clothes with pockets again.

Paula Laplante, the soulless woman at intake, apparently also handles discharge. She processes Adriana's with the same disaffected disinterest with which she might serve a burger and fries.

"Enjoy the world," she says flatly. Then Jameara leads Adriana into the final air lock . . .

. . . and through the outer door.

The air already seems to smell different. The sunlight is overwhelming—her eyes swim, making everything hard to see. This much light never reached the yard.

Lana, Colter, and her father are all there in the waiting area. Colter runs and jumps into Adriana's arms. "A-dana! A-dana!" Then corrects himself. "Adri-ana!" he says proudly.

"Hi, sweetie!" says Lana, giving her a kiss. "So happy to see you! You look great! You happy? Is everything okay? You have all your things?"

"Yes, yes, and yes," Adriana says with a smile. She turns to say a quick goodbye to Jameara, who just says, "Take care now," and heads back inside.

Her father, who has been hanging back, now steps forward. "Hi, honey." He gives her a hug that feels awkward, but that's just him. She's not going to cast aspersions on any of them today. She's genuinely happy to see all of them. Even Lana.

"Let's get the hell out of here," her father says.

"My sentiments exactly," says Adriana.

But all the way to the car, that letter Ms. Detrick gave her is just about burning a hole in her pocket.

Only when she's seated in the car does she dare to pull it out. Jameara said that the postmark was interesting, and said no more. But Adriana knows what's interesting about West-brook Township. Jolene used to get letters from there. From her asshole of a boyfriend, at the Westbrook Men's Correctional Facility. It's one of the places the male "graduates" of Compass go, if they're still serving time after they've aged out.

Lana's up front, going on about directions, traffic, and plans for what they might want to do with the rest of the day. But Adriana's not listening. All her attention is on the envelope. She takes a deep breath. Then a second. Then a third. Finally, she opens it.

Inside is a page with a single sentence. That's all. But it's everything.

"First order of business is lunch!" says Lana. "Wherever you want to eat, Adriana—just say it, and we'll take you there!"

"I . . . was thinking we could go to the mall," Adriana says.

Lana gives a knowing nod. "The food court! I'll bet you really missed that."

But the food court is the last thing on her mind. Adriana looks at the paper in her hands again, and its familiar handwriting.

The Beagle has landed.

"Actually, I was thinking we could go to that cute stationery store," she says. "I'd like to pick up a new journal."

Even as she says it, Adriana suddenly has to catch her breath . . . and she marvels at how her heart can pound so powerfully, and yet feel as light as walking on the moon.

A NOTE FROM THE AUTHORS

Dear Readers,

After visiting juvenile detention centers in both California and Texas, and speaking with people who have devoted time to working with incarcerated kids—such as media specialists Devo Carpenter and Amy Cheney—we became acutely aware of the harsh realities that these kids face daily within the confines of walls that can feel both inescapable and isolating. We quickly became committed to shedding light on the often-overlooked world of juvenile detention.

One striking discovery was realizing the role that reading plays in the lives of young detainees. Within the confines of their regimented facilities, books become lifelines—windows into a world beyond the bars.

With all this in mind, we embarked on an unlikely romance

between two people who find each other even though walls keep them apart, hoping to provide a glimpse into a world where love transcends boundaries and flourishes even within the harshest of environments.

It is our hope that, as you read *Break to You*, you will be reminded that there is more to life than the walls that surround us, more to incarcerated kids than the crimes and circumstances that put them in detention, and more we can all do to bring about positive change in the juvenile justice system.

Neal Shusterman
Michelle Knowlden
Debra Young

ACKNOWLEDGMENTS

Break to You has been a labor of love for us from beginning to end. We'd like to thank Rosemary Brosnan, our editor, who guided us and helped us shape the story through various drafts. Everyone at HarperCollins has been phenomenally supportive, from associate editor Courtney Stevenson, to Michael D'Angelo and Audrey Diestelkamp in marketing; Sheala Howley and Rachel Horowitz in subsidiary rights; Patty Rosati, the goddess of school and library marketing, and her team; Kathryn Silsand and Maya Myers in managing editorial; Allison Brown in production; art director Joel Tippie, who created the fantastic cover; and Liate Stehlik, the new conductor of the whole publishing symphony.

A very special thanks to Marty Bowen and Pete Harris at Temple Hill Entertainment for letting us run with the idea of a romance in a detention center!

Our gratitude goes to Amy Cheney, our expert on the troubling world of incarcerated youth. Thanks, Amy, for helping us keep it real!

Neal would like to thank the amazing people in his career: his literary agent, Andrea Brown; managers Trevor Engelson and Josh McGuire; foreign rights agent Taryn Fagerness; entertainment industry agents Steve Fisher and Debbie Deuble-Hill; contract attorneys Jennifer Justman and Shep Rosenman; social media managers Bianca Peries and Maya De Guzman; assistant/tour coordinator Claire Salmon; the family TikTok team of Jarrod Shusterman and Sofía Lapuente; and the rest of his family: Brendan, Joelle, and Erin Shusterman.

Michelle would like to thank her mom, Carol Knowlden, and siblings Linda and Gary, who have gone above and beyond in their support. Also a shout-out to Michelle's dear friends Robin Aquino, Rich and Shereen Glasgow, Marianne and Ross Iwamoto, Kris Klopfenstein, Ken Lew, Sue Masters, Deb Patterson, Jean Riddell, Gaylyn Smith, Pat Stout, Lori and Jeff Straw, Kathy Vallely, Michele Van Hulle, and Jeannie and Roland Walker.

Debra would like to thank her sisters and brothers—Valarie, Julie, Alesia, Robert, and Donald—for their loving support and belief in her, and although her parents, Georgie and Moses, have passed, Debra is grateful for their love, which helped her to believe in herself.

Thank you all for helping us break down the walls between concept and creation, and for helping us see this story to fruition!

NEAL SHUSTERMAN is the *New York Times* bestselling and award-winning author of more than fifty books, including *Challenger Deep*, which won the National Book Award; *Scythe*, a Michael L. Printz Honor Book; *Dry*, which he cowrote with his son, Jarrod Shusterman; *Unwind*, which won more than thirty domestic and international awards; *Bruiser*, which was on a dozen state lists; *The Schwa Was Here*, winner of the *Boston Globe–Horn Book* Award; and *Game Changer*, which debuted as an indie top-five bestseller. You can visit him online at storyman .com, on X, IG, and TikTok @NealShusterman, and on Facebook at Facebook.com/nealshusterman.

DEBRA YOUNG wrote fantasy, science fiction, and horror. She published stories in *The Horror Zine*, *Dark Fire Fiction*, *Swords and Sorcery Magazine*, and *Black Fox Literary Magazine*, and was the author of *Grave Shadows*, a story anthology. She died in 2024.

Once a space shuttle engineer and extreme hiker, **MICHELLE KNOWLDEN** now writes full-time. The Shamus Award nominee's stories have appeared in *Alfred Hitchcock's Mystery Magazine*, *Amazing Stories*, *Daily Science Fiction*, and in Neal Shusterman's *UnBound* and *Gleanings* anthologies. Her books include the Abishag Mysteries quartet, the Deluded Detective series, the Faith Interrupted Cozy Mysteries, *Her Last Mission*, and a 1930s novella, *The Admiral of Signal Hill*. Under the name Michelle Dutton, she wrote the fantasy series Ravenscar Shifters and the historical romance *Lillian in the Doorway*.

She splits her time between riverboats and the Arizona highlands with family, friends, and an Icelandic sponge named Marino.